Praise for *Bad Heir Day*

"Perfect."

—*Times* (London)

"Devilish satire."

—*Elle* (UK)

"Savagely amusing…the satire is deadly, the plot addictive, and the pace exhilarating."

—*Metro London*

"A romp of a novel…Wendy Holden writes with delicious verve and energy."

—*Mail on Sunday*

"Well observed and witty."

—*Mirror*

"Holden not only dissects social trends but also restores the pun to literary respectability—an amazing feat."

—*Esquire* (UK)

"Laugh-out-loud funny…a treat."

ess

"Deliciously wicked a

ist

Bad Heir Day

Bad Heir Day

A Comedy of High Class
and Dire Straits

wendy holden

sourcebooks
landmark

Published by Sourcebooks Landmark, an imprint of Sourcebooks, Inc.
P.O. Box 4410, Naperville, Illinois 60567-4410
(630) 961-3900
Fax: (630) 961-2168
www.sourcebooks.com

Originally published in 2000 in Great Britain by Headline Book Publishing.

Library of Congress Cataloging-in-Publication Data

Holden, Wendy.
 Bad heir day : a comedy of high class and dire straits / by Wendy Holden.
   p. cm.
 1. Nannies--Fiction. I. Title.
PR6058.O436B34 2010
823'.914--dc22

                              2010010667

Printed and bound in the United States of America.
    VP 10 9 8 7 6 5 4 3 2 1

Also by Wendy Holden

For my parents

Chapter One

THE BRIDE HAD STILL not arrived. Beside Anna, Seb fidgeted, sighed and tutted, and the surrounding cacophony of wailing babies and coughing increased. There seemed, Anna saw as she glanced round the candlelit chapel, to be an awful lot of people there. All better dressed than herself. As she caught the haughty eye of a skinny and impeccably turned-out brunette, Anna dropped her gaze to her feet. Realising that there had been no time even to clean her shoes, she immediately wished she hadn't.

Everything had been such a rush. After breakfasting at his usual leisurely pace, Seb had glanced at the invitation properly for the first time and, after much panicked scanning of the Scottish mainland, eventually discovered the location of the wedding in the middle of the Atlantic.

"Fucking hell, I thought it was in Edinburgh," he roared. "It's practically in Iceland." Seb thrust the *AA Road Atlas* at her, his stabbing finger a good quarter inch off the far northwest coast of Scotland. Anna stared at the white island amid the blue, whose shape bore a startling resemblance to a hand making an uncomplimentary gesture with its middle finger. She glanced at the invitation.

"Dampie Castle, Island of Skul," she read. "Well, I suppose getting married in a castle is rather romantic

"Castle my arse," cursed Seb. "Why can't they get married in Knightsbridge like everybody else?"

"Perhaps we shouldn't bother going," Anna said soothingly. After all, she had met neither component of the unit of Thoby and

Miranda whose merger they were invited to celebrate. All she knew was that Thoby, or Bollocks, as Seb insisted on calling him, was a schoolfriend of his. There seemed to be very few men who weren't. While his habit of referring to Miranda as Melons confirmed Anna's suspicions that she was one of his ex-girlfriends. Again, there seemed to be very few women who weren't.

Seb, however, was hell-bent on putting in an appearance. Abandoning plans to drive to Scotland, they flew first class from Heathrow to Inverness instead and drove like the wind in a hired Fiesta to the ferryport for Skul, Seb in a rage all the way. Being stopped by a highway patrol car and asked, "Having trouble taking off, sir?" had hardly improved his temper. In the end, they had arrived at Dampie too late to be shown their room, too late to look round the castle, too late to look at the castle at all in fact, as darkness had long since fallen. Too late to do anything but rush to the chapel, where the evening service would, Seb snarled as they screeched up the driveway, be halfway through by now at least. Only it wasn't.

Ten more brideless minutes passed, during which a small, sailor-suit-clad boy in front of Anna proceeded to climb all over the pew and fix anyone who happened to catch his eye with the most contemptuous of stares. Anna returned his gaze coolly as he bared his infant teeth at her. "I'm going to kill *all* the bridesmaids," he declared, producing a plastic sword from the depths of the pew and waving it threateningly about.

"I'm feeling rather the same way towards Melons," murmured Seb, testily, when, after a further half hour, the bride was still conspicuous by her absence. "Then again, she always did take bloody ages to come." He sniggered to himself. Anna pretended not to have heard.

"Thoby should think himself lucky," whispered a woman behind them as the vision in ivory finally appeared at the door. "Miranda is only fifty-five minutes late turning up to marry him. She's always at least an *hour* late whenever she arranges to meet *me*!"

"There's probably a good reason for that," muttered Seb.

"Shhh," said Anna, digging him in the ribs and noting enviously that Thoby clearly did think himself lucky. His inbred features positively blazed with pride as Miranda, her tiny waist pinched almost to invisibility by her champagne satin bustier, drew up beside him at the altar on a cloud of tulle and the arm of a distinguished-looking man with silver hair and a second-home-in-Provence tan.

"Stella McCartney," whispered the woman behind.

"*Where?*" hissed her companion.

"No, the dress, darling. *Achingly* hip."

"Aching hips, as well, I should think. It looks like agony. Poor Miranda."

"Still, it's worth it. Mrs. Thoby Boucher de Croix-Duroy sounds *terribly* grand. If not *terribly* Scottish."

"No. They're about as Scottish as pizza," whispered the second woman. "Hired this place because Miranda was *desperate* to get married in a castle. And I hear Thoby isn't quite so grand as he seems anyway. Apparently he's called Boucher de Croix-Duroy because his grandfather was a butcher from King's Cross."

"*Yes!* Shush, we've got to sing now. *Damn*, where *is* my order of service?"

As everyone vowed to thee, their country, Anna sneaked a proud, sidelong glance at Seb and felt her stomach begin its familiar yoyo of lust. His tanned neck rose from his brilliantly white collar, his tall frame, drooping slightly (Seb *hated* standing up), looked its best in a perfectly cut morning suit innocent of the merest hint of dandruff and his long lashes almost brushed his Himalayan cheekbones. He might make the odd thoughtless remark, but he was the best-looking man in the chapel by a mile, even—Anna prayed not to be struck down—counting the high-cheekboned, soft-lipped representation of

Jesus languishing elegantly against his cross. Seb was *gorgeous*. And, source though that was of the fiercest pride and delight, it was also rather terrifying. Seb attracted women like magnets attracted iron filings—and in about the same numbers. If being in love with a beautiful woman was hard, Anna thought, it was nothing to being in love with a beautiful man.

After Miranda had got all Thoby's names in the wrong order and, amid much rolling of eyes in the congregation, promised to obey, everyone returned to the castle's tapestry-festooned hall for the receiving line and *vin d'honneur*. Anna looked admiringly around, drinking in the vast fireplace blazing with heraldry and a fire of infernal proportions, the latticed windows and the stag's head-studded stone walls along with her rather flat champagne. Seb, meanwhile, made a beeline for the newlyweds.

"Bollocks, you old bastard!" he yelled, slapping the groom so hard on the back his eyes bulged. "Melons!" he whooped, pressing himself close to the bride whose chest, Anna noted, was flatter than pita bread. Seb's idea of a joke, obviously; Anna wondered what, in that case, the significance of Thoby's nickname could be. She maintained a fixed smile as Seb nuzzled Miranda's neck and stuck his tongue down her throat. "For old times' sake," he assured a distinctly tight-faced Thoby as he and Miranda came up for air.

"Darling, you look marvellous." An impeccable brunette Anna had spotted in the church was suddenly beside them. Silk Cut fumes pouring from her nostrils, gazing at Seb like a dog eyeing a bowl of Pedigree Chum. *My* pedigree chum, actually, thought Anna hotly, slipping her arm through Seb's, looking meaningfully at his patrician profile and trying not to notice that the brunette's brilliant white dress accentuated her spectacular tan just as Anna's own black dress accentuated her spectacular lack of one. But Seb did not return her glance.

"Anna, have you met Brie de Benham?" Seb shook off her hand.

"We were in the same year at university," Anna muttered. She did not add that they had actually sat next to each other throughout Finals and the girl had sobbed hysterically through each paper before eventually walking off with a First.

"We *were*? I don't remember," countered the brunette. She raked Anna's figure up and down and, like a hurt-seeking missile, homed in instantly on the vulnerable area of Anna's stomach. "How *very* clever of you to wear your money belt under your dress."

Anna went redder than a Mon Rouge lipstick. Come gym, come diet, come what may, the soft swag of flesh that clung around her hips had resisted all attempts to shift it. It had remained with all the knowing, grim relentlessness of the last guest at a party. She had been determined to lose it for the wedding. But it had been even more determined to attend.

Whipping round to display her fine-boned back, Brie de Benham began a lively conversation with a tousle-haired man in a velvet jacket of highlighter-pen neon green.

Seb had not heard the exchange. He had other matters at hand—quite literally. Anna turned, eyes pricking, back to Seb to see one of his palms wedged firmly inside the dress of a curvaceous blonde, the back of which was slashed to the top of her bottom.

"So I'm flying back to Hollywood next week," the blonde was saying in a deep, slow, seductive voice. "Darling, you should come too. You'd be wonderful in films. The new Rupert Everett…" She traced a slim finger round Seb's lips.

"Just saying hello to Olivia," Seb muttered to Anna. "Old friend of mine. Liv, darling, meet Anna."

The blonde's stare was the same chill blast as someone opening the lid of a freezer. "Hi. What did you say you did?"

Needled by the haughty tones, Anna was tempted to declare she cleaned loos at Watford Gap Services but, still reeling from Brie de Benham's opening gambit, failed to muster the necessary nerve. "Um, trying to do some writing…"

"Got an agent?"

"Um, no."

"*Oh.* Gosh, there's someone I absolutely must speak to over there. Big kiss, Seb, darling. Catch you later."

"Seb, how are you?" A girl so skinny that her eyes were quite literally bigger than her stomach had appeared in the blonde's powerfully scented slipstream. She did not even look at Anna. "It's been ages."

Since *what?* Anna wondered crossly, looking at the new arrival's puffed-up eyes, pneumatic lips, and bed hair. Rumpled, rough-cut, and a sexy, dirty blonde, it did not disguise in the least the girl's delicate face and air of fragile sensuality. Automatically, Anna sucked in her stomach and once more cursed the gene that had given her hair the colour of carrot soup.

"Strawberry!" Seb's eyes lit up. "You look amazing. I hear you're modelling."

"Yeah," drawled the girl. "A Storm scout just stopped me in the street…"

Typical, thought Anna. The only people who stop me in the street are tourists wanting to know where the Hard Rock Cafe is. She stood feeling utterly surplus to requirements—surplus, in fact, in every way—and listened to Seb chatting away animatedly to the exquisite newcomer. Strawberry was so thin as to be barely visible in profile; her perfectly flat front and back making Anna feel about as sexy as an overstuffed black bin-liner. She looked around wildly for the champagne tray.

A tall and slightly maladroit waiter was circulating uncertainly in her vicinity, looking as if he might drop his tray at any moment. Among the many lipstick-smeared empties which formed its contents, Anna spotted a single full glass of champagne. The waiter caught her eye and started towards her; at precisely the same time, something very large and colourful bore down from the opposite side of the room. Before Anna knew what was happening, a portly figure in a suit of wildly clashing checks had made a surgical strike on the champagne she had earmarked for herself. She and the waiter stared at each other in dismay, during which time Anna registered that he was really rather good-looking. He had wide-apart dark eyes into which locks of thick, dark hair intruded, making his progress through the crowded room more perilous than ever.

"And you are...?" Anna tore her eyes from the waiter's to realise with horror that the portly checked suit was barking at her, thrusting his heavy red face into hers. He was, Anna calculated, twenty-five going on at least fifty. The type of man who wore piglet print boxer shorts. Who teddy bear ties and novelty cufflinks were invented for; sliding her glance to his plump little wrists, she saw that, sure enough, a pair of miniature *Sun* front pages in enamel—one bearing the legend "Up Yours Delors" and the other "Gotcha"—were securing his French cuffs. As his glazed and lustful gaze slid slowly over her bare arms, Anna, out of the corner of her eye, saw Seb place a hand on Strawberry's naked back and steer her away into the crowd.

Chapter Two

"Er, I'm Anna. Anna Farrier."

"Orlando Gossett," boomed the check suit. "How do you do. And *what* do you do?"

"I, um, nothing much at the moment, as it happens," Anna stammered. As an expression of faint contempt seeped into the protruding blue eyes of her neighbour, she added, flustered, "Trying to write."

"Write, eh?" boomed Orlando. "Well, you're in good company. You see that dark-haired girl?" He pointed a fat red finger in the direction of the skinny brunette. "That's Brie de Benham. Works at the *Daily Telegraph*. Real rising star, they say. Does all their big interviews. And that chap with the white jacket on she's talking to?"

Anna nodded.

"Gawain St. George. Works in Washington for the *Sunday Times*. One to watch, apparently."

"Yes, I know Gawain," Anna said. "I know Brie too, as it happens. We all did the same university English course."

"*Did* you now? Well, in that case I wouldn't be wasting time talking to *me*. I'd be over there, trying to screw some work out of them. Ever heard of *networking*?" Orlando Gossett raised his eyebrows and gave her a patronising smile.

Natural politeness—or rank cowardice—stopped Anna pointing out that she'd had no desire to talk to him in the first place. It was with great difficulty she resisted the temptation to dash his glass of champagne into his scarlet jowls.

"Actually," she muttered, "the kind of writing I want to do isn't really journalism. More novel-writing, really. Books."

"Oh well, you'd better try and talk to Fustian Fisch. Chap with the very bright green jacket on? Got the most colossal book deal—well into six figures, I believe—before he'd even done his Finals. Something about a mass-murdering Welsh tree surgeon who's obsessed with Beethoven, apparently. Film rights went for a fortune..."

Anna glanced at Fustian Fisch. He was busily helping himself to three glasses from the replenished tray of the gangly waiter and looked extremely arrogant. *A six-figure book deal.* Anna sighed inwardly. So far, she had failed even to get a sentence published. And it wasn't for want of trying; before finally abandoning her attempts to write a novel she'd sent off screeds of manuscript to every magazine, agent, and publisher in the *Writers and Artists Yearbook*. The response hadn't even been the sound of one hand clapping—more one letterbox flapping as the rejections trickled slowly back. Still, at least the diary she had recently started was going well. Writing for a readership of one, it seemed, was easier than trying to hit the spot for thousands.

"...now Lavenham, over there, he's got the whole thing completely sussed." Orlando Gossett was gesturing at a group at the other side of the room. "Father's made a fortune out of the sewage business—been made a life peer as well—and the son will be rolling in it for the rest of his life. You could s-s-say," Gossett chortled, "that Lavenham won't have to give a *shit* about anything, in fact. Haw haw *haw*."

Anna shrank back as Gossett opened his surprisingly vast red mouth and roared, jerking his fat, tightly clad little body about in paroxysms of mirth for the best part of the following minute. "Quite eligible too," he gasped, wiping his streaming eyes with a chequered handkerchief, "although," he added in a conspiratorial whisper, "they do say his girlfriend's *quite* extraordinary."

"Do they?" Anna said, not at all sure what he meant. She reeled slightly. Orlando's breath was pure alcohol. One flick of a lighter and…

"Yah. Put it this way—Lavenham always says she screws like an animal."

"But that's rather flattering, isn't it?"

"Not really." Gossett paused, then nudged her. "Like a *dead dog*, he says. Haw haw *haw*."

Anna did not smile. "Have you met her?" she asked coldly.

"Not exactly, not in the flesh, no."

"You have, actually."

"Sorry?" Orlando looked blank.

"Met her. You're meeting her, in fact. Sebastian Lavenham is my boyfriend."

There was an exploding sound as Orlando Gossett choked on what Anna calculated to be his seventh glass of champagne. "*Christ*. Oh my goodness. Oh *fuck*. I really *didn't* mean…I'm *sure* he was joking…"

"Yes." Part of her refused to believe Seb could ever be so cruel. Part of her, however, feared the worst. "Excuse me, I really must go and powder my nose." At least she had an excuse to get away from him now.

"Well, you won't be alone," Gossett remarked cheerily. "Half of Kensington's chatting to Charlie in there. They say there's more snow in Strawberry St. Felix's bag than in the whole of St. Moritz."

Seb having completely disappeared, Anna decided to pass some of what promised to be a very long evening exploring the castle.

As she wandered from the thronging hall, ringing with the depressing sound of everyone but her having a good time, Anna wondered where she and Seb would be sleeping that night. And whether it would be the same place. The traumas of the journey were beginning to catch up with her. She longed for a lie-down.

The passage she was walking down was very dark, of a blackness so intense it almost felt solid. Anna inhaled the deep, cool, mildewed smell of centuries and wondered what it would be like to live somewhere so ancient. To have a past of burnished oak refectory tables, tapestries and mullions; Anna, whose own past was rather more semi-detached, G-plan, and Trimphones, was fascinated by the air of age and decay.

The darkness was now absolute. Anna, proceeding steadily onwards, stuck her hands out in front of her, terrified of being impaled on something sharp—perhaps another of the intimidating halberds she had noticed festooning the hall. The silence was ringing in its intensity—the noise from the hall having long receded. Yet, straining her ears, Anna thought she heard the faint sound of a door closing. A bolt of fear shot through her as she realised the castle might be haunted. That, of course, was the downside of old places. Say what you like about semis, Anna thought, you rarely saw head-less green ladies in them. Unless you'd knocked over one of Mum's china shepherdesses. On seeing a dim light in the distance, Anna felt weak with relief. Approaching, she saw that the faint glimmer was a large, diamond-paned oriel window, the deep recesses of which held two cushioned seats facing each other. She collapsed on one of them gratefully. A sense of calm ebbed slowly through her as she gazed out into the night.

Directly in front of her, picturesquely distorted through the ancient and tiny panes of glass, a full moon with a searchlight beam silvered the vast expanse of the loch. The water shimmered and wrinkled like liquid satin, edged with the thinnest of watery lace as it rippled peacefully up the pebbly shore. All was silence.

"Beautiful, isn't it?" said a voice beside her.

Anna leapt out of the seat and tried to scream, but found she could only manage a petrified croak. Yet even in her terror she couldn't help noticing that the voice was less marrow-chilling and deathly than low and well-spoken and shot through with a warm thread of Scots. Anna opened her eyes. The moonlight shone on tumbling dark locks. A shock of hair, in every sense of the word.

"Terribly sorry," gasped the diffident waiter. "Didn't mean to scare you."

"Well, I dread to think what happens when you do," Anna snapped, immediately regretting it. For some reason she didn't want him to think she was a harridan. As he put a nervous hand over his mouth to stifle a rather forced-sounding cough, she noticed the signet ring that glinted on his finger. Anna stared at it, surprised. But then why shouldn't a waiter wear a signet ring if he wanted? It was disturbing to realise that Seb's values—that only the wealthy and well-born were allowed rings with coats of arms—were seeping through.

"My name's Jamie Angus," he told her, proffering his hand. It felt cool and reassuring over hers.

"Anna. Anna Farrier," she mumbled, embarrassed both at how prosaic it sounded beside his own splendidly Caledonian affair and also at the waves of attraction thudding up her arm, down through her stomach, and straight into her gusset. I must be drunk, she thought wildly. Guiltily, even, until, suddenly, the memory of Seb's hand on Strawberry's naked back flashed into her mind. Slowly, reluctantly, she withdrew her hand from Jamie's and, looking at him, smiled.

His wide, dark eyes, Anna noticed, were as far removed from Seb's spiteful blue ones as soft malt was from a vodka martini.

"Did you come on your own?"

"I came with my boyfriend, actually." *Damn. Why the hell* had she said that?

The warm light in Jamie's eyes died away.

"Although," Anna gabbled, desperate to limit the damage, "he seems slightly more interested in one of the other women guests."

"Well, he must be mad," Jamie said, with what could have been no more than usual politeness. Silence descended. In an abrupt change of tack, Jamie asked her if she'd ever visited Scotland at the exact same time she asked him if he'd worked here for long. "No," was the mutual and simultaneous answer.

"Not exactly," Jamie elaborated. "I'm just helping out."

"I think it's beautiful," Anna said.

Another pause followed. Unwilling to risk banalities, Anna stared silently out of the window at the moonlit loch. The waves flexed tiny, tight muscles beneath the surface of the water, while the path of light lay sparkling above, leading to the distant horizon and the dawn. She stared hard at the stars glowing like Las Vegas in the blackness of the sky and tried to work out which of the constellations she could see.

"Is that a planet over there?" she ventured, pointing at a very bright star to the west. "It looks very bright. Is it Venus?"

"No. That's the planet easyjet." Jamie said it gently but sounded amused.

Anna reddened in the darkness as the star moved steadily through the sky, accompanied by a bright flashing light. Astronomy had never been her strength. Orion's belt was about her level, and she wasn't altogether certain of that. The one she was staring at seemed to have fewer notches than last time. Perhaps he'd been losing weight. Lucky old him.

"I'd better get back," Jamie said. "The cake needs cutting. And I think the disco has started in the Great Hall."

He led her back down the passage and gave her a swift, sweet, farewell peck on the cheek before propelling her through a door which, unexpectedly, opened directly into the cavernous, vaulted room, amidst whose friezes and flagstones the disco was indeed in full swing. Or swinger—a superannuated Ted with a thinning, greying quiff proudly presided over a console emblazoned with the words "Stornaway Wheels of Steel Mobile Disco." As the cacophonous blare of "The Locomotion" filled the air, Anna's heart sank in depressed recognition of the nuptial-attender's ritual nightmare, The Wedding Disco From Hell.

She glanced around the scattered strobe-lit crowd for any sign of Seb. Or Strawberry. Neither was in evidence. Taking care to position herself as far as possible from Orlando Gossett, currently investigating the buffet at one end of the room, Anna headed for the bar and drowned her sorrows in getting to know a group of delicious White Russians. After a while, emboldened by their company, she tottered unsteadily towards the dance floor and sank gratefully into a chair at the edge. The flashing lights made her head spin, as did the jerking forms of about thirty men in morning suits leaping around as the dying strains of "Love Shack" were replaced by "Come on Eileen." Roaring and foot-stomping floated through the speakers. When "Fever" succeeded "Mustang Sally," Anna felt the first urge to laugh she had experienced all day. The sight of Orlando Gossett writhing around and assuring some blonde, horsy woman in an Alice band that she gave him Fever All Through The Night made Anna snort with suppressed mirth.

It was odd, Anna mused with the intensity of the inebriated, how people seemed happy to sacrifice all dignity in the face of really terrible music. Just what *was* it about "Hi Ho Silver Lining" that got couples leaping up from their tables? Why did "I Will Survive" prompt mass histrionic role-playing, or "YMCA" and "D.I.S.C.O." have everyone waving their arms about like the compulsory morning workout at a Chinese ball-bearing factory? Most of all, why did the merest riff of Rolling Stones suddenly turn every man on the floor into Mick Jagger (in their dreams)? Even now, Orlando Gossett was prowling plumply around with one arm stuck straight out in front of him, rotating his wrist and imploring the horse-faced blonde to give him, give him, give him the honky tonk blues.

The music changed, as it was inevitable it would do, to *The Rocky Horror Picture Show*, and, as the heaving crowd on the dance floor shifted, Anna suddenly spotted her long-absent consort Doing the Time Warp Again. She watched, unsure whether the nauseous feeling in her stomach was because he was doing it a) at all, b) with a willowy, writhing someone bearing a striking resemblance to Brie de Benham, or c) because the effects of the White Russians were by now wearing off. Or possibly wearing on. Unable to reach a conclusion, or indeed anything else apart from the arm of the chair on which she kept a tight, stabilising grip, Anna watched their gyrating figures, oddly comforted by the fact that even the beautiful people looked ridiculous in the context of a really dreadful disco. It was a great leveller. Quite literally, she thought, as Orlando Gossett flicked to the right just a little bit too enthusiastically and went crashing heavily down on his well-upholstered bottom.

"*Desperate*, isn't it?" Anna had been too absorbed in watching the floorshow to notice that someone had sat down next to her. "Still, it beats L.A., I suppose," added the voice. It belonged, Anna saw, to an extremely pretty girl.

"It does?" Anna stared at her neighbour's glossy tan and radiant teeth. "But I thought L.A. was full of beautiful people."

"It is. All the men are gay and all the women are gorgeous. The competition's too stiff."

"But you look great," Anna said. Certainly, her new friend hardly looked the shrinking violet type when it came to men. The only thing shrunken and violet about her, in fact, was the tiny lilac cashmere cardigan out of whose casually unbuttoned front a pair of tanned and generous breasts rose like the morning sun. Even in the dim light her smile was electric, emphasised by plum-coloured lipstick applied with architectural precision.

"Thanks. As the lady said, it takes a lot of money to look this cheap." The girl grinned, smoothing a black satin skirt slit the entire length of her thigh over her slender hips. She flicked a heavily mascara'd glance around the room. "It's nice someone appreciates it. No one else seems to." A precision-plucked eyebrow shot peevishly upwards. "Can't say I'm too thrilled about having schlepped all the way up here," she added. "I only came because I was told this wedding would be thick with millionaires. But I suppose"—she lit up a cigarette—"they were right about the thick bit."

The girl blew smoke out in two streams from her nose. "And the *women…*" She stabbed her cigarette in the direction of Strawberry, who had suddenly reappeared and was glaring at Brie and Seb smooching to "(Everything I Do) I Do It For You." "Look at *that*. Hair like a badger's *arse*."

Anna looked determinedly away from the dance floor and bull-dozed a grin across her face. "Quite. I'm Anna, by the way."

"Geri. Lead me to the drinks. If I can't bag an heir, hair of the dog will have to do."

Chapter Three

"THEN THERE WAS HUGH." Geri struck the manicured pinnacle of her middle finger. "Gynaecologist. Met him at a BUPA checkup—it always pays to go private. Said I had the prettiest cervix he'd ever seen. Saved me a fortune on smear tests and breast examinations."

"Oh?" said Anna unsteadily. Geri had located the source of the champagne bottles behind a curtain beside the blazing hearth in the hall, grabbed three, and withdrawn with them and Anna to an alcove. Endless warmish fizz plus endless highlights of Geri's romantic history were proving a potent and anaesthetic brew. Even the sight of Seb grinding his pelvis into that of Brie de Benham was by now painless. More painless than for Seb probably, as the de Benham pelvis resembled two Cadillac fins and it could hardly have been comfortable up close. Seb, however, seemed to be rising to the occasion.

"Commitment problem," said Geri.

"Absolutely," said Anna, looking resignedly at Seb.

"Yes, except Hugh's was that *I* wouldn't commit," said Geri, oblivious to the connection between Anna and the couple on the dance floor currently in the throes of "2-4-6-8 Motorway."

"Wish I had now, really. But at the time, I wanted to play the field. Trouble is"—she rolled her long-lashed eyes—"if you play in the field, you come across a lot of shit. Like Guy, for example."

"Guy?" With difficulty, Anna shifted her bovine stare from the disco.

"A very rich banker. Or *was*. Complete ruthless shark. He was on the financial fast track until he got sacked."

"Insider dealing?" Anna hoped she sounded worldly wise.

"Nothing quite so glamorous as that, I'm afraid. Someone in the office—everyone there hated him—changed his computer screen-saver to say Fuck Off Cant. Unfortunately, Cant was the name of his immediate boss." Geri paused and grinned. "But we did have other problems, particularly in bed. He could barely raise his eyebrows, let alone anything else." She paused and sighed.

The disco, it suddenly dawned on Anna, had stopped. Everyone was milling about, many of them making a beeline for the cut-up wedding cake. This had suddenly arrived in their midst on plates borne by Jamie who looked on with contempt as two WAGs grabbed handfuls of icing and began to throw it at each other. Anna tried to catch his eye to throw him a sympathetic glance and perhaps experience that delicious frisson again, but, deliberately or otherwise, he failed to notice her. Wresting his wares from the WAGs, he disappeared into the crowd and was soon lost to sight. Resignedly, Anna tuned back into Geri.

"*Then*," Geri was saying, "there was James. Wanted sex three times a night at first. *Exhausting*. Nightmare, in fact. Then, after we'd been together a few months it went down to twice a night. I couldn't decide whether I was insulted or relieved. So I left him for Ivo. An academic. *Hopeless*."

"Oh?" said Anna, interested. She'd once entertained academic ambitions herself. "Why was he hopeless?"

"Oh, not academically. He was one of the best in the world at ancient languages. He spoke fluent Aramaic which, apparently, is only of any use if you happen to meet Jesus."

"So what happened?" asked Anna, grinning.

Geri sighed, "He was broke. And as far as I'm concerned, if there's no dough, it's no go. He could be awkward as well, which is no good either—you do it my way or hit the highway. But in the end, it was me who went. Took myself off to L.A. But now I've come back to London. Got offered this fantastic new job and there seemed no reason to turn it down."

A ripple of misgiving slid coldly through Anna's stomach. Her nose twitched suspiciously at the sweet smell of success. *A fantastic new job.* Just as she had started to regard Geri as a soul mate, as someone doing just as badly as she was.

Further questioning was rendered impossible by a sudden commotion in the hall. As everyone began to arrange themselves into pairs, Anna realised that Scottish dancing was about to begin. She shrank back against the hard wooden settle on which they sat. She hated country dancing. There were few people she loathed more than the Dashing White Sergeant, and could imagine nothing less gay than the Gordons.

"A new job as what?" Anna had to shout to make herself heard as the fiddling struck up.

"Executive development," Geri yelled back cheerfully, lighting up another cigarette. "Lots of travel, lots of responsibility. Lots of man management. A real challenge. I'm looking forward to it, although I must admit I was hoping to meet someone here who would save me the bother of working altogether. Anyway, enough about me. What do you do?"

"Oh, nothing much," Anna bawled. "I'm trying to write a book, actually." Hesitantly, then so fast that her words began to tumble over each other, she swiftly outlined her ambitions.

"That's *brilliant*," screeched Geri. "Can I be in it? I've always wanted to be in a novel."

"I'm afraid I haven't got very far with it," Anna shouted, feeling her voice beginning to break with the strain. "The trouble is, I'm not sure whether I'm any good or not. I think I need a bit of professional advice about the nuts and bolts of things." It was as near as she planned to come to admitting that she had neither agent, publisher, nor reason to believe she could write anything more than a postcard.

On the dance floor, the stomping, clapping, and shrieking had intensified. "Ow," yelled Geri as hairpins, shaken from their rightful positions by the frantic activity, began to fly in the direction of the oak settle. Brows streamed with perspiration, women's breasts sprang free from their moorings. An excited-looking Seb shot by with a fetchingly rumpled Brie de Benham, their pupils the size of pinpoints.

"This is dangerous." Geri was pulling someone's *skean dhu* out of her cleavage. "Let's get out of here."

Too late. The unmistakable form of Orlando Gossett, red-faced and polychromatic, was shoving its way purposefully through the heaving crowd towards their alcove like a vast tartan Sherman tank. "Would you," he asked, addressing Geri's cleavage, "do me the honour of partnering me for this dansh?"

Grasping Geri's thin brown arm in his plump, pink palm, he dragged her to her feet. With no time to do more than roll her eyes, Geri tottered after him and plunged into the heaving quicksand of the crowd.

Suddenly aware that tiredness was crashing over her in huge waves, Anna decided to try once more to locate her room. Numbed by the champagne, she felt too tired to mind that Seb—no longer visible among the dancers—would almost certainly not be joining her in it. It took several goes to extract Miranda from the whirling crowd, but Anna eventually secured directions bedwards; her progress through a series of dark corridors this time sadly unimpeded by dark-eyed young men.

Unlocking the door of her room, Anna had a vague impression of high ceilings and a four-poster bed silvered with moonlight before passing out with sheer exhaustion not to mention sheer alcohol. Hours later, she woke up. It was still dark but something was scrabbling at the door. The empty mattress stretched away beside her. Could it, at last, be Seb? Struggling out of bed, falling over her clothes and shoes on the way to the door, Anna opened it to reveal, not Seb, but Miranda leaning against the lintel. The formerly radiant bride now looked distinctly the worse for wear. Her ivory wedding dress, the epitome of taste and restraint mere hours ago, was now smeared here and there with smudges and stains. Such was the devastation wrought on her once-magnificent white cathedral-length veil that, stunted, ugly, and blackened, it was now more Methodist chapel. She cast an agonised glance at Anna, muttered something about needing a lie-down, and disappeared into the gloomy nether regions of the corridor.

Next morning, at breakfast, Anna was disappointed to see that Jamie was not presiding over the chafing dishes. Instead, a couple of Australian hired helps as wide as they were tall slammed the lids cheerfully on and off dishes of scrambled eggs and mackerel with a clang reverberating round the alcohol-swollen brains of all present.

Seb's brain—or what remained of it following what had clearly been a night of literally staggering excess—was so swollen that he was still in bed. He had appeared with the dawn, thankfully not with Brie de Benham, but inebriated beyond belief and surprisingly, unwelcomingly randy. Happily, his attempts to force his attentions on Anna were interrupted several times by his dashing to the bathroom to vomit—"drive the porcelain bus" as he called it. In the end, much to Anna's relief, he gave up and spent the rest of the night groaning for reasons that had little to do with ecstasy.

About five chairs away down the long dining table, Thoby slumped over his breakfast looking greyer at the gills than the mackerel he was pushing resignedly round his plate. Eventually, he put his fork down, his head in his hands, and emitted what sounded oddly like a groan. The memory of Miranda despairing at her door the night before confirmed Anna's suspicions that the wedding night had not been a brilliant success. Sympathetically, she steered her stare away from Thoby and focused on her surroundings instead.

Dampie Castle seemed to be entirely enveloped in a cloud. The windows of the dining room were long and elegant, even though the view outside bore a strong resemblance to that usually enjoyed by aeroplane passengers five minutes out of Gatwick. Nothing was visible apart from an ectoplasmic mist that pressed up against the panes and extended as far as the eye could see, which was not very far at all. The view inside, on the other hand, was pure old school patrician—long mahogany tables, towering bookcases, a vast armorial fireplace, and several patricians of indeterminate purity from Seb's old school. Anna was just beginning to wonder whether his condition was terminal when someone suddenly slammed a plate down on the next worn Scenes of Scotland place mat and threw herself into the chair beside her.

"What a night," said Geri, whom Anna had not seen since she disappeared to Strip the Willow with Orlando Gossett. She had spent the night hoping that was all Geri had stripped, but it appeared she had hoped in vain. Visions of large wardrobes with keys sticking out came flooding to mind.

"Oh dear." Anna swallowed hard. It really didn't bear thinking about. "Don't think about it," she counselled.

Geri put her fork down, her face as white as her unwarmed plate. "Well, I'm trying not to, only there are about a million bruises to remind me."

Anna swallowed. "He wasn't, well, *violent*, was he?"

Geri stared at her. "*Violent*? The man's a fucking Neanderthal. He practically threw me round the floor, stamped repeatedly on my new Jimmy Choos, knocked out one of my contact lenses, and then, *then*, he tried to get me to *sleep* with him. Can you imagine?"

"No," said Anna, even though she had.

"He couldn't understand why I *wouldn't* sleep with him though. Came over all indignant and said, 'I haven't got AIDS, you know.' 'Don't *worry*,' I said. 'I *believe* you.'"

"So how did you get rid of him?"

"Simple." Geri probed her fish with her fork. "Told him I was going to the bathroom. I just didn't mention I meant *my* bathroom in *my* room and I had no intention of coming down again."

"Ah," said Anna.

"But eventually I decided to sneak back down," Geri confessed, looking strangely furtive. "Had rather a good time in the end..." Her voice trailed off. "Anyway," she added briskly. "I've had a brilliant idea. About you."

"About *me?*" Anna felt a vague sense of panic. It seemed rather early for ideas. And hadn't Oscar Wilde said something about only dull people being brilliant at breakfast?

"Remember, management consultancy is what I do," said Geri confidently. "I'm paid to advise people on how to run their professional lives better. And I've got just the solution for you."

"You have?"

"Sure," said Geri, abandoning the mackerel and flinging her fork down with a flourish. "What you need is an apprenticeship."

Dickensian visions of workshops and boy sweeps loomed before Anna. "You mean long stands and striped paint?"

"Of course not. Stop being so rigid in your definitions," commanded Geri. "The first principle of management consultancy is creative thinking. I'm talking about a particular sort of apprenticeship. A *bestseller* apprenticeship."

"But where do they do those?"

"Lateral thinking," said Geri, tapping her forehead with a fingernail which, for all the night's traumas, remained impeccably manicured. "You need to find a writer who needs help. Be their dogsbody. Do their errands, take their post, make their life run smoothly. And in return..."

"They'll show me how they do it," said Anna slowly, catching the thread of thought. Her alcohol-sodden brain suddenly sparked into life like a match. "Or at the very least, I can pick up the nuts and bolts of it. Chapter construction, how one gets an agent, the different publishing houses…"

Geri nodded. "Exactly."

"Oh Geri, that's a *fantastic* idea."

Just then, Orlando Gossett entered the room and glided swiftly towards the chafing dishes. Having piled his plate high with eggs and fish, he turned his attention to finding somewhere to sit.

"Head down," Geri muttered, suddenly taking an intense interest in her Stirling Castle place mat.

"It's all right," Anna said. "He's sitting down next to Thoby, who doesn't look very pleased about it. But then, Thoby doesn't look very pleased about anything. He certainly doesn't look like a man who's spent a night of bliss with his new bride."

"That's because he didn't." Geri blushed. "He spent it with me."

Chapter Four

"FORTY-TWO, TWO TWENTY-EIGHT, FIVE fifty-seven." Cassandra squinted at the list of clothes beside the computerised wardrobe door and entered the numbers of her chosen garments into the keypad, taking great care not to damage her nails. Tyra the manicurist had just left; the fact she cost just over double what most painters of nails and buffers of cuticles charged demanded that her handiwork be shown a certain respect. She was worth it though; did she not count Nicole Kidman, Elizabeth Hurley, and the editor of *Vogue* among her clients? Though the fact that they probably paid nothing explained Cassandra's own exorbitant bills.

Still, full battle dress was essential today. Cassandra was not looking forward to the meeting with her publishers at which she would no doubt be expected to explain the whereabouts of *A Passionate Lover*, her long-promised but as yet unforthcoming new novel. So far, she'd pleaded writer's block, crashing laptop, even periodic bouts of mysterious illness, but now, floating faintly but definitely into her ear was the unmistakable sound of music that had to be faced. Cassandra was unsure how exactly she would break the news that no lover, passionate or otherwise, currently lurked in her laptop, still less in the left-hand side of her brain or wherever the creative part was supposed to be.

A PASSIONATE LOVER, screamed the poster pinned on the wall opposite her desk in bold letters of searing red. They were a searing reminder to Cassandra that her publishers had seen fit to start a poster campaign before seeing a single word of the novel it described. The apparent rationale was that if they proceeded as if the book existed, it might, through sheer force of corporate effort, actually materialise. "Love, lust, and betrayal—with a twist in the tail," declared the poster. "The new Number One bestseller from the author of *The Sins of the Father*, *Impossible Lust*, *Guilty*, and *Obsessions*," it went on in smaller letters running across the illustration of a tousle-haired Pierce Brosnan smoulderer in a frilled shirt who could pout and suck his cheeks in at the same time. Cassandra stared at him with loathing.

Love, lust, and betrayal—with a twist in the tail. Well, thought Cassandra bitterly, the publishers certainly had a head start on her. She hadn't even begun to think about the plot, let alone start trying to write it. And as for Number One bestseller, well, despite the publishers' best efforts—and often their worst and most underhand ones into the bargain—that was in the lap of the gods. It certainly wasn't, at this precise moment, in her laptop.

Forcing this uncomfortable and inconvenient fact from her mind, she stared at the electronic display beside the wardrobe door as it processed the numbers she had punched in. The figures were rippling like the destination boards used to do at Waterloo in those thankfully long-ago days when public transport and Cassandra were not the strangers they were now. She tapped her foot as impatiently as she could, given that each tap sank into inches-thick cream carpet.

What had gone wrong? Why had the inspiring spark, so reliable for so long, recently failed to spring into anything approximating a flame? "Everything I'm writing is shit," a panicked Cassandra had yelled at her editor recently. Harriet's lack of surprise, indeed the unspoken implication that that was entirely expected, did little to improve Cassandra's mood. But if shit it were, she thought indignantly, it was successful. Four bestsellers under her belt in as many years, spawning three mini-series and one talking book read by

Joanna Lumley. But lately…Cassandra swallowed. The thought of the flint-faced executives she would shortly face around the boardroom table make her heart sink.

She could no longer think of plots. The personalities of her characters vacillated as wildly as their gender, hair colour, and motivation; her development and consistency skills had gone, although, she thought, reddening, many of her reviewers had questioned the existence of those skills in the first place. *Bastards.* But far, far worse than the worst reviews (and there had been plenty of those and she never forgot the names and one day the score would be settled) was the fact that Cassandra couldn't seem to write sex scenes anymore.

Sex scenes had been Cassandra's stock in trade. Or stocking trade, as more than one razor-witted reviewer had pointed out in the past. Along with the smirking observation, following revelations that Cassandra was celebrated among the commuting classes for her ability to produce erections on the Circle Line at seven in the morning, that "here was a writer at the peak of her powers." But for the moment, those powers had deserted her—Cassandra doubted now she'd be able to produce an erection among a gang of footballers being lapdanced in Stringfellow's. Chronicling the most basic sexual encounter seemed beyond her; the springy breasts with their dark aureoles of nipple consistently failed to spring to mind. Likewise, the piston-like penises, so reliable of old, resolutely refused to come.

Cassandra was at a loss to explain, to Harriet or anybody else, why this should suddenly be the case. It was not, after all, as if her own sex life had suddenly slowed down to a splutter or that she had lost interest. She had never been interested in the first place. When push came to shove—and she rued every day that it did—Cassandra hated sex, at least, when she was sober. Her husband Jett, unfortunately, did not share her views and continued to press for his conjugal rights, although, admittedly, his requirements had gone down from a daily service to a Sunday one. Cassandra supposed she should be thankful for small mercies, even though there was nothing small or merciful about Jett at full throttle. The only point to sex, as far as she was concerned, was children. And after Zak's birth, eight years ago, Cassandra had dropped even the pretence that she was interested.

From briefly dwelling on the favourite subject of her son, that most gifted, charming, and beautiful of children, Cassandra's mind flitted to the rather less comfortable subject of Emma the nanny. Now *there* was a pressure, coping with the latest in that endless line of troublesome girls. *Five* in the last *twelve months*, Cassandra seethed to herself. Did staying power and commitment mean nothing anymore? Given what she had to put up with in her domestic life, was it any wonder that her storylines were about as sexy as an orthopaedic shoe?

They were all the same, these ridiculous girls; at least, they all said the same things about Zak. Emma had proved particularly unresponsive to Cassandra's standard line of nanny rebuttal, the argument that a child as brilliant as Zak was bound to be difficult from time to time, gifted children always were. And of *course* he was occasionally—*very* occasionally—disobedient. The respect of a child like Zak had to be *earned*. Cassandra decided not to dwell on Emma's mutinous expression the last time she had tried this tack, still less the pointed way she had turned her back and marched out of the room. She decided instead to concentrate on the matter in hand, which was the meeting and what to wear for it. It was eight o'clock, a blearily early hour for Cassandra to be up, and she was due in the boardroom at nine.

Forty-two, two twenty-eight, and five fifty-seven. It had been a difficult decision, but in the end, Cassandra was sure she had trodden the sartorial line between professionalism and plunging cleavage with consummate skill. Forty-two was the classic black YSL trouser suit with the big black buttons. Two twenty-eight was her new purple Prada shirt, and five fifty-seven her favourite pair of black elastic Manolo boots.

Boots? Was it, Cassandra thought, suddenly panicking, the *weather* for boots? She looked quickly at a second liquid crystal display beneath the keypad, which helpfully showed the temperature outside so you could pick your clothes to suit: 5°C. Christ, it was practically *freezing*. Amazing weather for June, but then, this *was* England, she supposed. She'd need a coat too, obviously. It could be the furs first outing since Gstaad in February. Cassandra scanned the list. Seven hundred and four was the silver-mink ankle-length. If that didn't wow them, nothing would.

There was a grinding sound, a faint rattle, then the door of the wardrobe slid back. Cassandra blinked as it revealed a pair of orange towelling sweatpants, a bright yellow jacket with shoulder pads of Thames Barrier proportions, and a bikini top in magenta satin. As Cassandra stared, aghast, a pair of olive-green Wellington boots hove into view along the conveyor belt at the bottom. "Jett!" she exploded. "Jett!"

"Whazzamatter?" A man in a red satin Chinese bathrobe far too small for him appeared in the doorway between the dressing room and the bedroom. His figure, with its round, protruding belly and long, skinny legs, was reminiscent of a lollipop. "Whazzup?" he asked, rubbing his eyes and yawning.

"This fucking computerised wardrobe you gave me," Cassandra almost spat.

"I didn't realise it fucked as well." Jett lounged against the doorjamb, his heavily bagged eyes narrowed in amusement. "The miracles of modern science. I'd have kept it for myself if I'd known."

"Don't be so bloody facetious, Jett," Cassandra snarled. "This wardrobe is *shit*." Losing her temper altogether, she slammed her clenched fists repeatedly against her sides with impotent rage, irrespective of Tyra's recent careful and costly efforts. "How the *fuck* am I supposed to wear *this* lot to meet my *publishers*?" She gestured furiously at the ensemble before her.

"Looks all right to me," Jett yawned, loping over and tweaking the bikini top. "Looks quite rock 'n' roll, actually."

"Rock 'n' roll my *arse*," hissed Cassandra.

"No, rock 'n' roll your goddamn *tits*." Jett thrust out a hairy, ring-festooned hand to grab Cassandra's breasts, half revealed by her flapping Janet Reger peignoir. Twisting deftly out of Jett's way, Cassandra heard the unmistakable crunch of her neck muscles going. Damn. Another fifty quid to the osteopath.

"This stupid sodding wardrobe's suggesting I wear nothing but this disgusting thing"—she tugged the yellow jacket—"outside when the temperature's more or less zero."

"Zero?" echoed Jett. "It's goddamn *baking* out there. Just look out of the window."

Cassandra turned and screwed up her face against the brilliant light streaming through the greige pashmina curtains, looped with studied artlessness over black iron rods.

It *did* look rather warm outside. "*Sod it*," she spat. "I've got to start all over again now. I'm going to be late. I need some help. Where's that useless nanny? Where's Emma?"

"I'm 'ere," said a northern accent in the doorway. "And I'm handing in me notice. With immediate effect."

Cassandra and Jett stared at the solid figure standing at the entrance to the room with two large bags in her hand. Then they stared at each other.

"You've been at it a-bloody-gain, haven't you?" Cassandra shrieked at Jett. "Trying to screw the sodding nanny. I thought as much when I caught you with her in your library last week. Showing her a few of your favorite *passages*, were you?"

"Well you can bloody well talk," Jett snapped. "Getting her to take those goddamn dresses back to the shops and saying they're not suitable, when you knew goddamn well you'd worn them. Poor cow. Sent packing by half of goddamn Bond Street."

"Well, if she'd ironed the linings properly like I told her, no one would have known," howled Cassandra, seemingly oblivious of the fact that Emma was still present and shifting from foot to sturdily shod foot. "And anyway, it's not as if she'd ever go in those shops of her own accord. I gave her an *education*, asking her to take them back. She should be bloody *grateful*. You, on the other hand, gave her an education of a completely different sort. *Why cant you keep your zip up?*" Cassandra yelled. "You're not a rock star being chased by every groupie in town anymore, you know. You're not a rock star, *full stop!*"

Jett's eyes flashed fire. Cassandra saw she had hit him where it hurt. "You haven't released anything for years," she taunted. "Apart from that *thing* in your trousers."

"Well, neither has anybody goddamn else," yelled Jett, furious. "You goddamn bitch. Solstice will be back with a bang, you'll see. You wait till the new goddamn album's mixed."

"Mixed? *Mixed?*" bawled Cassandra. "The only thing you know how to mix these days is bloody whisky and soda."

As Jett stormed out of the room, Emma stood aside, then stepped forward. "The real reason I'm leaving has nowt to do wi' what you just said," she said in dull Lancastrian tones, "although I'm not saying they didn't 'elp."

Cassandra stared at her in contempt. *Nowt* indeed. *Ghastly* northern vowels. She probably thought elocution was what happened if you dropped a hairdryer in the bath.

"Only summat happened this morning," Emma added, unbowed by her employer's freezing stare, "which made me realise I'd 'ad enough."

Summat. Ugh. And just *look* at *that hair.*

"Zak were complaining about feeling awful and wanted to stay off school. He said there were summat wrong wi' 'is insides." Emma paused. "'E said his poop were white."

"Poop? *Poop*?" Cassandra was incandescent. "We don't *poop* in this house. We *poo*."

"Course," Emma continued flatly, her stare concentrated at a corner of the room beyond her employer, "I tried to find out what were wrong before I got you involved. Zak took me into his bathroom and pointed at his toilet…"

"*Lavatory*."

"And there, bobbing around in the bottom of it, were these little round white thingies."

"*Really*?" Cassandra stared, intrigued at this concrete evidence—*white* poo, of all things—that the sun did indeed shine out of Zak's perfect ivory bottom.

"Well, obviously I were worried," Emma continued, still addressing the corner of the room. "Zak were screaming 'is head off saying he were in 'orrible agony and I were just about to call t' ambulance when summat about them white thingies struck me as funny, like."

"Well, of course they were *funny, like*," Cassandra barked. "What's remotely normal about white crap? *Poo*," she corrected herself.

"So I looked closer and picked one up," Emma said.

"Picked…one…up?" Cassandra's face was a mass of disgusted lines. Who did she think she was? Dr. Sam bloody Ryan?

"And it weren't poop at all. It were," Emma concluded with all the flat finality of the *Silent Witness* pathologist, "a can of tinned potatoes Zak had emptied down the toilet. Suppose 'e thought that were funny," she added. "But I didn't. Ta-ra." She turned on her sensible low heel and left.

Cassandra stared after her, the blood pounding in her temples. Oh *Christ*. She didn't need *this*. Not *now*. Not with this meeting, not with the book problems, husband problems, and problems of every other description she had to put up with. Did no one realise she was a *creative artist*? Where the hell would Shakespeare have been if he'd had the kind of crap—poo—she dealt with on a day-to-day basis, white or otherwise? Boy, did she need a *drink*.

Cassandra lunged with the last of her fury at the sweatpants and magenta bikini top, tearing them from their hangers as she sank to her knees. Sobbing, she crawled across the floor, her bony knees cracking painfully against the rubbed beech boards, towards the sustainable rainforest-wood bed draped with its white shahtoush duvet. "I'm sure I put one there," she muttered, feeling around underneath until her hand closed over a hard glass object. She pulled out the gin bottle, her nose almost touching the mirrored door of the wardrobe.

Cassandra stared at her reflection. In the harsh light of morning, her skin had all the bloom and smoothness of screwed-up tissue paper. Her hooded eyes, which in her more optimistic moments seemed Charlotte Rampling–like, today looked more like Rumpole. Cassandra reflected resentfully that, despite the fact that her face was the only well-fed thing about her, the gallons of expensive skin creams she rubbed in each night had clearly done nothing to help. Nor had last year's lift. She looked older even than her forty years. Her heart sank. She clamped a palm to her thin lips, shuddering as she saw the snaking veins on the back of it. Perhaps she could ask for a hand-lift for Christmas… "Bugger them all," Cassandra murmured as she unscrewed the top of the Bombay Sapphire.

Sometimes it felt like her only friend. The only one who understood the nightmare of her marriage, the challenges of her child, and the demands of her publishers. She'd started drinking it to soothe herself, to take the pain away, to give her courage to face and, more importantly, *do* things. Like the book. But lately she hadn't been able to do anything. And the only thing that made her feel better, Cassandra thought, as she put the bottle to her lips, was giving her little glass friend here a big, big kiss.

❖ ❖ ❖

When Jett returned to the house several hours later, he found it suspiciously silent. But then, he thought, most things seem pretty peaceful after you've been playing lead guitar at top screaming volume for hours on end. Boy, had he made that axe *weep* this afternoon. *Bleed*, even. Gone up to eleven and beyond. Whatever Cassandra might say, *Ass Me Anything* was shaping up to be a peach of an album; "Sex and Sexibility," if released as a single, might even make it to number one. What a blast that would be—Solstice's first chart-topper since "Bum Deal" in 1979. He'd show that bitch. Where *was* that bitch anyway? Hopefully recovered from that mother of all strops she'd been in this morning. But of course, it was the drink talking. Pity, thought Jett, the drink couldn't goddamn *write* as well. Because, since Cassandra had been on the sauce, she could hardly manage a sentence anymore.

There was, Jett noticed, a light downstairs in the kitchen. Had the impossible happened and Cassandra had decided to cook for a change? The usual rules of the house were that whatever nanny was currently in residence at the time fed Zak; Cassandra ate pretty much nothing and Jett was left with whatever happened to be in the fridge or on the menu of one of the local pubs. Although fancy bar food didn't always appeal—he'd have traded all the Thai prawn sausages and celeriac and Parmesan mash in Kensington for one steak and kidney pie—the beer certainly did. He'd been thinking of going down there later but, with Cassandra in the kitchen…he smiled to himself. At this rate he might even get a shag out of her as well.

Jett put his nose in the air and sniffed. He couldn't actually smell anything, but then, he reminded himself, he hadn't for about twenty years, thanks to all that shit he'd stuffed up there. In his time he'd snorted the equivalent of an entire fleet of Gulfstreams. Ah well. That was rock and roll for you. He shook his head and smiled ruefully as he dropped jauntily down the stairs.

His benevolent mood instantly disappeared as he entered the kitchen. "Aaargh!" screamed Jett, terror clenching his heart, which then leapt into his mouth and began to ricochet among the wisdom teeth he had never plucked up the courage to have out. "*Zak!*" he thundered. "Put that cat *down.*" He had arrived just in time to stop his eight-year-old son putting the neighbour's Bengal Blue into the microwave. "For Christ's sake, leave that animal alone."

"But Daddy, you once bit the head off a snake on stage," protested Zak.

"That's different," snapped Jett. "Snakes are two a penny. Have you any idea how much that sodding cat *costs?*"

"But it was *cold,*" Zak whinged, his shiny red lower lip shooting out like a cash till.

"Don't talk *shit.*" Jett felt calmer now. The prospect had receded, at least temporarily, of having to replace Ladymiss Starshine Icypaws Clutterbucket III, the prizewinning pride and joy of Lady Snitterton next door, an animal with a longer pedigree than the Queen and certainly Lady Snitterton herself, but one which possessed a strong self-destructive streak as well as a replacement price tag of about ten thousand pounds. He drew out a chair and sat down, admiring his long legs in their tight black jeans stretched out before him, but wincing slightly as the waistband cut into his belly.

"Where's your mother?" he asked.

"Upstairs," snuffled Zak, now occupied with turning the gas hobs of the cooker on and off.

"*Stop* that," demanded Jett. "What's she doing?"

"Praying."

"*Praying?*" Jett was astounded. "What sort of praying?" He could think of many words to describe his wife, but devout wasn't one of them.

"She's on her knees in front of the wardrobe mirror saying 'Oh my God.'"

Chapter Five

ANNA LOOKED LOVINGLY AT the tiny, coloured oblong—ENGLISH GRADUATE SEEKS WORK AS AUTHOR'S ASSISTANT—and blew it a surreptitious kiss as she pinned it to the noticeboard of Kensington Library. "Good luck," she whispered to it. In fact, acting on Geri's advice, she had left as little as possible to chance. Geri had stipulated she use hot pink card, neatly and clearly printed in ink, to distinguish it from the other dog-eared and sloppily Biro'd offerings usually found on noticeboards. And the noticeboard Geri had favoured, during her impromptu post-breakfast consultancy the morning after the wedding, was that of Kensington Library.

"Only bestseller-list regulars can afford to live there," Geri explained, as they stood in the castle entrance hall knee-deep in bags, most of which seemed to be hers. "Guess I'd better shoot," she added as a tense-looking Miranda appeared. "Before she shoots *me*. See you in London anyway. Good luck."

"Here's my address." Anna thrust it at Geri as she strode in high-heeled boots out of the Gothic arched doorway and disappeared into the mist. The roar of a powerful car engine could be heard almost immediately.

As she turned and left the library, Anna wondered what Geri was doing now. As yet she had had no word from her, although admittedly only a few days had passed since the wedding. She was probably out of town; Anna imagined her reclining in club class on her way to troubleshoot some international management crisis or other, head to foot in tailored pinstripes, exciting the discreet interest of a few tanned and handsome businessmen with cryptic smiles. Or sweeping through town in a limo, a mobile clamped to her ear. Or moving swiftly but authoritatively through an open-plan office, a gaggle of executives rushing after her, waving papers and vying for her attention.

Meanwhile, all Anna herself was doing was wandering vaguely down the library steps, having stuck a small pink card on the notice-board, and wondering whether she had done the right thing. It seemed pathetic in comparison. But what, as Geri had said, could go wrong?

Anna imagined listening raptly as Julian Barnes read aloud his latest chapter, or hovering helpfully in the shadow of Louis de Bernières' desk lamp. Perhaps her little pink plea might even be spotted by a visiting Gore Vidal or Garrison Keillor and she would be whisked away to the land of white picket fences, clapboard, clam bakes, and American literary legend. In the meantime, she boarded the number 10 bus and was whisked away to the land of Seb slouching in front of the television and a kitchen full of empty crisp packets, crusted cereal bowls, and ringed coffee mugs.

Staring out of the window as she juddered past Hyde Park, Anna's thoughts wandered due north to a soft-spoken Scotsman with wide-apart eyes and rumpled hair. As they fought through the traffic of Knightsbridge, Anna was lost in her memories of Dampie. The stone-flagged hall, the vast fireplace with carved canopy, the tapestries, the stags' heads, the ancient, misty, standing-stones-and-islands romance of it all...

Suddenly, Anna realised she'd missed her stop and was at the bottom of Oxford Street. She'd have to walk almost all the way back up to Seb's South Audley Street flat now. "*Fuck!*" she muttered.

"No need for that sort of language," snapped the conductor.

❖❖❖

"*Fuck!*" Cassandra threw down her pen and scowled at the Schnabel on the wall of her study. A present from her publishers when her fourth novel went through the five hundred thousand barrier, it only served to drive home the fact that she was getting precisely nowhere with her fifth. She flung herself theatrically back in her zebraskin chair, stretched her hands out before her, and tried to raise her spirits by examining the vast and glittering rings on her red-nailed fingers. Some people thought them vulgar, but they were wrong. If you could never be too rich or too thin—and she was hell bent on being both—you could certainly never have jewellery that was too big. She hadn't got where she was today by being subtle.

Cassandra reached for the small gold bell which always stood by her laptop and shook it. "Lil!" she screeched. "Lil!"

"Yes, Mrs. Knoight?"

A wrinkled apparition with orange-pencilled eyebrows, lips a painted purple bow, and hair the chewed yellow of a bathroom sponge poked its head round the door almost immediately. The cleaner, Cassandra realised, must have been next door attending to the latest interiors innovation, a perfume bathroom devoted entirely to scent bottles. *Cleaner*—that was a joke. *Filthier*, more like. Lil invariably left more smears behind her than she found, especially on the scented candles whose black smoky bits she never quite managed to clean off, to her employer's intense irritation. Nor, despite Cassandra's compiling and captioning an album of photographs of each room for her, showing exactly how each cushion, ornament, and curtain should be arranged, did the house ever look really up to scratch. But there were always lots of scratches. Cassandra groaned. She felt terrible after the party last night.

"I'd like a large gin and tonic, Lil," Cassandra ordered, thrusting a cigarette between her violently red lips. She always sat down to work in full makeup. After all, you never knew when a TV station might suddenly appear on her doorstep wanting to interview her, or whether a celebrity fan might pop in at a moment's notice. Princess Diana, she'd been told, had loved her books and, as Kensington Palace was practically at the end of her *garden*, Cassandra had always cherished the hope…until…Tears filled her eyes. "*Diet* tonic," she ordered, her hand suddenly shaking.

As the door closed behind Lil, Cassandra sucked on her cigarette like a Hoover in those hard-to-get-at corners of the staircase—well, Lil found them hard to get at anyway—and groaned anew at the memory of last night's gathering. The drink had been dreadful; it had, after all, only been warm white wine for the local Neighbourhood Watch coordinator's birthday. Admittedly, she'd had a glass or two more than was advisable—assuming any of it was advisable. It had come out of a *box*, for Christ's sake. In Cassandra's experience, the only good boxes worth opening were pale blue and marked "Tiffany & Co."

Still, she'd needed some rocket fuel after that wretched publishers' meeting. It had been tough, but she'd managed to buy more time—and half a case of Bombay Sapphire on the way back to help her recover. But she'd been left in no doubt it was her last chance. She simply *had* to get on with this book.

The thought of it made her feel sick. Compounding her nausea was the memory of last night's conversation with that *ghastly* Fenella Greatorex at number 24 who had banged on practically *all night* about her son getting one of the coveted invitations to Savannah and Siena Tressell's birthday party.

Cassandra's skin had almost *blistered* with the heat of her envy. Zak *had* to, she resolved, simply *had* to get an invitation too. Otherwise her life would not be worth living. And, hopefully, when—not if—Zak was invited, Otto Greatorex's wouldn't be worth living either.

Cassandra ground her teeth. Then she'd had to listen to Fenella Greatorex crapping on about her wonderful new nanny. This was doubly infuriating considering Fenella's new one was none other than Emma, Cassandra's old one. *Fuck* Fenella, thought Cassandra; still, she'd looked a lot less smug after Cassandra had pointed out a few home truths to her. "Oh yes," Cassandra sneered as the alcohol took hold. "You bloody well stopped at nothing to get that girl out of my house. Offering her money, cars, paid holidays, her own bathroom, the lot. You ought to be ashamed of yourself. You're nothing less than a thief."

That, Cassandra thought, had shown her. Only it hadn't. Murderous rage rose within her at the memory of Fenella piously pointing out that money, cars, paid holidays, and their own bathrooms were the bare minimum of what most nannies expected anyway and the sooner Cassandra realised that, the better. "No wonder you can't keep a nanny for more than a month," had been Fenella's parting shot.

Wheeling round on her chair, Cassandra stabbed her cigarette out in her Matthew Williamson ashtray and seethed. A *month*! She'd kept at least two nannies for *six weeks*; Isabel, that fat one from Wales, had lasted *two months* until that unfortunate business with the flower vase. Cassandra stuck by her guns, even now. That bunch of flowers had been unspeakably vulgar. *Carnations*, for Christ's sake. She'd been firm and unyielding. Isabel's boyfriend may have had every right to *give* her carnations but Isabel had no right—no right *whatsoever*—to expect to display them in Cassandra's house. She couldn't *quite* believe Isabel considered it a resigning issue, but so be it if she did. Cassandra permitted herself a slight sigh of regret. Isabel had been the best of a bad bunch—quite literally, in the case of those carnations—particularly because she had been so reassuringly plump and therefore Jett-proof. Her husband was not a big fat fan, unless you counted the beef dripping sessions he occasionally indulged in to keep in touch with his working-class roots.

At the thought of Jett, a chill suddenly swept through Cassandra. Was she meant to be doing the school run this morning?

She scrambled to her feet in panic. Anyone delivering the children late got an automatic black mark in the headmistress's book, and Cassandra had few lives left with Mrs. Gosschalk as it was. Last term she had been publicly humiliated when her car had been one of those named and shamed in the school magazine for parking on double yellow lines with the hazards on at dropping-off time. Still, at least she hadn't been on that *dreadful* list taking to task those mothers who turned up at the school gates in *jeans*, which had appeared in the same issue.

"Did Mr. St. Edmunds take Master Zak to school?" Cassandra demanded as Lil returned with a large cut-glass tumbler. The ice cubes crashed and shook together as Cassandra lifted it to her lips.

"Yars," rasped the cleaner in a voice so gravelly it sounded as if her oesophagus had been pebbledashed.

Cassandra was relieved and slightly amazed to hear that her husband had managed to perform at least one parental duty. For, despite the staff crises in which he had most certainly had a hand—in the case of Emma, Cassandra chose not to dwell on exactly where that hand had been—Jett was scarcely displaying Dunkirk spirit at the moment. More bunker mentality as he disappeared for days on end into a studio whose precise location had never been satisfactorily pinpointed.

Cassandra frowned hard at the screen of her laptop. It was a magnificent machine, customised in her trademark zebraskin, with a matching carrycase and special supersensitive keys designed not to break Tyra's nails. When she switched it on, an encouraging electro-musical burst of "Diamonds Are Forever" greeted her, while each time she completed five hundred words, a little pink cartoon figure appeared at the corner of the screen to blow her a kiss. It corrected the spelling for her, it suggested alternative words for her, it could do practically everything except write for her, something Cassandra profoundly regretted. Still, it did its level best to encourage her—its

Screensaver swirled with the affirming messages "Just Do It" and "Go For It" in about a hundred different typefaces, which, in her present mood, Cassandra found more irritating than motivating. The very fact she was sitting there staring at "Just Do It" meant she wasn't doing it. And the only It she felt like going for now was the sort you put in gin.

She decided to go for a walk. A walk would clear her head, Cassandra thought, emptying the last of the Bombay Sapphire down her throat.

"Just going to the library," she called to Lil, now busy bashing the paint off the skirting boards with the Hoover.

"I 'aven't done in there yet," Lil thundered over the vacuum cleaner.

"No, not our library," Cassandra screeched. "The local library."

She rarely, if ever, made an appearance in the mock-Victorian Gothic book repository Jett had had built for himself for his fortieth birthday—or what he claimed had been his fortieth birthday—the year before. God alone knew what he wanted it for, certainly not for reading. Jett's idea of quality fiction was the front and back pages of the tabloids. He had never read a single one of Cassandra's novels, although she derived some comfort from the fact that she was up there with Tolstoy and Dickens in that he had never read one of theirs either.

A walk round Kensington Library, Cassandra decided, was what she needed to stir her into action; the sight of all those volumes by other writers would ignite the petrol-soaked rag of her latent competitive spirit. It would also be interesting to see how many of hers were out on loan. All, hopefully.

Cassandra pulled on a shiny zebraskin mac and, conscious of the thick-waisted Lil watching her from the end of the hall, dragged the belt round her thin middle as tightly as it would go. Who cared if she had writer's block, husband problems, and a galloping staff crisis? She had the waist of a sixteen-year-old, didn't she? And the bottom of a twenty-year-old—Jett was always telling her she had the best arse in the business. A frown flitted across her face as she wondered for the first time what business he meant exactly.

Cassandra negotiated the front steps as well as she could in her high-heeled leopardskin ankle boots. She trotted unevenly down the street, glorying, as always, in the fact that it was one of Kensington's most recherché roads and her house one of the most expensive. They can't take *that* away from me, she thought, sticking her scrawny, plastic-covered chest out with pride and trying not to dwell on the fact that, if she didn't keep up with the mortgage payments, they most certainly could—and would. She simply *had* to get on with this book…

And to do that, she simply *had* to sort out a new nanny. The only *slight* hitch was her usual agency's flat refusal to supply her with any more staff. Cassandra twisted her glossy red lips as she recalled that morning's conversation with the head of Spong's Domestics.

"I'm sorry, Mrs. Knight," Mrs. Spong had told Cassandra. "I'm afraid we're unable to recommend you to our clients as employers anymore."

"What the hell do you mean?" Cassandra had raged, embarrassed as well as furious. Spong's was the smartest staff agency in the area. To be treated like this by them was humiliation of the first order, or rather it would be if anyone found out. She'd heard of *employees* being struck from agency books, but never *employers*. Really, this Spong woman had the most ludicrous airs. "Do you know who I *am*?"

There had been a polite silence before the agency head had, downright insolently, Cassandra considered, informed her that yes, she knew exactly who she was. "So what's the problem?" Cassandra had demanded.

"The problem, Mrs. Knight, is that we have supplied five nannies to you in the last twelve months, none of whom have managed to stay with you—or, more to the point, your son—for a period any longer than two months. It would seem that, ahem"—Mrs. Spong cleared her throat—"perhaps we are unable to supply quite the, um, *calibre* of staff you are looking for."

"Well, do you have any suggestions as to who might?" Cassandra had demanded. "I suppose it's back to trawling through *The Lady*," she had added furiously.

"I think, Mrs. Knight," Mrs. Spong had replied, utterly deadpan, "that you might have more luck with *Soldier of Fortune* magazine." Cassandra had never heard of it, but she liked the sound of it. It must be for rich military types. Another good reason for going to the library. She could save money by helping herself to their copy.

Cassandra swept into Kensington Library and sailed straight for the shelf with her works on it. She was horrified to see that the whole fat-spined four of them were in residence. Furious, she pulled out *Impossible Lust*, marched purposefully towards the display cabinet at the back of the room, and replaced *Captain Corelli's Mandolin* with it. Who wanted to read about a bloody *mandolin* anyway? Feeling better, Cassandra returned to her shelf and flicked to the front of *The Sins of the Father*, the book that had gone through the five hundred thousand barrier and netted her the Schnabel. She felt comforted by the date stamps tattooing the first and second pages—there had obviously been no shortage of borrowers. Then, absently, she flicked to the back, whose last page, she was disgusted to see, was covered in shaky initials in pale blue Biro; put there, she knew, by old women who couldn't remember what they'd read. Realising that the initials at the back tallied roughly with the number of date stamps at the front, anger coursed through Cassandra. If only the old bags would leave her books on the shelf for more than *five seconds*, perhaps some *fashionable* people would have a chance to borrow them.

Her mood did not improve as a stooping old woman with a slack, trembling jaw, thin grey hair, and skin like a raisin came shuffling into the room and made the sort of line a shaky, ancient bee might manage in the direction of Cassandra's shelf. Cassandra shrank against the Sidney Sheldons—at least they weren't all out either—and watched in disgust as the woman took *Impossible Lust* between her liver-spotted fingers and turned to the back page. Apparently unable to decipher her initials, the old woman grunted with satisfaction and shuffled off with the volume towards the librarians' counter. Cassandra's hand flew up to her skinny throat. She felt violated. Seeing that old woman's filthy old hands over her precious words was, she shuddered to herself, like being *raped*. Bile welled up within her. Cassandra hated most of her readers—the pitiful, pathetic, *poor* masses who bought her books in their hundreds of thousands. But even more despicable were the readers who got her books free from the libraries.

As best she could in her crippling heels, Cassandra rushed dramatically out of the room and into the library foyer, where she paused to catch her breath against the noticeboard. As her hammering heart calmed down, her eyes wandered across the many ruled and drawing-pinned pieces of card offering everything from Opera Camp for musical fives-and-up to wine appreciation courses for under-eights. There was hardly time for a panicked Cassandra to wonder whether she should be sending Zak on the latter before her eye fell upon the bright pink card pinned next to it. English Graduate Seeks…Cassandra did a double take. Her eyes narrowed. She read it, then read it again. Finally, she snatched it off the board, slipped it into her plastic zebraskin pocket, and left. It was only when she was halfway up Kensington Church Street that she realised she had forgotten to look for *Soldier of Fortune*. But hopefully she wouldn't be needing that now.

Chapter Six

ANNA HEARD THE SNAP of the letterbox and wandered slowly down the long, white-painted corridor to the post lying on the mat. Not *more* wedding invitations for Seb, she thought in amazement, picking them up and almost buckling under the weight of the thick, cream envelopes.

Over the few weeks since she had moved into his flat, the wedding invitations on Seb's solid Edwardian marble mantelpiece had grown from a mere spinney to a mighty forest. The rather hideous ormulu clock was now entirely obscured by folded cards in Palace script concealing lists from smart interiors stores and directions to receptions—including, once, instructions on how to arrive by helicopter or Gulfstream jet. None of them, however, bore Anna's name. "And Guest" seemed as far as most of Seb's friends were prepared to go. Given his track record with girls, it was probably a sensible policy; sometimes Anna wondered if he was only with her because he'd been out with everybody else.

Yet soon after they had met—at a wedding party, naturally—Seb had invited her to move in with him, which surely was an encouraging sign. Anna tried not to dwell on the fact that he had more or less had to. Having just lost the latest in the series of post-university, part-time dead end jobs she had taken while trying to get her writing off the ground, Anna could no longer afford to rent a flat of her own and was about to give up on London altogether and go back up north to her family.

It had seemed like a miracle, Seb's offer of free flat space, yet in Anna's more paranoid moments she wondered if he had merely calculated the cost to himself of losing not only her unquestioningly adoring company, but also a free laundress, cleaner, and cook. Anna performed these duties in lieu of rent and on the vague understanding that sooner or later she might move out. The feeling that she was living on borrowed time, both in the flat and in his affections, hung heavy. Yet, given that no one else was currently occupying either, squatter's rights didn't seem out of the question.

Anna came to the last of the envelopes. Another frightener. The steady stream of what Anna had come to think of as "frighteners"—routine rejection letters for the many jobs she applied for out of the Monday *Media Guardian*—continued their daily trickle through the front door. Anna swallowed as she bent to retrieve this one. Although it bore no corporate logo and was handwritten, the second-class stamp was a giveaway. Someone obviously thought she was not worth first. Anna slid her nail under the flap, wondering how they had phrased it this time. Overqualified? Underqualified? Overwhelmed by applications?

"I don't believe it," Anna muttered to herself. She stared at the white piece of paper in her shaking hand, heart thumping. "I don't *believe* it." She let out a whoop and rushed into the sitting room where Seb was crouched, fists clenched, in front of the lunchtime racing. Despite his marked and consistent inability to pick a winner, the delusion that he was a keen judge of horseflesh died hard. Perhaps, Anna thought nastily, this explained his attraction to the distinctly equine Brie de Benham. But this was no time to dwell on her, still less on the mysterious, anonymous click-burr answerphone messages that had appeared since the Scottish wedding. "It's fantastic!" Anna shrieked, jumping up and down in front of the television. "A writer saw my ad in the library and wants to see me straightaway. I've got to ring immediately. I could go this afternoon. *Wonderful*, isn't it?"

"Not as wonderful as you getting out of the way of the television would be," Seb drawled. "I've put a hundred on Friend of Dorothy at twelve to one. I could clean up."

Anna stood aside and watched as Friend of Dorothy started last, reared at the first hedge, and finally threw her hapless rider into the water jump. Having rid herself of the unwelcome burden, the horse then galloped merrily down the course, passed the leaders, and crossed the finishing line. Seb looked on furiously. "Bloody useless nag," he snarled. "That was the last of my sodding week's allowance. Still, I suppose I can always ask Mummy for some more tonight."

A 2000-volt electric charge went through Anna. "*Tonight?*" she stammered, the momentous piece of paper in her hand quite forgotten. "*Mummy?*" she croaked.

"Mm, Mummy's coming tonight," Seb yawned, his eyes still glued to the Newmarket paddock. Swallowing, Anna faced the terrifying prospect of meeting Seb's mother in the flesh. The only contact so far had been her tones, crisp and chill as an iceberg lettuce on the answerphone, barking out instructions for Seb to call her. "We're having dinner," Seb added.

"Why didn't you tell me before?" Anna was panic-stricken in the knowledge that the fridge and cupboards contained little beyond anchovy paste and Pop-Tarts.

"Forgot, I suppose," Seb said, over-casually. "But you don't have to meet her. Mummy will quite understand if you are out. I can take her to the Ivy or something."

"But of *course* I want to meet her." Anna gave Seb a puzzled smile. "And where else would I go? I *live* here, don't I? There's no need to take her out. I'll cook."

Dinner, it suddenly struck Anna, was a cast-iron if not a Le Creuset opportunity to impress Seb's mother with her cooking skills. Or at least the ones she planned hastily to acquire with the help of a notebook and an hour's browsing in the cookery section of W. H. Smith. "I'll do the shopping on my way back."

"Back from where?" asked Seb.

"From here." Anna waved the letter at him. Surely he hadn't forgotten about her interview already?

Seb looked at Anna blankly.

Anna had been up and down the smart Kensington street three times now. People were starting to appear at the corners of the windows to stare. Anna, however, had no option other than to continue squinting at their houses. For, among the figures painted neatly in black on the white pair of pillars framing each imposing doorway, number 54 did not seem to register.

Where 54 should, by process of elimination, have been, the letters Liv were painted. Liv. Odd name for a house, thought Anna. Then it hit her. LIV. Fifty-four in Roman numerals. *Of course.* A *tad* pretentious for a house name, perhaps; she hoped Cassandra had a classically educated postman. But then, most of the postmen round here were probably out of work ex-students like herself. Post-graduates, in fact.

Despite its number—or was it its name?—the house looked just like the rest of the street. A tall, wide slice of West London real estate heaven, its stucco gleaming white in the sunshine, its shining black railings thick and bumpy with a century and a half of paint. An Upstairs Downstairs house with a basement kitchen and five floors above it, their windows decreasing in size and grandeur towards the top. Anna went slowly up the paved path, jumping as the gate clanged treacherously behind her, and, using one of the many pieces of brass door furniture on offer, knocked.

"Yars?" The black-painted door swung back to reveal an overalled woman with electric yellow hair and a suspicious expression. "Can I ewp you?" She shook her peacock-blue feather duster enquiringly.

"Er, I've come to see Cassandra Knight," said Anna. "I've got an appointment."

"Carm in. You'll 'ave to wait in the kitchin. Mrs. Knoight's busy at the mowment."

In the kitchen, airforce-blue panelling coated every vertical surface including, Anna was interested to observe, the front of the dishwasher. A single lily stood atop the vast steel fridge. The black stone table was supported by skinny chrome legs fashioned into spirals; arranged in precisely-measured ranks beneath it were two rows of three tractor-seat stools in chrome. Anna heaved herself on to one, aware she had completely disrupted whatever visual concept prevailed.

The emphatic lack of any hint of food provoked a raging hunger in Anna's stomach. But the disproportionately vast antique station clock on the wall was to measure out a further lonely, unrefreshed half hour before footsteps could be heard on the stairs. An extremely thin woman with white-blonde hair in a straight, short bob, vast black sunglasses, and a white waffle bathrobe wafted through the doorway into the kitchen.

"Cassandra Knight," announced the apparition, sticking out a hand so thin it was practically transparent and as chill as if it had just come out of the freezer. Anna gazed at the bathrobe with admiration. So this was what real writers wore to work in.

She felt instantly disadvantaged by her own hot and sticky palm and not being able to see Cassandra's eyes properly. She could sense them moving behind the sunglasses, cold and invisible as fish at the bottom of a pond. The lenses were as impenetrable as they were inexplicable. Perhaps, Anna concluded, they were intended to combat the glare of Cassandra's computer screen.

"Yes, I recognise you from your book jacket photographs." Anna smiled, hoping to ingratiate herself. Panic flared in her stomach when, instead of looking flattered, Cassandra frowned.

"Which one?" she demanded imperiously.

Anna's mind whirled. She sensed something was at stake. One false move and all could be lost. "Er, the one on *Impossible Lust*," she hedged, plumping for the photograph which, when flicking through the volumes in the bookshop, had struck her as the softest lit, most touched up, and generally most flattering. She had guessed right. Cassandra preened.

"Yes, Tony—Snowdon—did quite a reasonable job on that one," Cassandra purred. "And he did say I was one of the most *challenging* people he had ever photographed. Let's get down to business, shall we?" she suddenly barked. "I haven't got all day. You want this job, I take it?"

Anna swallowed. "I'd love to work for you. It would be a wonderful training for *any* writer…" She stopped as Cassandra held up a hand.

"I *am not* offering a writing course," she snapped. "In my letter to you I said I wanted a *general assistant*. To assist me, er, generally."

"Of course," Anna echoed. "A general assistant."

"*Precisely*," said Cassandra, inhaling so hard on her cigarette her eyes watered. "An, um, *general* assistant is exactly what I want. I take it you're quite *versatile?*" Two plumes of smoke came flying out of her nostrils.

Anna jerked her head up and down eagerly. "Absolutely. I can type, research…even write," she added anxiously.

Cassandra nodded curtly.

"How are you with children?" she demanded.

"*Children?*" Anna vaguely recalled from the potted biographies on the book jackets that Cassandra had a son. Anyone working at close quarters with her would of course have to get along with her family. "Oh, fine," she stammered, recalling the occasional bout of unenjoyable teenage baby-sitting.

"Good," said Cassandra, grinding her cigarette out. "The job involves quite a lot of contact with Zak. He's, um, between nannies at the moment. You—ahem, I mean, whoever did the job—would have to help with the school run, his supper, that sort of thing."

"I see," said Anna, the dimmer switch of her enthusiasm turning down a jot. "But most of the job would be helping *you*, wouldn't it?"

Either Cassandra was nodding ferociously, Anna thought, or she was tossing that highly flammable-looking platinum bob out of the way as she ignited another Marlboro. "Absolutely," Cassandra confirmed. "You'd be helping me an *enormous* amount." She paused and pressed her lips together as the smoke poured out of her nostrils. "But of course if you feel it's not quite right for you…"

"Oh, no, I didn't mean…" stammered Anna, panicking. "I'm absolutely happy to do whatever…" One child, after all, surely couldn't be too much trouble.

"*Good*," said Cassandra, satisfied. She stared at her hands, pushing an amethyst the size of a door handle slowly round her forefinger. "Well, you seem all right to me. You can start tomorrow, if you like. The sooner the better as far as I'm concerned."

Anna felt a huge grin split her face. She was just about to stammer her thanks when Cassandra said, "We haven't discussed pay." She then named a weekly sum so ludicrously low that Anna gasped.

"I can't possibly live on that."

"You won't have to. The job is, of course, live-in."

Of course, thought Anna. That explained the awful money. Living in would be much cheaper for Cassandra. But surely it was unusual for assistants to live in? Nannies, of course, did it all the time. But she wasn't a nanny.

"I didn't realise." She spoke slowly, but Anna's heart started to slam against her chest like a moth trying to reach a lamp behind a windowpane.

"Well, obviously it's live-in," snapped Cassandra. "Children are a full-time job, you know. As is writing, of course," she added hurriedly. "You never know when the muse will strike."

❖ ❖ ❖

Half an hour later, Anna found herself standing, confused, beside the ready-packed salads in Ken High Street Marks and Spencer. She could not concentrate. Her ears were still ringing from Cassandra's furious reaction to being told she would think about the job.

"Most people would give anything to live for free in a house like this," Cassandra had snapped. "I would, for a start," she added acidly.

"Of course, it's the most wonderful house and most fantastic opportunity…" Anna had stammered.

"So what's stopping you?" Anna could feel Cassandra's eyes, turning from cold fish to lasers, blazing through the sunglasses.

"I need to discuss it with my, um, boyfriend," Anna had faltered.

"Your *boyfriend*? Can't you make your own decisions? Christ, if I asked my husband what he thought *I* should do with my life, I'd be permanently making full English breakfasts in between giving him blow jobs."

But Anna, albeit shakily, stood her ground. She would let Cassandra know in the morning. She was not sure she wanted to move out of Seb's so soon. And anyway, there was always the possibility—admittedly remote—that the prospect of her leaving would make him finally lay his cards on the table as far as their relationship was concerned.

She lunged for a bag of Mixed Herb salad, grabbed a box of baby potatoes, and headed finally towards the checkout.

❖ ❖ ❖

"Where the hell have you been?" Seb demanded as she staggered through the door at precisely the same time that the bulging plastic bags, strained beyond endurance, finally burst their flimsy moorings and spilled their contents all over the hall.

"For my interview, of course," Anna said. "I got the job," she added, scrabbling around on the floor after several mushrooms making good their escape.

"Did you get any wine?"

"What? Oh, *yes*, Chardonnay," Anna told him abstractedly. "But they want me to live in," she added, returning to the matter at hand.

"*What?*" said Seb in outraged tones.

"I *know*," Anna said, relief surging through her system. "I mean," she added, "they *do* live in W8, just off Ken Church Street, and their house *is* enormous, but…*oh*," Anna gasped, gazing rapturously at Seb. "I'm so *glad*. I thought you wouldn't care…"

"Of course I care. Chardonnays so *naff*, for Christ's sake. Why the hell couldn't you have got Chablis?"

Anna stared at Seb in disbelief. Had he not understood a word she had said? "So you don't care one way or the other?"

"Of course I care," Seb snarled, furiously thrusting a long-fingered hand through his unbrushed hair. "I don't want Mummy to think she's at a bachelorette party in a Peckham wine bar, do I?"

"Did you hear what I just said to you?" gasped Anna. "I've been offered a live-in job. Do you want me to stay here with you or not?"

"We'll talk about it later," said Seb. "There's too much to do just now." He disappeared into the sitting room, switched on the television, and put his feet up on the sofa arm. Whatever needed doing, someone else was evidently going to do it. Can't imagine who *that* might be, thought Anna, gathering the bags up and heading crossly for the kitchen.

There was something about the way Seb's mother rushed at him as if he were the first day of the Harvey Nicks sale that confirmed Anna's worst fears. Lady Lavenham was, Anna realised, a full-on, fully-paid-up Son Worshipper.

Anna could recognise the breed from a cruising height of thirty-three thousand feet. She had, after all, encountered them before. The boyfriend's mother before last had been one; a Welsh Italian who had made almost nightly phone calls and who had insisted on driving up from Cardiff to college to comfort Roberto practically every time he sneezed.

"Call me Diana," Seb's mother barked to Anna on arrival. The coda, "If you dare," hung unspoken in the air of the hallway, air that had suddenly thickened with expensive-smelling scent.

Anna had been expecting trouble. But she hadn't expected it to look like this. Diana was about as far removed from the tweedy battleaxe Anna had been anticipating as Cameron Diaz was from Margaret Rutherford. It wasn't just that Anna felt wrong-footed by Seb's mother. She felt wrong-haired, wrong-makeupped, wrong-dressed, and most of all wrong-shoed. Diana Lavenham had the type of long, thin, patrician feet that even looked graceful in wellies. A fully-paid-up Fulham blonde, she had thick wedges of expensive hair that shone brilliantly in the light of the hall chandelier, as did the single, polished platinum ring hanging loosely on one long, tanned hand. She had expensive skin too, opaque, glowing, and virtually unlined from a rich diet of face cream. Seb, who had suddenly shot into the kitchen, now emerged sporting an apron, a tea towel over his shoulder, and an air of cheerful culinary professionalism. "Anna, will you take Mummy into the sitting room while I get on with supper?"

"Darling, you're *so* clever," Diana purred at her son as she followed Anna down the hallway. "Are you sure its not *too* much trouble for you?"

"No trouble at all, Mummy, honestly."

That much was true, at least, Anna fumed silently.

Her mouth set rigidly into a smile, Diana regarded Anna with narrowed eyes as they sat at opposite ends of the leather sofa. The silence roared in Anna's nervous ears.

"Tell me about yourself," Diana said creamily. "Basty tells me you want to be a writer. I'd love to see some of your work."

"*Basty?*" echoed Anna, squirming at the thought of an unsympathetic stranger knowing such an intimate thing. Who the hell was Basty? Damn Seb for telling them, whoever they were.

"Se*bast*ian?" said Diana in the bright voice of one trying to communicate with an idiot. "My *son?*" She blinked repeatedly, her mouth turned up at the corners. "I call him that because I can't bear the thought of anyone calling him *Seb. Ghastly.* Makes him sound like an *estate agent.*" As opposed to an estate owner, I suppose, Anna thought.

Seb appeared. "Almost there with dinner," he said, obviously lying. Anna wondered if he had even managed to find his way into the packets of salmon fillets. Heaven knew what he thought the carton of ready-made hollandaise was. Custard, probably.

"I'll come and have a look, shall I?" She rose to her feet, for once grateful for the chance to slave over a hot stove. Anything to escape from this woman's icy, interrogative glare.

Following Anna's intervention, dinner was soon served. Throughout the meal, Diana chatted tinklingly yet pointedly to Seb about people Anna didn't know. "Yes, darling, they've just bought a house in what they call up-and-coming Acton but honestly, I ask you. *Acton?* I mean, where *is* Acton? *What* is Acton? Not even on the A–Z, is it?"

Anna opened her mouth. Here, at last, was something she could contribute to the discussion. "It *is* supposed to be getting slightly smarter, I believe. I have a friend who lives there."

"Oh really?" Diana had still not looked at her once since they sat down at table. She did not look at her now. "And where do *you* live, Anna?"

Anna watched Diana stab a baby potato with her fork. Surely Seb had *told* her they lived together? She shrank into silence and waited for him to take the initiative. It was up to him to explain their cohabiting arrangements to his mother. Who must, even if she didn't know, at least suspect it.

But the silence remained unbroken. Looking from Anna's flushed face to Seb's suddenly grey one, Diana raised a faintly amused eyebrow.

"*Kensington*," Seb burst out suddenly. "Anna lives in Kensington. Just off Ken Church Street, actually. With a writer. Anna's her assistant."

Diana looked coolly at Anna. Was it Anna's imagination, or did those narrow blue eyes hold a triumphal glitter? Diana smiled. "How *fascinating*."

"How *could* you?" Anna screeched at Seb after Diana, who had lingered as long as she possibly could in the obvious hope that Anna would leave first, had finally descended to her Dorchester-bound Dial-A-Cab.

Seb shrugged, unrepentant. "Well, what was I supposed to tell her? It's not as if we're married, is it? Anyway, I've done you a favour. She owns the place, after all. If I told her you lived here, she'd probably start charging you rent."

"Thanks a *million*," Anna snapped, having searched in vain for some appropriately reductive retort. She tried to console herself with the thought that even Oscar Wilde would have been stumped with Seb; all the *bons mots* in the world, after all, failed to get Bosie to behave himself.

"But it's probably time you moved out anyway," Seb muttered, not meeting her eye. Anna suddenly felt sick. Here it was then. It had finally come, the moment she had always been expecting, yet never really believed would happen. She was being given her marching orders. Like an employer dismissing an unsatisfactory servant, Seb had sacked her without batting an eyelid. There had been a steeliness to his tone which suggested attempts to plead for clemency would be useless. Not that she felt like pleading. She felt like taking the untouched hollandaise sauce and pouring it all over him. Especially when the mysterious person who refused to leave answerphone messages flickered once more into her mind.

Retreating to the bathroom, Anna slammed the door and set the water thundering from the taps to disguise the sobbing that suddenly overwhelmed her.

It was the humiliation. The helplessness. The sight of her naked body in the bath. The roll of flesh seemed bigger than ever; her stomach rose above the waterline like an island. An *island*. Anna sighed, wondering what Jamie was doing now, and suppressed the thought of what she could be doing with him, were she there too. Why the *hell* had she told him about Seb? What had there, after all, been to tell?

She lay in the bath, hot and shiny with misery and sausage pink with fury. Her anger mixed with the steam rising from the foam-free water; the final insult was that Seb had, at some point during the day, used up the last of the Floris Syringa her mother had given her for her birthday. Her mother would never meet Seb now. But it was unlikely either would have relished the occasion.

One good thing, Anna tried to persuade herself, was that if she wasn't going to be the wife of a sewage millionaire, at least she could take the job with Cassandra. This prospect, though it lacked the platinum charge card, sports coupe, and season ticket to Champneys that went with the former career option, at least offered a large and luxurious house in one of fashionable Kensington's most fashionable streets. Not to mention an apprenticeship with a successful writer. She'd show Seb. *And* his stuck-up horse of a mother. Anna permitted herself a delicious few minutes imagining their faces when she hit the bestseller lists.

If the job was still available, that was. Anna glanced at the watch on top of her pile of clothes on the loo seat. Just past midnight. Too late to ring Cassandra now. Please God she hadn't found someone else. She'd ring her first thing in the morning. In the meantime, Anna decided, as the silent sobs overtook her once more, she'd just sit in the bath and weep.

Chapter Seven

USUALLY, CASSANDRA NEVER SAW first thing in the morning. She usually hit it around fourth or fifth thing, but this particular ante-meridian was different. She'd had to get up *ridiculously* early to do an interview. In the normal course of events, Cassandra loved nothing better than talking endlessly about herself to journalists—friendly *OK!* and *Hello!* ones in particular. But there was nothing friendly about the sharp-faced, skinny woman sitting opposite her on the cowskin sofa with a tape recorder, a notebook, and a sceptical twist to her lips. Her eyes intermittently darted round the room, focusing in on, Cassandra was cringingly certain, every surface left respectively undusted, bashed, and unwiped by Lil as she had made her morning rounds. That was the trouble with minimalism; there was nowhere to run when it came to hiding dirt.

Lil herself had already been grilled; as Cassandra had clumped down the thin, stripped wood stairs to greet her inquisitor, she had overheard the cleaner being questioned about her mistress's working hours and daily routine. Although not a religious woman, Cassandra had sent a heartfelt prayer heavenwards to whichever benevolent deity had allowed her to appear on the scene before Lil had got on to the breakfast gin and tonics.

A curse on her publishers though, thought Cassandra, grimacing. The deal that had eventually been hammered out between her agent and the increasingly irascible people who commissioned her books had been that, the continued non-appearance of Cassandra's expected new manuscript notwithstanding, the planned publicity for the novel should continue to go ahead. Hence the presence of this spiky girl in her sitting room.

Cassandra sighed inwardly and gazed glassily at the journalist. The pre-interview nerve-soothing double gin had not only affected her concentration, but had dealt a temporary death blow to her ability to see straight.

"Sorry, can you rephrase that?" she asked.

The journalist looked astonished. "Er, yes. I just asked you what the name of your son was."

"Zachary Alaric St. Felix Knight." Alaric St. Felix had been the dashing hero of *Impossible Lust*, in whose heady, thrilling, champagne-and-cash-flooded wake (and particularly the former) Zak had been conceived. Repeating Alaric's name only reinforced Cassandra's awareness that she had so far failed to invent a hero to rival him.

"How do you *cope* with him?" the journalist asked next.

Cassandra's heart skipped a beat. What *exactly* had this woman heard about Zak? Surely she didn't know about the dreadful events of yesterday. "Theft, madam, is a criminal offence no matter *whose* son you are," that ghastly little Boots store detective had snapped. "How *could* you?" Cassandra had furiously admonished Zak all the way home. "Stealing like a common criminal."

It wasn't the *criminal* bit she minded—heaven knew, half the squillionaires in the City were crooks and she was fervently hoping Zak might join their ranks one day. It was the *common*. And from *Boots*, for Christ's sake. If Zak *had* to steal, he could at least have chosen Harvey Nicks.

"Cope?" she asked suspiciously. Was this woman trying to catch her out?

"Well, we've talked about your bestsellers and how you write them, but we haven't touched on how you also manage to run a house this size *and* have a family life. Not to mention how you keep yourself in such great shape."

Relief swept through Cassandra. This was more like it. "Oh, well, I find getting up at five and doing a couple of hours on the treadmill generally does the trick," she simpered. "I try and read all the papers at the same time."

The journalist looked astonished. "But surely you have some help with *something*? Do you have a nanny even?"

Cassandra shook her head vigorously. "No," she smiled. "No help at all."

"Why on earth not?"

Because that stupid fat Anna girl had had the unbelievable cheek to practically *beg* for the job and then announce, cool as a Decleor face pack, that she'd *think* about it, Cassandra thought viciously whilst training a look of melting sincerity on the journalist. "I suppose I can't bear to think of my child being brought up by *anyone* else but me," she said silkily. "It would be *desperately* sad to miss these crucial years when his character is forming, don't you think? He's so independent, Zak. Such an amazing little personality already."

The journalist nodded sympathetically; this argument, Cassandra was gratified to see, went down much better with her than it did with Mrs. Gosschalk. For Zak had taken full advantage of the inter-regnum in nannies and had, besides the shoplifting, recently been conspicuous by his absence at school.

The result was that the headmistress's office had been on the phone again complaining about his behaviour. Cassandra's blustering defence that it was proof of her son's extraordinarily entrepreneurial outlook and incredible creative spirit had cut no ice with Mrs. Gosschalk, although she had conceded "extraordinary" and "incredible" were accurate descriptions.

"And then of course," said the journalist, "you're half of a high-profile marriage."

Half, thought Cassandra indignantly. If you were talking profile, she was a good *two-thirds* of it, thank you very much. What on earth had Jett done this side of the Boer War? She very much doubted the re-formed Solstice would be a stadium-filler. If the tepid press reaction their reunion had prompted so far was anything to go by, they'd be lucky to be a stocking filler.

"Yes. Jett and I are truly blessed," Cassandra cooed through gritted teeth, "because, apart from being lovers, we're such good friends. We're very close. There's hardly ever a cross word…"

The sound of the slammed front door interrupted her musings. "Sandra?" roared a voice. "Where the hell are you? You've got to get someone else to take that *goddamn* brat to school. He's doing my goddamn head in."

The journalist stared in astonishment.

"In here, darling," trilled Cassandra, faking a sudden attack of coughing in the forlorn hope of drowning Jett's yells. The journalist's thin lips curved slowly upward.

"Hang on, I'm getting a goddamn drink first," yelled Jett, thundering down the stairs to the kitchen. "Zak made me park the goddamn Rolls round the corner *again*," he bellowed from below. "Said he was embarrassed in case the other kids saw it. And when I told him he should be goddamn *pleased*, not embarrassed, that his father had achieved enough to have a Rolls," Jett continued, his voice approaching up the kitchen stairs, accompanied by the rattling of ice cubes, "Zak said he was embarrassed because the Rolls was so *uncool* and *all the other kids' parents had groovy four-wheel drives*."

Cassandra had now coughed so much her face was red and streaming. That her efforts had been utterly in vain was obvious from the way the journalist was checking the red Record button of her tape recorder and scribbling maniacally on her pad. As Jett's raddled visage appeared round the sitting-room door, Cassandra was momentarily torn in deciding which of them she wanted to murder the most.

"What's going on?" he demanded, looking from Cassandra to the journalist. "Not another of your *goddamn* Mystic Meg sessions, for Christ's sake."

"If you're enquiring as to whether this is one of my metamorphic technique lessons, then the answer is no," said Cassandra, icily. "I'm being *interviewed*."

The revelation that he was in close proximity to a publicity opportunity had a more electric effect on Jett than the famous incident in Athens, Georgia, 1978, when his guitar had been accidentally (or was it? he was still not sure) plugged into the mains. Even by his optimistic lights, the reaction of the music press to the news Solstice were re-forming could hardly be described as ecstatic, with the result that "Sex and Sexibility" needed more of a push than overdue quadruplets. He could not afford to let golden opportunities like this pass.

"Hi. Jett St. Edmunds," Jett said, stretching out a hand to the journalist. Not bad, he thought. A bit skinny and pasty perhaps. "And you are?" he asked, pulling in his stomach and moving closer.

"Brie de Benham. *Daily Telegraph*."

"Hi, Brie. Know the name," Jett drawled, chewing on a nonexistent piece of chewing gum.

Yes, of course you do, Cassandra only just stopped herself saying. *From the Waitrose cheese counter*. She could spot Jett's thunder-stealing game a mile off. She was aware that "Sex and Sexibility" was hardly lined up to be the Christmas number one, but she'd be damned if it got publicity, however badly needed, at the expense of her new book.

"How's it going?" Jett asked, fixing Brie with his most charismatic stare.

"Fine," Brie smirked. "Miss Knight has been telling me how she gets up at five and reads all the newspapers while she's working out in the gym."

Jett stared at his wife, who returned his gaze unblinkingly. "Gets up at *five*?" he chuckled. "Oh yes, she gets up at *five*, all right. Five in the goddamn *afternoon*, that is. And working out? The only thing of Sandra's that gets regular exercise is her goddamn credit card."

In the hall, the telephone began to ring. Both Jett and Cassandra held their ground, locking eyes, neither willing to give up the valuable field of potential publicity to the other. "Phone's ringing," smirked Jett at his wife. "Probably that goddamn Gosschalk chick. She's never off the blower."

Silently telling herself she was doing it for her son, Cassandra gritted her teeth and stalked out of the room. Jett promptly sat down on the sofa beside Brie de Benham, who immediately rammed her elbows together to make the most of her skinny cleavage.

"*Ass Me Anything*," he breathed. Might as well get in a plug for the album straightaway.

"OK." Brie switched on her tape recorder again. "Is it true that Jett St. Edmunds isn't your real name and you're really called Gerald Sowerbutts?"

"*What*? What are you goddamn talking about?"

"You said to ask you anything."

"*Ass* me anything. Name of the new goddamn album."

"Oh. Right. Well, anyway, is it true? About the name?"

"Of course it bloody isn't," snarled Jett. "I'm called St. Edmunds because I come from there."

"From Bury St. Edmunds?" At least, he thought, she'd got off the Gerald bit.

"You gottit, baby."

This was, in fact, merely the version of the truth preferred by the record company who, having decided to ritz up Jett's Christian name, completed the exercise by surnaming him after the town where their A&R man first discovered him performing "House of the Rising Sun" *a capella* to an audience of two at a bus stop. Jett had objected to the name at first because he thought the town was pronounced Bury Street Edmunds, but preferred the story, as well as the rest of the tricky subject of his origins, to remain cloaked in mystery.

"And do you ever take your sunglasses off?"

Through the mirrored shades Jet invariably wore to do everything but sleep in, he saw Brie looking at him coolly. "Take them *off*?" He laughed theatrically. "Honey, I'm in showbiz." Brie smirked.

"Is it true what I've heard about you women journalists?" Jett murmured, moving his mouth close to her ear. "That you keep vibrating pagers in your knickers so you get a thrill when someone calls you?" He placed a hand heavy with silver skull rings on her thin, black-nyloned knee and began to work it slowly up her thigh. Hearing the phone slam back down in the hall, he hastily took it off again.

Cassandra swept back into the room looking triumphant. "Thank God," she declaimed. "That girl's finally seen sense. She's moving in tomorrow morning."

"What girl?" asked Jett, looking hopeful.

"The fat one who *inexplicably* lives in Mayfair. She's coming to be the nanny." Joy was not a regular visitor to Cassandra's fearful heart, but now she positively fizzed with it. No more interminable games of Monopoly with Zak, although it *was* gratifying how good he was at it. No more Harry bloody Potter at bedtime. Best of all, no more calls from Mrs. Gosschalk.

"The nanny?" echoed Brie, faintly mocking. "So you're getting some help after all." Cassandra did not like the tone of her voice.

"Not at all," she snapped. "This girl is an Oxbridge graduate. She is coming to be my assistant. It's just that," Cassandra added in an undertone, "she's going to be assisting me in rather more ways than she bargained for."

❖❖❖

The following morning, Anna let herself out of Seb's flat for the last time. As she headed for the bus stop and the Kensington-bound No. 10, she worked out that probably the most valuable thing she possessed was an old beaver coat which had a marked tendency to moult. It had been the only thing Seb had ever given her. Apart, that was, from an inferiority complex the size of Manchester.

Her recent emotional traumas, however, had not remotely affected her ability to be everywhere far too early. It made sense in a way; she had always suspected that her tendency to be unfashionably punctual had sprung from a lack of self-esteem. Following Seb's recent antics, it was surprising she wasn't even earlier—Cassandra had told her to present herself and her belongings at eight o'clock sharp, and here she was at a positively devil-may-care five to.

For reassurance more than warmth, Anna huddled further into the depths of the tatty coat. Seb had told her it gave her a Russian air. Doubtless, she thought sourly, he had meant less Anna Karenina than headscarved babushka with wrinkles deep enough to rappel down. *Bastard*.

Anna lifted the fountain-pen shaped knocker and let it crash back against the door. Following some vague sounds of shouting from within, it was opened by a man wearing studded black leather boots and a T-shirt bearing the Dayglo green legend, "My Probation Officer Went To London And All I Got Was This F***ing T-Shirt." Given its thinness and his age, his hair was longer than seemed advisable; his creased and baggy face was less lived in than marked for demolition.

"Your dog's obviously very fond of you." He looked pointedly at her upper thighs.

Anna glanced at her legs in mingled panic and fury. The coat had been shedding all over her. Her best Joseph trousers were covered in short black hairs.

"Oh, its not a dog," Anna said. "That's my beaver." The moment the words were out of her mouth she regretted them.

"Well, I can see we're going to get on splendidly," the man remarked, a broad grin splitting his stubbly face. He thrust out a hand. "You must be Anna. I'm Jett St. Edmunds, Sandra's husband." The palm that greeted Anna was as hot and moist as rice pudding. And rice pudding was one of the few—very few—desserts that Anna had never liked.

"Stick your bags in the hall. Sandra's in there." Beckoning her in, Jett gestured at the door of what Anna assumed to be the sitting room. "She's not," he added, with a conspiratorial wink, "in a very good mood."

Anna entered the vast white sitting room to be greeted by the sight of a bathrobed Cassandra prone on a chaise longue. She was wearing a sleep mask that failed to disguise that, beneath it, her expression was thunderous. Beside her on the floor lay a copy of the *Daily Telegraph*.

Cassandra raised herself a little. "You *bastard*," she hissed. "How dare you come in here after what you've done. You've ruined *everything*."

Anna swallowed, scared as well as confused. "Um, your husband told me…"

Cassandra whipped off her mask and stared at her in fury. "Oh, it's *you*," she said grudgingly. "At *last*. I've got to go out to an extremely important meeting."

Rather like those people who die and come back to life, Anna had a vague impression of lots of brilliant white. Rugs, cushions, curtains—apart from the two cowskin sofas, all was white. The floorboards were pale and interesting, as perhaps they were in heaven, Anna thought. Heaven, after all, was bound to be stylistically unimpeachable.

A small boy suddenly burst shouting into the room and stopped stock still when he saw Anna. He regarded her with approximately the same level of warmth and enthusiasm generally accorded to a heap of dog faeces. *After* one has just stepped in it.

"This," said Cassandra triumphantly, her *froideur* melting like ice-cream in the sun, "is Zak."

The boy wore grey tweed plus fours, a matching short jacket, black boots with buttons on the side, and, above his thick white-blond basin cut, a ribboned straw boater. He bore an equally close resemblance to his mother and the pre-Ekaterinburg Czarevitch.

"Don't you look wonderful?" smiled Anna encouragingly. "Very Railway Children."

"What's Railway Children?" demanded the boy.

Cassandra smiled indulgently. "I'm afraid, Anna, that the only railway Zak is familiar with is the first class Eurostar to Paris. But St. Midas's uniform *is* splendid, isn't it? *Everyone* recognises it—let's face it, there's no point shelling out four thousand a term otherwise, is there?"

"I suppose not," Anna agreed, faintly puzzled. She had always imagined high school fees reflected the quality of the teaching rather than the complexity of the uniform. And had Midas really been a saint?

"*One* of the governors," Cassandra added, "recently tried to vote to have Edwardian underwear as well but some of us felt that was a little, well, *excessive*. I believe"—she dropped her voice—"that the gentleman in question is under investigation by the Kensington police at the moment...But it's a marvellous school. Very *media*. Half the BBC top brass send their children there, not to mention practically every national newspaper editor." She flashed Anna a conspiratorial grin. "The opportunities for *networking* are excellent."

"That must be very useful for you," Anna remarked politely.

Cassandra's face froze. "Not for *me*," she snapped. "*For him*. You can never start too early, you know. After all, the children at St. Midas's now will probably be shaping the future of the country in twenty years' time."

Anna shot a glance at Zak who had by now climbed on the cowskin sofa and was jumping maniacally up and down on it with his boots on. It was not a comforting thought. Aware he was being watched, Zak then leapt down with a clatter on to the wooden floorboards and started kicking Anna's handbag with the tip of his boot. "I'm David Beckham," he shouted.

"Don't do that, darling," Cassandra murmured, as Anna bent and pulled her bag out of the way. "Those boots are very expensive."

"Is *she* my new nanny?" Zak pouted, looking sulkily at Anna.

"*Yes*," said Cassandra crisply.

"*Not exactly*," said Anna at the same time.

"Sort of," Cassandra compromised, giving Anna a dazzling, don't-argue-with-me smile.

There was an uncomfortable silence.

"She's not very *pretty*," said Zak loudly, staring boldly at Anna. "But she's got big tits. So you won't need to send her to the hospital like Imelda, Mummy."

Another uncomfortable silence. Bubbling under with rage, Anna felt she could not let this pass.

"What does he mean?" she asked. Cassandra had reddened slightly.

"Oh, he's referring to an operation one of his former nannies had," Cassandra said with a rather forced lightness. "*That's enough, darling*," she mouthed.

"Mummy wanted to have a tit job but didn't dare," Zak announced loudly. "So she made Imelda have one first to see what it looked like and to see if it hurt."

Anna was so astonished she forgot she was angry. Meanwhile, the unspeakable brat was speaking again.

"Has Daddy tried to shag you yet?" he demanded excitedly, fiddling covertly with his genitals through his pocket. "Don't worry. He will. He even shagged Imelda. Particularly after the tit job."

"*Zak!*" shrieked Cassandra. "My son has a very lively imagination," she added hastily. As Zak still rummaged frantically in his pocket, Anna felt her apprehension grow.

"Would you like to see my scab?" asked Zak, his hand emerging from his pocket balancing a matchbox on his palm. A matchbox which, Anna noticed, bore the logo of the Hotel Eden Roc, Cap d'Antibes. With a flick of his pink thumb, Zak pushed it open to reveal a very large, very green, and very nasty-looking scab, with specks of blood and shining green mucus still attached. It looked very fresh, although, darting a quick glance at Zak's smooth golden knees, Anna was unable to see where it had come from.

"It looks very painful," she said. "You must have been very brave when it came off."

"Oh, its not *mine*," said Zak, faintly contemptuous. "It's Otto Greatorex's. And *no*, actually, he wasn't *at all* brave. It took three of us to hold him down, but *I* ripped it off." He grinned at Anna, revealing gappy white teeth set in very pink gums. Behind him, Cassandra let out a light laugh.

"Such a *character* already, isn't he?" She smiled at Anna.

"You can say that again," growled Jett, suddenly entering the room behind them, the metalwork on his boots jangling irritably. "Look what he's done *now*."

The creature straining to be released from his hairy arms was not instantly recognisable. It looked, Anna thought, rather like a very large, very bald, and very angry rat. "This," said Jett, holding the furious animal up so it clawed wildly at the air, "is what remains of Lady Snitterton's Bengal Blue after Zak's had a go at it with my Remington."

Chapter Eight

THE ROOM CONTAINED A desk, a hard chair, and a sofabed that had clearly seen better days. Judging from the cracked and peeling paintwork, it was obviously between decorating jobs as well. Anna looked round in admiration. So *this* was where Cassandra did her writing. *This* was the inner sanctum.

"What do you think?" asked Cassandra.

"Wonderfully *plain*," Anna said brightly. "I imagine it's a marvellous place to concentrate."

"*Concentrate?*" Despite her permanent efforts to keep her face as expressionless and therefore wrinkle-free as possible, Cassandra could not prevent a slight frown rippling across her forehead. "Are you *Buddhist* or something?" she demanded, realising that, once her first, fierce instinctive opposition to anything unusual or foreign had worn off, she rather hoped so. After all, Baba Anstruther was always banging on about her wretched New Age Italian au pair, the sum total of whose duties seemed to be floating around the school gates in white, reeking of essential oils, and flirting wildly with the house husbands. Cassandra stared thoughtfully at Anna. Yes, a Buddhist would suit her very well. Very *Absolutely Fabulous*—and, Cassandra wondered, straining her sketchy grasp of theology to its limits, weren't they the ones who were supposed to renounce all worldly goods? That would sort out any remaining ifs and buts over Anna's wages very nicely.

"Oh, you're not a Buddhist," Cassandra said, disappointed, as Anna shook her head. "New Age then?" she hedged hopefully. "Oh well, I'll leave you to make yourself at home," she announced finally, a petulant note in her voice.

"You mean this is my *room*?" gasped Anna in horror.

"Yes, what did you think it was? A very *comfortable* room this is," Cassandra said defensively, in the face of all visual evidence to the contrary. She sat on the sofabed and bounced gingerly up and down on it. A hollow rattle ensued. "One of the best addresses in Kensington."

"I thought it was your writing room," Anna said boldly.

Cassandra's reptilian eyelids flickered for a moment. Better not push it *too* far, she realised. Time to concede a point or two; after all, she didn't want the wretched girl leaving. Not now she'd gone to the *enormous* trouble of showing her all over the house. But the sooner she snapped out of the idea of being a bestselling writer, the better. Everyone knew writers didn't look like *that*.

"Well, it's not," Cassandra said curtly. "My writing room is just off my bedroom, as it happens."

What was the creature saying now? Where was her bathroom? *Her* bathroom? What did she think this was, bloody Claridges? "You use the *downstairs* loo," Cassandra snapped. "And there's a shower in the garage."

"But…"

Closing the subject with a wave of her bejewelled hand, Cassandra led the way to the considerably warmer and smarter lower floor where she flung open a door to unleash a blaze of colour.

"Zak's room. Marvellous, don't you think?"

Anna blinked. "It's very, um, *bright*."

"Biodegradable, non-allergic paints in serotonin-stimulating primary colours," Cassandra announced briskly. "*Very* important to have a lot of brightness around—develops a child's senses, increases intelligence. Can't have Zak falling behind at school just because his bedroom is the wrong shade."

"I suppose not."

"Naturally, I've checked on what everyone else in Zak's year has, just in case. Otto *Greatorex*," Cassandra pronounced, as if a rotting kipper had been placed under her nose, "has a really rather *ill-advised* pirate theme in his nursery, while Savannah and Siena Tressell—well, of course, their father *is* an architect—have a trendy French thing in primary colours with lots of foam-rubber cubes and tubes everywhere. Mollie Anstruther has a giant Barbie bedroom—*ghastly*—and Ellie Fforbes has an appallingly *vulgar* fairy palace with chandeliers and a four-poster bed. Screamingly camp, but then, of course, there have always been question marks about which team her father bats for…"

"So," said Anna, looking at the walls and choosing her words carefully, "what's the theme here? The countryside?" Each wall crawled with animals and sprouted foliage in preternaturally bright colours. Small settlements appeared between gaps in the fat blades of grass—here sunny English villages, complete with church spires, there Eastern cities, minarets gleaming in a starry sky. It reminded Anna strongly of a pantomime set. Or perhaps a particularly cheesy birthday card.

"Well, originally it was supposed to be Narnia, as you can probably tell. I'd booked Damien Hirst to do it—he's a friend of my architect—but he had *absolutely no intention* of following my designs." Cassandra pursed her lips at the memory.

"What a shame," Anna said. A halved and pickled Zak would have added a certain *je ne sais quoi*.

"The only other bedroom I really rather envied," Cassandra said, "was Milo and Ivo Hope-Stanley's Nantucket-style one; terribly glamorous, all tongue and groove panelling, Navajo blankets, bunks based on ships' berths, and Stars and Stripes cushions—very Ralph Lauren. Caroline Hope-Stanley's housekeeper used to be a stylist for *World of Interiors* and she knows just how to arrange it. *Lil*, of course, wouldn't have had a *hope*. But that's all over, thankfully."

As if the horrors of that morning's *Telegraph* hadn't been enough, Cassandra had, just before Anna arrived, swept into the sitting room to discover Lil had failed to wipe the smoky smudges off the scented candle glasses *yet again*.

"If I've told her once…" Cassandra raged as she stormed round picking up and slamming down the black-tipped jars with the Diptyque label.

"Really gets on your wick, doesn't it?" Jett drawled. He spoke in a lightly insouciant tone precisely calculated to cause his wife maximum annoyance. He wasn't a musician for nothing.

Cassandra had stormed out of the room in search of the hapless domestic. She'd had enough. Something had to give. Notice, preferably.

Cassandra tsked now as she snatched down a poster of a grinning David Beckham. "Can't *bear* those boy bands, can you? That's Zak's bathroom, by the way," she added, gesturing at the vast white expanse visible through a door ajar at one end of the room. "Make sure you clean behind the sink pedestal. It gets filthy there for some reason."

"Me? *Clean?*"

"Yes, I've had to let Lil go, unfortunately," Cassandra trilled. "So if you could just step in for her for the moment, that would be lovely. Oh, and there's a pile of ironing downstairs for you—we iron all sheets and underwear here, I'm afraid—and if you could just run round with the Hoover that would be fabulous. Garden could do with a weed and I'm afraid I haven't had time to go to Waitrose either. To make your first day as easy as possible, Mr. St. Edmunds will do the school run this afternoon as well—you can take over tomorrow morning. Lunch is at one. Roast Mediterranean vegetable terrine, I thought."

"Lovely," mumbled Anna, still reeling from the list of tasks.

"So if you start to cook it at about eleven, that should be fine. Right, I'll leave you to sort yourself out."

Anna returned upstairs to "her" room and closed the door. She placed her back against it and slid slowly down into a crouch. Looking hopelessly at the bare and cheerless surroundings, she felt the familiar gulping in her throat. She wondered what Seb was doing now. Still in bed probably—it was hardly half past ten, after all. Probably not alone. As tears stung her eyes and began to roll slowly down her cheeks, she closed her eyes and swallowed hard. From millionaire's Mayfair apartment to skivvy's boxroom, she reflected. And all in the course of one morning. You've come a long way, baby.

Anna's first night on the sofabed was even worse than she had expected. After the endless fetching, carrying, and negotiating involved in putting Zak to bed, she had finally turned back the thin and smelly duvet, only to hear a bloodcurdling howl ricocheting wildly around the walls of the room. It took a few seconds for Anna to realise it was her own.

As the ghastly sight sank in, shock shuddered through her as if from a hairdryer dropped in the bath. There, on the grey-white sheet beneath the duvet, crouched the stark, black and hideously leggy forms of what looked like at least twenty enormous spiders. Anna *hated* spiders.

"Of course," Cassandra said, appearing in the room in a baby blue pashmina bathrobe, her eyes round islands of contempt in a sea of face cream, "had you been to *public school* you would have *instantly* realised that they were the tops of tomatoes and not real spiders. It's the oldest trick in the book, along with apple pie beds, although I understand duvets have put a stop to those. Really, I'm *amazed* you fell for it. Zak's *hilarious*, isn't he?"

Having been educated through a series of largely benign local state seminaries, Anna's knowledge of public school had come mostly from Enid Blyton and Seb, neither of whom had mentioned tomato tops. They would, anyway, have failed to register on the Richter scale of prep school nastiness that Seb had suffered—being made to swim outdoors naked in the freezing cold and have Matron smack your penis with a cold spoon were among the more lurid lowlights he had mentioned to Anna. Seen from this angle, it was no surprise Seb had turned out to be the person he was. It was amazing he wasn't worse.

"And making all that *ridiculous* noise as well," Cassandra continued mercilessly. "Zak needs his sleep, even if *you* don't. He, at *least*, has to work hard tomorrow morning. All you have to do is take him to school."

"I've done them this morning," Cassandra announced martyrishly next day. "But from now on, they're *your* responsibility." Collected in the hallway was a sprawling collection of extremely smart bags which looked like the personal effects of a visiting potentate. An entire suite of Louis Vuitton; a soft, buttery, buckled leather holdall; dark red crocodile Mulberry and any number of Bond Street carrier bags nestled up lovingly on the floor with the entrails of the vacuum cleaner, which Lil had evidently started to disembowel and then thought better of.

"Gosh," said Anna admiringly. "It looks like the luggage people take on Learjets." Some of the bags, in fact, had Learjet labels on them, albeit slightly ancient ones.

"*Learjets!*" Cassandra shot her a withering glance. "*No one* takes luggage on Learjets," she snapped.

Anna looked puzzled, previously unaware that the celebrated jet was luggage-free. She supposed it made sense—how else, after all, did it go so fast?

"All the luggage on Learjets," Cassandra explained, a pitying note in her voice, "is carried *on* and *off* by the cabin staff. Only tourists or the *terminally unsophisticated* take their *own* on."

"Oh. I see." Anna resolved to bear the tip in mind next time she flew supersonic.

"*These* are Zak's *school* things." As Cassandra produced a list and began performing a roll call of the contents and purpose of each bag, Anna's jaw dropped ever nearer to what Cassandra had already told her were the individually peasant-fired Tuscan tiles on the floor of the hallway. Wonderingly, she recalled the one satchel and single gym bag which had got her through her entire formal education.

"Young Futures and Options," barked Cassandra, pointing at a Vuitton attache case in the corner. "Operabugs and Junior Gastronauts," she added, stabbing at another bag. There was also a fixture for *extra* extra tennis—"His instructor says he's Wimbledon potential." Cassandra chose not to reveal that what the instructor had actually said was that, *yes*, Zak could easily get to Wimbledon, but only if you were talking about the Tube station. There was advanced French and dinner-party Chinese—"Well, Zak may as well learn how to pass them the mangetout if the bloody Chinks *are* taking over the world, after all." After being briefed about Madame Abricot's dance class and what sounded like tuition in every single instrument of the orchestra, Anna felt almost sorry for Zak.

Until, that was, he climbed into the brand new four-wheel drive—"We only got it yesterday and any damage comes straight out of your wages"—and turned the radio up to window-shattering volume. As Zak began throwing himself about on the front seat to the music, Anna inched through the Kensington High Street traffic, uncomfortably aware of the curious gaze of taxi, lorry, and double-decker bus drivers.

"Mummy's very cross with Daddy," shouted Zak suddenly. "There was an interview with him in the paper yesterday, about his new record. My daddy's a very famous pop star, you know."

"I see," said Anna, glancing frantically between the *A–Z* and the back bumper of the car in front.

"The interview was *supposed* to be about Mummy's book," added Zak. "But the only bits about Mummy were her shouting at Daddy."

"You've read it then?" asked Anna. She was surprised until she recalled Cassandra saying that reading and discussing the broadsheets was part of the daily curriculum at St. Midas's.

"No, but Mummy read lots of it out very loudly at Daddy, so I heard."

St. Midas's seemed to be at a particularly tricky-to-get-at end of the Cromwell Road, an area inconveniently plunged into the darkness of the *A–Z* gutter. Panicking, Anna snapped back the book's paper spine and stared fiercely at it for clues. It was only when other minivans, their back seats alive with squirming children in boaters, plus fours, and leg o' mutton sleeves, drew up in the lanes either side of her that Anna realised she was on the right track.

"Look, look," screeched Zak, clambering over the front and then the back seat to bang on the rear window. "It's Savannah and Siena! They're overtaking!" As the lights changed, a shining minivan containing two leg o' muttoned girls sped past.

"Put your foot down, *stupid*," Zak ordered Anna. "Catch them *up!*" Despising herself for being intimidated by an eight-year-old, Anna allowed the speed to creep up a fraction on the dial.

"I'm going to call them." Zak leant over the front seat, rifling through the Mulberry rucksack and eventually producing a miniature silver mobile phone. He stabbed at the keypad for a few seconds before diving into the bag again. "Bugger, I've forgotten their number," he cursed. "Where's my Air Book?"

That contact with Savannah and Siena had finally been established was confirmed a few seconds later by muffled whispering and giggling in the back. Anna swallowed and tried not to listen as "Yes…new nanny…I *know*…" floated over from the rear.

"No, you *don't* come in with me," Zak ordered imperiously as Anna parked beside the gates of the handsome pair of Queen Anne houses which, to judge from the boaters pouring within and the sign standing proudly without, was St. Midas's School. "Stay *there*." Slamming the door behind him with shattering violence, he ran off.

Waiting for her blood pressure to subside from Dangerous to merely High, Anna sat and watched what she assumed to be a collection of St. Midas's mothers and fathers milling about the entrance. Sartorial competition seemed stiff, if not positively cut-throat. Pashminas abounded and there seemed more racehorse legs around than at a Grand National starting line-up. The morning sunshine bounced off gleaming, well-cut hair, shining, straight white teeth, and gold and diamond rings. And that was just the men. These people, Anna realised, spent a lot longer preparing for school than their children did.

She stared through the windscreen as she conducted a gloomy résumé of life with Cassandra so far. The word *writing* had not been mentioned once, although the word *nanny* had, countless times. Feeling her spirits slump, Anna leant over and rested her forehead on the steering wheel. The view that met her was the far from uplifting one of her black-trousered thighs spread out like flattened sausages on the driving seat. She sighed heavily.

A sharp rap on the window disturbed her musings. Blearily, Anna looked up to see a grinning dark-haired girl wearing a great deal of plum-coloured lipstick. She rumbled in panic for the window button.

"*Geri!*"

"Hi, babe. Didn't realise it was *you* I was racing down the Cromwell Road in the Bratmobile."

"I didn't realise you had children," Anna said, bewildered. She stared at Geri with renewed admiration. Was there no end to her capabilities? Combining high-powered management executiveship with single motherhood and *still* finding time to put her lipstick on properly.

"Oh, they're not mine," Geri said breezily. "They're just part of my portfolio of responsibilities. But what about you? That was Zak Knight you had in the car, wasn't it? Surely…"—her eyes widened—"*surely* you're not…his latest nanny. Are you?"

"*Latest*?" Anna tried to keep the quaver out of her voice.

Geri glanced at her. "Got time for a coffee?"

"Probably not," said Anna, recalling the Augean list of chores Cassandra had barked at her as she had tottered out of the door en route to A Very Important Meeting. "But it sounds like I'd better."

Cassandra's hands shook as she took her seat at the long wooden table. Despite her distracted state, she could not help noticing that it was, as usual, polished to a mirror-like perfection infinitely beyond the capabilities of Lil. Lil hadn't even been able to polish mirrors to mirror-like perfection. Still, hopefully the new girl would do better. She certainly couldn't do worse.

Cassandra shot a nervous look at the set and determined faces around her, each one of which, she knew, had its own agenda as well as that which, neatly printed and bound, lay before each delegate on the glossy expanse of the table. She cleared her throat, took a swig of still water from the sparkling tumbler before her, and clicked the end of the pen which had been laid at a precise diagonal across the jotting pad bearing the letters SMSPA.

"May I call the meeting to attention." An imposing brunette with thin lips and elegantly understated makeup shuffled the sheets in her perfectly manicured hands, slipped on a pair of rimless glasses, and cast a steely glance over them and around the table. "Item one on the agenda. Funds…"

Boring *boring*. Why did they always have to trawl through the money bit first? The backs of her thighs, Cassandra realised, were well and truly stuck to the shining leather seat of her chair. Any movement would result in a ripping of flesh ten times more painful than the most inept bikini wax. She should have worn tights—but it was so easy to get the shade wrong and, anyway, leaving them off was an opportunity to show everyone else how unscarred, well moisturised, and, most importantly of all, *thin* her legs were. No hiding behind thick black opaques for her, thank you very much; it was vital at these meetings that you showed yourself off to the best possible advantage. One false outfit and you were sunk; your stock as irreversibly lowered as if your knickers had fallen down.

"...pleased to announce," enunciated the brunette in crisp tones, "that the Association finds itself in its best financial position *ever*..."

Bugger Polly Rice-Brown, thought Cassandra, glaring at the speaker and wincing as her left outer thigh peeled itself away from the seat. Why *leather* dining-room chairs, for God's sake? Surely that brat of hers wasn't *still* peeing everywhere? It had taken weeks to get rid of the smell of urine after Sholto Rice-Brown had stayed overnight with Zak; an occasion which Polly had had the *bloody* cheek to claim actually marked the *start* of Sholto's loss of control over his bowels. She'd tried to blame Zak, of all people, just because during the night he'd dressed up as a ghost and pretended—not *tried*, as Polly had insisted—to strangle Sholto. Honestly, Cassandra silently fumed. Some people had no sense of *humour*, let alone any appreciation of the exceptionally *imaginative* child Zak was.

No, Cassandra decided, an agonising tug at the bottom of her right buttock returning her abruptly to the present. She really shouldn't have worn quite so short a skirt; despite its being one of Enzo Boldanzo's signature bold prints (at his signature bold prices). But the computerised wardrobe had been playing up again...

She shot a careful glance to her left. Even Shayla Reeves was wearing what looked suspiciously like Prada trousers. *She'd* changed her sartorial tune, Cassandra thought viciously, hoping for the hundredth time that the rumour that Shayla had bagged her Premiership footballer husband whilst working as a lap dancer was true. If it was, Shayla had certainly ratcheted herself up a class or ten since—her son was called Caspar, for Christ's sake. Her interior-designed Notting Hill home, innocent of the merest trace of concrete lions, had recently been opened to *Hello!* magazine and her neatly side-parted hair had lost all trace of strip-club blonde and was now a tasteful fugue of beige and brown stripes not dissimilar to the top of a fine sideboard.

"...the St. Midas's School Parents Association," continued Polly, "would like to take this opportunity to put on record its thanks to Caroline Hope-Stanley for her careful stewardship of our funds..."

Cassandra pursed her lips. Just *what*, she thought to herself, is so bloody *amazing* about being a good treasurer when, like Caroline Hope-Stanley, you've been an investment banker for *ten years*. She glanced over at the offending official—lightly tanned, long blonde hair, slim figure in jeans and T-shirt, the latter brilliant white to match those great pearly gates of teeth of hers. Oh-so-relaxed, except that the jeans were Versace, the T-shirt Donna Karan, and the teeth the beneficiaries of the latest American bleaching treatment. Caroline's casual look, Cassandra estimated, cost twice as much as most people's smartest—certainly more than Polly Rice-Brown's, who had on what was quite obviously something from Topshop.

"...our Bolivian interests, in particular, have yielded high revenues..."

Now of course, Cassandra thought sardonically, Caroline wasn't a banker any longer. She was one of the gym-sleek, Knightsbridge-groomed breed of New Housewives; she'd packed the City in at the age of thirty-two in order to bring up her twins Milo and Ivo. *With* the help of a full-time nanny, a housekeeper, and an army of cleaners and gardeners. "I simply adore being at home," she had told more than one glossy magazine. "I now realise what I was missing out on." Well, the sack for one thing; if Cassandra could remember rightly,

Caroline's entire team of fund managers had been made redundant the week after she'd walked off with her golden handshake, due to question marks about the ethics of some of their South American investments. Drugs had been mentioned. Bolivian interests *indeed*.

"...some of the fund-raising initiatives have been particularly inspired..."

Cassandra ground her teeth. She was sick of Polly Rice-Brown's fund-raising initiatives. Ruthlessly determined to raise more in her stint as SMSPA chairman than anyone ever had before, she had already organised Himalayan treks, East to West bicycle tours of America, and blindfold bungee jumping. And, loath as Cassandra was to admit it, she *had* raised a great deal of money. By the end of it all, Cassandra thought sourly, St. Midas's would be able to send up its own space probe.

"The Bring Your Child To Work Day, of course, was a big hit..."

Bringing them to work being the only way *some* women ever saw their children, Cassandra thought piously, reflecting on the fact that she saw as much of Zak as possible. Whether she wanted to or not. She'd heard that tale, famous among St. Midas's mothers, of how Sholto's final act before going to sleep was to call up his mother at the newspaper plant where she worked as a picture editor and whisper "Night night" to her on his mobile. Not to mention the poignant rumour concerning Savannah and Siena Tressell, who supposedly spent one Christmas Day feeding turkey to the television, or, more precisely, to their absent TV presenter mother's talking head on the screen.

"For me, of course," Polly continued, "Bring Your Child To Work Day was wonderful. Sholto was such a hit with the editor that he was actually given his own newspaper column taking a sideways look at life as an under-nine..."

Precocious *brat*. Cassandra had been bored to death already during the pre-meeting coffee about the National Theatre's being

Sholto's second home these days, his forthcoming solo violin debut at the Wigmore Hall, and the sample chapters of his first novel that were already causing a stir in publishing circles.

"Aren't you a bit worried?" she had asked.

"About what?"

"Well, all this artsy stuff. Doesn't sound very…*masculine*, does it?"

"Oh, I see what you mean. Well, that's fine. We're quite happy to have one of each."

"One of each? But Sholto has a brother, doesn't he?"

"Exactly, one of *each*. One gay and one straight."

Well, what else did you expect from someone who worked on a bloody *leftie* paper? Cassandra thought. A *tabloid*, at that.

"…which of course led," Polly was saying now, "to the piece Sholto wrote about the dilemma of how to tell his old nanny about her appalling BO winning the coveted Columnist of the Year award…"

Cassandra fumed. Her own efforts having never earned anything other than derision from the literary establishment, it was hard to accept that an eight-year-old had won such an award. With a piece about a *nanny*, of all things. Well, she could give them pieces about nannies until they came out of her *ears*. *Christ* knew what the St. Midas's bunch had made of *her* new one. What had all the glamorous nannies everyone else seemed to employ so effortlessly thought of someone who quite obviously had never seen a full-length mirror? Or *any* mirror, judging by that *figure*. More visible panty line than the knicker department of M&S, not to mention tits like *coalsacks*. Cassandra glanced down complacently at her own neat little buds, still standing proud after thirty-nine years on the planet and a little help from the appropriately named Dr. Pertwee. Not forgetting Imelda, much as she'd like to. Shame Zak had brought all *that* up again. Especially after the pains she'd taken to keep Imelda and her family quiet about the pains Imelda had apparently suffered. As if, snorted Cassandra to herself. Girl had got a free tit job, hadn't she? Even if one *had* imploded, it hadn't *cost* her anything.

Still, the fact that the new girl was plumper than a Christmas goose should at least keep Jett from straying. He *hated* fat women. Mind you, she'd hired Emma on the grounds that she weighed a good twelve stone and look what had happened there.

Cassandra sighed at the thought of her husband. Jett was like a dog in heat at the moment. He was quite *literally* a pain in the arse. Whether it was the absence of Emma or an excess of testosterone generated by the incipient release of his comeback album, Cassandra was not sure. Whatever it was, it wasn't welcome. He'd wanted her in everything from whipped cream to Nutella over the past few days and when, last night, he had asked her to crawl under the glass-topped coffee table, Cassandra had decided enough was enough. "You pervert!" she had screeched.

"But I'm only asking you to pick up my goddamn lighter," Jett had protested. "You know I can't bend down that low with my goddamn back problems."

"I don't care," Cassandra had shrieked. "You've gone too far this time. You're disgusting."

"OK then, I'll pick it up myself," Jett had drawled. "And you can pay the goddamn osteopath's bill," he had grimaced a few minutes later, clutching his spine in one hand and flicking the tiny silver microphone lighter furiously on and off with the other as he headed through the door to spend the rest of the night in the spare bedroom. Cassandra sighed. Most men Jett's age only wanted sex once a year—and usually not from their wives even then.

"…a vote of thanks for Kate," Polly Rice-Brown was saying when Cassandra tuned back in. Cassandra glanced enviously down the table in the direction of Kate Tressell's flawlessly chic porridge linen Mao jacket. Then there was the Cartier Tank on the narrow wrist, whose thinness implied steely self-control and whose tan hinted at regular trips to the second home in Tuscany. Trust Kate Tressell always to wear the right thing, as well as have the right job being the nation's favourite current affairs anchorwoman, as respected for her brain as for her shapely bottom. She also had the right husband—happening architect Julian Tressell who combined building Britain's most talked-about edifices—such as his famous Tressell table which sank into the floor when not in use—with presenting a successful TV programme on the history of architecture. Kate also had the right haircut, dark-blonde and expensively tousled. And the waft of discreetly delicious perfume that had just entered Cassandra's nostrils from Kate's direction was, no doubt, the right smell.

"How does Kate manage to be the hottest thing in broadcasting, not to mention being one of the most proactive of St. Midas's mothers?" simpered Polly, echoing Cassandra's boiling thoughts. "Really, she's an example to us all…"

The rest of the table sat and listened to Polly's encomium about how, without Kate's determination and, more importantly, her contacts, the schools new state-of-the-art TV studio would never have got past first base. Or off the drawing board of Julian, who had designed it. The TV studio was intended not only to elevate St. Midas's facilities for its pupils into an entirely different league to that of even its closest competitors, but also to provide a training ground for the producers and presenters of tomorrow, amongst whose ranks Kate and Julian's daughters Savannah and Siena were obviously intended to feature.

Savannah and Siena, no doubt, would dominate the chattering classes of the future as easily as they excelled in the Kumon maths classes of today. They and their parents were easily the brightest stars in St. Midas's mini-firmament. And it was for this reason more than any other that Cassandra had come to the meeting.

Her mantelpiece—in infuriating contrast to Fenella Greatorex's—*still* being inexplicably innocent of an invitation to

Savannah and Siena's birthday party, Cassandra had decided to screw her courage to the sticking place and *force* Kate Tressell to invite Zak. After all, the children certainly *got on;* Savannah and Siena were almost unique among St. Midas's pupils for *not* having been the victims of some of Zak's more hilarious pranks. And there had been so many of those high-spirited expressions of Zak's boundless humour and creativity—Cassandra had only to raise her eyes and recall the time Zak had shut Milo Hope-Stanley in the garage overnight. Or when he had helped himself to the foie gras in Fenella Greatorex's fridge that was intended for a client-clinching dinner party. *Then* he had been sick all over the sisal. She quickly lowered her eyes again.

Zak had never done anything remotely like this to Savannah and Siena, although preventing him *had*, Cassandra thought ruefully, taken more persuasion than Jane Austen. So why, why, *why* had she not been granted dropping-off and picking-up rights to the birthday party? Cassandra clutched her fists so hard under the table that her knuckles turned white. Zak simply *had* to be there. After the appearance of Cherie Blair and the First Kids at last year's celebration had prompted a rash of newspaper articles about Power Children's Parties, the Tressell bash had become the most talked-about children's event since the Pied Piper hit Hamelin.

Cassandra hardly noticed the meeting moving on. Her mind was locked on to the party like a barnacle on the hull of a boat. She felt panic rising; had she not, for the past month at least, tried to impress on Zak that if he didn't get an invitation, there would be hell to pay? And there had been plenty to pay already—Zak had been connected to the Internet on the grounds that last year's summons had been sent out by e-mail. Cassandra had heard that this year's was some sort of smart card pass. Surely the invitation, whatever form it took, would come soon? She looked desperately at Kate's smiling face as she acknowledged the applause for her efforts. How on earth could she introduce the subject? Perhaps over a cup of coffee afterwards? But what would she *say*?

Kate's minimal makeup made Cassandra wonder anew if she'd needed *quite* so much lipstick on herself. But then, some of the mothers coming to these parents' meetings hired makeup artists for the occasion. And why not? St. Midas's, after all, was not any old school. It was a power prep of the first order. Which was why securing an invitation to its most sought-after event was so *vital*. Cassandra felt sick. She *couldn't* go home empty-handed. If Zak wasn't asked, they'd have to change schools; there would be nothing else for it, the shame would be too much to bear. But Zak had already changed schools so often due to what Cassandra could only put down to the lack of *imagination* of the head teachers, there were precious few left for him to go to—landing a place at St. Midas's had been a miracle of the first order. But even so, and without losing her sense of proportion *too* much, the rest of Zak's *life* depended on this party.

She swallowed hard and tried to refocus on the matter in hand. The meeting had by now moved on from the much-anticipated joys of the about-to-open studio—"Can you imagine, a mini *Question Time*? We could make a pilot and try and get the Beeb to squeeze it in between Blue Peter and the six o'clock news…"—to the next item on the agenda. Some group of bleeding hearts, Cassandra noted with scorn, were suggesting that St. Midas's set up an outreach link with London's underprivileged—"Holiday work with the homeless so that the children would gain some understanding of those considerably worse off than themselves," as the movement's main spokeswoman put it. Cassandra listened with contempt. Who in God's name wanted to understand anyone *worse off*? The whole *point* of St. Midas's was to meet as many rich and useful people as possible. But the bitter core of her loathing was reserved, not for these ludicrous sentiments, but the fact that their mouthpiece was that *bloody* Fenella Greatorex. Whose son *had* been invited to The Party.

"I mean, it's the *homeless* I just can't bear to see," Fenella sighed.

"Oh, *absolutely*," burst out Cassandra. "I mean, if they *have* to lie around all over the pavements, why can't they do it in nicer sleeping bags? Those disgusting blue flowery ones are *so* unstylish. They really ought to have more consideration."

A frozen silence followed. Cassandra smirked to herself. *That* put the bleeding heart lefties in their place once and for all. The shocked expressions round the table reminded her of the time, several meetings ago, when she had admitted to spending Zak's child benefit on Chateau Lafite.

"Um, well," Polly Rice-Brown said, after a plethora of throat clearing. "Perhaps we could think about that while we move on to the next item, the Promises auction. Which, hopefully, will get the fundraising for our next project, the film-editing suite, off to a great start."

Cassandra's dormant interest in any other subject but The Party was briefly stirred. The film-editing suite would, with luck, encourage Zak's obvious acting ability and get his film star career off to a great start as well. Her secret dream, apart from securing The Invitation, was that Zak star as Alaric St. Felix in the blockbuster film version of *Impossible Lust*, the only one of her books to be optioned by a film studio and still, as it had been for the past five years, stuck in Development Hell. "Impossible Film," Jett sneeringly called it.

To demonstrate her devotion to the project, Cassandra had come up with what she confidently expected to be the most sought-after item in the auction. Surely even Kate Tressell would be impressed with this.

"Well, thanks, everyone, for promising such wonderful things," Polly Rice-Brown said, half an hour later. Wonderful my *arse*, thought Cassandra sourly. What on earth was the use of Caroline Hope-Stanley's offer of a year's supply of horse manure from their weekend place in Oxfordshire? "For the garden, of course," Caroline had snapped when Cassandra had said as much. Or Polly Rice-Brown's wildly over-generous year's subscription to her bloody newspaper? Much as it pained Cassandra to admit it, the detox day at a health farm promised by Fenella Greatorex almost nudged the borders of reasonableness—until one reflected on the fact that Strydgel Grange was, quite apart from being firmly on the health spa B list, one of Fenella's own PR accounts.

Cassandra's own contribution had not quite been the one she had intended. Her original offer of an autographed boxed set of her own works was unexpectedly dismissed out of hand on the grounds that the purpose of the auction was to raise the school's profile, not any of the mothers' (Cassandra had dwelt bitterly but silently on Fenella Greatorex's spa at this point). *In extremis*, she had had to come up with a substitute. VIP seats at the Solstice reunion concert being deemed similarly unsuitable, Cassandra had eventually been pressed into offering to cook a dinner party for eight *at her home*. Or rather, offering Anna to cook for it, and the cheapest way possible. Was pasta and pesto, Cassandra wondered, a socially acceptable dish?

The end of the meeting was now in sight. As the smell of coffee drifted over from the kitchen wing, Cassandra braced herself to button-hole Kate Tressell—despite the fact that the latter's Mao jacket had no obvious buttons on it. Leaping to her feet, the leather seat ripping from the backs of her thighs, Cassandra stumbled, eyes watering, in Kate's wake as she headed with remarkable speed for the hallway.

"Just one thing," Polly called, holding up a hand to the half-dissolved meeting. "Kate's had to dash, but she wanted to suggest the auction be held at Siena and Savannah's birthday party. She thought it would be something for the parents there to do."

Cassandra's heart sank. Following the rest of the herd into Polly's Provençal-style kitchen, she wondered whether to commit hara-kiri with one of the large knives protruding from the olive-wood butchers block. The worst had happened. She had secured neither invitation nor word with Kate Tressell. Suicide seemed the only option.

Chapter Nine

ABOUT THE SAME TIME as Cassandra took her seat at the highly polished conference table, two men behind the counter of a little French cafe in Kensington burst into flamboyant and flirtatious life as a curvaceous girl with long brown hair and precisely applied lipstick made her entrance. Geri, Anna saw as she followed in her wake, was clearly a regular.

"So tell me what's going on," Geri said, as they sat nursing cappuccinos. "Why have you departed from my carefully constructed, individually tailored personal goal-achieving plan?"

Anna's face stayed frozen. "I *haven't*," she said evenly. "As a matter of fact I'm sticking to it like glue. I'm *supposed* to be Cassandra's assistant. She's *supposed to* be teaching me to write."

Geri raised an eyebrow and lit a cigarette. "I see. When did you start?"

"Today's my second day."

"Which means," Geri said, "you've been with her a full twenty-four hours. That puts you streets ahead of some of Cassandra's past nannies. One lasted about ten minutes, I believe."

"How many has she got through?" Anna's voice had lowered to a horrified croak. Her heart thumped against her rib cage and, despite the fact she was sitting down, her knees shook uncontrollably.

"Well," grinned Geri cheerfully, "you're the seventh this year, at a conservative estimate. I expect Cassandra just forgot to tell you about the others."

Anna was silent. It was all very well for high-powered career girl Geri to think her predicament the most enormous joke.

"But the good news," Geri continued, "is that you're in a *brilliant* position."

"I *am*?"

"Yes. All us nannies are."

"You're a *nanny*?" Anna gawped at Geri in amazement. "But what was all that about management consultancy and executive responsibility? I thought you were the head of Unilever at the very least. A captain of industry."

Geri took a bite from her croissant and grinned at Anna as she chewed. Her other hand still held the cigarette.

"But I *am*," she said. "We both are. We're valuable commodities in one of the most highly sought-after sectors of the economy. That of childcare provision."

Anna snorted. "You *are* joking? I feel about as valuable and sought-after as yesterday's copy of the *Sun*."

"Don't you *see*? It's a complete seller's market," Geri continued enthusiastically. "Play your cards right and you have the pick of who you work for, you can practically write your own salary cheque, you get glamorous holidays thrown in and get paid for going on them, you don't pay tax or National Insurance, there are no overheads whatsoever, and there are plenty of perks. I, for instance, have a company car."

Anna stared. "A *company* car?"

"Sure. You have to see the families you work for as companies. Some of which perform well, others not so well. Your job is to help them improve their performance."

"*Performance*?" gasped Anna, to whom the idea of the family as a unit floated on the stock exchange of life was an altogether new one. "But how on earth do you *measure* it?"

Geri gave a short laugh. "Let me count the ways," she grinned. "Like any company, through the achievements of its individual members and of the group as a whole. For children, there is a practically endless list of fields in which they are expected to compete and excel. Some of their timetables are more crammed than their parents'…"

Anna suddenly remembered the list of Zak's after-school lessons.

"Academic performance, for example," Geri continued. "The competition among parents even before the school stage is incredible. I've worked for people whose nursery floors are covered with rough sisal matting so the child will be discouraged from crawling and learn to walk more quickly."

"*No!*"

"Oh yes. Some of my past employers set up entire pay structures incorporating performance-related bonuses if the baby learned to talk by a certain date. At the moment, for instance, I have to make sure Savannah and Siena can talk about current affairs at their parents' power Sunday lunches. So every night we watch the six o'clock news and discuss it afterwards."

Anna was speechless. Geri, meanwhile, was anything but.

"The key," she said, stuffing in the last of the croissant, "is to identify your role in the corporate organisation and then exploit it. If you don't believe me, ask the others. They've just come in."

A laughing group were ordering at the counter. Anna recognised them as the same glamorous creatures she had seen milling about outside the gates of the school; a dark girl dressed entirely in white, a lanky man in a tight T-shirt, and two blondes—a rangy, bobbed one who sported loafers and cashmere, and a larger sporty-looking one. "You see that blonde with the bob?" Geri whispered. "That's Alice. Worked for Cassandra about three months ago." As a roar of laughter suddenly convulsed the group, Anna's heart fell out of her bottom and hit the stripped wood floor. The sick feeling in her stomach, she told herself sternly, must be due to her lack of breakfast.

"Hey, guys. Over here." As the group began to look about them for seats, Geri waved frantically. "Come and meet the new recruit."

Chairs borrowed from neighbouring tables were scraped across wooden floorboards as people shoved, exclaimed, giggled, and shuffled into position. In the end, everyone was squashed round the tiny marble table, which the waiter then attempted to pile with cappuccinos and croissants.

"This is Anna," Geri announced. "She's Zak Knight's new nanny." A collective gasp followed, then a silence interrupted by a giggle, followed by a snort which, much to Anna's annoyance and intense embarrassment, soon achieved fullblown laugh status. Alice, Anna noted, was laughing hardest of all.

"Well, you've got to laugh, haven't you?" she sniffed, mopping a streaming eye. "Otherwise you'd cry." She stopped as she caught Anna's baleful glare.

"Let me introduce everyone," Geri interrupted hastily. "This," she said, gesturing at the large blonde girl who, Anna saw with interest, had a perfectly round face the colour of strong tea, "is Trace. Works for a journalist called Polly Rice-Brown. Cassandra knows her. Zak tried to kill her son once."

"Wish she bladdy hed," pronounced Trace in broad Australian tones. "Wouldda sived me doin' it. Liddle *bastard*."

"Oh, come on, Trace, you know you don't mean that," interjected the lanky youth who, besides his rangy figure, had big lips, high cheekbones, a heavy Eastern European accent, and subscribed to that variety of sexiness known as brooding. "You love Sholto," he continued in the same flat monotone. "You just won't admit it."

Trace grinned. "Well, I suppose I *im* fond of the liddle *bastard* really. When I think what I could have inded up with…" She flicked a small-eyed glance at Anna.

"This is Slobodan," Geri intervened, introducing the lanky youth. "He looks after the children of someone called Caroline Hope-Stanley, another of the St. Midas's mothers."

"You're a nanny?" Anna exclaimed. "But you're a *man*."

Everyone laughed. Slobodan winked at her.

"Male nannies are *terribly* trendy at the moment," Geri explained. "Particularly exotic ones. One of the St. Midas's mothers has a rather dishy Japanese bloke called Hanuki, who was the first male Norlander. Slob's from Bosnia. Lots of the mothers are starting to want men to look after their children—they're more athletic and brilliant at games."

"Yes, Caroline loves my games." Slobodan narrowed his eyes and grinned. He shifted in his seat, drawing attention to the very tight jeans straining across his crotch, and pushed back his floppy dark hair with both strong, tanned forearms.

"Slob's a terrible flirt," Geri said, rather unnecessarily. "The St. Midas's mothers love him, despite the fact he insists on pickled fish sandwiches for breakfast. The Hope-Stanleys' stock has shot through the roof since he came on the scene—they get invited to everything so everyone can flirt with Slob. He's probably been through most of the mothers by now. And a few of the fathers as well."

"Ees not true, Geri," Slobodan protested, grinning. He winked at Anna. "Not *all*. Not *yet*."

He might be about as subtle as Benny Hill, Anna thought, smiling back, but he was *very* attractive. However, judging by the challenging way the dark-haired waif next to him was looking at her, she wasn't the only one who thought so.

"I'm Allegra," the girl breathed in an Italian accent of X-rated sexiness. "How do you do?" She over-pronounced the "H," Anna noticed, in a way that made her large lips pout even further forward.

"Allegra's even trendier than Slob," Geri supplied. "She's one of London's first New Age nannies. She smears her children with oil and makes them take baths with lots of dirt and leaves in them."

"Oh, Geri," protested Allegra, pushing her lips out like drawers. "You know the hoils are hessential hoils, for the calming of the bambini, and they are sage baths with horris root, to promote 'appiness."

"Allegra ees very good at massages as well," Slobodan added, grinning. Anna smiled back, feeling slightly better. It was, she decided, like being in a nanny version of *Friends*.

"And this is Alice." Geri waved at the girl with the blonde bob, whose face, Anna thought, was as long, flat, and pale as a new wooden spoon. "As I explained, she used to work for Cassandra and now works for someone called Shayla, whose husband's a footballer. Now you've met everyone. I've just been telling Anna that being a nanny's the best job in the world," Geri added, to general murmurs of assent. "That we've got our employers round our little fingers. Trace has, in any case. Almost didn't take her latest job because of the skiing—"

Anna nodded, feeling it was about time she said something. "Skiing's not my strong point either," she told Trace, who looked astonished.

Geri stepped in, grinning. "Trace *loves* skiing," she explained. "The problem was that the Rice-Browns wanted to take her to Val D'Isère with them and Trace never skis anywhere but Aspen."

Trace nodded triumphantly as she took a large mouthful of *pain au raisin*. "They daren't even take a holiday without checking with me whether it's somewhere I want to go to and that the dates are convenient for me," she assured Anna through a bad case of tumble-drier mouth. "I was saying to Polly only yesterday, do we have to go to Barbados *agin*? Why not splish out and try the Maldives? So thit's where we're going."

Anna stared.

"Trace gets poached more often than anyone else," Geri explained. "The Rice-Browns are desperate to keep her, but she'll go eventually. She gets great offers, all the time. Fighting off half the royal family at the moment, aren't you, Trace?"

"Not that that's saying *anything*," Alice chimed in. "I worked for some royals once and they were ghastly. Mean as mouseshit. Wrote the dates on the lightbulbs, for Christ's sake. Rock stars are the best ones—at least I used to think so before, um…" Her voice faded into a cough as she avoided Anna's gaze and pretended to splutter on her Marlboro. Anna blushed anew.

"But we're all very jealous of Allegra," Geri said hastily. "She's worked for loads of celebrities, from Tom and Katie to Richard and Judy. She's supposed to be writing a kids-and-tell book about it all, in fact." Allegra pouted and raised an eyebrow. "But she's got such a cushy number anyway," Geri added. "Her family, the Anstruthers, are so anxious not to lose her, they've given her a Saab convertible and her own apartment with a Jacuzzi bath. She's got them by the balls, haven't you, darling? Quite literally, if all that stuff about you and Oliver Anstruther is true."

Slobodan sucked his cheeks in thunderously, while Allegra smiled lazily. "*Si*, and I've already had offer of upgrade to Porsche Boxter from someone else."

Anna was fascinated. She had never thought of nannies as ruthless executives before. Less Mary Poppins, more Gordon Gekko. The only things Poppins about Geri, Anna noticed, as they all stood up to leave, were the top few silver buttons of the short-skirted blue dress straining to hold back the brown tide of cleavage. That was Poppins out all over.

"Is that a uniform?" Anna asked pointedly as everyone started to drift out of the cafe. After all Geri's self-determinist big talk, the clothes of subservience seemed something of a comedown. "Don't you mind having to wear one?"

Geri threw back her shoulders, thrusting out her impressive bosom yet further. "*Mind*?" she barked, slipping on a navy blue coat with distinct NHS overtones. "Far from it. I *insisted* on it, as a matter of fact. Best professional tool I've got. You look the part, no one argues with you when you're in one, and"—she lowered her voice—"men *love* them."

"Uh?" Anna was lost again.

Geri flashed her a sly smile. "Let's just say that at my current employer there are benefits I'm planning to avail myself of when the market situation is right." She paused and grinned. "I'm having some very interesting discussions with the CEO at the moment."

Anna frowned. "You mean the father?"

Geri nodded. "He's an architect and works a lot from home." She paused and gave Anna the benefit of her dazzling smile. "You might say the situation's building up nicely."

Cassandra roared through Kensington crashing her gears and grinding her teeth. The SMSPA meeting had been a nightmare, and not only because of the non-materialisation of the party invitation. As she was leaving, Cassandra had overheard Fenella Greatorex mention that St. Midas's was holding aptitude tests at the end of the week; when questioned, she had turned those huge cow's eyes on Cassandra and said, *yes*, absolutely, and hadn't Cassandra got a letter about it?

Back at Liv, Cassandra hunted high and low for the letter. Nothing. Bugger all in Zak's room, or in the wretched nanny's room, although there was a diary in one of the drawers that looked quite interesting, she'd come back to that later. She spent the rest of the afternoon with *A Passionate Lover* but, somehow, it failed to gel. Three double gins later it seemed to be gelling less. But that was only because the thought of The Tests was dominating everything. If Zak failed, his entire educational future would implode. Her dreams of him breezing through Common Entrance into whatever senior school topped the league tables at the time would have to be forgotten, along with those of Zak's Cambridge First and his being a Blue in everything from jousting to Footlights.

"I don't know what you're worrying about," Jett said when Cassandra came down for yet another gin and a consultation with him on the matter. "No point him going to university anyway. He can go to Clouds House like I did."

Cassandra almost choked on her Bombay Sapphire. "What, you mean the *detox centre*? Where you dried out?"

"Sure," breezed Jett. "The way you're spoiling him, he's going to end up there before he's eighteen anyway. May as well make an advance booking now."

Cassandra exploded. "How *dare* you accuse me of spoiling Zak? Can you *blame* me? It was *almost ten years* before I could have that child."

"Only because you wouldn't have sex for nine of them."

Cassandra stormed out of the room and returned to her study where she stared out of the window, thinking not of her book, but of her son. Her clever, charming son, who said the *sweetest* things.

"It took you *nine* years to have me, Mummy?" he had said when she told him. "You must have been *very* tired." Cassandra smiled a watery smile. Zak had such a very *particular* view of the world. There had been the time he had seen her getting dressed in the bathroom and rushed downstairs to tell the gathering dinner party, "Mummy's got hair on her bottom." Cassandra still blushed at the memory. Along with that of Zak telling the entire school gate set that "Mummy has been taken away by a policeman because of her straps." Reassuring everyone that she was not running an S&M brothel but had merely been driving without a seatbelt had been humiliation of the first order.

At half past seven, when Anna appeared through the door with Zak, Cassandra's grey mood had deepened to a thunderous black.

"Where the hell have *you* been?" she yelled.

"School run," murmured Anna.

"Well, what school did you bloody run to?" Cassandra shouted. "*Gordonstoun*?"

Anna could not frame a reply. Waiting outside Zak's endless extracurricular maths, music, judo, and dance classes, she had listened to so much radio news her mind was numb. In the interests of keeping her temper while Zak ground the fistfuls of cereal he had apparently been saving since breakfast into her hair, she had taken so many deep breaths on the way home she was practically hallucinating. She was also desperate for a pee.

"Excuse me, I must just…"

"What's that on your head?" Cassandra resumed her disdainful interrogation as soon as Anna emerged from the lavatory.

"Cereal. Zak was shoving it in my hair all the way home."

"I don't know what you're complaining about," Cassandra retorted. "Oatbran is very good for hair. Don't you ever read glossy magazines?" Mmmm. She raked Anna up and down with her chill glance. "Thought not."

"The loo stinks of *poo*," Zak announced loudly as he emerged from investigating it and came back into the sitting room. "Ugh!" he said, looking directly at Anna. Rage boiled within her. She'd had a pee, that was all. Little *bastard*.

"Darling, do you have a letter for me about some examinations?" Cassandra's voice was pure syrup.

"I don't think so," Anna began.

"Not *you*. Zak."

"No," snapped Zak. "Can we have a portable video disc player for the car?" he wheedled. "Siena and Savannah have one. They only cost a thousand pounds and then you can watch pop videos in the minivan. And can we have a minivan? Everyone else has one."

"If you pass your exams, darling," said Cassandra tightly. She didn't want to think about Savannah and Siena just now. "Right, this letter must be somewhere. Let's just look in your pockets, shall we—*ugh*."

Her face screwed up with revulsion as she unearthed a festering handful of paper, cloying cereal, and a substantial quantity of rotting green matter which may or may not have been more of Otto Greatorex's scabby knee.

"I don't know *how* you could allow him to go about with all *this* in his pockets," Cassandra ranted at Anna as she placed it gingerly on the table. "It's *disgusting*. Probably *dangerous*…ah, here's the letter." She smoothed out the chewed-up, screwed-up ball and scanned it quickly. "Oh, it's easy peasy, darling. All you need to be able to do is draw a triangle and a circle and that sort of thing."

She poked again at the matted mass on the table. Something shiny caught her eye. "*What's* this?" Cassandra's hand trembled as she held up what looked like a silver card. Her eyes blazed feverishly in her face. *Could* it possibly be…

"'Ninvitation," Zak said casually, his attention absorbed in setting fire to a pile of post with the microphone-shaped lighter which was once again under the coffee table.

"To *what*?" Cassandra's voice was trembling as well.

"S'vannah and Siena. Birthday party."

"H-*how* long have you had it?"

"'Bout a week. Not going to go, though. All *girls*."

Cassandra gasped, then dropped to her knees before her child. "Darling," she breathed, her voice cracking with emotion, "you *must* go. It's very *important* to Mummy that you go. Do it for Mummy, darling."

"Nah," said Zak, scowling.

"Isn't he wonderful?" Cassandra grinned rigidly at Anna. "*So* independent-minded. But *darling*," she addressed him again, waving a finger, "I'm afraid part of being grown up is that sometimes you have to do things you don't want to."

"Fuck *off*," said Zak and scampered out of the room.

Chapter Ten

AFTER THE FIRST WEEK as Cassandra's nanny, Anna found it hard to believe she had ever been anything else. It was impossible, as she crept, back bent, round the house, Hoover in one hand, *Harry Potter* in the other, to imagine the scale of her past achievements. Neither the fact that she had a university degree nor that she had had a dashing, blond heir—albeit to a sewage fortune—as a lover now seemed possible. Her utter and permanent exhaustion wiped out even the fierce pangs of longing for Seb that had, at first, lain in wait to ambush her when she was at her lowest. But before long she didn't have the spare energy to squander on emotional indulgence. Her entire previous existence—and most sentient hours of her present one—seemed to have been annihilated by the cycle of toil and bone-tiredness otherwise known as looking after Zak, as well as all the housework. Anna had never known a building which required as much attention as Liv. Not to mention its mistress. Several times, since entering Cassandra's service—and service in the below-stairs sense at that—Anna had felt life quite literally to be not worth Liv-ing.

She had heard, of course, that child care was drudgery—the screaming in the night, the endless demands—but she had always imagined that was the child, rather than the mother. Not in this case. After completing the school run and returning to the house, Anna's first duty of the morning was to go up the three flights from the kitchen to Cassandra's bedroom with a tray containing her breakfast requirements. These comprised one peeled and cored Egremont

Russet apple cut into eight identical sections, one slice of dry toast (lightly golden) with the crusts removed, Earl Grey tea in a china cup and saucer served with the merest dash of milk, and a vast number of different vitamin tablets—one each from the serried ranks of bottles kept in the kitchen. So vast, indeed, was the proportion of pills consumed compared to that of food that it seemed a miracle Cassandra didn't rattle when she moved. The gin, which swiftly followed half an hour after breakfast, may, Anna thought, possibly have had something to do with this.

Remarkably, Anna's first attempt at serving Cassandra's breakfast had gone without a hitch. She did not fall upstairs with the large and unwieldy tray, nor did she slip over on Cassandra's wooden bedroom floor and throw boiling hot water over her employer, tempting though it was. Anna went back down to the kitchen feeling ridiculously relieved. Until, that was, the already-familiar screech resonated through the house. Anna raced back up, her mind juddering with ghastly possibilities. Was the toast last season's tan rather than this season's pale gold? Had something unspeakable crept out of the slices of Egremont Russet? She arrived in Cassandra's bedroom to find her propped up against her pillows, her face contorted and purple with fury.

"The tea," Cassandra roared. "It's *disgusting*. I can't *possibly* drink *such filth*."

"But it's weak, like you asked. With a dash of…"

"It's not *stirred*," Cassandra yelled, seemingly oblivious to the teaspoon lying beside the saucer. "*Deal* with it, will you?"

"Perfect," she pronounced five minutes later when Anna reappeared with a cup stirred so vigorously that, its journey up three flights of stairs notwithstanding, the milk was still swirling around like a flamenco dancer's skirt. "You're learning, you see."

Anna was by now beginning to wonder if that was all she was learning. After days in the job, writing had not been mentioned once. There were, however, mitigating circumstances; as far as Anna could see, Cassandra had not written a line since she had arrived at Liv and seemed in any case to have been drunk or in a rage most of the time.

Night after night, when she had finished writing up her own diary, Anna would flick, uncomprehending, through the pages of Cassandra's novels, borrowed from the bookcase downstairs that held nothing else, and wonder what the secret was that lay locked behind those tight-set lines of type. How could such bilge have sold in its hundreds of thousands of copies? Perhaps, some time soon, Cassandra would have sobered up or simmered down enough to tell her.

Her days having been spent largely at Cassandra's tyrannical beck and call, Anna's nights, on the sofabed which managed, like an anorexic with cellulite, to be thin and lumpy at the same time, were usually rent with screams from the floor below. Cassandra's violent rows with Jett seemed at their most ear-splitting between midnight and morning, and generally accompanied by the sound of smashing glass or crockery. The day Anna had started, she had been subjected to a lecture on the great care that had to be taken when cleaning the perfume bathroom; seven days later, Cassandra seemed to have destroyed every piece in it by herself and quite deliberately.

Anna chose not to think about the psychological damage the nightly battles were having on Zak; although it seemed unlikely that anything could make him viler than he was now. She had spent several days trying to remember who he reminded her of—and then, having done so, wished she hadn't. With his blond basin cut, defiant expression, and turn-of-the-century school clothes, Zak bore a disturbing resemblance to a photograph of the infant Hitler she had once discovered in one of Seb's—admittedly also disturbing—many books on the subject of the Führer.

Having made this connection, Anna immediately dropped all pretence that it was from a sense of despair and powerlessness due to his parents' behaviour that Zak ordered her about, laughed at her clothes, and, after she had served his cereal, threw it on the floor because he preferred his Bran Flakes dry and his milk flavoured with strawberry syrup and served in a separate glass. The child was obviously even more of a tyrant than his mother—and was beginning to exhibit some of his father's personality traits into the bargain. On the second day of her employment, Anna had crawled up to her room at bedtime to find him standing over the rucksack which still served her as an underwear respository, sniffing hard at a pair of her knickers.

After he had swaggered back downstairs, and she had reached for her diary to confide the episode to the battered exercise book, Anna noticed it seemed to be at the back of the drawer rather than the front of it. Had Cassandra been reading it? Anna profoundly hoped not; the first impressions of Liv and its inhabitants recorded there were far from flattering. However, the next day Cassandra seemed no more poisonous than usual, and if it had been Zak she was safe anyway as, despite the thousands upon thousands being stumped up for his education, he still had difficulty pronouncing words of more than two syllables. If the grand plans his mother had for him didn't come off, Anna thought, he would still be on course for a brilliant career as a breakfast TV presenter.

One reason at least that Zak's parents rowed mostly at night seemed to be that Jett, thankfully, was rarely around during the day. The few glimpses she got of Cassandra's husband—with his long, patchy, pube-like hair, balloon-like stomach, limbs as wrinkled as left-over sausages abandoned overnight on a dying barbecue, and the unmistakable smell of armpit which seemed to fill the house whenever he was around—made Anna profoundly glad she had so far not had to suffer any of his attentions. Let alone the sort of attentions Alice had reported during the post-school-run morning coffee sessions in the cafe.

Yet one night Anna had woken and thought she had seen—in the bright light from the streetlamps afforded by the room's lack of curtain—the handle of the door slowly turning. Dragging herself up from the sofabed, she had quickly rammed the chair from the desk under the handle. Was it her imagination, or did the sound of retreating soft footsteps, and perhaps the faintest of rattles—as of the many chains, bracelets, and rings Jett liked to festoon his wrinkled self with—then drift to her strained and anxious ears? During the day, as far as a thankful Anna could work out, Jett was apparently too busy preparing for a tour with his geriatric rock band and finishing a new album to pay much attention to her. At least, that was the official version of what he was up to. There came a day, not long into Anna's employment, which illuminated some of his other activities.

It had quickly become a source of great irritation to Anna that Cassandra expected her to take painstakingly accurate telephone messages on which the date, time, and person were clearly marked, while evidently feeling no compunction whatsoever to return the compliment herself.

"Who was *that*?" she demanded one afternoon standing, arms folded, a foot away from the telephone after Anna, who had rushed right down from the top of the house to answer it, had completed taking down the message. "And come downstairs less heavily. Those treads aren't meant to take people who weigh over ten stone."

"It was the Earl of Wessex."

A brilliant smile irradiated Cassandra's face. She punched the air in triumph, her grin unwavering even when she sent the Alexander Calder mobile into an unscheduled flat spin.

"*Dearest* Edward! So like him to call in person. *So* unaffected! Such a *shame* we couldn't make it to his and *dear* Soph's wedding…"

Naturally you were asked, Anna thought sardonically.

"But I should have known they'd have us round for dinner just as soon as they could. After all, old friends *are* like gold. When do they want us?"

"Now," said Anna.

"Now?" Cassandra blinked rapidly. "You've obviously got the message wrong," she rapped out. "People like that book one for dinner at *least* six weeks in advance. What do you mean, *now*?"

"The Earl of Wessex in Golborne Road would like you to get there straightaway and fetch Mr. St. Edmunds who is apparently"— Anna struggled with her features—"drunk and disorderly."

Anna grinned as Cassandra tore, cursing, out of the door. She did not, however, have the last laugh for long.

Returning from the school run one morning, Anna opened the door at the end of the hall and instantly knew something was wrong. This was partly because the door had collided with something hard, hairy, and very strong-smelling. She yelped as the door opened fully to reveal a pair of naked hairy buttocks capering in the direction of the staircase. Unable to tear her horrified gaze away, she watched as they turned at the end to reveal a leopardskin thong. Above the beachball waistline, a collection of animal teeth threaded on leather nestled in the patchy spaces of a thin-haired chest. Behind purple mirrored shades, his eyes were invisible. A heavily beringed hand held an enormous joint.

Jett was evidently far too high to feel embarrassed. On the contrary, he seemed glad of an audience. He inhaled deeply then breathed out, wiggling the roll-up between his huge teeth and flashing a crazed, Jack Nicholson grin at her. Anna recoiled from the smell. She had never liked cannabis; it reminded her of dates with charmless students in search of easy sex who, having tried and failed to get her drunk on college lager, brought out the cigarette paper and lighters in the hope she would abandon her inhibiting senses. The only abandon that ever ensued was the contents of Anna's stomach—invariably a kebab from the shop on the corner which was her escort's idea of dinner for two.

"Just rehearsing my stage routine." Jett strutted back up the hall waggling his hips from side to side and pumping his arm in the air. The fanlight flashed in his mirrored sunglasses. "First gig in a fortnight."

"Oh really?" Anna gasped, wondering how she could beat a polite retreat. "Where? Wembley Arena?"

"You must be joking. Mandela Hall, Surbiton University, mate," Jett said, rotating his arm Pete Townshend style, until, hitting it on the banister, he yelped in agony and rubbed it hard. "We're going straight to the goddamn people this time. No messing about in massive goddamn impersonal stadiums where no one can see you." His voice held a hint of wistfulness. "That's where it all went tits-up last time. Got too far away from our fan base. This time we're taking everything that will goddamn have us…um, I mean, no chances. Playing small halls and small audiences. Back to our goddamn *roots*."

"I see," Anna said, still wondering how she could get away. Suddenly, Jett shot out his undamaged hand and grasped her wrist so hard, his rings cut into her flesh.

"C'mon. C'mon. I wanna show you something." She hoped, as he dragged her down the corridor, that it wasn't the contents of his thong.

"Wow," said Anna, a few minutes later. "It's incredible."

"Not bad, huh?" agreed Jett proudly.

Anna gazed in amazement at the rows of handsome leather-bound volumes filling every wall of Jett's library. He had hardly struck her as the literary type; more the sort to think *Vanity Fair* was a glossy magazine and Shelley a shoe shop selling platformed soles and silver Dr. Martens. This, however, was not the only reason the library was an anomaly; the style, classic Hammer Horror Gothic right down to the red velvet curtains and leaded windows, was utterly at odds with the aspirational minimalism of the rest of the house.

"Glad you like it," Jett breathed, coming closer. Overwhelmed by the powerful garlic aroma of his breath, Anna hardly dared think of the near proximity of his hairy, unclothed body, least of all his thong. Fortunately, the end of his joint chose just that moment to fall off and disappear into the intensely patterned carpet. "Damn," cursed Jett, flicking furiously at the remainder with the silver microphone-shaped lighter. At least, Anna hoped it was a microphone. Just as she hoped that vast pink object in the corner wasn't what she thought it was.

"I see you've spotted Dick," grinned Jett, waving an expansive arm towards the vast, thick, and hideously veined protrusion somewhat at odds with the bust of Shakespeare in the niche above it. "Ten-foot-tall rubber penis. Part of one of our old stage shows. Kept it out of sentiment—wanted to have it in the front garden at one point but Sandra wouldn't hear of it. Might take it on tour—it'll be good to get it up again."

Anna cleared her throat and edged away on the pretext of admiring some of the volumes.

"How fantastic," she enthused. "You've got *everything*. From *The Idylls of the King* to the complete works of Christopher Marlowe. Amazing."

"Yeah, and what's even *more* amazing," yelped Jett, evidently restored after a deep drag or two, "is that they've got the complete goddamn works of Martin Scorsese underneath them." He stabbed the shelf beneath the book spines with his beringed forefinger. *Tamburlaine* lurched forward, then, slowly lowering itself to the horizontal, revealed the video of *Mean Streets* fitted snugly behind the leather spine.

Anna stared. "What, they're all *DVDs*?

Jett nodded. "There's a button beneath each book which activates a spring at the back of the video and pushes it out," he explained proudly. "All filed by what you might call free association. Sixteenth-century playwrights equal mobster movies—I reckoned old Marlowe had probably seen some pretty goddamn mean streets in his time—while all those repressed Victorian chicks are the porn section." He flipped *Wuthering Heights* forward to reveal the lurid cover of *Debbie Does Dallas*.

"Yeah, I've read most of the classics," he told her. Anna could see her astonished face reflected in his lenses. "Can't beat 'em for song ideas. Wrote a great one about King Lear called 'Bitch Daddy,' and then of course you'll remember the *Bloodcastle* album inspired by Macbeth. Number one both sides of the Atlantic. Nineteen seventy-eight," he added, wistfully. "What a great goddamn year *that* was. Drove the Rolls into the goddamn swimming pool. Jagger was *furious...*" He took another long drag of his joint.

Why was it, Anna wondered, that all rock and roll anecdotes seemed to involve Mick Jagger and swimming pools?

"Specially as it was his neighbour's goddamn swimming pool. I'd got the wrong goddamn garden. Say, let's put some *goddamn music on*," Jett suddenly shouted. He threw himself into a vast, carved, throne-like chair and pressed a button apparently concealed on the left-hand inside of the red velvet-lined arm.

One of the walls of volumes on the opposite side of the room slid aside to expose a vast TV the size of a cinema screen. It instantly flicked into life to show a plump dark-haired girl, naked apart from a black leather bustier, whip, and black leather cap festooned with chains, thrusting away on top of a skinny, long-haired man wearing mirrored sunglasses and an ecstatic expression. He looked, Anna thought, vaguely familiar.

"Oops," giggled Jett, shoving his joint between his teeth again as he stabbed at the right-hand side of the chair. "My version of *Emma*. Not quite the same as Jane goddamn Austen's. Let's have some music instead." As the screen slid away behind the rows of Fieldings and Popes, a vast stereo appeared; what had been an entire wall of Shakespeare slid from sight.

"*You*," said Jett, jumping about in his seat and pointing the biggest remote control Anna had ever seen in the direction of the stereo, "are the luckiest goddamn woman on *earth*."

Anna, catching sight of the sprouts of salty growth under Jett's armpits, doubted it.

"Because *you*," Jett went on, "are about to have a private world prem-eer of Solstice's comeback album."

Anna said nothing.

"*Featuring*," Jett added, still fumbling with the remote control, "thanks to the miracles of modern technology, our former bassist Dirty del Amico, the greadest axeman rock and roll has ever seen until he perished in a mysterious gardening accident twenny years ago. *Play that axe, dead boy*," Jett screamed, leaping to his feet and puffing frantically on his spliff as a head-spinning blast of the loudest music Anna had ever heard suddenly shook the library to its foundations. She tried not to look as Jett, starting to headbang frantically, set all his wobbly bits reverberating like wind chimes in a gale. Suddenly, he rushed over to the stereo and, grinding his buttocks into its buttons while still facing Anna, started to jerk wildly up and down. She swallowed, fearing the worst, until she realised he was attempting to push the volume control up with his bottom.

"*Say, you're a really cool chick*," Jett screeched. He pulled Anna towards himself and breathed a mixture of garlic, sweat, and patchouli in her face. Something hard was pressing against her, somewhere in the region of the thong. "*I can instinctively tell you empathise with creadive people*," he bawled at her. "*My wife doesn't understand me ad all. Ad all. I'm just a money factory as far as she's concerned. A goddamn trophy husband…*"

"Trophy *husband*?"

Anna was suddenly aware the sound had been turned abruptly off. A ringing silence now filled the library.

"*Trophy* husband?" repeated the acid voice that Anna recognised, heart sinking, as Cassandra's. Wrapped in her pashmina bathrobe, Cassandra, barefoot, silently circled the pair. Her eyes were as mean and narrow as those of a boa constrictor about to strike. "Depends what you mean by *trophy*, I suppose," she hissed, her glance, now mocking, sliding from Anna to Jett and back again. "If you mean a *rotting moosehead* someone shot in nineteen fifty-eight, I suppose I'd have to go along with it. *Atrophy* husband, more like. Except when it comes to getting your end away with the sodding nanny. *Bloody hell, you don't waste much time, do you?*" she screamed at Jett, who pressed himself back against the stereo, the contents of his thong shrinking visibly.

"And as for *you*..." As Cassandra took a step towards her, Anna recoiled. But not soon enough. As Cassandra pressed her face threateningly close, an overpowering smell of gin suddenly filled Anna's nostrils. "I've been waiting," Cassandra hissed. "Waiting and *waiting*..." Anna felt herself start to shake. Yet the fact remained—if Cassandra had been so certain Jett would try to seduce her, why hadn't she stopped him? "And *waiting*," Cassandra continued. "So in the end I came downstairs." She paused again, eyes glittering, then struck. "Where the FUCK is my fucking breakfast?"

"Oh no. That's just too funny! Hope you put *that* in the diary." As Geri spluttered her café au lait all over her nurse's uniform, the waiters looked at them with interest.

Anna felt both irritated and gratified that someone found her ordeal amusing. Her legs still ached from the five times Cassandra had proceeded to send her tea back, and she had ironing blisters. The sheer scale of the pile Cassandra demanded she spend the day pressing had had a fairy tale quality—it had made Anna feel pretty Grimm, in any case. Still, it had been good material for the diary, whatever purpose *that* might eventually serve.

"Actually," Geri confessed, "she accused *me* yesterday of having a fling with him."

"What?" Fear began to grow in Anna's heart.

"She called me on my private line and told me to fuck off and stop ringing her husband."

"And were you?" Remembering the aftermath of Thoby's wedding, Anna braced herself for the worst.

"*Of course not!*" Geri looked outraged. "When I'm *that* desperate, I'll stick my mobile up myself. It vibrates," she explained, catching Anna's puzzled glance. "No, Cassandra pressed one four seven one. It must have been after I'd tried to call you. When I answered she must have thought I was one of his slappers. So do I take it he *is* on the loose again, then?"

"You could say that," said Anna, thinking of the thong. "Last night she flung an entire dinner service at him whilst yelling she was a woman who loved too much."

"What *she* loves too much is gin," Geri grinned. "No wonder she can't write anymore."

There was a silence. Then Anna remembered something.

"Did you say you had a private line?"

"Of course. Naturally the family pay for all the calls...even if my bill does sometimes look like an international phone book." Geri grinned guiltily.

"I can't believe it. Cassandra makes me pay whenever I use her phone. Even if I don't get through."

"That's ridiculous. She should bloody well give you your own phone. Insist on a digital answerphone as well, and while you're at it, get the stingy cow to give you a mobile. Preferably a vibrating one like mine. Hours of fun, I promise you."

"Some hope." The nearest she was going to get to a mobile, Anna thought miserably, was Alexander Calder in the hallway.

"So," said Geri, a careful look creeping into her eyes. "She given you any writing lessons yet?"

Anna's heart sank. At the back of the café she could hear Slob, Allegra, Trace, and Alice laughing with each other. No doubt because,

Anna reflected jealously, they had all probably had two changes of sports car and three pay raises since yesterday. Reluctantly, she shook her head.

"Shall I tell you something?" Geri looked at her. "I think you're wasting your time with Cassandra. Time for a change of focus. I've been thinking about you, and—"

Anna took a deep breath. Her measured tones, she hoped, gave no hint of the fury suddenly filling her. "As I recall, you'd been thinking about me when you encouraged me to get a writing apprenticeship in the first place. And look where *that's* got me."

"*Quite*," said Geri, not batting an eyelid. "But we need to approach it a different way. It's obvious that you don't want to be a nanny despite us all spelling out to you the advantages. If you still want to write books, well, fine. But you need more than a great novel to get what you want out of life."

"I do?" How did Geri always manage to completely wrong-foot her?

"Absolutely. What you need is a great *man*. A rich one, so you don't have to work and can write your books without having to wait hand and foot on Cassandra and rush off to Operabugs and junior Cordon Bleu every five minutes. And *I'm* going to help you find him." She grinned broadly at Anna. "There. What about it?"

"But I'm a complete failure with men," Anna wailed.

"Rubbish. You may not be in a brilliant position bookwise, but you're certainly in one manwise."

"*What?*" The dreadful suspicion that Geri was encouraging her to have a fling with Jett dawned horribly on Anna. She blinked hard to eradicate the memory of his scrawny, hairy buttocks bouncing around in front of her in the hall.

"I mean that when nannies pick the family they're going to work for, they should do it with two things in mind. One is everything we discussed last time. The other"—Geri paused, her Malteser brown eyes coyly disappearing under her lowering lashes—"is the man-meeting potential. High-profile, high-earning families, such as the one I work for, attract high-profile and high-earning men to their dinner parties. The type of men no nanny could hope to meet in normal circumstances." Geri leant forward, eyes glowing. "You coming to Savannah and Siena's birthday party on Saturday?"

Anna nodded. "Cassandra bribed Zak with a digital camera to get him to go."

"Good. Because, let me tell you, it's a man *magnet*. Those kids have so many godfathers, it's not true. Kate and Julian asked practically every mover and shaker in the country to come and move and shake by the font. Establishment, high society, the arts, the lot. You can't *fail to* score."

"Just watch me," said Anna miserably.

Chapter Eleven

BY DAWN ON THE day of Savannah and Siena's party, Cassandra had already been up for several hours struggling with the computerised wardrobe. Denim shirt and jeans for that wholesome, Hope-Stanley, yoghurt-ad look? Or more smart Sloane with the loafers and stand-up collar? Casual yet stylish was what she was going for; you couldn't join in Sardines and Pass the Parcel in Givenchy couture (although some, like Shayla Reeves, would probably try to). What she wanted was something scruffy enough for games but smart enough to translate to the Number Ten dinner table, should Cherie suddenly find herself a body short of a *placement* and remember that perfectly charming writer at Kate's children's party.

Cassandra had prepared for the party like a military offensive. Every grooming eventuality was anticipated. By the end of the week, she had had a full-peel facial, manicure and pedicure, and even a bikini wax. Well, you never knew. It might be sunny and she didn't want to be sprouting around the gusset of her Versace swimsuit.

The remainder of her time had been spent finding exactly the right presents. Ignoring Zak's insistence that what Savannah and Siena really wanted was a plastic ray gun and a light sabre respectively, Cassandra had rifled the racks of Oilily, Petit Bateau, and half junior Bond Street before settling on two fabulously sequinned and frill-festooned party dresses, complete with huge net underskirts, from Please Mum. She was, Cassandra told herself as she left the shop with her bags, now ready for all eventualities. The only thing that remained out of her control was the SMSPA Promises auction to be held at the party.

Cassandra bitterly regretted her offer—well, as much as anything you were *forced into* could possibly be an offer—to cook a dinner party for eight at her home. She quailed at the thought of who might win it and, in order to prevent such ghastly eventualities as having to wait on Fenella Greatorex and friends hand and foot, almost considered bringing Jett along to outbid everyone else. Financial considerations—Jett, after all, was the man who bid ten thousand pounds for one of Eric Clapton's guitar strings during that dreadful period when he was trying to set up a rock and roll museum—had forced her to abandon the plan. The added risk that Cherie might clap eyes on Jett had been judged worse than Fenella Greatorex's being the highest bidder for the dinner. If that happened, Cassandra decided philosophically, she would just have to put Liquid Paper in the sauce.

Anna too had been up for hours. Saturday was glass day—after doing all the windows, Anna had now moved on to the mirrors. She sprayed furniture polish on the hall's vast, frameless looking-glass and rubbed it while trying not to look at her dejected reflection. It was difficult to avoid it—the sheer misery in her eyes drew the viewer. Once sparkling, they were now as flat as week-old Bellinger; her hair looked redder and lanker than ever beside the grey of her exhausted face. The only comfort was that she looked thinner—cheekbones, faint but discernible, ridged each side of her formerly shapeless cheeks. Her mouth too, though pale and dry, seemed bigger. Anna tried to smile at herself, but the lips didn't move. I don't do smiling anymore, she thought.

I must get out of here, she repeated mantra-like to herself with each circle or her duster. God knows how, though. Or *where*. I've no money, nowhere to live, and no skills to speak of, especially housework…*damn* this polish. Every stroke of the cloth left wild white streaks elsewhere on the mirror's surface. Cleaning, Anna was beginning to realise, was more exacting an art than she had imagined.

Depressing though it was to admit it, Geri was right. Cassandra had absolutely no intention of teaching her anything at all about writing and Zak had no intention of doing anything other than making her life a misery. The only mercy was that the library incident with Jett had thankfully not been repeated—Anna had kept well away from its Gothic portals, especially after having, during one of Cassandra's rants about her being more useless even than her predecessors, worked out who the Emma in the video must be. Less thankfully, Jett had recently taken to squeezing past her in the corridor and, less excusably, in rooms containing sufficient space for two articulated lorries to pass each other, let alone two people. On each occasion, Anna had been aware of something large and hard in the region formerly occupied by the leopardskin thong.

"Sue him for sexual harassment," Geri had urged her. "I would. I knew a nanny who sued her employer's husband for coming into her bathroom by mistake. She wasn't even in it at the time. *You'd* make a fortune."

"And be all over the papers?" protested Anna. "Spend the rest of my life being the woman who was groped by some has-been old celebrity? At least Monica Lewinsky was groped by the president of the United States."

"Well, he'll be a has-been old celebrity soon," said Geri.

"Yes, but imagine it all over the *News of the World*—The Rock Star, Me, And That Leopardskin Thong."

"Well, it's got more of a ring to it than that boring old blue dress. I think you should consider it."

Anna sighed and rubbed her polish harder. The sound of the telephone ringing in the hall was a welcome diversion.

"Guest list for the party's looking *great*," Geri whispered on the other end. "Two financiers, three actors, four TV executives, a lord, and a couple of national newspaper editors, and that's just for starters. *Your* best bet is one of the financiers. *Stinking* rich and—although admittedly this *is* a drawback—*young*."

"Why is that a drawback?"

"They're best old, really, then they drop off the perch after the honeymoon and leave you all their money. The good news is, no emotional baggage or, worse, grabby first wife wanting tons of alimony. He's unmarried—never has been, from what I can work out—but *seems* to be straight. Reasonable-looking, as well, apparently, although I've never seen him in the flesh to confirm this."

"Sounds like a real dreamboat."

"Hey, well, you've got to know what you're dealing with in this game," Geri said huffily. "No point me steering you towards some sex god who turns out to be penniless and as gay as New Year's Eve into the bargain."

"No, *absolutely*," said Anna, realising Geri sounded annoyed. Alienating her would not be a good idea. Not now, when, however mad her schemes sounded, they represented a better route to escape than any she could think up herself. "Thanks. Really, he sounds *wonderful*. Just the job."

"Good," said Geri, mollified. "Anyway, get here as early as you can. And don't forget—look *gorgeous*."

How *amazingly* self-confident, thought Cassandra as she trotted into the entrance hall holding her invitation like a shield. How almost *show-offy* for the Tressells to have the party *in their own house*. Only people with nothing to hide and everything to reveal dared expose their homes to the scrutiny of other St. Midas's mothers and fathers, most of whom, when their own children's birthdays came round, preferred to pay up the thousands demanded by Hollywood theme restaurants for a couple of burgers, a shake, and a photo opportunity with an Arnold Schwarzenegger lookalike.

"It's very cutting edge," was all Geri had said to Anna of the Tressell home and current world headquarters of her operations, a converted former prison in Islington. Well, Anna thought, entering in Cassandra's Gucci-heeled wake, there was certainly plenty of glass. Through the transparent hall roof, the grey London sky brooded above. She wondered what the drill was when, as it occasionally must, a passing pigeon let fly a splatter or two. She glanced briefly at the shattered-blue-glass-effect floor, before realising that banging noise was Zak trying to shatter it further by removing his black patent shoes and using the heels as hammers.

"Stop that *now*." Geri detached herself from a milling group in the light, circular hall where, stuffed as usual into her plunging uniform, she was rounding up the arrivals and their broods with the efficiency of a sheepdog.

Among the throng, Anna spotted Allegra shepherding a child in a pink net tutu. Slobodan shuffled in behind her with a pair of basin-cut boys, looking, as usual, as if he'd just got out of bed; Anna wondered whose. A plump, dark-haired girl who confirmed Anna's worst suspicions about Jett's video was being clung to by a pale, frightened-looking child with noticeably scarred knees— Otto Greatorex, Anna realised. A slender and extremely handsome Japanese man was visibly buckling under the weight of a very large, pink-faced child in a—possibly real—tiara, whom he held in his arms; this, Anna realised, must be Hanuki, the first male Japanese Norlander. Well, he'd certainly got his hands full.

The parents and godparents, distinguishable by their un-hassled expressions, brimming glasses of champagne, and complete absence of any children near them, stood chatting in one group while the nannies and children formed a loose collective at the other end of the vast hall. The pink-faced child, Anna noticed, had already thrown up something purple and sticky down the front of Hanuki's white shirt. Beside her, Zak was banging on the floor again.

"Children and nannies in there," Geri shouted above the chaos, pointing at a room in which serried ranks of forms and tables could be glimpsed. "Parents and godparents this way." She pointed to where a waitress stood by a door bearing a tray with yet more champagne glasses.

"Not so fast," Geri murmured as Anna headed automatically after Slobodan, Alice, Trace, and the rest of them. "You're helping me with the nibbles. Best way for you to meet people. I've OK'd it with Kate, so Cassandra can't object. Leave Zak with Trace."

Zak looked mutinous as the massive Trace, her face set, clasped his fat wrist in her strong grip and whisked him off into the children's room.

"You look very smart, by the way," Geri said. "Lost weight, haven't you?"

Anna nodded and grinned. "All thanks to dish soap."

Geri stared. Then her face relaxed. "Oh, I see, that old Fairy Liquid trick. Do that, do you?"

"No, not me," said Anna. "*Cassandra.*"

Although the housework workout had no doubt helped, it had been Cassandra's habit of obliterating temptation by squeezing dish soap over Zak's leftovers and any other cooked food she found in the kitchen that had really made the difference. A pizza and several sandwiches Anna had made for her own supper had, several times, been rendered inedible this way. She had been furious at the time, but now, given that her trousers hung slackly from her waist and she'd managed to tuck her shirt in, she felt almost grateful to Cassandra. Almost.

"The idea," Geri was explaining, "is that the grown-ups have their party while the children have their tea, their games, and the party entertainer. Then we all get together for the Promises auction and the disco." Gingerly, she touched the skin beneath her eyes, careful not to smudge any of her precisely applied makeup. "I'm *knackered*. I was up more or less all night wrapping forty Pass the Parcels in recycled paper containing Third World–friendly items. Did you realise that these days you have to have a present between *every layer?*"

As yet more sleek parents and sleeker offspring arrived, Geri hustled Anna into a vast kitchen off the main hall in which a production line of chefs was busy making faces from basil, mozzarella, anchovies, and olives on a collection of mini pizzas. "Olives!" whispered Anna. "I didn't think children liked olives."

"Well, these ones do," said Geri. "What's more, they can distinguish between about ten different types. Olive oil as well—they spend so much time in Tuscany they think 'Like A Virgin' is a song about first cold pressings."

Anna giggled. "They're very glamorous, these chefs," she muttered. Male and female, each one had the heavy eyebrows, lithe limbs, and bee-stung lips of a supermodel. They smouldered at each other as they arranged the anchovies into smiles.

"They're from some screamingly expensive Italian restaurant by the river, apparently," Geri hissed. "But I've got better things lined up for you than them. Take these." She thrust a plateful of perfect miniature bacon sandwiches at Anna, each complete with tiny rind, baby crusts, and heart-shaped dab of tomato ketchup beside it. Each bore a plastic skewer bearing the initials SS. "Make sure you eavesdrop on all the conversations," Geri warned, as they sailed forth through a sliding aluminium side door that led from the kitchen to a large, light, glass-walled reception room. "They're hilarious. I once overheard three women talking for hours about vaginal sprays and how much their husbands earned."

Giggling, they swept into the crowd.

"Why *do* people in England despise success so much?" a woman in violently coloured clothes was saying to a toned, tanned man with close-cropped white hair as Anna and Geri started to circle the room.

"*Who's* that?" Anna mouthed.

"Julian, of course," said Geri, her eyes fixed longingly on her employer's face. "Oh, the woman? Son at St. Midas's. He's got the concentration span of a gnat. They're hoping he's autistic, I believe. *She's* a happening fashion editor."

"Looks more like a what's happened fashion editor," observed Anna, taking in the pink hair, yellow dress, and orange tights, topped off with a large black fedora. She looked with interest at Julian Tressell, short-cropped, sandalled, and dressed from head to foot in white linen, his only decoration a CCCP Soviet–era Lenin badge in deep red enamel and gold.

"Yes, she is rather post-nuclear."

"And who's that?" Anna slid her eyes meaningfully at Kate Tressell talking to a pneumatic blonde in a tight white dress and hot pink heels that added at least a foot to her height. Beside her exuberant beauty, Kate's hemp suit, though doubtless eye-wideningly expensive, looked drab and monastic.

"Champagne D'Vyne," whispered Geri. "You know, that spectacularly thick society columnist. She's supposed to be getting married next month to an unfeasibly rich landowner called Juan Legge, but it'll never happen. She always trades them in at the last minute for something better."

"Lucky her." Anna took in Champagne's ripples of ice-blonde hair, undulating figure, and spectacular tan. Netting landowners must be a breeze when you looked like that. She strained to hear the conversation.

"Are you thrilled about the wedding?" Kate was asking.

"Oh yah," Champagne replied in a bored voice. "*Beside* myself."

"Will you be wearing white?"

"God no. I thought Versace."

Anna and Geri caught each other's eye.

"You go that way and I'll go this," Geri hissed, shoulders shaking. "Meet you in a minute."

Anna veered away and headed towards a pair of matronly thirty-somethings in sensible heels.

"...well, at the moment we've got what you might describe as a *below stairs* problem."

"Oh *really*? Does it involve wearing paper pants?"

"No, the *nanny*, silly."

"Oh. Of course. The *nanny*. Oh, yes please. Bacon sandwiches, how *adorable*."

Anna now bore down on a thin woman with an Anna Wintour crop and a lilac cashmere cardigan listening to a tall, haughty blonde in a lime green lacy dress.

"We know he's a boy, yes. Well, if he has my looks and Marco's brains, he's bound to be fine."

And both of your modesty, thought Anna, proffering her wares.

"*No* thank you." Both women looked at the food in horror. "What are we going to call him?" continued the blonde. "Well, we were thinking about Wyndham, but it sounds a bit *bottomy*, and then Louis, but when you come to think of it, that's rather redolent of lavatories as *well...*"

Anna stood as the woman in the cardigan, apparently unable to stop herself, slid out the skewers from a couple of sandwiches, peeled off the bread topping and, without moving anything from the tray, crammed the pieces of bacon hurriedly into her mouth.

"Yes, you've got to be careful," she agreed, amid much loud sucking of red-tipped fingers. "You need to steer clear of anything that's going to be pilfered by centre forwards or triplicated in the nursery. We had the most awful time—our first choices were Atlanta or Aurora, both once solidly B1, but now skidding firmly into C2 territory, I'm afraid. We considered Cheyenne, but..."

"*So* trailer trash."

"Mmm, so in the end we called her Doris."

"*Lovely*. So *millennium*."

Anna drifted away to where a reed-thin woman in a linen dress with eyebrows plucked into surprised-looking arcs was talking animatedly to an exhausted-looking man. "I went *straight* to my homeopathic doctor, and she said my stomach was like a pond that hadn't been cleaned for years."

The man paled. They both shook their heads at the sandwiches.

"Vegetarian," said the man.

The woman's eyes lit up. "Really? *Are* you? How very interesting…"

"That was Frank Gibbons," whispered Geri as she swung by with her plate of sandwiches. "Siena's godfather. Edits the *Guardian*."

"Really? Who's that he's with?"

"His wife. He's so busy that the only time they get to speak to each other is at parties."

Anna grinned. Geri, she noticed, had got rid of even fewer sandwiches than she had herself.

"Last round before we refuel," Geri said as they parted ways again. "We'll need to reheat. I'm not sure your financier has arrived yet, by the way. Probably delayed closing the deal that will make his fortune. Even *more* of his fortune," she added hurriedly.

Anna moved off in the direction of two more glamorous women in skimpy dresses and the type of strappy sandals that, on lesser mortals, would have been a display case for bunions and stubbed, square toes.

"…unfortunately he's at that stage where he thinks bottoms and poo are *hilarious*," one was saying to the other.

"Tell me about it," said the other woman. "Marcus's hand is practically *welded* to his *you know what*. Dreadfully embarrassing when we were on holiday—there we were, outside the Fairfaxes' wonderful *palazzo*, feasting on pasta, when Mango Fairfax suddenly says *what on earth* is Marcus doing? And we all look and—well, frankly, he had his hand on it and was yanking it up and down for all it was *worth*…don't suppose we'll be asked there again. No thank you, I don't eat bacon."

Or anything else by the look of you, Anna thought as she sailed off, almost colliding with Geri who was hurrying urgently towards her.

"Look, look, he's over there. Just arrived. Your financier. Talking to those men," hissed Geri. "Grey suit. Quick, girl, get over there with your nibbles."

Obediently, Anna wove her way through the throng to the other side of the room where a group of smartly dressed men were having a loud and braying conversation. She approached the grey back—it seemed rather broad—and hovered. A narrower navy one next to it turned and grinned at her. "Delicious," he said, stuffing two in his mouth at once. "Sandwiches aren't bad either."

Anna rolled her eyes. The old ones, she thought, were most definitely the old ones. Irritatingly, the grey back was the last of the group to turn and attack the sandwiches. And when he did, Anna wished he hadn't bothered. Not only was he plump, pink-faced, and almost bald, he was also Orlando Gossett. Anna threw a burning mortar of a glance over to where Geri stood, open-mouthed, on the other side of the room. Was this her idea of a joke? Her pale face and shocked expression, however, suggested she was as surprised as Anna was.

"Orlando…what…what on earth are you doing here?" Anna stammered. Gossett looked at her in astonishment.

"You're very *familiar*," he boomed. "But, since you ask, I'm one of Savannah's *thousands* of godfathers."

"Oh, are you?" asked the navy suit. "Me too."

"Yah, Julian's an old mucker of mine—built me an outdoor sauna recently, as it happens," honked Gossett. "Quite an achievement considering I live in a mansion block in Fulham. Actually," he said, screwing his small blue eyes up at Anna, "you know…you *are* familiar actually. Didn't we meet at a wedding or something?"

"Yes, in Scotland," said Anna. "Thoby and Miranda's."

"Gosh, your company gets around, doesn't it? Well, the eats here are a damn sight better than they were at Bollocks's. Worst food in the world, that was. Canapés looked like cat sick. Tasted like it too."

"Can't say I've ever tasted cat sick," Anna retorted. "But the food *was* dreadful." Even if the waiters weren't, she added mentally, a sudden vision of Jamie sliding across the screen behind her. She was jolted from her musings by what felt like her spine leaping out from between her shoulderblades. Orlando Gossett was slapping her on the back.

"*I* remember now. Course. Friend of Lavenham's, weren't you?"

Anna nodded.

"Enjoy the other day?"

"What other day?"

"Lavenham's wedding, of course."

It felt as if a bucket of freezing water had been flung in her face. "*Wedding*?"

"Yah. Whirlwind stuff. You didn't go? Actually, I didn't either. No one did—tiny private do at the Chelsea Register Office, Lavenhams and de Benhams only, and then off to this island—Knacker, I think it's called."

"You mean Necker," said Geri, who had just floated up. "How *ghastly*. Necker's so five minutes ago. Anyone who's anyone's honeymooning in the Maldives. Or going backpacking, like Lachlan Murdoch…" The jaunty note in her voice dried up as she saw Anna's white-green face.

"*De Benhams*?" stammered Anna, her tongue moving slowly around her dry mouth. "Seb's married *Brie de Benham*?"

Orlando nodded emphatically. His eye caught one of the waitresses circulating with glasses of champagne and he threw back his head to drain his existing flute. Champagne cascaded down his shirt front. "Yah," he bubbled, foaming at the mouth. "Everyone's *thrilled*. Lavenham's mother, particularly. Apparently couldn't *wait* to see the back of the last girlfriend."

Anna staggered away with her tray and headed out to the kitchen. It was empty; the chefs were presumably busy with the children. She sat down at the counter and stared, stunned, into space, unable to decide whether the numb feeling inside her was devastation or indifference. Seb married to Brie de Benham. It was so utterly predictable she almost wanted to laugh. So expected—and yet not expected at all. Geri rubbed her sympathetically on the back. "Never mind. He was a bastard. Treated you like shit."

Anna's eyes pricked. Her throat ached. She sniffed. No, she told herself. I *will not cry*. She wiped a hand across her nose. "It's the shock, I suppose. Not that it's that much of a surprise. He was always going to marry someone like her."

"*Were* you *in love* with him?" Geri's voice, though incredulous, had softened.

Anna nodded miserably. "Yes. Yes I was. He was very good-looking. Impossibly handsome. But in the end he turned out to be just impossible." Geri rubbed her back again. "Yes, I loved him. But I was very let down." Anna stopped and forced a smile at her friend. "Sound like Princess Di, don't I?"

Geri thrust a brimming glass of champagne at her. "Sounded like a nasty piece of work to me. Looked like one too—that handsome but shifty type. I vaguely remember him from that Scottish wedding."

"Shame you didn't remember Orlando Gossett as well," Anna sniffed, mopping her eyes with a piece of kitchen towel. "I'm amazed you forgot *him*. He more or less smashed you to bits during the eightsome reels."

"Believe me, I haven't forgotten," Geri said. "I've still got the scars. But he never actually told me what he was called. So when I saw his name on the party list, I was none the wiser. I judged solely on his other criteria, although I have to say," she added, wrinkling her brow, "my informant who claimed he was reasonable looking has rather low standards. Subterranean, even."

Anna managed a smile. Geri looked at her. "Come on. We're wasting valuable man-meeting time. Once more into the breeches."

By now, miniature bacon sandwiches had given way to tiny vegetarian burgers, each with their Savannah and Siena skewer and a V-shaped blob of mustard on the side denoting their meat-free state. Anna again approached the *Guardian* editor and his wife.

"J.J.—you know, the one who has a decoupage shop in Fulham—rang me yesterday," Mrs. Gibbons was twittering. "Ooh, *thank* you. Look, darling, little *veggie burgers*...well, she's just got back from running with the sheep. Ovine alignment therapy, it's called."

Frank Gibbons, although heavily occupied stuffing in two burgers and balancing another two in his napkin, stared in astonishment at his wife. "*Uuggghhh*?"

"*Terribly* good for you. You go to an Australian sheep ranch, live in a tent, and run with the baa-baas all day. Gets rid of all your city neuroses, apparently. Mmm, *may* I just have another one? *So* delicious."

"*That*," said Gibbons decisively, "is a feature." Placing his burgers down on a nearby construction of plastic and wood whose function was not immediately apparent, he fished out his mobile and started to stab the keys.

"So I might stop having monkey gland injections in my bottom and try that," Mrs. Gibbons was saying. "I'm not sure they did me much good anyway. But lots of people swear by them. *Ooh*, just one more then."

"Well, you swore by them when you came home," Gibbons observed, pressing his mobile to his ear. "The air was blue until the pain wore off and you could sit down again...Hello? Editor here. Get me Features."

The Gibbonses having decimated her supplies, Anna returned to the kitchen. Geri was peering through a porthole in the connecting door to the children's room. "Entertainer's going down a storm," she reported. "He's getting them all to pretend to be animals."

"*Pretend?*" said Anna with feeling.

"I always find it amazing how entertainers remember the children's names," Geri mused. "But then I suppose they're called either Venetia, Jack, or something ending in 'o' so it's not that difficult." She turned back into the kitchen.

"Puddings now," she announced. "I'll take the little tartes au citron and you take the miniature jam roly-polys. Don't forget the thimbles of custard."

As they opened the door into the adult room, the sound of braying voices hit them like a wall.

As Anna took a deep breath and prepared to plunge in, a soft voice beside her said, "Hello."

Anna turned. Someone with floppy dark hair and wide-apart eyes looked back at her. Dressed in a smart three-piece suit in Prince of Wales check, Jamie looked very different from his last appearance as the uncertain bearer of a tray full of dirty glasses.

"Er…just going to the loo," trilled Geri, over-obviously making herself scarce.

Chapter Twelve

Spreadeagled on the loo seat, Cassandra was feeling distinctly inebriated. She'd had a good four glasses to calm her nerves and had now retired to the bathroom to regroup her forces. After all, the two great challenges of the day were still to come—the meeting with Cherie Blair, *still* not here but expected, and that wretched Promises auction. It was imperative that things went well at both.

Cassandra's head swam. Champagne always had a devastating effect on delicate nervous systems like hers, particularly in the quantities she'd consumed it. She tried to focus on her surroundings, but immediately wished she hadn't. *Damn*, thought Cassandra, looking about her with twisted and envious lips at the blanket-sized taupe towels, the vast greige granite bath, the recycled green glass cistern in which a number of tropical fish glided serenely around, and the tiny chrome pushbutton taps tucked away above the granite sink.

It was all *so bloody tasteful*. It made her own attempts at minimalism look about as stylish and assured as those things they used to make on Blue Peter with sticky-back plastic and toilet rolls. *Loo* rolls, Cassandra corrected herself. But then, the Tressells' converted Islington prison was universally acknowledged to be a modern masterpiece, even though some dissenting voices—Jett's for one—had been contemptuous of its pointed eschewal of obvious luxury. "Still looks like the inside of Pentonville," Jett had scoffed when Cassandra had shown him the feature on it in *House and Garden*.

She had been so busy condemning him as a Philistine that it only occurred to her later to wonder how he *knew*.   ·

It was odd, but Cassandra could not wrest her thoughts away from Julian Tressell. She'd always found him handsome, but today… well, she'd initially had trouble identifying the unfamiliar feeling but she felt positively *randy* towards him. But architects *were* sexy, she thought. All that talk about pillars and erections…

Standing up, she looked in the mirror that covered the whole of one wall. She looked *stunning* today. This skirt, well, she had wondered if it was a *bit* short, but *no*, how could it be—it showed almost the entire length of her still-excellent legs. No man could resist a really cracking pair of pins and Julian was a better judge of fine structures than most. Cassandra moved closer to the mirror, ran her tongue round her lips, and thrust her hips out. Her nipples pinged erect under the thin fabric of her top. Christ, she was a sexy beast.

Cassandra lowered herself with difficulty onto the marble floor. You never knew, it *might* still work, and there were few better ways of relieving tension. Flipping off her knickers—not that there was enough of *those* to seriously get in the way—Cassandra slid a hand between her legs. Christ, it was like a swimming pool down there. Somewhere down here was *that bit*…ah, here it was. Cassandra began to rub slowly up and down, caressing her nipple with her free hand, running her tongue around her lips and thinking of Julian Tressell. Mmm.

This was *good*. That sort of electric build-up feeling in her legs… She raised her pelvis and rubbed harder. Damn, lost it…ah, no, here it was again. "Mmmm. *Mmmmm…oh, oh…*" Cassandra gasped.

"You OK?"

Cassandra shot upright and stared wildly at the doorway. Peering round the blond wooden door was that *bitch* of a United Nations nanny.

"Can I help at all?" said Geri, struggling to control her facial expression.

"No thank you," gasped Cassandra. "Period pains. You know," she added hurriedly.

As Geri withdrew and audibly exploded with mirth in the corridor, Cassandra lay on her back again. Well, it had worked, in a way. It had relieved her former worries. The thought of the Promises auction and the Prime Minister's wife faded into insignificance beside the thought of Geri telling Julian she'd caught Cassandra wanking in his bathroom.

"You look different," Jamie said to Anna.

"I'm thinner." Wonderful to be able to say it as a mere statement of fact. But sad that there had been no joy in achieving it.

"That's it. Thinner. Suits you. Not that you didn't look great before…"

Seen in full daylight—or at least under Julian Tressell's concept spotlights—Jamie, too, looked better. Suited and booted, he looked even handsomer than she remembered. Anna had lost no time in telling him she no longer had a boyfriend. Unfortunately, she had not left it at that, not left the door open for a pleasant, ego-boosting flirty conversation. Oh no. Instead, she had stupidly ploughed on through the events of recent weeks, told him all about Cassandra, all about Zak and Jett, and how miserable she was, becoming increasingly aware as she did so that none of it reflected particularly well on her judgement and intelligence. He probably thinks I'm more stupid than even I think I am, she reflected miserably, drawing the sorry tale to a close.

Jamie looked at her speculatively. He did not speak.

"Anyway, enough of me," Anna said hurriedly, plastering a vast smile over the exposed cracks in her life. "How's the wonderful world of waiting?"

Jamie's composure dramatically slipped at this. "Sorry? *Waiting*? Waiting for what?" His eyes, most unexpectedly, appeared to narrow in suspicion.

"When I met you," Anna persisted, puzzled, "you were a waiter at the wedding."

An unmistakable expression of relief crossed Jamie's face. "Oh, er, um, yes, well, actually, I'm not a waiter."

"You're not?" This at least explained why he had been so bad at it. "You're a student then? Holiday job?" He looked too old for that, though.

"No, I live at the castle, you see. It belongs to my, er, family."

"*Oh.*" Anna felt her mind ripple with the effort of reassessment. That explained the signet ring still gleaming—she shot it a look—on his finger. He actually *lived* in the castle. Probably owned the island. How *wonderful.* "So you're a laird?" How *romantic.* "Skul is so pretty." As Jamie's expression changed from faint gratification to utter astonishment Anna panicked that she had said the wrong thing.

"Pretty? Do you think so?" he demanded, amazement still tingeing his tone. He smiled incredulously. Anna nodded, relieved. For she *had* thought so. In the few snatched seconds she had been allowed to take her eyes off the map book, she had admired from the car window great misty sweeps of grass and heather. Pewter lochs, air as cold and clear as water, Seb cursing that the signposts in Gaelic read like a monkey let loose on a typewriter. "Bloody stupid language. Like the worst possible letters in Scrabble."

Jamie shook his head so his hair flopped once again into his eyes. Needs someone to cut that for him, Anna thought, longing to reach up a hand to push the errant lock aside. His smile was dazzling now. Good teeth.

"And did you like the castle?"

"Loved it," Anna said, thinking of the view of the moon from the oriel window. Did Jamie remember? she wondered, blushing.

Suddenly, she asked him, "So how come *you* were handing out the drinks?"

"Well, Dampie gets rented out for weddings sometimes, and I was just helping."

"How *wonderful* to actually live there."

"Bit damp sometimes."

"But I'm sure that doesn't matter, does it?" For how could living in a castle not be wonderful? "It must be *so* romantic." As she said this, Geri came past and gave her a huge, encouraging wink.

"Actually, I do rather like it myself, but it's not everyone's cup of tea. Some people find it a bit too remote."

"Do they?" Anna could see their point, but chose not to say so. Such a shame he was stuck up there in the middle of the Atlantic. That ruled out any taking up where they had left off after the wedding. Although, come to think of it, they had left off almost immediately.

She looked at him again and lowered her eyes. There was silence. Anna was aware, from the other side of the room, of Geri shooting her a concerned gaze. She was also aware of the tray of untouched miniature jam roly-polys in her hands. People were looking meaningfully at her, obviously wanting her wares. Time was running out. If she didn't say something—anything—soon, he could just turn on his shining leather heel and leave, having had no more than a pleasant/meaningless exchange with someone once met at a wedding. Anna cudgelled her brains for a topic. Something to catch his imagination. Something original. "Er, um," she finally said, as inspiration struck. "How do you know the Tressells?"

"Met Kate ages ago when she did some report about Scottish nobility for *Harpers & Queen*. And now I'm Siena's godfather."

Siena had, Anna concluded, more godfathers than the whole of Southern Italy.

"And your firm," Jamie was saying. "Do you often get asked to cater…?"

"Oh, I'm not a waitress. I'm a writer. But frankly," Anna sighed as, out of the corner of her eye, she saw Cassandra picking her way down the spiral metal staircase, "my writing's been more trouble than it's worth. And that's the reason why." She pointed out her employer to Jamie. "My boss."

Jamie looked hard at Cassandra. "Christ."

Anna suddenly noticed Julian Tressell heading towards them. He whirled up and seized Jamie's Prince of Wales checked wrist. "Cherie's *refused* to do the Promises auction; says it's her day *off*," he sighed theatrically. "So Kate and I were wondering whether, as our resident squire, *you'd* get us out of jail…"

"See you later," Jamie whispered, as he was led away.

Anna hoped so. As she nodded eagerly, every nerve in her body thrilled.

Every nerve in Cassandra's body jangled. Not because of the recent events in the bathroom—by the look of it, that wretched Geri had kept her trap shut and the story had got no further.

But the auction was now about to begin. Just let Fenella Greatorex *dare* bid for the dinner. Cassandra shot her a vicious look from where she huddled on the floor cross-legged. Cross everything, in fact. Chairs, it seemed, were banned throughout the house.

"An enemy to good posture, apparently," someone behind Cassandra whispered. "Julian and Kate eat dinner by candlelight on leather cushions on the floor."

"That sounds like an enemy to good digestion to me," replied her companion. "Oh look, the auction's starting."

Anna watched, impressed, as Jamie immediately got into the swing of the auction. He had a natural authority—she supposed it went with the territory; aristocrats, after all, spent half their lives in salerooms, buying or selling according to how their luck was going. There was even a wicked gleam in Jamie's eye; like a naughty little boy, Anna thought fondly, until she remembered Zak. Still, at least he was next door for the moment. *Pretending* to be an animal.

Bidding for the health club, newspaper subscription, and an organic food box delivery service which had mysteriously appeared from somewhere swiftly dispensed with, it didn't take long for the moment Cassandra dreaded.

"Dinner party for eight at the home of, um, Sandra Knight." Jamie peered at the card in his hand, then brandished the Philippe Starck toffee hammer that stood in for a gavel.

"*Cass*andra," yelled Cassandra furiously.

"The bidding starts at fifty pounds," announced Jamie.

Cassandra bristled. *Fifty pounds*? It had better raise more than *that*. She'd be a laughing stock.

"Do I hear a hundred pounds?" said Jamie in his soft Scottish voice, cupping a hand to his ear. "Wonderful menu. Foie gras to start with, partnered with the most wonderful old Sauternes, then noisettes of Highgrove lamb, served with a Chateau Margaux nineteen fifty-nine.

There was a stirring of interest. Hands sprouted in the air. Cassandra goggled. *Sauternes…Margaux…*what was this ridiculous man *talking* about? It would cost a *fortune*. She hadn't been thinking beyond boeuf bourguignon and supermarket plonk. "Er," she called, raising her hand.

"No, sorry," Jamie said, all charming Caledonian firmness. "You can't bid for your own promise. Dessert is, um, yes, of course, champagne sorbet followed by tarte au citron especially flown in from Fauchon. Do I hear a hundred pounds? The lady over there."

Fenella Greatorex. Cassandra's spine froze. This was worse than the worst nightmare. She looked desperately at Cherie Blair. Entertaining the Prime Minister would put an entirely different complexion on things; one might well run to the Margaux then. Something chateau-bottled, at least. But Cherie Blair's hand remained resolutely on the shoulders of her son Nicky. Her large brown eyes swivelled round the room in amusement.

"One hundred and fifty pounds. To the gentleman in the grey suit."

Orlando Gossett, Anna saw with dismay. For once she was with Cassandra in wanting the bidding to get higher.

"At this point," Jamie said, grinning, "I'm going to depart from convention and put a bid in myself. Three hundred pounds."

There was a surprised murmur, then silence. "Sold to the Scotsman," smiled Jamie as Kate rushed up and shoved a note in his fist. "Now, um, I hold in my hand a piece of paper saying the disco's started. Ladies and gentlemen, everyone into the next room and join the children for the disco." As the room scrambled to its feet, Anna glimpsed Cassandra sitting, stunned, in the middle of the floor. Then she saw Jamie coming towards her, looking very pleased with himself.

"What on *earth* did you do that for? You know who'll have to cook it all, don't you? *Moi.*"

Jamie looked astonished. "You surely don't think I'm going to take her *up* on it, do you? Go to her wretched house and have dinner? Not to mention waste three hundred pounds."

"Yes, why bother," said Anna, grinning with relief. "You'd have to be a masochist, not to mention stinking rich."

"You've seen Dampie," Jamie said. "Does it look stinking rich? Stinking, certainly, particularly when the tide is out and the sun heats up the rotting seaweed…um…but it's absolutely beautiful, of course. Wouldn't live anywhere else."

Anna smiled. The disco could now be heard thumping away in the room previously occupied by the forms, trestle tables, and pizzas with faces on them. Jamie placed a hand on her bare arm, the shock of his touch shuddering all over her body. He put his mouth close to her ear. "Did it for you. Call it bribery if you like. Now, I have to go, but perhaps I could take you out to dinner later? What's your address?"

Hoping desperately that he meant it, Anna scribbled Liv's location down in a tiny leather-backed notebook Jamie produced from the inside of his jacket. "Pick you up at seven thirty. But not a word to *her* about the dinner party. Let her sweat a bit."

"You *see*. You *see*." As Anna entered the disco, someone shot to her side and nudged her hard. It was Geri, looking smugger than Mrs. Bennet at the wedding of Elizabeth and Darcy. "Told you you'd score with someone. Very *nice*, I must say. Actually, I'm rather jealous."

"Well, there's nothing to be jealous of," Anna told her. "He's only asked me out for dinner."

"*Only*?" teased Geri. "That's pretty fast work considering you only met him this afternoon. *And* he bought Cassandra's wretched dinner party. I call that gallantry beyond the call of duty."

"Actually, I *had* met him before. He was at the wedding in Scotland."

"*Was* he? I don't remember."

"Yes, well, your memory of that event isn't exactly *perfect*, is it?" Anna prodded Geri as Orlando Gossett took the floor, Savannah and Siena each holding one of his plump red hands. Anna looked about her in surprise. She had been expecting a ghettoblaster with a few infants staggering around it. Instead, a pair of intimidatingly trendy-looking DJs presided over a console and the full complement of flashing lights; the disco was indistinguishable from a grown-up one, and a good deal better than most. Miranda's and Thoby's sprang particularly to Anna's mind.

"Now," boomed one of the DJs, "we have our first competition. Every child on to the floor, please."

As a hundred plus parental hands pushed their little darlings forward, Cassandra looked wildly around for Zak. There he was, behind the console, busily pulling the wires out. So technically minded already, Cassandra thought proudly, clawing her way through the crowd to get to him. Within seconds, he had been propelled on to the floor. Zak may not be making his debut at the Wigmore Hall or Pinewood Studios, Cassandra thought fiercely, but here was a wonderful opportunity to display his Madame Abricot dancing skills.

"We're going to play some music," one of the DJs announced as Fatboy Slim began to pulsate through the room, "and you're all going to dance like your mummy does."

As the parents laughed and clapped, the children stood uncertainly in the strobe lights. One or two, Otto Greatorex among them, Cassandra noted furiously, started to sway to the music and move their feet from side to side. Come on, Zak, she urged silently from the sidelines. *Dance*, you *sod*.

"Like your *mummies*, remember." The DJs turned the sound up until the room throbbed. Anna wondered how loud it had to be before the glass, of which there was plenty, shattered and showered down on them all.

Savannah and Siena, Cassandra saw with panic, were stepping neatly from foot to foot in perfect time, making graceful and economical movements with their arms. Kate Tressell obviously danced as perfectly as she did everything else. Cassandra derived some comfort from the fact that, beside her, Polly Rice-Brown was clearing her throat embarrassedly as Sholto stood swaying his hands from side to side, an ecstatic expression on his face. Otto Greatorex presented a similarly heart-warming sight, galumphing around determinedly off the beat, an inane grin stretching from cheek to cheek. On the sidelines behind him, Fenella looked thunderous.

"Ooh, is *this* how your mummies dance?" mocked the DJs.

Cassandra grinned to herself. She was beginning to enjoy this. More satisfactory still was the arrival onto the floor of Milo and Ivo Hope-Stanley, who began to jerk wildly around in a sort of graceless bop that Cassandra did not at all connect with Caroline until she spotted her mortified face through the crowds. She shook with laughter. This really was *hilarious*.

"What on earth is Zak *doing*?" Geri suddenly whispered to Anna. Cassandra's son had suddenly appeared in the midst of the now heaving dance floor, clutching a bottle of champagne he had found somewhere. He proceeded to stick it in his mouth, tip his head back and stagger around the floor, deliberately colliding with as many people as possible.

"Don't ask," Anna murmured, gazing from between her fingers at the rapidly clearing floor. Zak was now ripping off his shirt and waving the bottle around. As they watched in horror, he rushed up to Milo Hope-Stanley and began grinding into his pelvis, the hand not holding the bottle now clasped firmly to Milo's behind. Milo squealed in terror and rushed to his mother on the sidelines.

"Look at Cassandra," Anna whispered, glancing at where the strobe lights sporadically illuminated a mini-skirted, horror-transfixed figure by the edge of the dance floor.

"I can't. I might miss something," Geri hissed back. Miming that the bottle was empty, Zak now proceeded to strut in an unsteady circle, both hands thrusting his imaginary breasts forward, a lascivious expression on his face. "But look at Cherie Blair!"

Across the dance floor, the Prime Minister's wife looked on in amazement as, the music fading, Zak slid to his knees by way of a finale, lay on his back, spread his legs wide apart and yelled to the assembled company, "I don't suppose there's any chance of a shag?"

Chapter Thirteen

ANNA HAD NEVER HAD a date with a laird before. Apart, that was, from a landlaird—Mr. McGrabbie, the owner of the tiny, scruffy terrace house in which she had occupied a small room during her last year at university, had practically haunted the place. He had, Anna recalled without affection, been particularly fond of appearing either early in the morning or late in the evening, hours which a cynic might assume to be timed in the hope of finding Anna in a state of undress.

A laird. It was really rather exciting. Admittedly, Seb had been an Hon, but one, despite his own wealth, relentlessly Hon The Make. Anna had not been surprised to see, the once or twice she had glimpsed the *Daily Telegraph* recently, that Seb had been given a racing tipsters column. Seeing that he was married to one of the paper's leading writers, the coincidence was really no less than astonishing. What was more genuinely amazing was that, glancing at his byline picture smirking from the page, Anna felt nothing at all. Seb now seemed to have been part of someone else's life altogether, but then again, most things BC (Before Cassandra) seemed to have been part of someone else's life.

It had not been easy to extricate Zak from the party and get back to the house in time to get ready for her date. He was not only having the time of his life stabbing the party entertainer hard in the backside with a plastic sword, but unsurprisingly seemed in no hurry to face his mother, who had suddenly found it necessary to leave the party during his dance routine. Anna was equally unenthusiastic at the prospect of seeing Cassandra; no doubt she would in some way be to blame for the embarrassing turn the afternoon's events had taken.

For once, united in fear, Anna and Zak entered Liv to find it silent. Neither Cassandra nor Jett was anywhere to be seen. Obviously vastly relieved, Zak shot like greased lightning up to his room whence, before too many seconds had elapsed, the unmistakable sound of Warlord Bloodlust II could be heard emanating from the direction of his Playstation. Anna, it seemed, had the house to herself. Or, more significantly, one of the bathrooms. The shower in the garage—fitful, sulky, and invariably occupied by some hideous insect or other—hardly seemed the place to prepare for a hot date with someone like Jamie. Not least because it was always freezing cold. Anna padded up the stairs silently and approached Cassandra's bathroom with the trepidation of Hercules entering the lair of the Minotaur. Dare she?

Before she could change her mind, Anna took her ancient toilet bag and a deep breath and slid through the bathroom door, locking it behind her. Turning on the mock-Edwardian tangle of shower head and mixer tap, she smiled in delicious anticipation at the thundering, warm Niagara pouring into the familiar—and emphatically un-Edwardian—circular bath she spent much of each morning wiping and polishing. Sometimes, admittedly, with her own spit. She burrowed her toes into the thick white carpet which stretched away to the room's distant corners and up the three stairs leading to the platform on which the bath was placed. Cassandra's ablutions, like everything else in her life, had to be a performance.

As the bath slowly filled, Anna, undressing, stared at herself in the mirror. It gave her a distinctly mixed message, the good news being that the wretched swag of flesh had almost disappeared. Even better was the fact that, if Anna raised her arms above her head, she could even see her ribs, although this exercise also revealed the less satisfactory sight of sprouts of russet hair from her armpits. That, plus the unruly thatch between her thighs and the white and flaking expanse of her calves, was the bad news. Christ, thought Anna, surveying with horror the auburn fuzz on her long-neglected lower limbs. I look like a Yeti.

More bad news was that the brilliant light of Cassandra's bulb-and-gilt encircled Hollywood-style mirror only accentuated her pale, dry lips and the exhausted dark smudges under her eyes. As if, Anna thought, she'd gone ten rounds with Prince Naseem. There was no obvious solution to this. Anna's own slim stock of makeup had run out weeks ago, and in any case it would take more than a quick slick of Boots Own Brand to reverse—much less repair—the damage she was now contemplating. It called for spackling paste, at the very least.

The bath was now ready. Stepping in, Anna sank back thankfully among the few bubbles she had dared add. Not that Cassandra was exactly short on unguents—there seemed to be enough royal jelly for a globewide celebration of the Queen Mum's hundredth birthday. Now the excavations could begin: taking her ancient Ladyshave from her washbag, Anna took the first tentative strokes at her armpits, reflecting as she did so that, this being Saturday night, millions of other girls all over the country would be doing the same thing. Men too, very possibly. As she watched the hairs floating on the water's surface, Anna briefly wondered what happened to all the excess fuzz removed from the arms, legs, and pubes of the nation during such preparations. Was there, somewhere underground, a compacted mass of unwanted hair, like the hugest bathroom plug clot ever seen? It was a disgusting thought.

Anna lay back fully now. The delicious and unaccustomed warmth of the water seeped into her bones. She felt sleepy. Exhausted, in fact. That light above the bath was a bit bright; Anna reached for the cord to switch it off, then, a nanosecond later, was forced to stifle a scream as the whole bath erupted around her. Powerful jets of water were pummelling her on every side—in the ribs, under the arms, in the small of the back, and, rather enjoyably, a particularly strong and focused one pouring into the space between her legs. As the delicious tension grew, Anna realised that she had stumbled across not only Cassandra's Jacuzzi—so that was what all those tiny holes had been for—but very possibly also the source of inspiration for the racier scenes in her novels. Given that Cassandra and Jett seemed to go in for steaming rows far more than steamy sex, Anna had never really understood what had fuelled her employer's high-octane literary raunchathons. It was now obvious it wasn't Jett, but another jet altogether.

Anna gasped as the water drilled on, pleasurably, painfully, direct into her inner nerve centre. She'd had no idea that a bath could be so much fun. The blood pounded round her head as a slow throbbing spread through her body; simultaneously, the thudding in her brain seemed to intensify. Anna lifted her head slowly from the water. It was as she had feared. The thudding was coming from the door.

"Who's that in my fucking bathroom?" Cassandra's furious shriek was practically glass-shattering. Climbing reluctantly out of the bath and bracing herself, Anna reflected that at least the description was right.

Anna looked at Jamie over the artificial carnation. The soft glow of the food warmer flickered over his cheekbones as he smiled at her. He seemed to be finding the story of Cassandra and the bathroom extremely diverting. It was almost worth having had her eardrums practically punctured with the force of Cassandra's wrath. Anna's excuse that she was giving the bathroom a steam clean and her hair was wet not with shampoo and bathwater but with the sweat of her exertions had cut little ice with her employer. Until, that was, Cassandra had thrown a handful of cubes into a glass and topped it up with neat Bombay Sapphire. The resulting stupor had afforded

Anna the opportunity to sneak into Cassandra's drinks fridge and help herself to the makeup and perfume that were stored there for reasons Anna had been unable to get to the bottom of, beyond Cassandra's snapped assertion that "All the supermodels do it." After all, thought Anna, dragging the ice-cold tip of the eyebrow pencil painfully across her brow, one may as well be hung for a sheep as a Lancôme.

For her first date with Jamie, Anna had imagined someone with a Scottish island to their credit would have come up with something slightly smarter than the King's Cross tandoori Jamie eventually ushered her into. Even if, as he explained, the sag aloo was to die for and it was convenient for Euston, where he was due to catch the sleeper back to Scotland later. The fact that, come midnight, Jamie would be somewhere in the region of Newcastle did at least solve the problem—raised by Geri—of whether to sleep with him on the first date. As it was, the murky-looking vegetable curries currently being deposited by the waiter on the table looked likely to scupper any plans to kiss him into the bargain. Those plans, anyway, were under constant revision. Jamie smiled a lot, especially at the bath story; he was perfectly friendly, yet Anna detected a guardedness, a tendency to withhold personal information, revealed via a veritable barrage of questions about her. It was difficult not to be flattered however— no one, after all, had ever been *this* interested in her before. Seb, certainly, had barely bothered to find out her surname, let alone any family details. Not that Anna had blamed him overmuch for that; there certainly wasn't anything obviously fascinating about the fact that her civil servant father had died when she was ten, and that she had no siblings and a polite but distant relationship with her part-time librarian mother. Jamie, however, seemed riveted.

There was no time to ask him questions anyway. Having exhausted Anna's stock of answers, Jamie spent the rest of the evening talking about Dampie, while Anna, listening patiently, tried hard to be fascinated by sheep figures, fishing statistics, and dry stone wall replacement programmes and supposed it went with the territory. Quite literally—growing up on a Scottish estate probably did spark a lifelong interest in Tudor oak settles and eighteenth-century portraiture, although growing up in her mother's spotless semi had correspondingly failed to ignite any fascination on her part with MDF and Anaglypta. A faint tremor slid through her stomach as she realised that, in order to have any chance at all with the person sitting opposite, she was going to have to watch a great many *Antiques Roadshows*.

She learned, for her part, a handful of facts about Jamie's background. Her eyes pricked, his terse and dispassionate delivery notwithstanding, on being told how, after his parents died in an aircrash when he was fifteen, the young Jamie had divided his time between school and the Dampie estate.

Despite his obvious reluctance to talk about it, Anna managed to gather that, due to some complication in his father's will, he had only inherited the estate fairly recently and even now the process was not complete. Something about the right personnel not being in place.

"And do you like the countryside?" Anna nodded, her cheeks bulging with onion bhaji, and wondered why he always managed to ask her a question when her mouth was full. He still hadn't shown the slightest inclination to flirt with her, and Anna was beginning to wonder sadly, after the endless questions about old houses in rural locations, if getting the right personnel was the point of the evening and he was merely sounding her out as a potential housekeeper. After all, he knew she was a dab hand with a duster and could manage basic meals. She had hardly held back on her descriptions of life with Cassandra. And there was no doubt that Jamie was far more interested in the domestic details of her day than her ambition to be a writer. She hadn't even told him about the existence of the diary, whose entries seemed daily to get longer and more clogged with telling detail. It seemed to be occupying the same role in her life as the bottle did in Cassandra's—as a comforter. She was a diaryholic.

The miserable conviction that Jamie wasn't remotely romantically interested in her grew as the waiter replaced their plates (hers empty, his full) with the extremely modest bill (he paid it), and the complimentary After Eights (he left them). By the time they both stood up to leave—he still banging on about the reroofing needed at Dampie—she felt the distance between them to roughly resemble that between Land's End and John O'Groats. That's it then, she thought, looking her longing last on his rangy frame as she followed it out defeatedly into the rain-slicked, greasy street. Another one bites the dust. The inimitable Farrier line in charm and conversation had reeled in yet another willing victim. *Not.*

It was with astonishment that she heard him mutter, as he pecked her distantly on the cheek, that he would like to see her again. She spent the whole journey back in the taxi in a state of cautious bliss only slightly punctured by the discovery, when dismounting at Liv, that Jamie hadn't paid for it as she had assumed. Honestly, she thought, handing over her last ten-pound note, I'd have got the bus home had I known. The fact that Cassandra hadn't paid her beyond the first week, and not in full even then, desperately needed addressing. Still, what did that matter? thought Anna, letting herself quietly back into the house, skipping silently up to her sofabedroom, taking her pen, and opening her diary. I'm through to the second interview.

Cassandra, naturally, seized upon the fact of Anna's having a suitor with a bitchy glee. "Aren't you going to get changed, then?" she enquired nastily as, early one evening, Anna gingerly descended the green glass staircase.

"Actually, I'm ready." Having done her best to sponge the marks off her faithful black Joseph trousers, Anna felt reasonably respectable in the white cotton shirt she had slipped in among that afternoon's Everest of ironing. The suspicious way Cassandra was looking at it suggested she might well deduct the three minutes not spent ironing Zak's underpants out of her wages, a further half of which had, after much hand-twistingly embarrassed enquiry, just materialised. This had almost created more problems than it solved—Anna had been torn between paying off some of her student loans and investing in new makeup. Torn, that was, until Geri had intervened and, rolling her eyes, steered her firmly off to the Ruby and Millie cosmetics counter at Boots.

"Didn't realise you had another job as a waitress," Cassandra remarked spitefully before drifting back into the sitting room. As Anna, prompted by the taxi honking outside, left the house, she heard the unmistakable clink of the Bombay Sapphire bottle; crossing the road to the throbbing black car, she was conscious of Cassandra's laser stare penetrating the sitting-room window. So far Cassandra, despite her hints and questions, had not met Jamie and Anna intended to keep it that way. Thankfully, even her basilisk gaze could not penetrate the gloomy depths of the back of the taxi. Jamie, inside, was practically invisible.

It was their second date and, imagining it would be romantic, Anna had suggested they went to see a film. The intervening several months since her last visit to the cinema had, however, obliterated its universal laws from her mind. Such as the one dictating that, directly after she took her seat, the Person With the Biggest Head in the World would sit down slap bang in front of her. And then that the Person With the Noisiest Sweet Wrappers in the World would arrive to sit directly behind her. Thus flanked, Anna spent the whole of the film stiff with rage and frustration, or cringing with embarrassment during the sex scenes. Meanwhile Jamie, back like a ramrod beside her, didn't as much as move his hand to take hers. The few sneaked sideways glances she dared to steal showed his profile, rigid and tight-lipped, staring stonily at the screen in front of him. The last straw had been that the film—one of the must-sees of the moment—was worse than terrible. Its cheesy plot, impossible twists, gratuitous sex, and utterly unbelievable and unsympathetic characters almost, Anna thought, made it comparable to Cassandra's worst.

"I'm so sorry," she gasped afterwards, as they filed down a back staircase which, like all cinema back staircases, stank of urine. "That film was *desperate*. You must think I'm a moron."

"Actually, I didn't notice," Jamie, all gallantry, reassured her. "To tell you the truth, I was thinking about the drainage."

"The *what*?" Had the reek of urine wafted into the cinema as well? She thought she had smelt something else unpleasant, but imagined that to be connected with the bowel movements of the Person With the Biggest Head in the World, from whose direction the smell seemed to be seeping.

"The drainage at Dampie," Jamie explained. "It needs replacing."

Anna sighed. "Let's go and eat something, shall we?" she said. "There's a Pizza Express round the corner."

Clad in the three-piece suit he had also worn for their last date, Jamie looked slightly out of place among the tourists in their pastel polo shirts. He glanced, irritated, down the list of elaborately named pizzas, discounted them all, and asked for lasagne. Afterwards, Anna watched as he unenthusiastically pushed a hard disc of individually portioned vanilla ice-cream around his plate. "Looks like a breast implant, doesn't it?" she grinned.

Jamie looked from her to the ice-cream. "Does it?" he asked, looking both puzzled and disgusted.

❖ ❖ ❖

"It's a disaster," Anna wailed to Geri as soon as the other nannies had left the café the next morning. "He spent the rest of the evening talking about flashing."

"What?" Geri's face darkened. "You mean…*macs* and things?"

"No." Anna permitted herself a faint smile. "The lead flashing on the roof at Dampie. Needs doing, along with everything else, apparently. He's obsessed with that place."

Geri sighed. "Sweetie, it could be much worse. Better that he's obsessed with something glamorous like his ancestral home than *trains* or *football* or something. Or," she grimaced, "DIY. I once had a boyfriend who…"

Anna cut in. She wasn't in the mood to hear about yet another of Geri's erstwhile swains. "Well it is DIY of a sort," she retorted. "I'm sure if there was a Do-It-All on Skul, he'd be down there every five minutes. And, from the sound of the place, so would I. Apparently there's one pub on the whole island and the nearest M&S is in Inverness. Imagine what the clothes must be like."

Geri looked stern. "I don't think you're approaching this quite the right way," she said sharply. "Is Jamie or is Jamie not the best chance of escape you're ever going to have? Don't you want to get away from Cassandra? Don't you want to get *married*?"

"*Married*?" Anna echoed. "I…I can't say I'd ever actually thought about it. I mean, I hardly know him. We've only had two dates…"

"The trouble with *you*," Geri began, as Anna's back stiffened defensively, "is that you never think far ahead enough. What's the point of you going out with Jamie unless you've decided what you want from him? Where's your game plan? *Your* problem is that you just drift along. Take life by the balls, or you'll just end up being taken for a ride."

Anna squirmed. She wished Geri would drop her dictatorial tone. As a matter of fact, the thought of taking Jamie by the balls *had* crossed her mind, although not quite in the way Geri meant.

"You have to visualise the end result you want," Geri stated firmly, grinding her spoon round and round in her coffee cup. "Approach each date like a board meeting—ground you need to cover, subjects discussed, etc., and make sure you prepare for *every eventuality*. You've slept with him, of course?"

Anna recoiled, shocked. She felt her face flood a sizzling, mortified red. "Well, as a matter of fact, I haven't," she muttered. "There haven't really been any opportunities."

Geri was gazing at her in amazement. *What do you mean, there haven't been opportunities?* said her eyes. *You've been alone with him for two whole evenings. What do you think back rows of cinemas are for? People have sex in taxis, you know. What do you need? A four-poster bed and full set of love toys?* In the event, however, Geri confined herself to an emphatic "Why not?"

"It's just that," Anna stammered, blushing ever more furiously and tearing the last corner of her croissant fanatically into pieces, "I'm not very good at sex, you see. Seb told his friends…um," Anna flinched at the memory, "that I was like a corpse in bed."

Geri's eyes flashed fire. "Well, take it from me, sweetie, that there are some men out there who think having a corpse in bed is *very sexy* indeed."

Anna sighed. She did not feel up to confessing that the corpse in question was a dog's. And what was Geri suggesting anyway—that she target necrophiliacs?

"Look, don't worry about all that," Geri ordered. "I've got an idea. When did you say your next date was?"

Anna sighed, more deeply this time. "I didn't. There isn't one."

Anna drove home, wondering if Geri was right. Part of her thought that perhaps she *didn't* control her own destiny enough. Part of her thought she'd got into enough trouble already by allowing Geri to, but given that Seb had practically thrown her out, working for Cassandra had been a good idea at the time.

That, of course, had turned out to be an utter dead end. But perhaps if she had insisted more…As Geri was fond of saying, a tad defensively, "It *was a* good idea. It *might* have worked." But now it hadn't, Anna felt powerless to do anything about it. She was too exhausted, for one thing. Having the self-esteem of a lugworm didn't help either.

Perhaps Jamie was the answer to all her prayers. She was strongly attracted to him, but it was very early days and she hadn't thought—hadn't dared think—of him as a potential husband and saviour. But was that symptomatic of her general lack of direction? Perhaps a great opportunity was staring her in the face—although she had noticed Jamie seemed reluctant to look her in the eyes for too long.

Anna bit a nail on one hand as she absently steered the minivan with the other. Her heart sank as she contemplated last night's date. What exactly had gone wrong? The dreadful film with the faint, seeping smell of fart from the stalls in front? The painful scares over the pizza later, when the conversation had dried up to such an extent they had been reduced to discussing the number of regional Pizza Express branches listed on the back of the menu? The way he had, after stabbing quickly at her cheek with his lips in farewell, shrugged his broad shoulders as if to apologise for wasting both their time? It seemed, Anna thought, vaguely conscious of having jumped a red light, as if it was less a case of what had gone wrong. More what had gone right.

Her heart sank still further when she entered Liv to find Cassandra lurking in the hallway. Her eyes were blazing with fury—or possibly alcohol; the difference, after all, was minuscule.

"Hello, Cassandra," Anna ventured. She'd better try and make the best of it now. After all, she'd blown her one good chance of escape. As Cassandra raked her up and down with her glittering gaze, Anna instantly felt all wrong, despite the fact that her employer was the one wearing a bathrobe and had obviously only just got up.

"Message for you," she spat, stabbing at a piece of paper by the telephone. Anna tried to walk as composedly as she could in

Cassandra's direction. After all, it might only be the bank manager, thwarted by Anna's persistent inability to address her financial problems by mail. Unlikely. There was only one person in Anna's life that Cassandra would be sufficiently interested in to take a message from. Anna picked up the paper. The name, written in wildly veering handwriting—no wonder Cassandra used a laptop—was not the one she had been expecting.

"*Johnny*?" she repeated, puzzled.

"Your…er…*admirer*," Cassandra snarled. "Just called about a minute ago. Wanted your address."

"My *address*?" But Jamie had picked her up from Liv only last night. "Here, you mean?"

Cassandra's eyes narrowed. She shrugged. "No idea," she drawled. "He called this morning as well, now I come to think of it. Zak took the message. I heard him telling whoever it was that you didn't live here anymore. *Such* a sense of humour, that boy." She swept off, grinning, into the sitting room and Anna, still standing stunned in the hall, heard the familiar clink of bottles. Cassandra reappeared unsteadily in the sitting-room doorway. "To Romance," she announced theatrically, raising her tumbler in the air.

It was two evenings later. Anna, taking the small flight of steps to the left of the garden as instructed, found herself facing a neat little door painted a glowing lavender blue. She pressed the small gold bell and waited.

"Geri! It's gorgeous." Anna stepped under the recessed spotlights beaming down into the smart, white-painted hallway. "Is all this really yours?"

Geri nodded nonchalantly. "It's the granny flat. Only both Kate and Julian have such rich mothers that they don't need it. So now it's the nanny flat." Walking down the hall, Anna glimpsed both a shining white bathroom and a roomy bedroom with powder blue bedding piled on a white iron bedstead before Geri showed her into a small, neat sitting room with big squashy sofas. The faint scent of lavender drifted over from a scented candle on an oak coffee table whose sturdy little legs nestled into a fat sheepskin rug. On another side table sat the state-of-the-art answerphone, next to a charging-up mobile.

"I can't believe it," Anna gasped, noting the low lighting and the fashionable slatted wooden blinds at the big windows, and recalling her own stark boxroom with its bare bulb and curtainless, bird-spattered panes. She sank gratefully into the sofa's comforting embrace. It seemed like—indeed, it had been—ages since she had sat on anything so luxurious. Cassandra's chrome tractor-seat kitchen stools, for all their stylishness, were about as comfortable and supportive as their owner.

"Drink?" At the back of the room, below a large, spotless, frameless mirror, Geri was rummaging in an antique-looking box with brass fittings. "Birthday present from Savannah and Siena," she said, seeing Anna looking at it. "An eighteenth-century tea chest, although I like to keep something a bit stronger than Earl Grey in it. And boy, do I need a drink today. G and T?"

"I'd rather have vodka, if you have it." Gin and tonic, formerly one of Anna's favourites, was now too reminiscent of Cassandra. "Why do *you* need a drink? What's up?" Geri rarely, if ever, seemed stressed.

"Slight turbulence at the high tea table." Lighting a Marlboro, Geri blew smoke from her nostrils like the con trail from a plane. "Savannah finished everything on her plate. Kate went *ballistic*!"

"What's wrong with that? Isn't that what children are supposed to do?" Apart, she thought, from Zak, who took the view that eating anything she had cooked was tantamount to expressing affection for her and invented excuses not to, ranging from "it looks like dogshit" to "it's got bugs." Anna had come to derive an intense comfort from this—there was always the hope he might die from malnutrition.

"They're only ever supposed to eat half of everything," Geri explained. "Kate's strict instructions. If they eat everything on their plate they only get half as much at their next meal. She's terrified they're going to grow up fat. She won't let them have any sweets and once even tried to convince them that sugar was salt so they wouldn't develop a sweet tooth. Needless to say, as soon as they're away from the house they're *desperate* for chocolate."

She inhaled deeply and blew smoke out of her nose again. "Anyway, enough of that. The main thing is, he's called you again."

Anna grinned. Kicking her shoes off, she hugged her knees excitedly on the sofa. "Not exactly. I called him."

Geri frowned. "That's not in the Rules," she said. "The man should always call you. Treat him mean and…"

"I *know*. But I didn't have much choice. Zak told him I'd left the country. Thank *God* for one four seven one. I managed to get Jamie's number just before Cassandra staggered out of the sitting room again and caught me."

"Good thinking." Geri looked at her approvingly. "So, down to business. How much time do we have before you're meeting him?"

"Two hours. Pasha at nine."

"*Pasha*? Hope he's paying."

"My treat," Anna said firmly. "After all, I made the call. And he paid for the pizza."

"Big fucking deal," said Geri, looking considerably less approving. "So, let's get to work. This way to the bedroom."

Ten minutes later, Anna was beginning to regret having agreed to come to Geri's for a makeover, clothes-borrow, and pep talk. It had seemed such a good idea at the time. "Success is all in the psychology," Geri had told her. "You need to have your tactics sorted out. More importantly, you need some sexy clothes."

Standing in Geri's bedroom, knee-deep in the contents of her wardrobe, Anna was beginning to have second thoughts. Her breasts had been cantilevered almost to chin level by the most aggressive push-up bra she had ever encountered. She looked doubtfully at her rear in Geri's leopardskin-printed trousers. "Does my bum look big in…" she began.

"No," snapped Geri. "You look fantastic. More curves than a Rococo ceiling, as Julian would say." Anna glanced at her suspiciously. When exactly, she wondered, would Julian say that? Things were obviously going well. Geri had already mentioned that she was accompanying the family on holiday at his special insistence, even though the other family they were going with had two nannies of its own. She turned back to the mirror.

"This shirt is far too tight," she protested, gazing disconsolately at her reflection. Geri was at least two sizes smaller than she was.

Geri sighed. "Shirts," she stated patiently, as if talking to an idiot, "can *never* be too tight."

"But I look fat."

"Rubbish. You look fabulous. And next time you get depressed about your weight—which is nothing, by the way—remember that a ten-stone person weighs seven pounds on Pluto."

"I don't think this is really Jamie's sort of thing," Anna ventured as, after half an hour's backcombing, eyelash-curling, mascara-applying, and lipgloss-slicking, Geri stood back, said, "There!" and held up a mirror to Anna's face. The dark-eyed, pneumatic-lipped stranger with the wild red hair staring back at her looked, Anna thought, rather terrifying.

Geri recognised doubt when she saw it. "Well thanks a lot," she huffed. "I turn you into a raunchy sexbabe and this is the thanks I get."

"But I'm not sure Jamie likes raunchy sexbabes," said Anna, recalling his set face during the film's more explicit scenes.

Geri put her hands on her hips, exasperated. "Well, he'll be the first man ever in the history of the universe who doesn't. *Every* man likes raunchy sexbabes. Get *real*, will you?"

Anna's appearance being, in Geri's eyes at least, satisfactory, they then moved on to tactics. "For Christ's sake look *interested* if he talks about the castle…"

"You mean *when*," said Anna. "There's no if about it."

"Well, do you want to be Cassandra's slave for the rest of your life or would you rather be lady of the manor? Doesn't seem much of a choice to me."

Anna was forced to admit this was true. Nonetheless, she had a sense of events moving out of her control. Did she really want to marry Jamie? More to the point, did he want to marry her? "Mere details," scoffed Geri. "Just *make* him want to marry you, that's all. You like him, don't you? If the marriage goes tits up you can always leave him and get half his property into the bargain. It's not what I'd call a great risk. He's good-looking, isn't he? Which ninety-nine per cent of men aren't. And anyway, what other options do you have?"

Put like that, it sounded almost reasonable. Anna, in any case, had barely had a chance to wonder aloud about love, sex, and having to want to spend your whole life with the other person before Geri cut in with a single word. "Guff."

Anna had no idea why a small part of her still believed that marriage should be for love. Certainly, she had never seen any evidence to the contrary. From her own parents' squabbles—so far as she could dimly remember them—to the vicious battles between Cassandra and Jett, not to mention her own miserable co-habiting experiences with Seb, there seemed no reason to believe marriages were ever idyllic.

"Marriage," Geri declared, "is like a tornado. It starts with a lot of blowing and sucking, then it ends up taking your house."

"Did you make that up?" Anna looked at her admiringly.

"No, James Caan did, as it happens. Told me that at a dinner party once. So stick with Jamie and, whatever happens, you'll get his house. Half of it, at least."

"Hopefully the half with the roof and plumbing," grinned Anna.

"Stop splitting hairs and go out there and get yourself one. An heir, I mean."

Somehow implicit in her tones was the suggestion that if Anna didn't, Geri would. It was this more than anything else—apart from the taxi hooting outside—that finally propelled Anna out of the lavender front door.

"Remember," Geri called after her, "it's all about tactics. Think Premier League. The manager gives the team a pep talk before the game, and again at halftime." There was a sound of running footsteps and then something small and hard was slipped into Anna's hand. "Take the mobile and call me from the loos before the pudding. Which, of course, you'll have refused."

Jamie was late. Anna shifted uncomfortably in Geri's tight trousers, trying to relieve the pressure on her bladder. In twenty-five minutes, she'd got through almost the entire bottle of rosé provided by the kaftaned waiter. Her nerves now felt much better, but she was dying for the loo. Two things prevented her from going: the thought of missing Jamie when—*if*—he finally appeared through the carved front door; and, almost worse, the thought of everyone else in the restaurant scrutinising her too-tight clothes as she walked past their tables and descended the look-at-me staircase leading down past the petal-strewn fountain to the loos.

The girls at the next table, she knew, would be merciless in their criticism. There were about eight of them, strappy dresses flopping off their tanned shoulders, spindly, high-heeled ankles poking out in all directions from under the table, taking quick, nervous puffs on their cigarettes as their narrowed eyes flicked speculatively at each other and around the room. They had already cast her a few pitying, been-stood-up-have-you glances made worse by Anna's surmising that, judging from what the ringleader, a naughty-looking blonde chignon with a dirty laugh, was saying, they were a bachelorette party. "Yah, and the worst thing is that so many people are buying off-list," complained the chignon. "I mean, this morning I got sent some *Italian millennium toasting flutes*, for fuck's sake."

"Is that the same as toasting forks?" asked the very thin dark crop next to her.

"No it isn't. And while we're on the subject of Italy," added the blonde, "I'm sick of people ringing me up and asking where it is. *Unbelievable*. I'd no idea my friends were so thick."

Anna smiled to herself and reached for another piece of pickled carrot. Jamie was now half an hour late. The many scenarios she and Geri had rehearsed—what to say, how to sit, how to look ("Catch his eye, drop yours, and then, with a sweeping glance back upwards, look at him directly again and give him a slight, full-lipped smile," Geri counselled. "It's called The Flirt. Never fails.")—had not included a complete no-show on his part. She'd give him another ten minutes, thought Anna, pouring the last of the rosé into her glass. Until then, she'd practise The Flirt in the mirror opposite the table and hope the girls didn't think she was trying to pick them up.

The restaurant buzzed with laughter and conversation. Tiny alcoves were let into the walls, each containing a softly radiant oil lamp; from the ceiling above the stairs hung a collection of about twenty magnificent brass Moorish lanterns, all of different sizes and heights. Rugs were scattered over the wooden floors, providing a challenge for the waiters as they slid back and forth with huge brass trays of food. It was every bit as romantic as the glossy magazines she had consulted said it was, as well as being deliciously camp—Disney Moroccan—into the bargain. The only fly in the ointment was the food—for someone like Jamie, who had been barely able to cope with a choice of pizzas, Pasha's suggestions of yoghurt chicken, seafood tagine, and prawn chermoula would probably be completely unnavigable. But that was a bridge she would cross when she came to it; at this rate, she wouldn't have to bother.

A flurry of interest among the bachelorette party suddenly impressed itself on the daydreaming Anna (the rosé had been more potent than she had thought, the restaurant was deliciously warm, and she had finally found a way to sit that didn't make her want to wet herself). Something tall and imposing was walking through the restaurant—and straight to her table.

"Anna, I'm so sorry." Jamie. At last. "Got delayed, I'm afraid, and couldn't remember the name of the restaurant. Just came back to me in the taxi—thank God."

Aware that the bachelorette party—and a good many of the waiters—were staring at Jamie in open admiration, Anna levered herself halfway out of her chair to receive his kiss on both her cheeks. She was surprised to see that he, too, seemed to have made a considerable sartorial effort. His crisp white shirt set off his wide, dark eyes and Mediterranean tumble of thick black hair to perfection, despite the emphatic crease across the nipples and lower stomach revealing that he'd just got it out of the packet. A pair of Argyll check trousers fell in a long, graceful line the ten feet or so between the floor and Jamie's waistline. There were other transformations too. Instead of sitting down, as expected, and glancing suspiciously at the menu, Jamie picked it up enthusiastically. He did not quite say, "Oh, chermoula, my favourite," but he did make interested noises about the chicken. Anna, encouraged, and clenching her buttocks to strengthen her resolve, tried out The Flirt on him.

Jamie looked back at her. She felt her stomach tense and her lower bowels turn to liquid—which at the moment, was pretty much what they were anyway. Finally, after a long, sexy silence pregnant with possibility, Jamie, still gazing at her, spoke.

"Got something in your eye?" he asked.

Anna buried her face in the menu. Fortunately, the waiter chose that moment to mince up.

But that was the only wrong note of the evening, apart from when Anna, helping herself to the mixed mezes with more enthusiasm than skill, accidentally knocked her hand against his. As the usual electric shock shot deliciously up her arm, the spoon wobbled and a great dollop of aubergine and tomato splattered onto the glaringly white tablecloth. Anna blushed furiously and, in her confusion, promptly set a spoonful of tabbouleh scattering across the table as well. She felt like a four-year-old. Seb, she knew, would have left the splodge where it was and stared at it meaningfully all evening. Jamie, however, simply moved one of the many terracotta meze dishes over the mark, pressed it firmly down on top, and grinned at her.

As they talked—or, rather, as Anna listened to Jamie talking—it struck her that he seemed to be making an effort to charm similar to the pains he had taken to dress well. As Jamie, again neatly sidestepping the subject of himself directly, related a string of anecdotes about his ancestors, it seemed to Anna that never had someone talking about their relations seemed so sexy. Or amusing.

"Yes, Granny Angus was quite a character. She used to stick her teeth in with exactly the same mortar she used to mend the walls—you see, as a family we've always been patching up the old place." Jamie paused and flashed her a gusset-immolating grin. "After she had her fifth heart attack, my father was at her bedside thinking she was about to peg it when she opened her eyes, looked straight at him, and demanded, 'Fetch me my compact mirror.'"

Anna giggled. She had rarely felt so happy. More rosé was ordered, food arrived, and plates were taken away. Suffused with wine, glowing brass, and the soft light of oil lamps, she felt herself relaxing under Jamie's barrage of charm. Enough even to go to the loo, at last.

There was something different about the table when she returned to it. Anna's stomach did a double loop of nervous delight when she spotted, nestling against the knife blade next to her plate, a small, rather tatty blue box. Sitting down quickly before her knees gave way beneath her, she gazed from it to Jamie, her eyes wide with hope and fear.

"Well, aren't you going to open it?"

Anna put out a trembling hand, hoping Jamie wouldn't notice how bitten her nails were. Inside the box, nestling on a bed of rather moth-eaten cream satin, was a diamond of impressive dimensions. Anna gasped. Inside her, the mezes and the prawn chermoula attempted a pas de deux.

"It was my mother's."

"It's lovely." Never having been one to count her chickens, Anna could not yet be sure he hadn't just brought it along as a Dampie curio to show her, rather as some people got out their holiday snaps.

"Aren't you going to try it on?"

"Do you think I should?" Her heart beat a tattoo as she gazed unsteadily at him. His face was fading in and out of focus. Its strong, well-defined edges disappeared in places into a watery mass. As she bent her head, something wet and warm trickled down her cheek.

He rolled his eyes to the ceiling. "Well, of course it's up to you, but it might be an idea as I'm asking you to marry me."

Anna stared at him. She was conscious of feeling nothing beyond being perfectly stunned and immobile. Opposite her, Jamie, as if in slow motion, smiled, gestured, and, finally, picked the ring out of its box and slid it on to her hand. In the watery world of utter shock she now inhabited, Anna was dimly aware of the cold metal sliding up her finger, of the bachelorette party at the next table turning to stare in unadulterated envy.

"…know it seems sudden…thought you would be perfect," Jamie was saying in a slow, gloopy, surreal voice that didn't sound like him at all. She tuned out again in panic. "…share all the same interests, love of old buildings, the countryside…" he was mouthing at her as she picked up his voice again. She felt her head, heavy as a rock, moving slowly up and down in assent. "…saw no point in waiting for years to ask you…one just knows, doesn't one…important to have a wife who shares one's interests…very happy," Jamie was adding, a hint of concern now creeping into his wide eyes at her lack of response. "Thought you could come back to Dampie with me…going up in a couple of days…sooner you move in the better…can plan the wedding from there…chapel in the castle grounds…are you all right?"

There was a crash. Waiters rushed to the scene as Anna fled in the opposite direction, leaving a trail of the glasses she had swept from the table as she leapt up. She was conscious both of Jamie's concerned stare and the laser hatred of the bachelorette party as she rushed headlong down the tiled staircase beneath the lanterns, past the fountain, and into the sheltering space of the lavatory cubicle. Hanging over the shining enamel hole, she realised she didn't want to be sick after all. It was exultation rushing up her throat, not half-digested couscous.

Suddenly, the mobile in her pocket buzzed. "Half-time team talk," hissed Geri. "Decided whether you're going to shag him or not?"

"I'm not sure," Anna said slowly, "that I'm going to have to bother. Yet, at any rate."

The next day was Sunday, yet Anna and an unusually grumpy Geri were drinking coffee together as usual. Operabugs, the junior appreciation society designed to ensure St. Midas's pupils shone in the corporate Covent Garden boxes of the future, had been moved to Sundays, there no longer being space on the weekday timetables to give it the attention it was felt it deserved. Puccini was currently under the microscope, and "One Fine Day" was pouring out of the St. Midas's windows into Cassandra's rain-spattered minivan, where Geri and Anna sat like a couple of Bank Holiday coach drivers awaiting their cargo of pensioners. Their usual café being closed, they cradled plastic cups of distinctly inferior coffee from a fourth-rate builders' café round the corner and watched the rain run down the windscreen.

"Geri," said Anna after another silence had elapsed, "how long do I have to hold my cup like this before…"

"Omigod!" Geri, beside her, shot upright on the seat, her eyeballs large, rigid with excitement and clamped, mesmerised and unwavering, on the vast and glittering gem on Anna's finger. "*Christ*. It's colossal. That's *incredible*. I mean, from what you said when I called you, that you weren't going to sleep with him, I thought the whole thing was off. Was quite cross, actually." Geri suddenly grinned at her. "After all the advice I gave you and everything…"

So that explained the grump. Anna pressed her hand. "Well, I couldn't have done it without you. You were brilliant."

"So, can I be bridesmaid?"

Anna smiled at her nervously. "Course you can. But the wedding date's not set yet—I'm supposed to be moving up to Scotland with him and sorting it out from there."

"When are you going?" Geri's face suddenly fell. "I'll miss you."

"And I you." Anna squeezed her hand.

"So what happens next?" asked Geri, her eyes darting back and forth in wonderment from Anna's face to her finger.

Anna felt a tremor of fear course through her intestines. The wedding, certainly, was an intimidating prospect. In the back of her mind was the worry that she had not done the right thing by accepting, that she had allowed herself to be carried along on a tide of reckless romance at the expense of common sense. But it wasn't this that had caused the tremor. Geri, Anna knew, would shoot down her doubts in a few emphatic and eloquent sentences. The fear was caused by something else altogether.

"Well," Anna said slowly, "I suppose I'd better tell Cassandra."

"Zak! ZA-AA-AAK!" Having scanned the envelope's contents, Cassandra had bounded up the stairs two at a time, oblivious for once of the damage the Gucci spikes inflicted on the treads, and burst into his nursery to find her son slinging what looked like a dressing-gown cord over the hook on the back of the door. The vague, dreadful suspicion of what he might be up to—she, like all the other mothers, had read the reports of the Eton Strangling Game—stirred in Cassandra's mind but there was no time for that now. Besides, everyone knew that dicing with death one way or another, be it sadistic prefects, capital punishment, or initiation rites involving everything from buggery to bogflushing, was an occupational hazard at public schools. It was part of what you paid for.

"What the hell is all this about?" she shrieked, waving the letter with the St. Midas's crest at Zak whose spoilt face faded from pampered pink to haunted grey. He had never seen his mother so angry. He had never, for that matter, seen her angry at all.

"It says here," Cassandra said in the low, dead voice of one forced to accept that their profoundest fears have become reality, "that you failed the mid-term exams. *How has this happened?*" Cassandra's voice sank to the agonised whisper of Macbeth at the point it dawns on him that life's but a walking shadow. "It says here that you failed at *drawing*. How *could* you? After all that *work* I put in. I spent *weeks* showing you how to do a triangle…" Tears rose in her eyes.

Zak nodded, his eyes slits beneath his thick blond-and-honey-striped fringe.

"So why the hell *didn't* you draw a triangle?"

"Because," Zak said contemptuously, "they wanted me to draw a *circle* in the exam."

Cassandra howled, smacked her head with the base of her palm, and waved the letter again. "And apparently you were asked to draw a woman."

Zak nodded. "I *did*."

"But you drew one *with one leg*."

Zak sniggered. Cassandra glared at him, torn between murderous fury and blind despair. Then, most unexpectedly, an idea occurred to her. Her fury with her son evaporated as she weighed up the worth of her inspiration. It really was a good one, Cassandra thought. Rather *brilliant*, actually. She tottered to the telephone and dialled the school's number.

"But Mrs. Gosschalk, did Zak not tell you about my *amputation*…?"

Five minutes later, Cassandra put the phone down, her face magenta with fury. Not only had Mrs. Gosschalk not believed her—Cassandra could tell from her tone of voice, despite the sympathetic noises, although, come to think of it, they had not been *that* sympathetic—but she had mentioned The Party. Cassandra had cherished the wild hope that Zak's behaviour at Savannah and Siena's birthday had been brushed under the sisal—after all, it had not been mentioned since. The reason for this, it now turned out, was because the school—which took a keen interest in its pupils' behaviour both on and off the premises—had been deliberating on what action to take. It had, Mrs. Gosschalk had just informed Cassandra, decided to hold a kangaroo court on Zak's future at St. Midas's, at which the entire SMSPA (apart from Cassandra) would be present. She would, Gosschalk had said, be informed of the results of its deliberations in due course. Cassandra's blood boiled. That *bloody* Fenella Greatorex would be sitting in judgement on *her*. A woman whose property was at best borderline where the St.

Midas's catchment area was concerned. Borderline in every other respect as well. The *humiliation* of it.

Things, Cassandra thought, could not get any worse this morning. But that was before Anna dropped her bombshell.

"*What?*" Only her spike heels, anchored firmly if ruinously in the kitchen floor, stopped Cassandra from collapsing. She glared at Anna with blazing loathing. "*What* the *fuck* did you just say?"

"Jamie says he doesn't want to take you up on the dinner party. He just, um, wanted to make, um, a donation to St. Midas's." Anna, feeling the hatred burning into her like a laser, paused.

"No, not that," Cassandra snapped. "The *other* thing you said."

Anna swallowed. "And, um, he's asked me to marry him."

"Oh my *God*. I've got to sit down." Cassandra collapsed dramatically into a chair and stared at the delta of thin blue veins in the heel of her hand. Should she end it all now?

"*Give me air,*" she yelled at Anna as she fired up a Full Strength Ultratar. Hot tears began to flow over her foundation like lava over the cragged face of Etna. Her mascara—part of a new range called Rock Star she was celebrity test-driving for one of the few glossy magazines still aware she existed—began to run in black streams down her face.

"So I'm afraid I'll have to be leaving rather sooner than I had planned," Anna muttered. She genuinely felt almost apologetic. She'd seen earthquaked cities look less devastated than Cassandra at that moment. "Jamie wants me to move up to Scotland with him."

Anna spent her last night in Liv hearing Cassandra and Jett screaming more violently at each other than they ever had before. Unable to sleep, she was red-eyed and exhausted when Jamie came round in the morning to pick her up in a hire car specially rented for the occasion. Doubtless he had thought, Anna realised as, embarrassed, she stuffed her one piece of luggage into the boot, that she had slightly more possessions than was the case. Or even the rucksack. "What time will we arrive at Dampie?" she asked him, over-brightly, as they headed up through Hampstead.

"Oh, about midnight, I should think." At least, Anna thought, he knew his way there; there would be no repeat of Seb's cold fury at her inability to tell right from left.

"We'll be starving."

"Don't worry. Nanny will have left something for us to eat."

"*Nanny?*" Anna shot upright in her seat. "You've still got a *nanny?* You never mentioned *her* before."

"Oh, didn't I?" Did Jamie sound over-casual? "She still lives at Dampie. She's, um, well, sort of the housekeeper now—been in the family forever. *Great* old character. You'll *love* her."

There was a silence as Anna tried to suppress a sense of rising panic. She gazed out of the window, unseeing, as Golders Green flashed past.

"What's Nanny like?" she asked, as they turned on to the M1.

"Mm?" Jamie was absorbed in indicating to move into the middle lane.

"*Nanny,*" repeated Anna. "Tell me about her."

Jamie didn't miss a beat. "Oh, Nanny. She's wonderful. You'll love her. Actually," he added smoothly, "you might find her quite useful as well. Thought you could talk to her about the wedding. Organising it and all that…Nanny's very good at organising things."

It was a while before Anna spoke again.

"Are you very close to her?" she eventually asked, choosing her words carefully.

"Well, she looked after me after my parents died. Used to knit me scratchy jerseys." Jamie laughed fondly as they sailed past Northampton. "Still does, as a matter of fact. Bright yellow. Keeps the fleas off, she says."

"*Fleas?*"

"And always a bit tight," Jamie continued.

"What? Gin?" Not another alcoholic, Anna hoped. Cassandra had been bad enough. But bad enough, thankfully, to still be in bed when they left.

Jamie's shocked jerk sent the car spinning into the fast lane. Quickly, he pulled it back into the centre of the middle lane. "God, no. Nanny never drinks. She knitted the jerseys a bit tight, I mean. She's always been a bit funny about clothes. She thinks T-shirts are very scruffy and once drew a collar and tie on a picture of me in one. I looked rather strange beside the rest of the school cross-country running team." He grinned uncertainly at her across the handbrake. "But I'm sure you girls will have a wonderful time planning the wedding."

Girls. Even at best, Nanny would hardly qualify as a twenty-something. Difficult to imagine giggling over the wedding dress with a white-haired pensioner, however twinkling the eyes, apple-like the cheeks, and benevolent the smile.

"Did she spoil you?" If Nanny was generous, that at least would be something. They could giggle over the lavish menu and champagne instead.

"*Spoil me?*" Another amazed swerve. "Oh no. Nanny was *very* firm. She thought running water was immoral and used to make me break the ice on the horse troughs before I could wash. Even in summer. And long after we'd stopped using horses."

As far as Nanny was concerned, Anna quickly decided, what remaining ignorance there was bliss. She made no further enquiries and spent the rest of the journey either dozing or listening to Jamie describe the various repairs to the castle he had planned. From what he said, the place seemed to be falling apart; the weather since she had been there must have been appalling. She didn't remember it being so bad at Thoby's wedding. Although, come to think of it, it had been a bit cloudy.

By the time they reached Dampie, Anna realised there was a lot she didn't remember from Thoby's wedding. Such as the drive being a moonscape of yawning holes with the castle itself lurking glumly at the end in a cloak of swirling mist. The moss-slimed steps leading to the cracked and peeling front door had also slipped her memory. Indeed, so far was Dampie from being the Disneyland palace of light she remembered that Anna wondered if the wedding had been somewhere else altogether.

Anna gripped Jamie's hand tightly and tried not to shudder as something unimaginably ancient opened the door and thrust a battered, kerosene-scented lantern almost in their faces. The light blazed on the brimming red rims of the creature's rheumy eyeballs and caught the slimy stumps of its teeth. Flecks of phlegm were speared on the unshaven wastes of its chin like cuckoo-spit on grass, and a strong smell of whisky clung to the shabby layers of its clothing. It took all Anna's self-control, never high and currently at its lowest, for her not to recoil in disgust.

"MacLoggie!" exclaimed Jamie, much to Anna's relief. The unshaven chin had been a hint but hadn't necessarily ruled out the possibility of this being Nanny.

"Hame safely," the ancient retainer gasped at Jamie, apparently deeply affected, although whether by alcohol or by emotion, it was impossible to tell.

"D'ye want anything ta eat? Nanny's left you some stovies in the kitchen."

Jamie brightened. "Nanny's stovies," he informed Anna, "are a force to be reckoned with."

Anna had no idea what stovies were, except that they sounded like something you presented to your doctor in a glass jar for examination. "Too late for me," she muttered. "If you don't mind, I think I'll turn in."

"I'll take ye up to bed then," the ancient heap growled.

Anna swallowed, trying to stifle the almost unimaginable

thought of snuggling down with such a creature. She lifted her ring finger half in protection. The diamond glimmered dully in the lamp light. But MacLoggie showed no signs of noticing it.

"Take Miss Farrier to Dr. Johnson," said Jamie.

"Dr. Johnson?" echoed Anna. "But I feel perfectly all right. I know I was slightly carsick around Scotch Corner but I'm fine now."

"The Dr. Johnson *suite*," said Jamie. "He slept in it when he visited Dampie on his tour of the Highlands. Thought that might appeal to your literary side. He really enjoyed himself here," Jamie added. "Wrote in his diaries that Dampie was 'a most impressive ruin…the first sight of which weighed very solemnly on me.'"

"Oh." It didn't sound like a five-star recommendation to Anna.

The weak light from MacLoggie's lantern had faded to a pinprick in the all-absorbing gloom of the back of the hall; Anna, stumbling in his wake, found a far more reliable guide to be the strong smell of whisky trailing after him, and the faint rattling of keys. Endless passages and stairways were negotiated, one spiral. As she pushed her shoulders up the claustrophobically tight and twisting stairwell, Anna had the impression the walls were pressing in and squeezing her. She wondered which of the many dark passages contained Nanny.

"Hae we are," MacLoggie said as they finally emerged on a red-carpeted landing where a number of low, wide white doors with brass handles were set deep into their respective frames. He unlocked the door and, turning on his heel, disappeared into the darkness without another word. The blackness descended on Anna with the intimidating suddenness of a kidnapper's cloak.

As she felt for the bedroom door and opened it, the chill air hit her like a fist. She fumbled and found a light switch, revealing a room vaguely similar to that she recalled occupying with Seb. This was, however, much larger and presumably much grander, so vast were its proportions, so impressive in size if possibly not in comfort the large four-poster bed which stood in the centre of it, scented slightly with mildew and mothballs. A honeymoon suite for the Addams Family, thought Anna, peering closely at a murky oil which hung between two deeply recessed windows and depicted what looked like a soldier dying in the arms of a tragic-looking woman. A spaniel apparently also breathing its last lay nearby; the picture was entitled "The Double Sacrifice." A door in one wall of the room led to a cavernous Edwardian bathroom with a rust-scabbed container of Ajax standing on the bathside where the Crabtree and Evelyn ought to be.

Anna returned to the bedroom, knelt in the recessed window and squinted out through the diamond panes. One was missing, and the draught shot through Anna's thin Ghost dress—a good luck present from Geri—like a bullet. She shivered, hoping it was the only Ghost in residence.

A hideous and heavy mahogany piece of furniture, seeking to combine the functions of desk, dressing table, and decorative object and failing singularly at all three, stood against the faded floral paper of one wall. Anna debated whether to put her underwear in it, but having taken one sniff at the damp and dusty interior, decided not to. The flat, wide drawer just below the mirror in the centre would, however, be the perfect place for her diary. After she had written today's entry, of course. Fishing the small exercise book out of the front pocket of her bag, Anna crouched on the end of the bed and scribbled her account of leaving the vibrancy and crowds of London—never had she thought of them with such attention before—for a land where both the warmth and the light seemed permanently switched off. She shivered as she scribbled, noting at the end of her entry that she seemed to be further from writing a novel than ever. But perhaps the silence and space of the castle might prove an inspiration. After all, hadn't Dr. Johnson stayed here?

Anna unpacked quickly and thrust her clothes into the dank and icy wardrobe. After finally screwing up the courage to get between the sheets—just as cold and old-smelling as anticipated, and very possibly the very same the eminent lexicographer had slept in—Anna lay and waited for Jamie. As the fatigue of the journey overcame her, she drifted in and out of dreams where she was being chased up an endless and ever-shrinking spiral staircase by a large, bewigged, and whisky-scented creature who may have been Dr. Johnson. Or Nanny.

Chapter Fourteen

THE DOCTOR PUT HIS pen down on his desk, sighed, and looked at Cassandra.

"Mrs. Knight. Is there anything in Zachary's past, any experience he may have had, that could have left a deep and abiding impression on him?"

"Certainly not," snapped Cassandra. "Zak's very resilient. Nothing ever makes an impression on him."

"Yes," said the child psychologist. "That's roughly what I'd heard from Mrs. Gosschalk." He sighed, picked up his pen again, and tapped it on the desk. Mont Blanc, Cassandra noticed crossly. *And* the desk was antique. Bound to be with the fees she was paying him.

"Children are very sensitive, you know. It could have been something minor."

"Zak's never met a miner. I try and keep him away from *that* sort of person." Cassandra narrowed her eyes and hoped the psychologist—all too obviously *that* sort of person himself—would get her drift. Large, red-faced, and florid, with a distinctly regional accent; it was *ludicrous*. What on *earth* could a creature like this tell her about Zak?

"So, no trigger that you can think of?"

"Well, he does have a number of guns piled under his bed."

"He *does*, Mrs. Knight?"

"All toy ones, of course. *Almost* all, at any rate."

Still, she had had no choice but to come, such had been the verdict of the St. Midas's parents in that *bloody* extraordinary general meeting held after Zak's performance at the Tressell birthday party. Cassandra boiled inside at the memory of that *wretched* Fenella Greatorex, now risen to chairman of the SMSPA, telephoning her afterwards and telling her in a voice *saturated* with sugary condescension that, given his obvious degree of mental disturbance, Zak needed to be referred to a child psychologist, on the basis of whose report Zak's future at St. Midas's would finally be assessed. Stay of execution, then. But executions there would be, Cassandra was determined. Eventually.

"Never mind, darling," Cassandra had reassured her son. "What goes around, comes around, and when you're head of MI5, you can have them all stabbed to death with poisoned umbrellas." Zak's eyes had lit up; Cassandra had tried not to notice when, several hours later, she spotted him looking with interest at the furled inhabitants of the Jade Jagger umbrella stand in the corner of the hall.

Great though the relief that Zak could—at least temporarily—stay at the school had been, the expense of fulfilling the conditions had been greater. Cassandra had been amazed to discover the waiting list for a child psychologist was almost as long as that for a Hermés Kelly bag. She'd virtually had to found a whole ward before she could leapfrog it. But it was unthinkable that Zak lose his place at St. Midas's.

"So." The psychologist looked up at Cassandra from his notes. "As far as you are concerned, Zachary's childhood has passed entirely without any violent or emotionally upsetting incident?"

"Yes."

"Sure?"

"Well, there was a *slight* scene on the Ghost Train at Chessington when he was about six years old, but I never managed to find out whether it was Zak or his father who burst into tears during the ride."

"Mmm." The psychologist raised an eyebrow. "Is that all?"

"And I suppose I was a *bit* cross with him when he only came second in the hundred metres sprint at the school sports day last year. But I was entitled to my view—after all, I'd won the mothers' race only after *months* of intensive daily training with a former Olympic athlete. I felt Zak was rather letting the side down."

"Ah." The psychologist brightened. "Now we're getting somewhere. You must beware of ambitious parent syndrome, Mrs. Knight."

"*Tell* me about it," Cassandra sighed dramatically. "The parents at St. Midas's are so pushy it's *embarrassing*. One of them is talking about getting his child selected for Labour at the age of twelve. He says if William Pitt can do it, so can Mungo, although I suppose William Pitt must be at another school somewhere. I don't think he's at St. Midas's."

The psychologist's eyes boggled slightly. He rippled his fingers repeatedly on the desktop as if playing an overture. "Zachary, Mrs. Knight, is a child. Not a racehorse."

It was Cassandra's turn to stare. "Dr. Leake," she said, flaring her nostrils, "I find it hard to believe that I am paying good money—and rather a lot of it at that—to be told my son is *not* a racehorse. Do you think I wouldn't have noticed when he was born?"

"You misinterpret my meaning, Mrs. Knight. What I am trying to say is that parenting is not a competition. Pushing him too hard can result in burnout syndrome. You don't want him to win cups at eight only to drop out at sixteen."

"No, of course not. I want him to win cups at sixteen as well."

The psychologist sighed. "Mrs. Knight. Like many parents you are over-anxious that your child should be a success. You are perhaps expecting too much of him. Parents who want their children to be MPs at ludicrously early ages are not really doing them any favours."

"I agree. The very least they should expect is Prime Minister. Aim high, that's what I say."

"Thank you, Mrs. Knight. I think that's quite enough for one afternoon."

Put *him* in his place, Cassandra thought triumphantly as she drove home. How dare anyone suggest Zak was anything other than an angel?

"I mean, really," she declared to Jett on arriving back at Liv. "How could anyone possibly take any of this *seriously*? Just because Zak's a chip off his father's old performing block and has a powerful stage presence. What's happened to everyone's sense *of humour...*?" Her voice tailed off as, having finished flinging off her pashmina and checking her makeup in the hall mirror, she turned and caught Jett's expression. It was one of unbounded fury.

"Yes, well, the little *bastard's* done more than demonstrate stage *presence*," snarled Jett. "He's been demonstrating some of the *goddamn props* as well." He shook a fist at the ceiling from where lengths of wire dangled like beheaded flower stems.

Zak, it emerged, had discovered a broadsword from the forthcoming Solstice stage show under the chaise longue in Jett's study and, with the aid of judiciously-placed chairs and tables, had immediately set about hacking every ceiling light in the house from its flex on the pretext that he was playing at pirates.

"Well, quite right too," yelled Cassandra, determined to defend her son. "Everyone knows ceiling roses are hopelessly passé. Zak's just taken the first step on the road to uplighters."

"Trust you to take his side," roared Jett. "You let him get away with goddamn *murder*—almost literally in the case of Otto Greatorex. Gave his goddamn arm so many Chinese burns yesterday he nearly burst into goddamn flames. What sort of example are you setting him?"

"*You fucking hypocrite!*" shrieked Cassandra. "If we're talking examples, just hang on in there while I get the lawyer on conference call. What about you and that Yugoslavian *slapper*?"

"Ethnic Albanian, actually," huffed Jett. "She lost her entire family in the Kosovo war."

"And then she came here and got screwed by *you*. I wonder which was worse."

Svetlana, the East European nanny, had seemed manna from heaven the day, almost a week after Anna had left, that Cassandra had spotted her ad in the local freesheet. She had been irresistible to Cassandra because she was cheap; to Jett she had been merely irresistible. Just as Zak could not pass over the opportunity to call her Sweaty instead of the approved diminutive of Sveti, Jett could not pass over the opportunity of making a pass.

"I didn't screw her."

"Oh no? What about all those scratches and squeeze marks on your back?"

Jett's protestations and excuses that Sveti had been a dermatologist before the war in Kosovo and was giving him some free treatment cut no ice with his wife.

"A *dermatologist*?" Cassandra hissed. "She's got a face like a *pizza*. Probably thinks cathiodermie is an *Irish barmaid*." She was, Cassandra suddenly decided, *sick* of playing host plant to a parasitic philanderer. The last strumpet had sounded. She'd had enough.

Seeing the genuine light of battle in her eyes rather than just the drunken rage he had privately come to think of as the Warninks signals, Jett panicked. A large house in Kensington and a lavishly subsidised lifestyle seemed to rise up before him and disappear out of the window.

"Um," he stuttered. "I can explain…"

Cassandra held up a hand. "And besides," she spat, "what the *hell* do you want with dermatology anyway? You've got skin like an old teabag that's been buried for years. Just *look* at you."

Jett bristled. He stared at his wife with a mixture of fear and loathing. Finally, squeezing through the decayed and dripping cells of his brain came the dim memory that attack was the best form of defence.

"You're jealous," he hurled back. "You can't bear to think another woman finds me attractive." As Cassandra stared at him in disbelief, he wondered whether he had got it wrong. Perhaps defence was the best form of attack. "So what harm does it do?" he wheedled. "It's not as if *you* give two hoots. I'm not *hurting* anyone."

"*That*," snapped Cassandra, "depends whether you're wearing your Five Gates of Hell penis strap or not. I imagine that could hurt quite a lot."

"How do you know about *that*?" Jett demanded as what colour there was in his face drained out of it. "Been opening my post again, I suppose?"

"Never mind how I know. The point is," Cassandra said, feeling suddenly exhausted, "it's over. Our marriage. I've had enough."

"I'd say you haven't had anything *like* enough," Jett said bitterly. "That's the problem."

"You're a dead loss," snarled Cassandra. "Or, to be more specific, you look dead and you make a loss. I can't afford to have a sponge like you hanging round me any longer."

"Dead loss?" expostulated Jett. "What about the band getting back together? The TV deal?"

"TV deal?" snorted Cassandra. "You mean that cowboy outfit wanting to make a fly on the wall documentary about your shitty band re-forming and going on the road? Hardly your own *chat* show, is it? Fly on the wall documentary my arse—fly on the *fly* is what they should make about *you*."

Desperate, Jett produced his trump card. "So what about Zak? How's he going to feel when he finds we're splitting up?"

"Delighted," Cassandra returned triumphantly. "I've already discussed it with him and he's thrilled. Very keen it should go through as soon as possible, in fact."

"*Bastard.*"

"Sadly, no," Cassandra said. "I wish he was but, unfortunately, my child *has* a father. *You.*"

"Worse luck," said Jett, to whom it had now become evident that resistance was useless.

"For *you*, yes," spat Cassandra. "Zak, as a matter of fact, was the one who alerted me to your antics in the first place."

"*What?*" Jett's hands clenched and unclenched as best they could while sporting a row of rings like knuckledusters.

"Oh *yes*," Cassandra said. "Asked me why does Daddy have Sweaty in bed with him when you're not there, Mummy? I had to tell him it was because Daddy was frightened of the dark. He thought that was pathetic and that I should divorce you."

"I bet he did," Jett snarled. "He's set the whole thing up. I *knew* it."

"How *dare* you?" shrieked Cassandra. "Typical! You'd blame your own eight-year-old son rather than take responsibility for your inability to keep your trousers zipped."

"Yes, because as far as he's concerned, us splitting up means two lots of Christmas and birthday presents for *him*. Can't you *see*?"

"Don't be *ridiculous*," snapped Cassandra, recalling that, now Jett came to mention it, Zak *had* raised the matter of presents during the divorce discussions she had had with him. Quite frequently, in fact.

Chapter Fifteen

IT HADN'T BEEN—*ABSOLUTELY* IT hadn't been—Jamie's fault; he was obviously *completely* exhausted by the drive and, well, if the expected first night of passion had boiled down to nothing more than him dragging it in and out a few times, at least, Anna thought, he'd made some effort to mark the occasion of their homecoming. If not the bedsheet.

"I'm sorry," he had the grace to say as they lay, silent and several feet apart, in the darkness. "I'm afraid I wasn't really in the mood."

Anna reached across and squeezed his hand. "You're tired."

"Yes, and I was just reading the most depressing report about how the curtain walls are going to need completely rebuilding. I'm afraid," he added, "that the wedding probably can't be as lavish as we'd hoped." Anna said nothing. "Still," Jamie concluded brightly, "you need to discuss all that with Nanny. You'll see her at breakfast." So saying, he turned over and went to sleep.

Anna woke up alone. Jamie, she imagined, had gone to inspect some decaying part of the castle or other. She hugged her knees to her chest beneath the covers as she tried to preserve the precious pocket of warmth between her thighs and her stomach for as long as possible. In the cold air outside the bed, she could even see her breath.

Thin grey light divided the curtains, and as Anna stared at it, she noticed that the line didn't seem to be increasing much in brightness.

If anything, it had faded slightly, as if the day had dawned, thought better of it, and gone away again. And what on earth was that odd noise? That strange, wailing sound, like a soul in torment, coming from the direction of the window. The wind trapped under one of the panes? Christ, but it was loud. As the ghastly yowling seemed to reach a peak of high-pitched, hopeless misery, Anna, suddenly deciding not to go and check, took the boldest action she was capable of and stuck her fingers in her ears.

She yawned. She really must get up now, find out what Jamie was up to. A cold wave passed through her stomach as she remembered this morning held her first encounter with Nanny. Fighting the urge to burrow back beneath the blankets, Anna told herself sternly not to be so stupid. Reluctantly, she peeled back the covers and shuddered as the cold rushed to embrace her like a long-lost relative. Perhaps she would brave the plumbing first, and have a bath to warm up…

After wandering aimlessly about the seemingly endless corridors in search of the breakfast room, Anna found Jamie in what, to judge by the long oak table in its centre and heavy, dark, carved sideboards against its walls, was a dining room. It seemed to be a different room to that where, over breakfast, Geri had confessed to taking Miranda's place on Thoby's wedding night, but without the milling people, deafening clang of the chafing dishes, and, most of all, the electric light which had *definitely* been on then, it was hard to say. The silence was absolute, interrupted only by the bad-tempered spatter of rain against the windows. Outside, nothing could be seen but fog. *That* much, Anna thought, she could remember.

Jamie sat calmly at one end of the table blowing the dust off a pile of ledgers, documents, and receipts. "There you are," he remarked distantly, noting something down in a margin. Somewhere in his tone, Anna felt, lay rebuke.

"What time is it?"

"Ten past nine."

"Christ. I had no idea. *Sorry.*"

"Didn't MacLoggie wake you up?"

Anna started. The thought of the bent old man creeping into her bedroom to lay a clammy, whisky hand on her sleeping arm… she suppressed a shudder. "No, he certainly did not."

"But surely you heard the pipes." Jamie looked at her with surprise.

"Oh yes." Come to think of it, she had heard some rushes and rattles and gurgles, counterpointed by the occasional distant explosion, immediately after their abortive lovemaking. Still, noisy plumbing was preferable to no plumbing at all. And the eccentric-sounding pipe layout may have had something to do with her recent experiences in the bathroom, experiences she intended to bring up with Jamie. But in the meantime she was determined to put a brave facecloth on it.

"Oh, and there was the most *appalling* yowling noise an hour or so ago," Anna added. "*Horrible* row. Like a cat being tortured to death."

Jamie looked annoyed. "Yes. That's what I mean. The *bagpipes.* When the laird is in residence, MacLoggie plays under the windows every morning at six. Has done for centuries. His family, I mean."

"*Oh.*" Anna blushed furiously. So *that* was what the ghastly noise had been. Dr. Johnson's sudden flight was starting to make sense.

"Yes. The MacLoggies have been pipers to the Anguses for as long as anyone can remember. Far back into the mists of time."

Mists was right, Anna thought, glancing at the grey cotton wool beyond the windows.

"But darling," Anna said, "does he *have* to do it so early?" She wondered where she might get a cup of tea or even, luxury of luxuries, a slice of toast. The rack in front of Jamie was empty.

"Early!" Jamie sounded indignant. "He *usually* does it at six. This morning he did it at eight as a special favour. You were very honoured."

Anna plastered what she hoped was a suitably awestruck expression across her face and drew out a chair to sit down. She promptly jumped about seven feet in the air as she suddenly became conscious of something massive and frightening in the doorway behind her.

"Nanny," Jamie said as the figure moved slowly forward like a juggernaut. "This is Anna. My fiancée." It was difficult not to notice the apprehension in his tone.

"How do you do," stammered Anna, whose tongue suddenly felt as dry and rasping as a piece of biltong. Call her a scaredy-cat, but there was something ever so slightly intimidating about the large, thickset, late-middle-aged woman before her. Perhaps it was the huge and hairy mole nestling beside the thick boxer's nose. Perhaps the eyes, like ice chips behind glasses as thick as a crateful of bottle bottoms. Perhaps it was the line of her mouth, as flat and unrelenting as that on a switched-off life-support machine; perhaps the few strands of hair scraped back to expose the huge and pouchy face. Perhaps it was the way the very dining room seemed to shrink in her presence. Because this woman came from the other end of the childcare spectrum from the apple-cheeked, lavender-scented, *Brideshead Revisited* variety of cradle-rocker. Nanny looked as if she could bite the bollocks off a brontosaurus. And frequently did. In an act of instinctive self-protection, Anna spread her fingers out across the table, so the ring shone as best it could in the gloom. But if Nanny saw it, she showed no sign.

"Nanny's an extraordinary woman," Jamie said appreciatively as the vast figure, armed with an order for a cup of tea which was as much as Anna dared ask for, left the room.

"Yes, she looks it." Anna, feeling the colour slowly start to return to her face, realised Nanny also looked like the last person on earth she wanted to discuss her wedding with.

"She can see things we can't. Fairies, ghosts, images from the past and the future. She's got second sight," said Jamie admiringly.

Just as well, thought Anna. If those glasses are anything to go by she obviously hasn't got first. She lapsed into depressed silence.

Jamie, meanwhile, returned to perusing his papers. Anna watched him as, handsome brow furrowed in concentration, he ran his finger slowly up the page.

"What are you looking at?" It seemed reasonable to try and strike up a conversation with her fiancé on their first morning in their future home.

"Just checking the figures for the deer herd."

Looking round the dining room, it seemed a miracle there were any deer left. The walls bristled with antlers. Above large dark oblongs which she imagined must be paintings, hundreds of stags' heads ran like a frieze round the room. She jumped as Jamie abruptly closed the deer book. Her hopes of engaging him in discussion were swiftly dashed as he instantly opened another.

"What's that one about?"

"Refurbishment."

"Can I help?" Anna asked eagerly. At last, something she knew about. The annual university ritual of rolling white paint over the walls of dingy student rooms would prove to be useful experience after all. She could come to Jamie's emulsional rescue.

"Any good at roofing?" asked Jamie, a shade sarcastically. "And there are a few walls that need rebuilding as well."

By the time Nanny returned with the tea, which was tepid and thoroughly stewed, silence had descended once more. Seeing Jamie turn to yet another ledger, Anna tried again. Third time lucky.

"Er…"

"Tenants' complaints," rapped out Jamie before she could get the words out. He did not sound as if he wished to discuss what they were.

Silence. As Anna replaced her cup in its saucer, the noise seemed window-shattering. Perhaps that was why so many of them were broken.

"Um, about tenants' complaints," she ventured.

"Yes?"

"Well, I've got one. There's something very wrong with the water supply."

"What do you mean?" She'd got his attention now. His head had lifted, at least.

"When I ran my bath this morning, it was absolutely filthy."

"*Filthy?*" Anna was conscious of both Jamie and Nanny staring at her in amazement. "It can't be," Jamie said. "It's as fresh as a daisy. Comes straight out of the local burn."

"Well, this looked as if it came straight out of the local pub. Horrible dirty brown. Looked just like beer."

A fork clattered dramatically and possibly deliberately to the floor. Nanny bent to retrieve it. A faint creaking sound accompanied her efforts, and Anna cast an awed glance in the direction of her corset. Evidently a triumph of civil engineering, it was probably holding back as much raw force as the wall of the Aswan dam.

"*That,*" said Jamie, casting a nervous glance in Nanny's direction, "is because all the water here runs through peat. There's nothing wrong with it. On the contrary, it's some of the best and freshest around."

Not for the first time since arriving at Dampie, Anna wanted the floor to swallow her up. Still, there was one saving grace. At least she hadn't mentioned she'd flushed the toilet several times as well, unable to understand why the pee wouldn't go away.

"Oh dear," she said, grinning apologetically. "I can see I've got rather a lot to learn about Skul. Perhaps you could tell me a few things."

"Absolutely," said Jamie, recovering his equilibrium instantly. "Skul is a fascinating island. Besides the castle, there's the Old Man Rock, the Mount o'Many Stanes, the Cairns of Bogster, and Mad Angus Angus's Burn."

Was that like a Chinese burn? Anna wondered, trying not to notice Nanny's massive red hands as she cleared the last of the plates away. "How interesting," she said.

"Yes, well you should certainly explore the lie of the land a bit," Jamie continued. "After all, you're about to become mistress of the place."

A strange feeling—as of her heart soaring and her stomach sinking simultaneously—gripped Anna. Then a stray ray of light, bolder than its fellows, suddenly shot through the gloomy dining-room window and scored a direct hit on the ring on her finger. The stone may have been old and slightly yellow, but it still packed a considerable punch. Both she and Jamie gazed at it, Anna in a kind of dazzled delight; Jamie slightly more speculatively.

"Yes, that would be lovely." Anna beamed. A walk with Jamie round the island would be absolutely the most romantic introduction to her new home. Perhaps, she thought, they could even take a picnic. One glance at the weather brooding outside the windows, however, and even one of Anna's newly optimistic bent was forced to admit that looked unlikely. She glanced away from the grey mist pressing up pleadingly against the panes as if wishing to be let in to get warm. Some hope. In the space of a single breakfast-time, it was already evident to Anna that Dampie's most testing social challenge was the ability to hold a conversation whilst suppressing ones teeth from chattering with the chill. It could, she reasoned, hardly be colder outside than it was inside. "When shall we go?" she asked.

"We?" Jamie looked astonished. "I'm awfully sorry, but I've got a few things to sort out this morning. Turns out that yet another section of roof caved in last night, this time over the old wine store."

"Oh no." Anna looked at him, her eyes wide with concern. "Does that mean all the drink for the wedding…?"

Jamie looked even more astonished. "Well, actually, the cellar was empty. The point of it is that the wine store connects to the kitchen and we don't want the roof there collapsing in on Nanny."

Aware that Nanny was clearing up the rest of the breakfast things as slowly as possible with the obvious intention of listening to every word of their conversation, Anna tried hard to look as if this was absolutely the last thing she wanted. Not that Jamie noticed.

"No," he was musing. "I think the last wine in there was taken out for my father's twenty-first birthday party, as a matter of fact. For the wedding we'll most probably get in some boxes of plonk from Tesco's in Inverness…" His voice died away as his glance once again settled on Anna's diamond ring. "Because unfortunately we won't be able to afford champagne. Not unless we sell something…"

Seeing what he was looking at, Anna closed up her fingers into a fist. "I'll go on my own, then," she said, trying, more for her own benefit than his, to sound as if she felt this to be an attractive prospect.

"Perhaps someone else could show you round," Jamie said vaguely. "MacLoggie, for example. Or…" His glance fluttered speculatively towards the wide doorway through which Nanny's almost equally wide back was at that moment retreating. "Perhaps…"

With a deafening scrape of her chair, Anna stood up. "No, really, I'd rather go by myself." It was clear, in any case, from the sudden acceleration of Nanny's back through the door that Nanny felt as eager as Anna about the prospect of taking a walk together. So they could agree on one thing, at least.

Jamie looked relieved. "Oh well, if you're sure. Thought it might be an opportunity for you to talk to Nanny about…"

His voice was drowned in a sudden deafening clatter from the corridor. Nanny, by the sound of it, had consigned most of the breakfast service to the stone-flagged floor. Anna's nerves jangled wildly, both at the noise and the prospect of discussing something so intimate with such a terrifying creature. As the sound of Nanny scraping up china drifted into her ears, it occurred to her that here was another subject on which they probably held identical views.

"Yes, I must get round to doing that," muttered Anna.

"Yes, and I must get in touch with the vicar," muttered Jamie, as if to himself. "The whole thing should have been done and dusted by now. If it wasn't for the fact that the whole bloody place is suddenly collapsing."

His eye flickered towards Anna's ring again. "I'll go for my walk, then," said Anna.

Once outside the front door, the first thing about the lie of the land she discovered was that the land didn't as much lie as desiccate in wiry tufts. Each was surrounded by a sticky sauce of black and oozing mud, over which Anna had to pick her way carefully as she headed automatically towards the loch which, grey and bloated this morning, lapped the rocks on which the castle was built. The waves made a slapping sound which, for some reason, immediately reminded Anna of Nanny. She shuddered. Nanny and the wedding were fast fusing into the same thing, and she was starting to dread the one at the thought of the other.

Glancing back at her new home-to-be from the shore, Anna saw with surprise that the ever-present clouds had parted sufficiently to allow her first proper look at Dampie in daylight. It was not a sight to lift the heart. The rocks leading down to the water from the castle were slimy and rather brutal-looking. The building itself was a long, thin construction, its sheer sides punctured with slitty, sullen-looking windows. Any romantic effect the turreted top may have had was undermined by the walls being coated with a grey pebbledash and concrete mixture across which the dampness spread in a huge unsightly stain. So unprepossessing and prison-like was its aspect that, as the softening mists embraced the building once again, Anna felt almost relieved to see it go.

Her left hand clasped comfortingly round the Panasonic in her pocket that Geri had given her along with the Ghost dress as a farewell gift. "Think of it as an early wedding present," she had said. The "w" word again. Geri, of course, would be in the People's Republic of Tuscany now. Probably at this moment lying by a palazzo pool-side sipping Prosecco, nibbling Parma ham, and chatting to Tony and Cherie, who had apparently been due to drop by.

Picking her way with difficulty along a soggy glen on either side of which the hills rose sheer as walls, Anna determinedly quashed the frisson of envy that contemplation of Geri's prob-able lot provoked. Skul's beauty, she told herself, was not of the *obvious* Mediterranean sort. It was a more subtle matter altogether. Very subtle, she thought, scanning the grey and green horizon and noticing the threatening grey clouds squatting sullenly atop each twisted hill. As one suddenly, bomber-like, dropped its load of hail straight in her retinas, Anna closed her eyelids hard. Opening them again, she looked once more on the desolate scene, noting that the bumpy spines of the hills reminded her of stegosauruses and trying not to dwell on how strongly their particular shade of bilious green resembled mould. More depressing still was the collective effect of the jagged hills ringing the grey sky above her—making her feel as if she were trapped inside a giant, just-cracked, soft-boiled egg.

The grey mists on one of the summits suddenly drifted suffi-ciently for Anna to glimpse a tall, thin rock in profile on its upper slopes. Its very particular shape, combined with the forty-five-degree angle at which it leant from its fellow rocks, reminded her irresistibly of a penis. She smiled before reflecting, rather sourly, that it was the nearest thing to an erection she'd seen so far on Skul. Could this, she wondered, be the Old Man Rock?

The hail began again and put an end to her curiosity.

Visions of steaming baths drifting before her—which she already knew better than to expect to be realised—Anna set off back towards the castle, hoping fervently she was going the way she had come. The mists were fast closing in, and it was becoming impossible to tell. After spending several worrying minutes skirting the edge of a large and very troublesome bog, she recognised, through the now almost opaque swirls of fog, Dampie's familiar, damp-stained walls rising gloomily up before her, albeit from a slightly different angle to that expected. She was much lower than she had thought. Practically in the loch, it seemed. No wonder it had been boggy.

The slippery remains of what had once been a stone path stretched up before her. Gritting her teeth and grasping at clumps of grass to support herself, Anna slowly ascended, eventually emerging through a thicket of extremely wet bracken to what could almost feasibly have been, long ago, part of a garden. There was even some sort of building there, small and squat, lurking behind the vegetation. Moving forward through knee-high grass, Anna used both arms to heave aside the lolling fronds of an enormous rhubarb plant and reveal a half-ruined pile of stones whose relatively imposing arched entrance seemed to hint at some ecclesiastical function.

It could not, thought Anna, the cold hand of panic gripping her stomach, surely *not* be the chapel Jamie had mentioned. The chapel he had marked out for their wedding ceremony? But surely, when Thoby and Miranda had got married...? Obviously, she now realised, they had been married in the castle itself. A room must have been adapted for the occasion, somewhere small and cavelike, which had passed at the time for a chapel. The wine store, most probably. At least they'd tied the knot before the roof had caved in. She and Jamie, Anna thought, looking at the sodden pile of stones, would have no such luck. Just to recap, Anna thought miserably, I'm getting married in a ruin, toasting my good fortune with wine box plonk, and arranging the whole thing with Hagar the Horrible's twin sister because my husband-to-be is too busy trying to prop up our collapsing home to do anything about it. *Marvellous.* Turning her back on the chapel, Anna walked in what she imagined to be the direction of the castle, now invisible above her. A loud rushing sound, accompanied by a steep downward movement of her path, alerted her to the possibility that she might be about to slip. Parting more fronds of vegetation, Anna suddenly realised in terror that she had stopped just short of certain death down a deep and profoundly gloomy chasm, at the bottom of which lay a voracious-looking river flowing into the loch. The rushing noise was now explained. Deafening now, it came from a waterfall thundering, spitting, and spraying over the glistening rocks just to the right of where Anna was standing.

"Aaargh." Anna jerked in shock. Her feet slithered nearer the treacherous edge. "MacLoggie." She had not quite framed who she thought had suddenly crept up directly behind her, but she was relieved nonetheless that it was not Nanny. So relieved, in fact, that it did not occur to her to wonder what the ancient retainer was doing here, wandering about in the wet, abandoned garden. MacLoggie did not react. Nor did he make the slightest noise of apology. Instead, he fixed her with his rheumy eyes and demanded to know what she was doing by Mad Angus Angus's Burn.

"Oh, is that what it is?" Anna did her best to sound unfazed.

"Aye. It's said that it was the only thing that calmed him down. He had a dreadful temper," MacLoggie explained. "He especially liked to listen to it at night. In bed." His watery eyes glistened unpleasantly. He was, Anna thought uneasily, being unusually friendly. His mouth was stretched in a way that, on someone resembling a human being to a slightly greater degree, might almost have passed for a leer.

"I see." Jamie would be impressed. Two of the island's hotspots before lunch. Not bad going. The weak sun that had finally deemed it safe to come out glanced against her ring. There was no doubt, this time, that MacLoggie had spotted it.

"But this is nae place for a woman engaged to be married," MacLoggie suddenly growled. He stretched his splitting, scabbed lips still wider.

"No, I'm sure you're right." Relieved, Anna grabbed the chance of escape with both hands. "I'd better go then."

"Too late." MacLoggie grinned at her evilly. Anna suddenly felt rather ill.

"What do you mean?" She was not at all sure that she wanted to know.

"Tradition is that the unmarried woman who walks down to Mad Angus Angus's Burn before noon marries the first man who claps eyes on her."

Anna glanced up nervously at the steep wall of the castle. A mean slit of a window could just about be seen through the dripping fronds of the trees. As MacLoggie strode off, cackling, she hoped fervently that sometime in the last twenty minutes Jamie had looked out and seen her here.

"Total *bollocks!*" Cassandra stormed.

Twisted old bitch, she seethed. What did Gosschalk *mean* about the psychologist's report confirming her own impression that Zak's unstable parental background affected his attitudes and aptitudes? Call herself a *headmistress*. *Head case*, more like.

"I'm sorry, Mrs. Knight?" Mrs. Gosschalk looked sternly over her bifocals.

"*Absolute shit.*"

True, she'd had a gin or three before coming here, but even Barack Obama would probably need Dutch courage before facing this shrivelled-up old bluestocking. On second thoughts, Gosschalk was probably a stranger to stockings. Blue *tights*, more like, the thick, knitted sort with the gusset you can't get above your knees.

"I read a survey only recently," Cassandra spluttered. "In fact"— she rummaged in her bag—"I have it *right here.*" She produced a crumpled piece of the *Times* over which foundation from her makeup bag had liberally leaked. "Which says that parents with, um, *volatile* relationships are the best thing that can happen to a child, and that there's nothing like seeing your parents scream blue murder to kindle the creative spirit. For *Christ's sake*, Jett and I are doing Zak *a favour*."

Mrs. Gosschalk took the piece of newsprint between finger and thumb—bloody cheek, thought Cassandra, as if it was smeared with old chip fat and not my best MAC foundation.

"My dear Mrs. Knight," she said in a voice so cutting it could have given the de Beers machinery a run for its money, "you are no doubt aware that newspapers are full of surveys of questionable value on the subject of education. Only yesterday I read one claiming that giving your child a ludicrous name guaranteed its future success, as the struggle it would have to overcome the teasing in the playground would teach it independent habits of mind. *Obviously* ridiculous."

"*Absolutely*," burst out Cassandra. "Teasing in the playground?" she added scornfully, relieved to have found a theory both she and the headmistress could agree to despise. "There *is* no teasing in the playground at St. Midas's. *Everyone* has ludicrous names."

"Quite," said Mrs. Gosschalk. Why were the corners of her mouth quivering like that? Cassandra wondered. Nervous tic, obviously. The mad old bat was obviously off her rocker. "So naturally you will understand when I fail to take the dysfunctional parent theory quite as seriously as you seem to."

Mrs. Gosschalk compressed her lips which were, Cassandra noticed, resolutely lipstick-free. Perhaps she should have held back on her own facial ensemble; the startling Ruby Tuesday lipstick from the Rock Star range was, she was aware, possibly visible from Venus, but the cashpoint was boringly refusing to play ball at the moment so visits to the Harvey Nicks makeup counters were, for the moment, on hold.

Mrs. Gosschalk stood up. Cassandra's heavily made-up eyes— well, she'd had to balance the lipstick somehow—flicked over the sensible suit and crisp shirt which seemed miraculously free of creases. Everything everyone else was wearing seemed miraculously free of creases at the moment; Cassandra, for the first time in her life having to grapple with an iron on a regular basis, was constantly frustrated by the fact that whenever she tried to use it, her clothes looked worse than they had to start with.

She was aware that the grey linen trousers she was wearing looked as if they had spent the last fortnight buried at the bottom of the garden; also that their greyness was more the result of a spin-cycle confrontation with one of Jett's new tour T-shirts than a conscious attempt to look businesslike before Mrs. Gosschalk. Jett, thank God, was finally away on Solstice's "Back From The Dead" tour, promoting the *Ass Me Anything* comeback album. Comeback *indeed*, thought Cassandra. The thought of Jett coming back from anywhere but the pub was almost hilarious enough to cheer her up. Although, maddeningly, he was going for half of everything they had in the divorce. Or half of everything that was left after the man from Mishcon de Reya had been paid. He had at least put up no resistance whatsoever to Cassandra's claim for custody of Zak. One would almost think—*ha ha*—that Jett didn't want to see his son at *all*.

"I'm terribly sorry, but I'm afraid I cannot allow your son to remain in the school," said Mrs. Gosschalk. "That is my final word. Now, if you'll excuse me, good afternoon, Mrs. Knight."

"But you can't do this," Cassandra gabbled as Mrs. Gosschalk showed her firmly to the door. "Zak is autistic, he's got Tourette's syndrome, he's got special needs, *and* he's a gifted child."

"I'm sorry, Mrs. Knight. I wasn't going to mention it, but there is also the additional matter of the school fees. As you know, your payments lately have not been as regular as they might have been."

Cassandra's eyes blazed and a lump rose up her throat. Her week had hardly been enhanced by the demand of the publishers that she pay back her advance for *A Passionate Lover* on the grounds that no manuscript of any description had neared her editor's desk and it was a good six months past the deadline. For the moment at least, money was tighter than a gnat's arse. The fact that Gosschalk probably knew it made her blood boil.

"Have you thought of sending Zachary to boarding school?" Mrs. Gosschalk suggested. "There are ways of getting help with the fees, you know."

Reduced fees. The horror of it. Something in Cassandra suddenly snapped—something quite apart from the bra strap currently hanging on by a thread. "Why don't you stuff your school up your leathery old *arse?*" Cassandra yelled. "And yes, I might well send him to boarding school. You'll be laughing on the other side of your raddled old face when Zak comes out top of his year at Eton."

"Come the glorious day, no one would be more delighted than me, Mrs. Knight. When he's the right age, of course. Although, given your recent remarks and his general attitude, I see no reason in keeping from you the fact that the only boarding school I can see Zachary getting a place at is Borstal."

Chapter Sixteen

"MIDGIES." THE WORD HUNG in the damp, heavy air.

"Sorry?" Anna whirled round to see who had spoken. A cloud of tiny black insects half obscured the unedifying sight of the ancient retainer MacLoggie, grinning malevolently through his tooth stumps.

Her heart sank. She had been avoiding MacLoggie for ten days since the Mad Angus Angus's Burn encounter, the memory of which still made her shudder. She had not mentioned it to Jamie—partly out of suspicion that he was far more likely to have been inspecting a septic tank than looking out of the window at the time, and partly because, given his manic respect for Dampie and its traditions and legends, he might hold her to it.

"What did you say?"

"Midgies. Those wee black flies there. They bite like *bastards*."

"*Really?*" Disbelieving, Anna flapped her hands half-heartedly in front of her face. "They don't look big enough to."

MacLoggie smirked. "Ye"ll see."

"Well, thanks for the advice, MacLoggie. I'm sure there are lots of things I've yet to learn about living up here."

MacLoggie snickered. "Ye can say tha' again."

"Well, then, perhaps you could tell me how I get to the nearest town."

Her enquiry was rewarded by yet another glimpse of the ancient creature's slimy stumps. "'Orrible's over there. That way." MacLoggie pointed vaguely beyond the end of the loch and staggered off in the opposite direction. *Horrible*? Anna echoed, silently. There couldn't, not even *here*, be a village called *that*. Could there?

She walked off at a brisk pace in the direction indicated, along the side of the loch. The pewter platter of the water, bordered by the rust and sodden green of the heather, reflected a chill, white sky. The only signs of life were a few Highland cattle in the distance and a group of sorry-looking sheep limping over the rocky hillside. A slight stinging sensation she had noticed earlier continued; looking down, she saw that small red marks like strawberry-juice stains had appeared on her wrists.

Some time later, quite a long time later, long after she had left the loch behind and had continued onward without even as much as a signpost to confirm she was headed in the right direction, Anna wondered if she should perhaps have pressed MacLoggie for more details. A steel-keen wind began to slice at her across the rock spurs and skim over the heather like a Stealth bomber. Surely MacLoggie would not have let her set off alone and directionless if the village really were a long way? She looked at her ring for reassurance. It gleamed dully back at her. Far more vivid was the memory of MacLoggie's insolent leer. *Would* he?

By the time she gained the village—not the cheerful cluster of white-painted cottages she had imagined, but a sullen, sodden huddle called, not Horrible, but Oribal—the rain was lashing down like stair rods and bouncing off the deserted—and only—street. Shivering in the bus stop, Anna looked speculatively across the road to the only establishment in the immediate vicinity featuring electric light. The low, grey-white pebbledashed building with frosted windows looked as if it might be a pub.

Though desperate for a vodka and tonic, Anna decided to give it a miss and, taking advantage of a hiatus in the deluge, walked towards a damp wooden hut with "Village Hall" in rotting letters above the door. Before it was a glass-fronted noticeboard containing a Met Office declaration that Oribal had had the most rainfall and least hours of sunshine of any place in the British Isles in the previous year. It was difficult to shake off the impression, fostered by the prominent position the notice commanded on the board, that the village was rather proud of this distinction.

Another notice offered the services of a Mrs. McLeod and her ironing board at what Anna considered to be the extremely reasonable rate of a pound per ten items, "discretion assured." Either people round these parts wore things they didn't want others to know about, thought Anna, or to be suspected of not doing one's own ironing in Oribal was to be suspected of sin beyond redemption. Perhaps both.

Rather grudgingly displayed at the board's bottom was a card advertising evening classes in flower-pressing and the bagpipes. Neither appealed to her much; having failed so far to spot a single bloom she doubted the feasibility of the former, and the idea of learning how to make the sort of ghastly row that woke her every morning similarly held few attractions. MacLoggie, on the other hand, could clearly do with a lesson or two. Perhaps she'd suggest it to Jamie when she saw him at lunchtime; the thought of which reminded her that it was probably time that she was heading back to the castle.

Just then a vibrating sensation somewhere around her lower pelvis announced that either she was having an unexpected orgasm or someone was attempting to make telephonic communication. The latter seemed most likely. Dragging the mobile out, Anna stabbed frantically at the buttons and slammed the instrument against her ear several times before finally the voice came through.

"Hi, babe."

"*Geri!*" Anna shrieked in delight.

"So, life is bliss, is it? Set a date yet? I'm desperate to get my bridesmaid dress—I've seen just the thing in Gucci. White, tight, and with a huge slit up the side."

"Sounds amazing," said Anna truthfully. "We're still sorting the date out, as it happens—no, nothing's wrong." Anna crossed her fingers behind her back, keen to get off the tricky subject. "So how are *you*? Your voice sounds funny. *Deeper*."

"All that screaming at those *bloody* kids," said Geri with feeling.

"*What*? But I thought Siena and Savannah were supposed to be angels. Wasn't the holiday good then?"

"Absolute fucking *disaster*. Mostly because their cousin came with them—ghastly brat called Titus. Fought *all the sodding time*."

"Oh dear." Yet Anna felt a faint sense of relief that even a take-no-prisoners nanny like Geri was powerless in the face of a truly intractable child.

"And so bloody *noisy*—had a scream that could shatter glass. *Could*, but didn't have to—he managed very well at that with just his hands. Looked like Kristallnacht in the kitchen when he'd been looking for something to put his pomegranate juice in."

"What a shame. And the place looked so peaceful." Anna remembered the snaps Geri had shown her of the magnificently well-appointed and stupendously expensive-looking palazzo that Julian Tressell had restored to its former glory after many years serving as a rural bus station.

"Was until Titus got there. Then we became the cabaret for the entire village—walking through these *completely* silent old squares with all the kids screaming and hitting each other with their Barbies."

"Did Titus have a Barbie as well then?"

"'Fraid so. His parents are against sexual stereotyping. Which in my experience has one of two results. Either he becomes a complete wuss who embroiders his own bookmarks, or he turns into Attila the Hun. Titus is the latter. Obsessed with bums, willies, and toilets. Loved nothing better than watching himself pee in the bath."

"Didn't know Attila the Hun did that."

"Ha bloody *ha*. Well, anyway, I'm thinking of suing retrospectively for mental distress. Had a long discussion about it over lunch with a gobsmackingly rich barrister who has a place out there as well. He agreed it would make an interesting test case, and said he'd be only too happy to take the brief. Except I think he had other briefs in mind."

"But what's wrong with that?" asked Anna. "A rich barrister with a place in Tuscany?"

"And a face like a basket of fruit. Rotten fruit, at that," said Geri with her trademark crushing frankness. "Even *I've* got standards, sadly. But enough of me. Any gossip?"

"Gossip?" The last gossip on Skul, Anna imagined, was when Flora MacDonald dressed Bonnie Prince Charlie as a woman to help him escape. That rumour was probably still doing the rounds. "Not as *such*. What's going on down there?"

"Oh, the usual. Otto Greatorex has got a place in the choir of St. Pauls and Fenella is beside herself."

"I bet she is."

"But not for the reasons you'd think. It's a nightmare, apparently. She's got choir school mother's bottom, sitting on a hard pew for hours every week, and has Otto under her feet all the time because he's not allowed to go out in case he gets a cold and loses his voice. But she says the worst thing is that all that time sitting in cathedrals contemplating the Almighty means she's getting rather worried that He might actually exist."

"Oh dear. I see."

"Yes, the parents are rather suffering at the moment," Geri said breezily. "The Rice-Browns are mortified because their new nanny drives around in an Audi while they make do with an old Volvo. Polly said to Kate the other day how ghastly it is when your nanny is so much richer than you are. Then Hanuki—you know, that Japanese male nanny you met? Well, he's won the nannying equivalent of the Lottery. The Pottery, I suppose you'd call it. People have tried to poach him so often he's on double pay, works no more than thirty-six hours a week, and gets his breakfast in bed. It's rather gone to his head. He refuses to come anywhere near the kitchen until the dishwasher has been unloaded nor anywhere near the children until they've been washed and dressed."

Dishwashers! Anna determinedly suppressed a pang of envy. Even the thought of Liv seemed suddenly tempting—it was warm, if nothing else. Downstairs, at least. "I can see now that I never quite got the hang of nannying," she sighed. "I practically had to wash and dress Cassandra as well as Zak. Particularly after she'd been at the Bombay Sapphire." Anna shuddered. Yes. *That* was what it had been like.

"Oh, that reminds me. Cassandra's divorcing Jett."

"No! Why?"

"Cassandra realised he was shagging her new nanny when she saw someone else had been squeezing the spots on his back." With a sense of a cliff-hanger ending that *Days of our Lives* would do well to emulate, the mobile abruptly cut itself off.

As Anna put it away and prepared to return to Dampie, something caught her eye. Something typewritten, white, and tucked right into the edge of the board. "Robbie MacAskill. Poet. Creative Writing Classes Given." Anna gazed at it in astonishment. A *poet*? The only man of letters she'd imagined ever braving this place was the postman—and Dr. Johnson, of course. As the rain began again, she scribbled down the number with one of the family of leaky Biros that seemed to have a member in the pocket of every coat she had ever owned.

Jamie was nowhere to be seen when Anna returned, sodden and demoralised, to the castle. Thanks to her nonexistent breakfast, her stomach felt as if it were almost touching her backbone, but she resisted the temptation to seek out the kitchens for fear of encountering Nanny. She made do with some furry, age-softened Polos from the bottom of her bag and spent the afternoon blowing on her purple fingers in the bedroom and trying to write up the morning's events in her diary. The thought of there being a poet in the area intrigued her. She determined to ask Jamie about it at dinner—it was a topic concerning the island, so hopefully she'd get a response. And then perhaps she could tackle the increasingly tricky subject of who was organising the wedding as well. Why couldn't Jamie speak to Nanny about it? After all, he'd known her since birth. It occurred to Anna that perhaps this was precisely the reason the task had been delegated to her.

Dinner came and, more thankfully, went with Jamie, as usual, distant and absorbed in paperwork, muttering, this time, about damp proof courses. So when a window of conversational opportunity presented itself during coffee in the upstairs sitting room, Anna seized it.

The sitting room stretched the entire length of the second floor of the castle. Outside the three long deep-silled windows along one wall, the sulky grey of day had sunk into the coma of night. Inside the cavernous chamber, a few inadequate lamps made it gloomier still. There were a few gilt-framed and watery Highland scenes on the walls, a number of small, padded chairs, a couple of battered sofas, and a rather experienced-looking china tea set on a side table. The most arresting item in the room was a large portrait opposite her chair. Suddenly it became obvious what her opening gambit should be.

"Is that the Angus tartan?" she asked, wondering if she should be wearing eclipse glasses to view the blazing yellow and orange of the kilt being worn by the large, hostile-looking bearded gentleman with the extremely red face who was the subject of the portrait canvas. Despite the considerable degree of age and fading, the tartan glowed as retina-fryingly brightly as the day it was first painted.

"Absolutely. Yes. That's Mad Angus Angus wearing it." Jamie, as predicted, looked up eagerly from his books. As in Burn, thought Anna. She looked at the picture again. "Why was he mad?" she asked.

Jamie's head shot up again. "He had what would probably be called an anger management problem today."

"Oh, I see. Mad as in cross." That figured. The very portrait looked ready to explode with rage. "The tartan's very, um, yellow." There was no polite way of saying it was the most hideous pattern she had ever seen—yellow, orange, and brown shot through with bilious green.

"Oh. Yes." Jamie was now happily back on track. "Yellow, *yes*. There's rather a funny story connected with that. The family motto is Hold Fast. Unfortunately, for many years that did not extend to the colours of the tartan. Ran horribly in the wash."

Anna decided to change the subject, but did not feel confident enough yet to tackle The Subject.

"Gosh, that's huge," she remarked presently.

"*Magnificent*, isn't it?" Jamie said proudly.

"I've *never* seen one like *that* before."

"Glad you appreciate it. Mad Angus Angus's lucky war axes are the pride of the Dampie collection."

"Unlucky for some, I should imagine," Anna observed, thinking meanly that they were probably the only thing in the Dampie collection.

"Yes, he killed fifty Englishmen in battle with those," Jamie said proudly. "Sharp as a knife, even now. Nanny keeps them in tiptop condition."

"Does she now?"

There was a silence.

"Very impressive suits of armour you've got over there in the corner," said Anna.

"Yes. In actual fact, they're terribly rusty and not really very valuable at all," said Jamie. "Don't know why I bother keeping them. Should throw them away really."

"Oh, it's probably worth hanging on to them," said Anna flippantly. "You never know. You might get called up." Oh why had she said that?

The look Jamie gave her as he opened his ledger again quelled further discussion. Now was obviously not the time to ask about the poet. Or, for that matter, the wedding. After an hour or so's silent contemplation of sheep figures (Jamie) and a 1962 edition of the *People's Friend* found behind a cushion and fallen on as if it were the latest *Vogue* (Anna), they went to bed.

As she undressed, Anna saw with horror that her neck, arms, shoulders, and cheeks were covered in violently red, itching spots. They looked disgusting, red at the bottom and yellow and hard on top, mini volcanoes against the whiteness of her skin. "My God, what are they?" she shrieked, showing an ankle bearing at least five of them to Jamie who, already in bed, was sitting up with plans of the castle spread all around him.

He looked up. "Midgies." He looked down again.

"What, those tiny black flies? I can't believe it."

But she had lost his attention already. Still, Anna thought as her fingers ran over the hard, painful lumps, at least the midgies fancy me. There was a gap large enough to drive an articulated lorry down between Jamie and herself. It was almost as if he were trying to avoid a situation where he had to have sex with her.

But *why*? Anna fretted. Her appearance had not changed for the worse since arriving at Dampie almost two weeks ago; on the contrary, the atrocious food and long walks through the mist had resulted in her losing yet more weight. She could feel her rib cage all day long now, not just first thing in the morning when she was flat on her back. So what was the problem? Anna had read enough "When

Sex Dies" magazine stories to realise keeping the sensual spark alive in a relationship was a challenge to most couples. But even in the direst of these tales the spark hadn't disappeared immediately, as it appeared to have done with them. Why was Jamie so much more interested in making walls than love? All she had managed to glean from him today was that he'd spent the afternoon repairing rotten fencing. Did that account for the barrier now between them?

"Look, you can tell me if there's a problem," she ventured gently as they lay side by side in the darkness. Like two marble sarcophagi, she thought, only without the passion and commitment that implied.

"Oh, there's a problem all right," Jamie said. "Several, in fact."

"Is there?" Anna hadn't expected such frankness. Suddenly fearful, she wondered if she was ready to be told.

"Yes. Well, for a start, the guttering's rotten and the roof on the old guardroom is—"

"Not *that*. Not the bloody *building*. Us."

"Us?" Jamie sounded surprised. "What's the matter with us? Aren't you happy? We're getting married, aren't we?"

Anna felt an odd mixture of relief and fear. "Call me paranoid," she said, "but I can't help noticing that you don't seem to like having sex with me."

Jamie was silent for a few moments. Then he said, "No. I don't."

"He said *what?*" Geri demanded.

"He said *no*, he didn't," Anna shouted into the mobile the next morning, crouching unsteadily behind a rock as the wind hurled a spiteful spatter of rain in her direction. "He said that I wasn't to worry though, it was nothing personal."

In normal circumstances, Anna thought longingly, she and Geri would have been having this conversation in hushed whispers in the darkened corner of a wine bar, fuelled by large glasses of chilled

Chardonnay. Normal circumstances, however, were now a thing of the past. As was normal anything.

"*Sounds pretty personal to me*," shouted Geri. "Sounds about as personal as it gets."

"He said he'd gone off sex at school. Apparently he was bullied very badly, frequently beaten and buggered on a regular basis."

"But I thought that was the whole *point* of public school," Geri yelled. "That's what every boy in St. Midas's has to look forward to. And the girls when they get married."

"I know. But it seems to have turned Jamie off sex for good. He says he's still getting over the horror of having to do it when we first got to the castle."

"He really knows how to make a girl feel good, doesn't he?" shouted Geri. "Sure he's not gay?"

"Well, I did wonder, of course." Anna pictured Geri in the minivan with the entire Tressell school run's ears out on stalks. "But I couldn't see why he would have bothered asking me to marry him if he was. I mean, why drag me all the way up here?"

There was silence for a few minutes. "Hello? Hello?" yelled Anna in a panic. Please don't cut me off again, she prayed.

"*Just thinking*," Geri bawled. "Basically, you need to awaken his interest in sex again. Take the initiative. Come up with a love strategy."

"A *what*?" The wind whipped by Anna's ear, as if trying to eavesdrop on the conversation.

"*A love strategy*," Geri screeched. "Seduce him. Wear garters. Buy some red underwear and bonk his brains out. That *always* works."

At this point, the phone cut out and Anna sat back on her heels on the sodden grass wondering dully where one got garters on Skul. No doubt Nanny had on more rigging than your average tea clipper, but it seemed unlikely Jamie would find it a turn-on. As for red underwear, the only possibility of that, she imagined, would be if something ran in the wash.

Chapter Seventeen

CASSANDRA SLAMMED THE FRONT door in fury. The girl had to be *joking*. A new Mégane coupe in a colour of her choice—*to keep*! Paid-for membership of the Harbour Club *and* the Ivy Club! Tickets for all the best shows in town! On top of this, a salary approximately *ten times* what she had ever paid a nanny before. Cassandra seethed as, from a corner of the window, she watched the girl sashaying nonchalantly away down the street, apparently confident that if Cassandra would not meet her requirements, some other family would be only too pleased to. Those tits *had* to be fake, thought Cassandra. So pneumatic-looking—you probably had to stick a pressure gauge on the nipple every four weeks to check the air.

Cassandra grimaced as a bilious intestinal twinge almost bent her double. But was it any wonder she had stomach problems? She'd been stuffing herself lately—she'd eaten a whole lettuce sandwich and a ricecake yesterday before reading the fortuitous *Daily Mail* article about how skinny women in New York kept their weight down by eating naked in front of mirrors. Seizing another ricecake, Cassandra had straightaway gone into the bathroom, stripped off, and sat with her legs apart. It certainly removed the urge to eat. The problem was, contemplating her dry patches, thread veins, incipient turkey gobble, and wrinkled labia in the mirror almost removed the urge to live as well.

Unfortunately, it didn't bring back the urge to write. Since being dumped by its publishers, *A Passionate Lover* was currently as high and dry as a hallucinating bone. Of late, the only occasions

Cassandra had ventured into her study were to rifle her gin fund to satisfy Zak's incessant demands for money. On these visits, she had tried not to notice the dust thickening on the laptop lid. Her writer's block had become an entire thousand-foot-thick barrier; the Great Wall of Writing China. Her agent was getting frantic.

"Try anything," he urged, whilst privately wondering if he should dump Cassandra. Half literary London was calling her the day before yesterday's woman; having her on his books was getting embarrassing. Not that it hadn't always been, but at least she used to make money. Perhaps, he suggested, colonic irrigation might help unplug the flow.

Cassandra liked the idea of recharging her creative batteries with alternative therapy. Especially if it meant charging Jett's platinum card.

"I want to feel *inspired* again," Cassandra told a New Age therapist in Hampstead, who advised "the all-over spiritual spring clean approach. You wash yourself from the *inside*," he explained. Ugh, like those bristly things you put inside bottles, Cassandra shuddered. The white witch in Camden she consulted next advised flushing out the system by sticking her bottom in cold water and her feet in hot. Or was it the other way round? But sitting with her buttocks in a warm sink with her feet dangling in the loo didn't feel very inspiring.

By the time the crystal therapist in Crouch End advised she stick crystals up her bottom, Cassandra was beginning to doubt alternative therapy could do the trick. On the other hand, the engagement ring Jett had given her could scarcely meet a more suitable fate. She'd try anything once.

Once. Having placed the sapphire in her sphincter, Cassandra quickly became aware that her writer's block had suddenly changed from being a metaphoric to a literal condition. She would have sued the therapist had she not been fearful of all the publicity that would, given her celebrity status, no doubt follow. As it was, she was not entirely convinced that her regular Harley Street doctor had believed her protestations that she had fallen over in her bedroom and landed on her jewellery box. Had she not known better she would have sworn that, as she was leaving, the bellow of loud laughter following her down the corridor had definitely come from Dr. Monson's office. From now on, she vowed, the only crystal I'm prepared to take internally is the sort with Louis Roederer on the label.

The end finally came when the Tufnell Park thalassotherapist told her not to "sweat the small stuff." Cassandra had indignantly pointed out that she didn't sweat *any* stuff, thank you, she'd had the botox injections to close up any glands of *that* nature, and swept out. She decided to return to the Bombay Sapphire.

Bloody nannies, she thought, sloshing another measure furiously into her glass. Her thoughts returned to the Mégane-coupé-demanding one she'd just seen. Bloody *cheek*. And there'd been plenty of *that* on show as well—Ivana, or whatever her name was, had been wearing a miniskirt practically up to her *pubes*.

Cassandra sighed. As if the Nanny Question wasn't enough, there was the continued and worsening matter of finding a school that would take Zak. It was hardly surprising she hadn't written a sentence for weeks. Every ounce of her literary ability was currently employed in restricting to a few scant paragraphs the wonders of her son in letters to boarding school headmasters.

The clang of the letterbox alerted her to the arrival of the post. Cassandra ground her teeth as she opened the usual fistful of rejection letters from schools. Until a thought occurred to her. Why not educate Zak at home? Much cheaper, for a start. And talking of starts, there was no time like the present. She tripped up the stairs to his room.

❖ ❖ ❖

"Oh, *Mum*."

"*Mama.* Come on, darling."

"Only if you buy me a mini CD player."

"Yes, all right then, darling. Come on. Let's count up to ten in French."

Around two hours was the approximate time it took Cassandra—and Zak—to realise that she had forgotten every French phrase she had ever learnt, with the notable exception of *haute couture*. Switching subjects to maths, she realised she had never, in the first place, grasped the principles of long division. Similarly, the only geographical fact she was in possession of was that a by-product of the Australian sheep industry was lanolin for lipstick and the sort of moisturisers that gave you a hairy face. Even Cassandra realised that this probably wasn't going to get Zak very far.

Finding a boarding school was of the utmost urgency. For Zak was beginning to get out of hand in other ways as well. Only last week he had threatened to sue her retrospectively over his unsatisfactory Christmas presents and there had been ugly scenes just yesterday when the tooth fairy had left only ten pounds and not the twenty pounds Zak had apparently been expecting. Adore him as she did, it was beginning to dawn on Cassandra that the costs of keeping him at home were astronomical, psychologically as well as financially.

Anna's love strategy had not got off to the most brilliant of starts. Taking the initiative, as Geri had suggested, she had arrayed herself in her best underwear, used the last of her Chanel No. 5, fanned her hair out across the pillow in approved bra-model-ad fashion, put a candle by the bedside—and waited. And waited. And waited. And, eventually, fell asleep.

She woke to find the candle out and Jamie snoring gently beside her. *Damn.* She'd missed the opportunity. Take the initiative, she urged herself.

Taking a deep breath, Anna stole a hand across the customary foot of uninhabited sheet that separated her from her husband-to-be. As usual, Jamie was wearing thick flannel pyjamas, but she deftly circumnavigated the folds and ties to slip her hand through the gap in his bottoms. Running her hand swiftly over the bristle of his pubic hair she at last gained what she was seeking: his warm, soft, sleeping penis. To her astonishment, it was rigid. More than that, it was as thick and as hard as an oak.

A thrill ran through Anna as she lay on her back in the darkness. Had her underwear had the desired effect after all? Smiling, she circled the warm, wet, and rubbery tip of his penis with her finger. She stroked his hot, swollen, bristly balls and was gratified to hear the steady breathing interrupted by a faint but distinct groan of pleasure. As she increased the pressure of her fingers, the groans increased. Without giving herself time to worry about the consequences, Anna slid down under the covers and pushed her face straight into his salt-scented pubic hair.

His penis was almost too big for her mouth; it seemed the approximate size and solidity of a cricket bat handle as she began inexpertly to circumnavigate it with her lips and tongue. Still, as she was buried beneath the covers, Jamie would be unable to hear any slurping sounds and anyway, from the still louder moans of pleasure she could hear from above the blankets, she was having roughly the effect she was intending. As matters quite literally seemed about to come to a head, Anna pulled herself up, over, and on to her fiancé's body. Wet with excitement herself, she slid him inside her just as he came.

"*Aaaargggh.* Uuugghh. Headmaster! Headmaster! *What's going on?*" Jamie, wide awake now, was thrashing around wildly in terror. For a few seconds, Anna held on as if to a bucking bronco, hoping for an orgasm, but she realised she might as well hope for a miracle as the engorged muscle inside her shrank to the proportions she was more familiar with.

"*What's happening?*" The night being blacker than the inside of a Highland cow, it was impossible for Anna to see Jamie's expression but his voice still held traces of genuine fear.

"Oh, nothing," said Anna bitterly. She swallowed hard to keep down the choking in her throat. The love strategy had been a dismal failure. Everything about coming to Dampie had been a dismal failure. *She* was a dismal failure.

As soon as, after breakfast, Jamie had headed off muttering something about drains, Anna had gone outside with the mobile and called Geri.

"He was definitely thinking about someone. Another woman."

"Doubt it," said Geri. "He was probably fantasising about a lovely stretch of releaded roof."

"Can't you come up? *Please?*" Only Geri, Anna was certain, was capable of sorting out the mess she had got herself in.

"Mmm. As it happens, this is a good time. Savannah and Siena are off to Opera Camp for a week and I could do with a change of scene. What are the men like up there? I rather fancy getting my hands on something big, hairy, and Highland."

"Well, there's plenty of that about," Anna said. No need to tell Geri she meant cattle.

"*Fantastic.* I'm *desperate.* I've even started doing yoga classes," Geri continued, "hoping I'd get the chance to do the lotus position with some supple young sex god. But everyone in my class is either pregnant, gay, or has nasty toenails." Geri sighed. "So here I am with this lovely flexible pelvis and no one to flex it on."

"Poor you." Anna tried to sound as if she wasn't smiling. Funny how Geri could cheer her up even in the most wretched of circumstances. "But at least you must be full of inner calm."

"Funnily enough, I've never felt so ratty as I have since starting yoga classes. But that's probably a lot to do with the nasty toenails. We're always being told we need to keep our anuses soft as well, which as you can imagine makes for some rather ripe results. Which tend to interfere with one's contemplation of the immortal."

"But at least it explains levitation," Anna said. "There's plenty of fresh air up here, anyway."

"Right. That's settled then. I'll come up on the plane. After all this jetting around with the family I've got enough air miles to practically get to Pluto."

"Oh Geri," Anna breathed in relief. "That would be fantastic. I'll go straightaway and get Nanny to sort out a room for you. The best one the castle has, promise."

"Well, that's not saying a lot."

Re-entering the castle, Anna firmly squashed the qualms of marrow-freezing fear that the thought of an encounter with Nanny provoked. She marched with as authoritative a step as she could muster down the stairs, back down the corridor, and into the stone-flagged kitchen beyond. Nanny was nowhere to be seen.

From an open door leading to an outhouse, the vague murmur of voices could be heard. Loud and vaguely obscene noises seemed to be punctuating the conversation. As she crept nearer it sounded, to Anna's quailing ears, horribly like naked flesh being slapped.

"Do ye think she's worked it out yet?" The man's voice, Anna realised, was MacLoggie's. Slap. Squelch.

"Nae idea," Nanny said in her slow, deliberate monotone. "She's nae too bright, ye know." Slap.

Anna stood frozen to the spot. She would have been in any case, given the plunging temperatures of the kitchen passage, but the realisation that they were talking about her sent an additional chill down the cord of her spine.

MacLoggie snorted. "Surely even someone *that* stupid must have realised by now," he drawled in a contemptuous tone accentuated by his Scots accent. "After all, why else would someone as bonny as him want to marry someone like *her*?"

Nanny snorted. Anna flamed with indignation. *That* was rich, coming from MacLoggie, who even in a good light looked as if he'd been pile-driven into a brick wall. As for Nanny, the only good light was no light at all. She looked as if her idea of sartorial effort was to shave the hairs off her moles.

"All because the old laird put that clause in saying the young maister had to have a *wife* before he could properly inherit," MacLoggie observed laconically. *Slap slap slap.*

Anna breathed in deeply and slowly. Her knees had gone weak, and something seemed to have stopped her moving. Something else, however, was slipping slowly into place. Was this the reason Jamie wanted to marry her?

"Well, ye canna blame the old laird for wanting to make sure there'd be an heir," Nanny pronounced. A strange flubbery noise like the breaking of wind accompanied her remark.

"Well, and *will* there be, do yereckon?"

"Well, not if ye're judging by the bed," Nanny cackled. Anna's stomach hit the flagstones. "I've looked every morn and there's ne'er anything on the sheets." *Squelch.*

Anna ground her teeth, her fury now overtaking her surprise. The thought of Nanny on the loose in their bedroom—as, to judge by the rigidly tucked-under sheets, she was on a daily basis—had never been a comfortable one. But never in her worst, most paranoid moments had Anna imagined Nanny checking the bed for stains of activity.

"Aye, bu' that might not be the lassie's fault," cackled MacLoggie. "There've always been a few question marks over the maister in that department. That's wha' comes o' sendin' him to public school in England."

Anna decided she had heard enough. She gave a loud cough and stepped forward. As she entered the outbuilding, the far door was still swinging in the wake of MacLoggie's sudden departure. The slapping noise continued and was explained by the fact that Nanny was noisily rinsing something wobbly and bloody in a shallow stone sink. She turned her heavy face to Anna. "Can I help you?"

Anna boiled at Nanny's level tones, salted with just a hint of insolence. To think that Jamie had wanted her to discuss a wedding with this termagant. Well, the old battleaxe had asked for it. She'd make her squirm. Anna took a deep breath. "I couldn't help overhearing…" Yet, somewhere along the lines the words came out differently. "I'd like you to get the best room in the castle ready please, Nanny."

The slapping continued. Looking around her, Anna saw that a deer carcass hung from one of the hooks in the stark white walls. Near the sink, a vast wooden block on which lay a hatchet, several knives, and a considerable quantity of blood confirmed that Nanny had recently been indulging in a little light butchery.

"Did you hear me, Nanny?" Anna was aware that her voice had gone up an octave or two.

"Aye."

Suddenly, Anna realised that the bunch of unidentified organs hanging from a hook on the wall were the bowels of some unfortunate deer. She knew this because she could see a passage protruding from the organ mass in which small, round black pellets of deer poo were held in their own separate sacs, like the French sweets sold in long ropes of individual plastic packets. Looking at the unexpunged faeces, Anna had an overwhelming sense of life and all its natural rhythms suspended.

"I'd be grateful if you could do it immediately," Anna said tightly. "I have a friend coming to stay."

Chapter Eighteen

GERI'S EYES FLICKED OPEN. Something strange was going on. It wasn't *just* that she was slammed into the nasty-smelling grey carpet wall of her bunk every time the train rounded a bend, or grappled with the wrong sort of leaves, snow, or, more probably, rail. It wasn't even that the lid of the cabin's tiny sink, theoretically held up by a catch on the wall, kept being loosened from its moorings by the locomotive's wilder lurches and slamming down with the force and violence of a maniac's fist. Nor was it that the cabin was so airless she could barely breathe, and small enough to satisfy the most rampant agoraphobic. She could barely turn round standing up; lying down, on the other hand, had involved a different set of challenges altogether. When first entering the sleeper, Geri had laughed aloud at the size of it. Now, in the shaking, rattling watches of the night, it didn't seem nearly so amusing. Anna, she thought. The things I do for you. The opportunities I set you up with, and the minute I take my eye off the ball…Fancy not even having managed a *wedding date* yet. Still, hopefully it wouldn't take long to get everything back on track. After all, she hadn't bought that Gucci dress for nothing.

Irritating though her inability to get on a flight to Scotland had been—when *was* she going to use all those air miles?—the news that the quickest way up had been by sleeper had not worried Geri unduly. There was, after all, something very romantic about spending the night on a train. Geri's fond visions of walnut panelling, lamplit buffet cars, and steam trains puffing gracefully across northern uplands in the sunset had, however, reached the end of the line rather sooner than she had anticipated. At Euston, in fact. Before the train had even set off.

For Geri, any romance the journey might have held was quickly obliterated by the sound of the couple next door going at it hammer and tongs before the rear engine even pulled away from the buffers. "Didn't even *bother* putting my knickers on this morning," gasped a woman's voice. "Didn't see the point—you *always* want it the *minute* we get on." Brief encounter, thought Geri, it wasn't. Literally.

The rest of Geri's Orient Express–inspired expectations met with much the same disappointments. There was no walnut panelling; the only thing in sight even coming close to resembling a walnut was the short and intensely wrinkled old steward who asked her if she wanted tea or coffee in the morning (and quickly gave up on his attempts to elicit the same information from her neighbours). The lamplit buffet car had turned out to be an ordinary carriage filled with the sort of drunken, disappointed, rootless, and downright strange human flotsam and jetsam one might expect to find in a sleeper bar on a weekday evening.

Having secured herself a paper bag containing two miniature bottles of gin and two tins of tonic, Geri headed back to her telephone-box-sized compartment and locked the door, intending not to emerge until the train reached Inverness. She did not even intend to make the long, cold trek in her nightclothes to the loo, having decided on an impromptu but, she suspected, by no means infrequently employed system involving an empty plastic cup and the sink.

One blessing at least was that the couple next door had temporarily ceased their activities, having reached something of a crescendo at Stevenage. Geri downed her second gin and tonic and, having prised apart sheets so firmly tucked together they made opening an oyster with bare hands look easy, made a determined attempt to sleep.

Something in the compartment on the *other* side, however, seemed just as determined to stop her. Something that shouted, screeched, and banged itself periodically against the very wall—against the very section of the very wall, in fact—that Geri's face lay closest to in quest of slumber. As the noises increased in volume and the thuds in violence, she half expected the interconnecting door between the compartments to open and a madman with a carving knife to loom above her. The madman, however, did not seem to be the only person in the cabin. Someone else was shrieking as well. *Two nutters*. Finally, Geri stuffed tissue paper from the complementary toilet bag in her ears and pulled the blanket over her head.

But now something had woken her. Not a noise, but a smell. Geri sniffed hard. Something was burning. She gasped and sat up, visions of a rolling fireball filling the corridor outside springing terrifyingly and irrepressibly to mind. There was another scent besides, something heavy, slightly acrid. Geri had never smelt burning flesh before, but…

Flinging the compartment door open, Geri stuck her head out into the corridor. No fireball in sight, no nothing, in fact. But the smell here was definitely stronger and coming from the compartment next door, the one with the nutters in it. Geri hesitated for a nanosecond before rapping hard on the door. As shouts within greeted her knock and the door eventually opened to allow the throat-punching fumes within to escape, Geri saw she had not been wrong about the inmates. The person standing before her was, without a doubt, the most insane she'd ever seen.

"*Cassandra*! What the hell are you doing here? And *what on earth is that stink?*"

Cassandra gasped. Her eyes boggled and her mouth fell open. *Was there no escape?* Here she was, trying to leave everything behind her. Trying to forget the theatres of humiliation and degradation otherwise known as Kensington, Jett, St. Midas's, Mrs. Gosschalk, and most of all the Tressells' *wretched party* which had started it all. And who should be in the carriage next to her but the Tressells' ghastly nanny whom she had last encountered whilst in a very compromising position on the Tressells' bathroom floor.

"Got a body in there or something?"

"As it happens, I've got Zak in here." Cassandra spoke with as much hauteur as she could muster. Was the creature *spying* on her? Would the shameful truth—that she had been reduced to travelling in a second-class sleeper, and a pre-booked, reduced-price Apex one at that—filter back to W8? But now that the divorce was underway and the mortgage payments had fallen behind, did it much matter if it did? The Mrs. Curtaintwitchers down the road had had a field day as it was; Cassandra knew she would never be able to hold her head up in Kensington again. Or her hand up either; taxis were, temporarily at least, a thing of the past. She and Zak had suffered the ultimate indignity of coming to Euston on the Tube, a shattering experience for both of them. Having to actually *hold* those *disgusting* yellow poles that a million filthy commuter hands had gripped before her had turned Cassandra's stomach like a skipping rope.

"So what's the smell?" asked Geri. "I thought the carriage was on fire."

"South American Sage Stressbuster, since you ask," said Cassandra, as haughtily as she could. For she had salvaged one item from the wreck of the luxury liner of her life. The last of her scented candles. Not only did the smell remind her of happier—well, *wealthier*—times, it also reminded her of the joyous fact that Fenella Greatorex had recently burned her entire house down by leaving a scented candle alight while out at a parents' meeting.

"Oh, I see. Well, I am surprised to find you here, Cassandra," Geri said. "Didn't have you down as a user of public transport. Unless it's the sort that flies."

Cassandra swallowed. "Yes, well, it's really for Zak's benefit, of course." Over Cassandra's bony shoulder Geri could see him lurking on the top bunk, computer game in hand, watching her malevolently.

"How do you mean?"

"Well, as he'll be going to a Scottish boarding school and they're supposed to be *terribly* basic, I thought it best he got used to travelling rough straightaway. As a matter of fact," Cassandra tittered hysterically, "I took him to Euston on the *Underground*!"

"Heavens above," drawled Geri. "You'll be throwing caution to the winds and going on a bus next. So which school is Zak going to? Excuse me for saying this, but I thought he hadn't got a place *anywhere*."

"Of course he had," Cassandra snapped. "There were plenty of offers."

"Well, I'm glad to hear it," said Geri, unable to resist turning the knife. "I've obviously been getting the wrong information. Last I heard, you were looking into Christ's Hospital."

Cassandra's lip curled in a snarl. "Yes, well, I wouldn't have sent Zak there anyway."

"Why not?" asked Geri. "The academic standards are supposed to be excellent, aren't they?"

"Well, it can't have been a very good *hospital*," Cassandra barked. "Didn't do Christ much good, did it?"

She shifted forward into the doorway so less of the cabin behind could be seen. The last thing she wanted was for this wretched creature to see the handful of headmasters' letters scattered over the bed behind her, grudgingly agreeing to see Cassandra and her son for five minutes despite there emphatically being no possibility of a place. "And what are you doing here?" she asked Geri. Time they got off this subject.

"Well, I'm going to see your old nanny as it happens," Geri said, recognising another opportunity to rub Cassandra's nose in it. "At her *castle*."

"Oh. Yes. You must give me the address." A light went on

in Cassandra's eyes. Or was it, Geri thought, merely the fact that they were drawing into a station? They were stopping, at any rate. Rather abruptly, as well. As the train shuddered with screeching suddenness to a halt, she turned behind her to the window and looked out.

"How bizarre," Geri said. "We seem to be stopping in the middle of nowhere." She grinned at Cassandra, unable to resist the urge to tease her. "Zak's not pulled the communication cord, has he?"

Cassandra glared. "Of *course* he hasn't. Zak would *never* do such a thing." She darted a nervous glance over her shoulder, threw a startled look back at Geri, and disappeared inside the cabin.

Geri slipped back into her own compartment just as the train guard strode as furiously up the narrow passageway as his well-built frame would permit.

"How *dare* you say that about my son?" she heard Cassandra yelling as she fitted the tissue paper back in her ears. "He's just *curious*. A sign of very high intelligence. He pulled it because he thought it was something to do with the air conditioning."

"But what *did* MacLoggie mean about your father's will?" Anna was trying to get Jamie to meet her eyes, but so far hadn't even managed to set up an appointment. This made her angrier than ever.

"Here, have some of Nanny's shortbread," Jamie said quickly, proffering a plate of thick-cut brown blocks. "She's spent all morning making it."

Staggered by the inadequacy of the diversionary tactic, Anna took the plate anyway. As her wrist plunged floorwards, she bit back the urge to enquire whether a concrete mixer had been employed in the construction of the shortbread and if so, why didn't Jamie prop up the crumbling curtain wall with it? She looked for the smallest piece possible. None seemed less than a foot across.

"Nice, isn't it?" said Jamie, chewing away so violently his eyes watered with the strain.

Thanks to Nanny's lurking in the shadows all through dinner, it had been impossible for Anna to bring up the subject of what she had overheard in the kitchen. Her chance had, as usual, only arisen during after-dinner coffee—and shortbread—in the castle's upstairs sitting room.

"Let me put it another way," Anna said when Jamie's jaws had finally stopped moving. "*Why did you ask me to marry you*? You don't *love* me, do you?"

Jamie did not respond immediately. "We-e-ll…" he hedged.

"Well *what*?" A frigid calm, far more disturbing than anger, spread through Anna. She was, she knew, emotionally anaesthetising herself against what was to come.

"Well, of course I *like* you," Jamie murmured, crossing one yellow-corduroyed leg slowly over the other. "But I'm not really sure what *love*, such as it is, really *is*."

"Oh *really*," Anna snapped. "You sound like Prince bloody Charles. You know what I mean."

There was a pause.

"Well, love's never really, um, been an issue in our family as far as, er, marriages are concerned," Jamie said, still avoiding her gaze. "There's an estate to consider. Anguses usually marry for a reason."

"Yes, so I heard. Your father put it in his will that you had to have a wife in order to make the inheritance final."

"Yes, um, well, there *is* that," Jamie said.

"But why? That's not normal, is it?" Anna felt furious, yet oddly detached. Like a cross-examining barrister. A very cross examining barrister.

"No," Jamie admitted, turning his wide dark eyes on her almost pleadingly. "But my father realised that, after being beaten and buggered by the other boys at school, I wasn't either. At the start of one term, I begged him not to send me back and told him what was happening. He was worried about the effect it would have on me and my future relationships with women."

"That sounds very enlightened," Anna remarked.

"Not really. He told me it hadn't done him any harm, thrashed me senseless, packed me off, and went straight round to his lawyer and stuck in that clause."

"Oh. Oh dear." For a few moments, sympathy for the crushed little boy Jamie must have been welled up in Anna. Then she remembered what they were supposed to be talking about. "That explains why you want to get *married*, but not why you want to get married to *me*. I'm not remotely grand."

"Which is why we were the perfect match."

"Sorry? Am I missing something?"

"Simple." Jamie darted a look at her. "You had no money and nowhere to live and were desperate to get away from that boss of yours. I needed someone to come here and marry me in order to properly inherit the estate. What better arrangement could there possibly have been?"

Anna stared at him for a few seconds. "None, I suppose," she said, slowly. "Except for the fact I was the only person—on this entire island, by the sound of it—who didn't realise it *was* an arrangement."

Jamie cleared his throat. He sounded almost bored now, so distant had his tone become. "Well, that didn't seem necessary," he drawled, "because you seemed to find me rather, um, attractive when we met."

Anna blushed furiously. "But I *still* don't understand why you picked me," she hit back. "Surely half the smartest girls in Scotland would have been *desperate* to marry you."

Jamie took a deep breath and closed his eyes—a brief but eloquent gesture implying that this was an extremely unpleasant business he heartily wished was over. "It's true that in the past there *have* been some women—some rich, some beautiful, some even both—who thought they wanted to marry me," he muttered. "But they all changed their minds."

How rich? *How* beautiful? More to the point, *how dare he?* Anna gazed at him indignantly. "Why?"

"I'm not sure," Jamie said, not entirely convincingly. "I think when they came here they realised that perhaps living in an isolated castle in the middle of nowhere wasn't their idea of heaven."

You mean they didn't realise they would have to play second fiddle to a pile of old stones, Anna thought. She glanced at the engagement ring. Belonged to his mother, indeed. His mother and God knew how many other women since. Like an upmarket Pass the Parcel.

"I see what you're getting at," she said with just a trace of sarcasm. "It's not so much a matter of not being able to get the staff these days as not being able to get the ladies of the manor." So this is what he had meant in the tandoori about not having the right personnel in place.

Jamie wrinkled his brow slightly. "Something like that," he confirmed. "But another advantage you had was that you had at least been up here and knew what it was like."

What I *thought* it was like, thought Anna. Dampie dressed up with flowers and laughter for a wedding and Dampie in its everyday habit had turned out to be very different places. God, she'd been a fool.

"So to a certain extent, you knew what you were taking on," Jamie continued.

"So it's all my fault, is it?" Anna felt the anger rise again.

"To a certain extent, well, um, yes."

Anna stared at him hard. There was something, she felt, that Jamie wasn't telling her. Something wasn't quite adding up. Plenty of women, after all, willingly married into remote estates. There must be some other reason why only someone poor and desperate would want to marry him.

"This is just a thought," she said slowly, as it suddenly struck her. "Just an idea. But did they, did *any* of these beautiful, rich women happen to meet Nanny?"

Jamie looked away quickly.

"*Thought* as much," said Anna, as triumphantly as she could, given the circumstances.

Chapter Nineteen

OFFICIALLY, IT WAS MORNING, yet as the light stayed that way all day, it could be any time at all. Jamie once had tried to persuade her that the failing light was a consequence of their position in the far north, a sort of Grey Days of Skul answer to the White Nights of Scandinavia. Anna's private theory, however, was that there was only so much light to go around and what there was simply didn't stretch as far as Dampie.

As she walked away from the castle, Anna clenched her fists and stared desperately into the grey half-darkness. Dawn rambles were getting to be a habit with her, as was not sleeping. She had stayed awake almost the entire night after Jamie's bombshell, first pouring out her battered heart to her diary and then lying sleepless in the darkness. She was alone—Jamie had gone off to a bedroom somewhere else. As soon as ashen-fingered dawn appeared between the crack in her curtains, Anna had got up. A walk might clear her head, as well as give her some idea of what the hell to do next. Jamie had asked her not to make any sudden decisions, but to think about things. He'd refused even to take back the ring which she had yanked painfully from her finger and hurled across the mouldering carpet at him. Eventually, she had been persuaded to pick it up again; this time, however, it was going in her pocket.

But...*think about things*? What was she to think? She must, of course, leave the castle. But go where? In the not-so-broad light of day, the idea of returning to London struck her as lamer than a sheep with foot rot. She was, Anna dolefully told herself, unemployed, unskilled, impecunious, and effectively homeless. She was back to square one, square minus one now she'd failed at being engaged as well as everything else. As the mist rolled over her like steam from a kettle, gathering her into its ethereal embrace, Anna let out an agonised howl.

It was a howl of hurt, of betrayal. Of fury with herself for having been so easily taken in. Having failed even at *writing* romantic novels, how had she ever thought it possible to *live* them? She felt exploited, more used than an old five-pound note. And lurking darkly behind all the sound and fury of her disappointment was the maddening knowledge that Jamie had had a point. It *had* suited her to agree to marry him at the time. No one had forced her. She had only herself to blame.

Anna stumbled blindly onward, heading she knew not where and caring less. She felt as if the earth had given way beneath her—which, given the muddy ground and the careless way she was negotiating it, was more or less the case. The violent jolts of her ankles as they twisted and slid onward over the uneven humps of marshy grass were intensely painful; throwing back her head, Anna howled again, investing in the sound all the indignation, betrayal, remorse, and shame one might have expected to find given the circumstances. It was a howl that reverberated with perfectly understandable panic and pain. Only one thing about Anna's howl was a surprise. It was answered.

At first, she thought the sound was an echo bouncing off the rocks and drifting back across the water, except that the water she saw before her, she suddenly realised, was the sea. She must have stumbled for miles and did not now recognise the shore she found herself standing on, heels sinking into an expanse of sand as white as bone. She listened in awe as the full aural expression of her agony was borne thunderously back to her on the waves. It was impressive. Terrifying, even, a wild, abandoned shriek, the cry of a banshee, the scream of a soul in purgatory. As she listened, it came again. Exactly the same but with the crucial difference that this time she had not yelled first. Someone else was howling by the shore.

Anna's first instinct was to duck out of sight behind one of the rocks and wait for her fellow hollerer to reveal himself. Yet, as the minutes went by and no one appeared, Anna started to wonder whether what she had heard had, in retrospect, been MacLoggie at the pipes again. Failing that, a howling dog.

"And you are?"

Anna's throat contracted with terror before she could fully release another scream. A strangled yelp emerged, like an indignant puppy. Having focused all her attention on the shore in front of her, she hadn't heard anyone coming up from behind.

"Come on, you can do better than that," said the voice. "I heard you. Very impressive. You were doing a much better job than I was."

Anna felt her back crunch as she whipped round to find herself staring at a tall, broad-shouldered, and very untidy-looking young man. She was suddenly intensely aware of being a woman alone in the last landscape on earth; easy prey for any psychopath who happened to be passing. Perhaps she was jumping to conclusions, but this strange man, given that he was the person she had heard emitting terrifying howls a mere few minutes before, hardly struck her as particularly normal.

"Oh. You heard me then?" Anna spoke steadily and quietly. *Better not do anything to agitate him.* But it was just her luck. Even on the remotest beach on the remotest island she'd not only ended up engaged to Mr. Wrong but meeting Mr. Possibly Extremely Dangerous into the bargain. Five minutes ago, she had wanted to die but was now acutely conscious that she hadn't meant it *really*.

"Yes," he replied. "You see, I've been out yowling all morning as well."

It was fatal, she knew, to make eye contact with lunatics, but there being just the two of them, it was difficult not to. Anna drew a measure of relief from the fact that his pupils seemed warm rather than blazing insanely and that the grin looked more full of friendly enquiry than murderous intent. Yet complete peace of mind was prevented by the fact that, standing like a hedge between herself and reassurance was—a beard.

Anna had read enough of Cassandra's glossy magazines to know that beards, hitherto firmly beyond the style pale, had recently experienced a renaissance. She was aware that, when cut and shaped, they could even be fashionable. But there was nothing trimmed about this one. It was an out-of-control leylandii; large, abundant, and the sort of thing neighbours complain about. It was firmly of the variety favoured by geography teachers, vicars, and lunatics. Free range, to say the least. And very possibly organic.

"Why *were* you yowling?" she asked him.

The bearded youth smiled again. Looking at his extraordinarily strong-looking white teeth, Anna tried to banish all thoughts about *The Silence of the Lambs*. She also noticed that, apart from the bad hair day at the end of his chin, he had some distinctly deranged-looking clothes on. Torn and faded jeans that seemed to have been attacked by a wild animal and a cotton jumper that had more holes than a mesh tank peeped from under the wrinkled flaps of an ancient Barbour. "Yowling helps me in my work," he said. "When I'm really letting it all out, I feel as if I'm communicating with a higher, creative force. With the Great One."

That rules out the geography teacher then, thought Anna. Which left only vicar or lunatic. Could be either, except that he'd mentioned his *work*. Vicar then. Must be.

"An unusual approach to work."

"Not to mine."

"Really?" Some island parishes, Anna knew, adhered to practices considered extreme and unusual by those of more liberal beliefs and downright bizarre by those of no beliefs whatsoever.

But those island priests, the ones who forbade even heating up tins of beans on Sundays on the grounds that it counted as work, hardly struck her as likely to go in for screaming on hillsides. Perhaps, Anna thought, the man before her was some sort of charismatic prophet, marrying people on clifftops and baptising others in the freezing real-ale coloured waves breaking ever closer up the shore behind them.

"But what do your congregation think?"

It was his turn to look wary. "Congregation?"

"Aren't you the vicar?"

"No, I'm a writer. My name's Robbie MacAskill. I'm the—"

"*Poet!*" Anna finished. "Oh, it's *you.* I read about you on the noticeboard. You give classes in creative writing. I'm *so sorry.*"

"Well, they're not *that* bad."

Anna had not expected to return to the castle feeling calmer than when she had left it. It was amazing how a few hours' talking about writing soothed the nerves. Robbie was impressively passionate about it. The hilariously trite diktats he had invented for his creative writing classes had made her laugh for the first time in weeks.

"You have to take the *fear* out of it," he explained as they walked slowly back over the dripping heather. "Most people would rather show you their bottoms than their writing." He turned to smile at her, his large teeth glinting in his beard. "You're a writer, of course?"

Anna nodded, flushing with both embarrassment and gratification. "In theory. How did you know?" Was it her eyes? Her hands? The creative aura around her?

"Well, *everyone's* a writer," came the rather less flattering reply. "I tell everyone at the start of my course that a book is like an arsehole. Everyone's got one in them. And most of what comes out is, of course, usually shit."

"*Oh.*" Anna wasn't sure what she thought of this. Then Cassandra came to mind and she smiled.

"But the point is," said Robbie, helping her negotiate a shallow stream which would otherwise have flooded all over her shoes, "it's better out than in. Most people feel a lot better afterwards, anyway. It helps them work out their frustrations. I'm a great believer in the therapeutic value of writing things down. If everyone did it, the world would be a better, calmer, less hysterical place. And if that means there are more bad novels about, so what?"

With surprise, Anna saw that they were already approaching the castle entrance. She stopped and smiled at him. "This is where I live." This, she decided, was as much as she would tell him.

"I know." But of course he did, she thought, feeling her former sour mood returning. Everyone on this island knew everything. Except her.

"Come in for a coffee…or a drink?"

"Thanks, but I'd better be getting back. I have a class to prepare. Mrs. McLeod has given me another chapter of her novel and I need to have read it with comments by tomorrow afternoon."

"Mrs. McLeod? The one who irons with discretion?"

"The very same. And writes the raunchiest stuff I've seen this side of a Soho porn parlour. All that steam must go to her head."

"Not to mention all that underwear."

They said their goodbyes. "Come to my class," Robbie told her. "Come tomorrow afternoon, if you feel like it." He swung on his way back down the drive without looking back. But then, if he had, Anna realised, he would have probably broken his neck in a pothole.

She stepped, heart sinking, into the flagged chill of the hall and wondered what on earth to do with herself. Where exactly did she go from here—in every sense of the word? But as she paused at the foot of the stairs, a strange, faint, and entirely new sound greeted her. A sound she had not heard since coming to Dampie. Someone, somewhere, was laughing.

It seemed to be coming from somewhere upstairs. As Anna mounted the wide treads with their rotting red runner, she wondered who on earth it could be. Kate Tressell? Had one of the girls who had jilted Jamie dropped in for old times' sake? The laughter rang out again down the second-floor passage. It was coming from the sitting room. Anna rounded the corner to the sitting-room doorway, and gasped as Nanny, looming terrifyingly out of the gloom like the *Hound of the Baskervilles*, rolled on past her down the corridor with the force of a juggernaut and a face like thunder.

Whoever was laughing had made Nanny livid, which must by definition be good news. And, if she was not mistaken, before she had surprised her, Nanny had been bent double in the corridor with her ear shoved against the door. Which, come to think of it, seemed rather a good idea.

"Is that the Angus tartan?" a woman's voice was asking as Anna put her ear to the keyhole. *Geri*. It was *Geri's* voice. *Christ, she'd completely forgotten she was coming.* Even though there didn't seem much point in her being here now, Anna suddenly felt overwhelmingly glad she was.

"*Absolutely.*" Jamie sounded almost incoherent with enthusiasm.

Fools rush in, Anna told herself, taking her hand away from the doorknob she had been about to turn. *Not* that *bloody* tartan story again. On the other hand, what a heaven-sent opportunity to let Jamie reveal his true colours to Geri—in every sense of the word.

Chapter Twenty

CASSANDRA HAD HAD NO idea she had such *resilience*. Driving around in a *hire* car. And by no means the biggest available at that. And actually *surviving* the experience. She'd rather have died than do this in Kensington, yet here she was just west of Inverness in her Weekend Bargain Class A three-door "Disco" with its denim-effect seats and tan plastic trim, and the God of Style had not struck her down. Not yet, anyway.

It was, Cassandra reflected, *amazing* what the human spirit could bear. A fortnight ago, failure to get a table at Bam Bou or an on-the-day appointment with Jo Hansford would have seen her booking straight into the Priory. Were she to go to Jo Hansford now, Cassandra thought, the celebrated colourist might be in need of a spot of trauma counselling herself, given the state of her highlights. For, at the base of each platinum coloured hair shaft lurked a good one and a half black and sinister inches. Cassandra ruffled them ruefully in the driving mirror. Talk about going back to one's roots. For the time being, at least, she would have to go cold turkey on blonde. Gold turkey, if you liked. She hadn't really had much choice.

She hadn't had much choice about the car either. It had been impossible to book a flight to Inverness for herself and Zak. How was she supposed to have remembered, with all the *millions* of other things she had to worry about, that Zak had been banned by BA after an incident involving an injured member of staff and unlocked central emergency doors eight miles above the Atlantic several months before? Those sorts of things just slipped one's mind, although in this case they had been forcibly helped back into it again by the bookings clerk.

Honestly, Cassandra thought. Some people were so *petty*. It wasn't as if anyone *important* had been injured. Admittedly that *ridiculous* hostess Zak had been playing catch-the-gin-miniature with *had* ended up requiring plastic surgery, but quite frankly she'd needed that anyway. Face like a baboon's bottom, learnt her makeup tips on the set of *Star Wars*, by the looks of things. Forget launching a thousand ships, you wouldn't want to launch a range of frozen peas with that. Anyway, Cassandra thought indignantly, was it *her* fault they'd been stuck on the tarmac for at least ten minutes waiting for Air Traffic Control to relent? Which had hardly helped with the Zak situation. He'd got bored and playful, that was all.

And harmless fun was all it had been—the door incident itself was merely the result of Zak *playing* at being an air steward. He'd only wanted to see what his emergency mask looked like when he pulled it down, and had only wanted to play at being a pilot when the captain—somewhat *reluctantly*, it had to be admitted—had allowed him into the cabin. Best draw a veil over *that* one, Cassandra thought. The memory of the sudden plummeting of the Boeing 747 made her blood run cold, just as it had made her Bloody Mary run cold all over her white Sulka shirt at the time.

Still, hiring the car and booking the sleeper had worked out very well—not to mention *cheaply*. Once she had got over the shock of realising that the box on the train she had thought must be her wardrobe area was actually the *entire cabin*, the journey had passed without too much incident. Apart, of course, from that ludicrous nanny of the Tressells' occupying the next door cabin and Zak's ever-curious and enquiring mind bringing itself to bear on the communication cord.

Bumping into Geri had proved useful, however; she'd now got Anna's address and fully intended to use it. It had been obvious from the way Geri had so determinedly talked Dampie Castle down, dismissing it as freezing, tiny, and so damp it was probably *wringing*, that the place was vast, luxurious, and ramblingly romantic, probably complete with Jacuzzis and aubergine guest bathrooms. And, quite apart from the weight it would take off her bank account, staying in the castle would, Cassandra decided, prove a useful source of ideas. In the last few days she had been thinking the previously unthinkable—moving out of London. Property was so much cheaper up here; hopefully there'd be enough left after the divorce from Jett for a *starter* castle, at least. Reluctantly, Cassandra recognised she had to get out of her Kensington mind-set. She soon wouldn't be able to afford anything more than a shoebox in W8 anymore. Location, location, location was all very well. But not if it was broom cupboard, broom cupboard, broom cupboard.

And there were other reasons for being in Scotland. No school in England having been prepared to rise to what Cassandra, in her letters to the headmaster, called "the particular challenge of Zak," the virtues of Scottish education were now being explored. Chief among these virtues, Cassandra decided, was instilling in the pupil the appropriate degree of fiscal ambition. She had little on which to base this conviction other than the names of some of the places—but how, after all, could anyone at school in Stirling have anything other than a healthy respect for cash in all its forms? Unfortunately, the headmaster hadn't seemed interested in any of hers. The school called Dollar Academy had also struck, so to speak, the right note with Cassandra, and so it had been devastating to receive a letter pleading a waiting list longer than an M1 Bank Holiday traffic jam. In the end, Cassandra had decided she had no option but to take the bull—and the headmasters—by the horns and come up and sort things out herself. So far, her in-person surgical strikes on the schools had failed to make much difference—it had, incidentally, been *amazing* how many of them knew Mrs. Gosschalk. Bloody woman got everywhere.

Cassandra had now moved on to the northwest Highlands, although getting around the place was driving her mad. These *ridiculous* little single tracks full of even more ridiculous people expecting her to *stop* for them, for some reason. Now she'd finally persuaded Zak he didn't need to get out of the car to pee, be sick, or be bought things every five minutes, Cassandra had no intention of stopping for anyone. Zak had latched on with greater interest than she had anticipated to the idea of peeing into a plastic cup, although Cassandra had correctly assumed that anything to do with his willy would fascinate him.

"It's a good job you're a boy," Cassandra observed, hearing the gushing of urine into the cup behind her. Unusually, Zak had insisted on sitting in the back seat.

"Why?"

"Because you can aim straight."

"Cant *bints* aim straight?" demanded Zak, thrilled to be at last discussing his beloved subject. "Why don't *birds* have cocks and balls?"

Cassandra sighed. Buttock-clenchingly uncomfortable though she found sexual organs herself—both literally and metaphorically—she knew it was vital to be as patient as possible with Zak. His young mind, after all, was still forming and misunderstandings in this very delicate area—*very delicate area*—could result in a lifelong psychiatric condition. Everything had to be explained very carefully and accurately. "Ladies have whiskers and gentlemen have tails," Cassandra said. "I told you on the train."

"But why don't blokes have *cunts*?" yelled Zak with relish. "After all, everyone has *arseholes*."

Cassandra swallowed. "Darling, you know we call them front bottoms and back bottoms," she said faintly, almost grateful for the sudden distraction of the flashing, frantic headlights of a car looming in her driving mirror. A few minutes later, Cassandra found herself faced with a furious dental supplies salesman from Aberdeen who had just received an unscheduled golden shower through the air conditioning system of his car. It suddenly became clear why Zak had insisted on being in the back seat.

"When I said you could aim straight," she said as she got back in the car having spent a fortune on mouthwash, enough dental floss to last the rest of her life, and a state-of-the-art laser toothbrush apparently developed aboard a space shuttle, "I didn't mean throwing the contents of your cup at any car that happened to be following us." Sometimes, she thought ruefully, Zak really took the piss.

Zak did not reply.

Fearing one of his world-class sulks, Cassandra turned to see her son sitting rapt with the mobile glued to his ear. "Darling, give me that. I've told you before about dialling those 0898 numbers."

Cassandra wrested the mobile out of Zak's grasp and decided to call the London answerphone again. You never knew. Of late, she had become addicted to dialling the Knightsbridge phone number and listening with bated breath as the pitiless woman on the other end informed her "you have *no* new messages." Yet Cassandra could still not shake off the conviction that in her absence, every glossy magazine and national newspaper in Britain had called leaving urgent messages on the answerphone wanting interviews. One never, after all, knew when the *Larry King Live* show would get in touch. And there was always the possibility that another publisher would ring with a huge offer.

Cassandra stabbed the autodial and listened. *Fifteen messages!* *Fifteen!* It was unbelievable. Clearly, her fortunes had undergone a transformation more dramatic than Jocelyn Wildenstein after plastic surgery. Hand shaking, Cassandra pressed two.

Her dreams had come true. The *Guardian*, the *Independent*, the *Daily Telegraph*, *The Times*, the *Daily Mail*, and the *Express* had all called wanting interviews. *Vogue* wanted to set up a photoshoot and

Harpers & Queen wanted to do an At Home. Radios One, Two, and Four had called, as had the long-awaited *Larry King Live* researcher and about three representatives of prestigious publishing houses. It was overwhelming. In the bright blue sky of Cassandra's happiness, there was but one small cloud. None of the messages were for her.

The phrases "ironic," "cult," and "the real-life Spinal Tap" were repeated again and again. "Jett St. Edmunds," the Radio One researcher breathed reverently, "you are, quite literally, the new black." Slowly, Cassandra worked out that not only was Jett's nationwide tour of student halls proving a massive success, but "Sex and Sexibility," the first single released from the *Ass Me Anything* comeback album, had gone straight to number one.

"With a bullet," some of the journalists added, whatever that meant. She wouldn't mind pumping a few bullets into Jett now. *Number one.* Cassandra's heart plummeted faster and colder than a block of frozen urine from a plane.

Cassandra slammed the mobile back into the glove compartment. It was just so *sodding typical* of him to get successful now she was in the middle of divorcing him. Having sat on his *arse* doing *fuck all* for the past ten years at least, he would choose *now*, of all times, to get his act together and become famous. *And*, no doubt, rich. *Bastard*, thought Cassandra furiously. No wonder she was divorcing him.

Geri, Anna considered, was proving something of a disappointment on the moral support front. So far, she had failed to detect any of the expected *froideur* between her faithful friend and her conniving fiancé. On the contrary, they were getting on like a castle on fire. Geri seemed to be drinking in every detail about Dampie as enthusiastically as she was downing the gin and flat tonics Anna had been relegated to preparing from the rudimentary contents of the drinks tray.

"You know," Geri said, "you should really think about promoting this place more. It's so romantic and interesting. Have you ever thought of opening it to the public?"

Anna was unable to suppress a snort. Jamie shot her an indignant look.

"This place is a tourist gold mine." Geri looked around decisively. "You've got turrets, towers, suits of armour, Dr. Johnson, and Mad Angus Thingy's romantic burn, and that's just for starters. You've even got a monster."

"Have we?" Jamie looked amazed.

"Yes. That woman who showed me up to the sitting room was just about the scariest thing I've ever seen." There was a silence. Anna looked keenly at Jamie.

"You mean Nanny?" Jamie's voice was noncommittal. Then, confounding all expectation, his mouth moved up at the corners. "I suppose she is a bit fearsome," he admitted.

Anna almost fell off her—admittedly rickety—chair. Jamie had never said anything before that implied Nanny was one whit less beautiful than Kate Moss.

"Any dungeons?" Geri enquired briskly. "Tourists love a good dungeon."

"How come you know so much about it?" Anna asked.

"Actually," Jamie interrupted, looking hurriedly at his watch, "I think we'd better go down to dinner. Nanny will be very cross if we're late."

"I was a hotel PR for years," Geri confessed once they were seated at opposite ends and in the middle of the long dining table. "I quite enjoyed it, until…"

"What?" asked Anna.

"Until it all went horribly wrong when A. A. Gill was supposed to be going to one of the restaurants I represented. Everyone got in such a state because they didn't know what he looked like that they made me do a drawing of him and fax it through."

"No!" said Jamie. "How ridiculous."

"Yes, and it all went more pear-shaped than the chef's Belle Hélène. They ended up making the most *tremendous* fuss of someone who looked exactly like my drawing but turned out to be Jimmy Tarbuck. Poor Adrian Gill got completely ignored, was really pissed off, and slagged off the restaurant all over the *Sunday Times*."

Anna laughed. It was impossible not to find Geri funny, despite her abject failure to find Jamie as appalling as she was supposed to.

"Then I decided to go into travel PR, but I left it when I found myself."

"Found yourself?" Jamie looked nonplussed. "But isn't that a good thing?"

"Found myself halfway up some mountain in Grenada with some old git from the travel pages looking up my skirt and asking for my room number, I mean," said Geri. "After that, I decided to pack it in. Gosh, what's this?"

Nanny had arrived in the dining room, her large, reddened thumbs firmly pushed over the rim into whatever was piled on the pitilessly large plates. A teaspoonful of grey flakes that might have been some sort of fish cowered at the foothills of an Everest of pulverised vegetable.

"Yummy," said Geri. "I love mashed potato."

"Champit tatties, you mean." Jamie glanced nervously into the shadows where Nanny lurked.

"Do I?"

"Yes, and that orange stuff next to it is bashed neeps."

"Oh well, never mind. I'm sure they taste just as good as ordinary neeps, whatever they are."

"Actually," Jamie said hurriedly, "Nanny's cooking is renowned the length and breadth of the island."

"I bet it is," giggled Geri, flinging him a flirtatious glance as devastating as a mortar. "Well, nobody's perfect. I expect there are lots of other things she can do."

Anna was not in the least surprised when Nanny turned

massively in her shadow and stomped furiously out of the room. What was amazing was that Jamie did not immediately scuttle after her. Instead, he shrugged his shoulders and grinned apologetically at Geri.

Past one in the morning, they were still all in the sitting room. Egged on by Geri, Jamie had returned to the subject of Dampie and had even dug out some mouldering and ancient pamphlets about the island. Anna, meanwhile, had felt compelled to stay through a mixture of masochism and curiosity. Geri was up to something, it was obvious. But what?

"And this is Old Man Rock." Clouds of dust wafted from the pamphlet Jamie waved at Geri. "It's supposed to look like an old man."

Anna recalled the penis-shaped rock she had glimpsed fleetingly in the mist. No doubt the keen-to-impress-Jamie Geri would think of a more suitable way to describe it.

"Looks exactly like a penis to me," said Geri, staring at the grey, grainy picture.

Anna muffled a giggle.

"*Well...*" began Jamie, doubtfully.

"But don't you see?" said Geri. "That's a great *asset*. If you think about how many people go and look at a lump of stone shaped like four presidents, just think how many will come to see a rock that's shaped like a *penis*."

Jamie did not look entirely convinced. "I *suppose* I see what you're getting at," he muttered.

"And what's this?" Geri reached for another pamphlet and sneezed as she prised apart its long unopened pages. "The Mount O'Many Stanes?"

"A construction in the islands west comprising concentric circles of stone slabs on a hilltop," supplied Jamie instantly. Both women looked at each other, and then at Jamie, in astonishment.

"Various guesses—graveyard, remains of extraterrestrial

settlement, early form of calculator—have been hazarded through the centuries," Jamie added, "but no one really knows what they're there for. The latest research thinks it has something to do with working out the best time for planting crops."

"Fine," said Geri, breezily. "You're looking at the world's first Filofax in that case, aren't you? The cake-and-a-crap crowd will love it."

"*Sorry?*" said Jamie.

"*Cake-and-a-crap crowd*," Geri enunciated emphatically. "Tourists, in other words. They like to have a look at something before going to what they really came for—the café and the loo."

As Geri and Jamie proceeded to discuss Dampie's potential as the Alton Towers of the North, Anna found following the conversation increasingly impossible. Her thoughts kept drifting to a smiling poet with big teeth. She resolved to add every detail of her encounter with Robbie to tonight's diary entry, especially her impression that she had met someone with a heart almost as big as his muscles. "Come to my class tomorrow if you feel like it," he had said. *Such* a shame he had a beard. But even given that rather considerable drawback, Anna was surprised by how much she felt like it.

Chapter Twenty-one

WHEN GERI FAILED TO appear at breakfast, Anna seized the opportunity to take it up to her. Doubtless after a night on one of Dampie's rock-stuffed mattresses, she would have an altogether different view of both the castle and its laird. At last they'd be able to have the heart to heart she'd been longing for.

"Ugh, that smells *disgusting*," groaned Geri, turning her face away from the plate of tepid egg on toast. Anna tried not to mind the ingratitude—following Geri's comments the night before it had taken the diplomatic skills of Kofi Annan to get any breakfast at all out of Nanny this morning. Only by pretending the eggs were for him had Jamie acquired them. Anna had stepped in before he could take them upstairs himself, but not before hearing about little other than Geri all breakfast-time. "So positive," Jamie kept repeating. "So full of good ideas."

"*Oh my head*. Someone's tightening a rope around my brain." Geri's usually tanned face was almost as sludge green as the blankets. "It was that fish we had last night. I'm sure it was off. I've had," she added, "what you might call a long dark night of the sole."

Anna suspected there might be another reason for Geri's condition and wondered guiltily whether she really should have compensated for the flatness of the tonic by adding twice as much gin. Geri's Malteser eyes were now rather more reminiscent of a red-rimmed multi-hued gobstopper.

"And I'm sure this horrible seventies wallpaper's not helping," grinned Anna, nodding her head towards the vast orange and brown flowers crawling all over the walls. To her surprise, Geri refused to rise to the bait.

"Well, I wasn't expecting Claridges. And if you think this is bad, you should have seen the room I got last time."

"I think its probably the room I've got now," sighed Anna. As the familiar drone of MacLoggie started up outside the windows, she looked at her watch. Three hours later than usual—Jamie must have asked him specially to serenade Geri. And, Anna saw gleefully, it wasn't having quite the effect he was intending.

"*What the hell is that?*" Geri shot up in bed like a scalded cat. "Christ, my head. My brain's slamming around in there like a squash ball."

"Since the dawn of time," Anna declaimed dramatically, "MacLoggies have lived and died as pipers to the Anguses."

"Died, by the sound of that," Geri groaned. "One's heart rather goes out to the Anguses."

As MacLoggie's attempts to launch into "Scotland the Brave" collapsed into a cacophony of choking coughs, Geri covered her ears. "I'm not sure about the bagpipes," she groaned, "but he does a great catarrh solo."

Anna stuck her fingers in her ears. "See what I have to put up with?"

"Oh, the poor old boy's in a bad way," Geri chided. "When he showed me to my room last night, his knees were cracking like a firing squad."

"I wish I'd never seen this place." Anna, overcome by a fit of despair, dramatically buried her head in the musty-smelling quilt on Geri's bed. "Come for a walk with me?"

"I couldn't. The only walk I'm capable of making is to the bathroom to throw up."

"But I need to talk to you. My life's fallen apart at the seams."

"Bit like these sheets then."

Something in Anna suddenly snapped. She rounded on Geri with fury. "All very well for you to come up here and find the whole thing side-splitting," she snapped. "I thought you were supposed to be my friend."

"I *am*. But I feel slightly as if I've been dragged up on false pretences."

"*False pretences?*"

"Well, you made it sound as if you were more or less rotting alive in a dungeon, helpless in the grip of an evil and ruthless brute of a fiancé and his stone-hearted female accomplice…" Geri held up a hand as Anna tried to interrupt. "…And I arrive to find you in the company of nothing more disturbing than a slightly preoccupied and really rather sweet Scottish aristo and his nanny who, though admittedly not at the front of the queue when looks were given out, isn't exactly Frankenstein. In other words, I think you might have things *slightly* out of proportion."

"*Well*." Anna's mouth opened and shut like a guppy catching flies. "There's nothing much in proportion about Nanny, for a start."

"Nanny's easily dealt with. She just needs showing who's boss. Take the piss out of her a bit, like I did last night. Better still, just sack her."

"And what," demanded Anna furiously, "is so wonderfully in proportion about Jamie only wanting to marry me so he'll inherit the estate? What about the fact that he lured me up here on *false pretences?*"

"*Darling*," Geri sighed ostentatiously, "*every* husband, to some extent, lures his wife on false pretences. If every woman knew exactly who and *what* she was marrying, there wouldn't be any weddings at all."

The blood pounded in Anna's head. Her brain whirled. How *dare*, how *could* Geri be so flippant about her situation—a situation she was only in, after all, largely thanks to Geri. Right, well, she'd let her have it with both barrels.

"What about Jamie not wanting to have sex with me?" There. Get out of *that*.

There was a pause. *Got* her, Anna thought, darkly triumphant.

"Well, sweetheart," Geri eventually remarked, "I suppose you have to look on the bright side."

"*Bright side?*" Anna was staggered. "What *bright side?*"

"Well, a lot of wives would give anything for a husband who doesn't want to have sex with them. Kate for one. Julian gives her a UTI practically every time. She has to sit on the loo for *hours* pouring water on her clit from a milk bottle."

"But this is practically an arranged marriage," blustered an aghast Anna. "Except for the fact that no one ever got around to arranging it," she added.

"Well, in that case perhaps you should get on with it," said Geri calmly. "Jamie's very good-looking. Just get real, will you? You could have ended up with a lot worse."

Anna felt she was about to hyperventilate with shock and disappointment.

"OK, so your sex life isn't exactly electric," said Geri, "but you can be friends. Lots of couples are and have affairs on the side. It would be rather fun. *Very* French."

"But I don't want to have affairs on the side," wailed Anna. "I wanted to marry for love. I thought I was *going* to."

Geri looked at her with a mixture of exasperation and pity. "Your trouble is that you're a fully paid up, hearts and flowers hopeless romantic, aren't you?"

"And what's wrong with that? Better *that* than viewing every relationship as a business opportunity," she snapped, immediately regretting it.

There was a silence.

"Knights on white chargers don't exist in real life," said Geri. She sounded more sad than triumphant. "At least, not without the charger being weighed down with more baggage than the Heathrow arrivals hall."

Anna's top lip quivered, her throat ached, and her eyes brimmed with tears. *She would not cry.*

"I just don't understand," Geri continued, "why you seem incapable of seeing what a brilliant position you're in."

Anna closed her eyes. "You've lost me," she said faintly. The only position she was aware of was sitting in a rickety armchair from which entire handfuls of smelly stuffing were making a bid for freedom.

"The castle, of course." Geri's voice was now hard with impatience. "Absolutely *bursting* with opportunities. Wake up and smell the coffee—not to mention the tearoom, the conference dinners, the five-star restaurant specialising in local produce—you name it. Just stop being so *bloody sensitive*. You could really make a go of this place."

"*Well, why don't you?*" sobbed Anna, reaching both the end of her tether and her ability to hold the tears back. "As you've got so many brilliant ideas for it. Personally speaking, I'm finding it less than wonderful to be stuck in a rotting pile in the middle of nowhere with a fiancé who literally doesn't give a fuck." Tearing out of the room, Anna headed for her bedroom. Her first instinct was to go straight to her diary and confide to its unconditionally sympathetic bosom every shocking detail of Geri's shameless betrayal.

Sitting on the musty quilt, she flicked back randomly through the pages, reliving the humiliation of the overheard conversation between Nanny and MacLoggie and the heart-sinking misery of Jamie confessing he was marrying her for a reason. *Get real* indeed. Was there something wrong with her that she didn't immediately feel able to pick herself up, dust herself down and channel her frustrations into a tourist boutique? Reading on, however, she suddenly felt self-conscious. She imagined Geri's mocking tones. "To paraphrase Oscar Wilde, it would take a heart of stone to read the diaries of Little Anna and not laugh."

Looking at the battered pad, its pages covered with her embarrassingly large and juvenile-looking scrawl, Anna was suddenly overpowered by a sense of futility. What was the point of writing things down in a filthy old book when no one but herself would ever see them? What had happened to the wonderful writing career—writing *real* books—that she had promised herself? Hopeless romantic, quite literally. She stared at the creased and battered old notebook with sudden loathing. It seemed less a repository for observations, dreams, and ambitions than a chronicle of abject defeat.

Grasping the now-hated notebook by its cover, Anna walked slowly out of the room, down the stairs, out of the front door, and down the pitted and scabby drive, pausing only to stuff the entire volume firmly into the dustbin that stood by the peeling and half-unhinged gate for collection. Rubbish to rubbish, she thought.

"Her nipple pinged erect under the urgent rasp of his flickering tongue. She groaned as, tracing her long, red-painted fingernails down the matted hair on his chest, her hand touched the thick, insistent swell of his tumescent and throbbing cock…"

Cassandra switched off her Dictaphone and paused. Could cocks be both throbbing *and* tumescent? She wasn't even sure she knew what tumescent meant. Was it a bit like *fluorescent?* she wondered.

Whichever way you looked at it, it certainly put the dick into Dictaphone. Which her machine wasn't really, not in the strictest sense of the word; but cassette recorders were all they had had in Ullapool, the point in the journey where Cassandra realised the floodgates of literary inspiration were opening once more. Like a glacier in the sun, her writer's block seemed to have melted. She was beginning to have ideas again.

This was a relief, explaining as it did the persistent and rather unpleasant erotic fantasies that had coloured her dreams over the two preceding nights. As it was, she certainly intended to use the scene involving the horse, the dog, and the masturbating hermaphrodites in *A Passionate Lover*, although, as she had left the protagonist in a Knightsbridge office block, it was difficult to see exactly where, so to speak, they would all fit in.

Although in no circumstances could the new flow of ideas be described as a torrent, Cassandra was nonetheless as puzzled as she was pleased by its advent. Perhaps the long hours she had spent driving the denim-seated Disco and poring, largely in vain, over maps had used up her conscious mind and freed up her id for creative activity? Maybe books conformed to similar physical principles as a watched kettle; a constantly monitored steamy novel constantly never got to the boil either. But this couldn't be right—all the driving had, after all, cut her off from the gin bottle. The fact of her precious son's being in the car with her had stopped Cassandra drinking anything stronger than the occasional Perrier or Diet Coke ever since the Scottish trip had started. Oddly enough, now she came to think of it, it had been around that time she had first been aware of the occasional plot idea struggling to get through. But that, Cassandra reasoned, must be impossible. Gin was the source from which all her inspiration had traditionally flowed. Wasn't it?

Pulsating cock, Cassandra suddenly thought. *That* was it. She whipped out her Dictaphone and, still keeping one hand on the wheel, whispered fervently into it, whilst casting a nervous glance in the driving mirror to make sure that Zak was still asleep in the back seat. She thought she saw his eyelids flicker, but no, he was sleeping like a baby, bless him. As he had been, interestingly enough, ever since she'd started working this way. She'd never known him to be so tired. It seemed all she had to do to keep him quiet was get out her Dictaphone; something in the cadences of her voice, something redolent of the womb, she assumed, lulled him to sleep. At first, she'd been afraid he was listening but he'd assured her he wasn't, and Zak was always a *very* truthful boy.

Oh *yes*, thought Cassandra as she bowled merrily past a passing place and forced yet another approaching farmer to reverse for miles to the last one. Some writers would find muttering erotic scenes into a tape recorder while driving around some island off the coast of northwest Scotland something of an eccentric way to go about one's business. But it was working very well for *her*.

Time to celebrate, Cassandra decided. Nonalcoholically, of course. But it would be nice just to be *near* some real drink, just to *look* at it. Smell it, even. The small and rather ugly little village she was driving through—Orrible, it seemed rather aptly to be called, judging from the sign she had shot past at its entrance—did not, on the face of it, have much in the way of hostelries. But Cassandra could smell booze a mile off and, if she was not very much mistaken, that building by the side of the road that looked rather like a loo was in fact a pub. Deciding to leave Zak in the car—he looked so peaceful—she closed the door of the Disco as quietly as she could and tottered across the road in her skin-tight ponyskin jeans and leopardskin high-heeled ankle boots.

Cassandra had not, from the moment she had arrived in Scotland, seen any need whatsoever to drop her standards of dress. If Scottish women's idea of style was something that didn't show the cat hairs, that was fine by her, as long as she wasn't expected to follow suit. Especially if the suit was tweed, a fabric hideously reminiscent of Mrs. Gosschalk. Cassandra was prepared to go as far as cashmere, but no further. Unless you were talking pashmina.

She pushed open the toilet-glass door. A fug of smoke and a deafening silence greeted her. Cassandra swallowed on catching sight of the occupants. She'd never seen such a collection of inbreds—at least, not since the last St. Midas's sports day.

Letting the door slam loudly behind her, Cassandra crossed the thick, dusty, and hostile space between the threshold and the bar. "A glass of mineral water, please," she commanded. From beneath brows so protruding they seemed almost to need scaffolding, the landlord shot her a suspicious look. Unbowed, Cassandra met it with a freezing stare.

"We daen't have *mineral water*," he growled. "This is a pub. Nae a *health farm*."

"*That*," Cassandra snapped back, "is obvious enough." She fixed the landlord with a gimlet eye, aware that this was a trial of sorts, a test of nerve. *High Noon*, although her current Cooper aspirations were rather more Jilly than Gary.

"No mineral water—that's *ridiculous*." Cassandra's eye did not move from mine host's. "You're missing out on a potential *gold mine*. Only last week I took my son to a restaurant where there was a mineral water *menu*. You could," Cassandra blasted, "mix two or even *three* different waters in the *same glass* to make a *cocktail*."

The landlord looked stonier than ever, but Cassandra did not flinch. Mine host indeed. *Mean* host, more like. She recognised this belligerent, macho, brazen-it-out stare. It reminded her of Jett, which, free association being what it is, also reminded her of Jett being so *bloody inconsiderate* as to hit number one at the precise time she had chosen to divorce him. The memory packed her backbone with ice and her voice with fire.

"Well, as you haven't got any *mineral water*," she hissed, "I'll have a *Diet Coke*."

Somewhere in the depths beneath the bar counter, mean host detached the tab from a can with a venomous rip.

A few minutes later, as she tottered, drink in hand, across the rickety, sawdust-and-fag-strewn wooden floor, Cassandra stopped dead. The room, which had started to murmur to itself again, immediately fell silent. The ice cubes clanked belligerently together in Cassandra's glass as she turned and hit the landlord straight between the eyes with a glare like a laser.

"This is *not* Diet Coke." She stalked back to the bar and slammed her drink down on its sticky surface. Mine host took an involuntary step back. "*This*," Cassandra snarled, brandishing the glass, her face a mask of cold fury, "is *fat* Coke. Which means"—she leant over the bar, pressing her face as close to the alarmed landlord's as she could—"that you have *knowingly* force fed me a total of *one hundred and twenty calories* I had not allowed for. *Force fed* me. *Without my say-so, permission, or go-ahead.*" She waited, then delivered the coup de grâce. "For all you know, I could be a *diabetic*," she roared at the by now quite openly cowering landlord. "*I could sue you.*"

She'd forgotten how good it felt to reduce a man to rubble. Ten minutes later, Cassandra sat, satisfied and reflective, in an inglenook by the pub's rather *odd* fire which seemed to be burning strips of lawn. A rather sorry-looking blaze, on the whole. But nowhere near, Cassandra thought triumphantly, as sorry as the landlord had looked when she'd finished with him. After the magic word "sue" had been uttered, he'd showered Cassandra with every gin bottle in the house in an attempt to placate her.

Cassandra had decided to limit herself to one sip only. Just for appearance's sake. Just to be polite. It was the least she could do. After the way she had just humiliated him, the landlord would probably have to sell up and leave, or bear the tale's constant repetition for the next thousand years or so. Probably nothing so exciting had happened since Mel Gibson had dropped by in the thirteenth century to raise his troops.

She took a sip. And then another. Was there anything *quite* like that powerful shot of juniper-infused spirit ricocheting round one's empty intestines? It was, Cassandra thought, finishing her third double in as many minutes, like the blissful reunion of lovers after many months apart. Like herself and *A Passionate Lover*, in fact. With his *pulsating, throbbing, tumescent, fluorescent cock*—no, *no*, that couldn't be right. Perhaps *pulsating* wasn't really the right word after all. If only she had a tyrannosaurus to look it up in. Funny how she couldn't seem to think anymore. Again.

Plastering on her best grin, Cassandra leant over and shook the ancient, shrunken character slumped the other side of the inglenook, a white river of saliva running steadily down into his beard. "*Shcuse* me," she boomed in a loud, shrill voice as MacLoggie lurched, terrified, back into wakefulness. Silence dropped like a stone on the rest of the bar. "Wonder if you could help me. Could you tell me… have you notished…Doesh your penis ever pulsate, throb, swell, and *tumesh* all at the shame time?"

Chapter Twenty-two

STRETCHING AWAY ON ALL sides, the wiry russet grass made the island seem like the broad back of a massive Highland cow. Anna had been walking for hours now, higher and higher, striding furiously so the pounding of the blood in her brain would be louder than the cacophony of her thoughts. She paused, panting.

Below her, the loch opened up like a giant silver oyster; beyond, the sea stretched into misty infinity, the horizon hidden by a grey stretch of storm cloud. It was, as usual, raining. Anna sat down at the summit and peered into the distance. She could see the village from here, the odd person—very odd person probably—moving about, and wondered if what Robbie had told her the previous day was true, about the island being cut off from civilisation for the first half of the century and its inhabitants having to mate with whatever came to hand. "They screwed anything. Animal, vegetable, or mineral." Anna had wondered aloud what mineral Nanny's mother had screwed. Robbie's claim that she had been a Gloucestershire Old Spot didn't quite ring true. Had he said Lincolnshire White, though, that would have been quite different.

She twisted her lips in what was half-smile, half-grimace. Geri's lack of sympathy made her feel both vulnerable and foolish, her despairing stride round the island seemed increasingly the self-aggrandising act of a drama queen. Lear, of course, had strode the blasted heath in a much more convincing manner, but he *had* lost a whole kingdom and he *did* have Shakespeare arguing his case, which obviously helped. He'd never had to cope with Geri telling him to pull himself together and concentrate on the business opportunities.

But, loath as Anna was to admit it, in some ways Geri was right. Nanny *was* an annoying old monster but she was hardly life-threatening, even if she undoubtedly represented a higher than usual risk of salmonella. Even more irritatingly, Geri was right about Jamie. He hadn't deliberately lied to her, there had just been facts he hadn't bothered to reveal. Economical with the actualité, if you liked. As well as everything else. She hadn't felt warm since she'd got here. And there had been bottles on the drinks tray whose only known exact contemporaries were in the wreck of the *Titanic*.

And it *was* pointless to blame everything on the engagement. After all, she'd been willing enough to go along with it; she, too, as Jamie had pointed out, had had her agenda. They were quits then, in a sense. And it was probably just as well she had found out that she was about to plight her troth to a pile of old stones before she did so. The love of Jamie's life was undoubtedly Dampie; last night, he had been wildly excited by Geri's increasingly drunken suggestions—about the castle, of course—especially her recommendation that he try and turn Dampie into the Glastonbury of the north and promote it as a rock venue. "Imagine," Geri had shouted up into the chilly rafters of the sitting room, which no heat had penetrated since the great summer of 1538, "you could have floating stages in the loch." Floodlight the castle in pink and purple. Have fireworks. It would be *amazing*."

And then there were Geri's other suggestions. The ones she had made to Anna over the cold egg on toast. It might be possible to stay at Dampie with Jamie and just be friends. But could she really settle for so little?

As for the taking lovers proposal, well, that really *was* foolish. Only someone, like Geri, who had been on the island a mere matter of hours, could have failed to notice the howling absence of suitable partners on Skul. The bearded poet suddenly slipped into her mind; yes, Robbie *might* have been a possibility. Witty, sensitive, poetic; she could tick all those boxes, but there was the problem of that permanent bad hair day on the end of his chin. Try as she might, Anna could never love a man with facial fungus, especially grown to that extent. It was impossible to imagine kissing him—she'd probably come out in a rash with the friction. Still, it was probably very useful for scouring pans.

Yes, thought Anna, looking over the wide, low-lit, sea-girt land around her, I should definitely stick to writing books rather than trying to live them. Somewhere along the line she had, quite literally, lost the plot. Whatever spanners Fate had thrown in her works in the past, at least she had always had her writing. It had comforted her through Seb, encouraged her through Cassandra. But since becoming engaged to Jamie, it had disappeared altogether. She thought ruefully of the diary buried in the rubbish bin.

Once she was writing again—and this time she planned actually to finish the wretched thing—everything else would fall into place, even if she had doubts that that place was Dampie. But that all lay in the future. Time now to get herself back on track. She would write, she needed to write; all she required was a little prod in the right direction. A little encouragement. She looked at her watch. She'd been here *hours*. But if she hurried, she could get to the village hall in time for Robbie MacAskill's afternoon class.

"*Fuck me. Fuck me.* I want you to come inside me, big boy. Fuck me *hard*."

Anna, about to push open the door of the village hall, drew back in embarrassed astonishment. The voice was a woman's. Soft, Scots, and urgent with lust.

"That's *fantastic*, Mrs. McLeod. Don't stop." *Robbie.* Anna's stomach plunged with disappointment. For some reason, possibly the beard, it had never occurred to her that there might be a woman in Robbie's life. Yet here he was with Mrs. McLeod, going at it like a steam train. A steam iron even. It might only be—Anna glanced at her wrist—a quarter to two, but presumably on Skul one had to get ones kicks where and when one could.

"I'm *wet*," the voice continued. Anna felt white-hot knives of jealousy plunging into her stomach. There was, she realised, nothing like competition to make you realise you liked someone. And *what* competition. "Just *feel* how wet I am," Mrs. McLeod panted. "I'm a *river* down here. Taste it, here, lick it off me. *Oh, fuck* me. *Harder.* I want you to come *like a fire hose.*"

Well, it certainly gave a whole new meaning to ironing board cover, thought Anna. What on earth did Mrs. McLeod look like, she wondered—a wild-haired Hebridean Carmen, no doubt, full-breasted, with a lusty glint in her eye. I should go, Anna thought as the Hebridean Carmen began once again to speak.

"Panting, running her tongue round her wet lips, and staring at him through hazel eyes glazed with lust, she ripped off her shirt. Her breasts sprang out like dogs let out for a walk—"

"Hang on a minute, Mrs. McLeod. I'm not sure that's working. The image of dogs being let out for a walk is *slightly* at odds with the rest of the passage. And I'm not too wild about that fire hose either."

"Are ye not, Mr. MacAskill?"

"No, well, the whole point of this exercise is to read aloud to see what works and what doesn't," said Robbie, completely matter-of-factly. "The problem with very erotic passages often is that they can sound slightly, well, *excessive*. The trick is to err on the side of believability. Otherwise you end up being awarded things like the *Literary Review* Bad Sex Award, which I don't think you'd appreciate, Mrs. McLeod. Not least because you'd have to go to London to receive it, and you know what you think of England."

"Particularly when you lie back," Anna murmured as, grinning in relief, she pushed the door wide open.

"Sorry I'm late," she said, "but better to come late than never to come at all. As I'm sure Mrs. McLeod would agree—" she stopped short in amazement. "*You've shaved your beard off.*"

He looked so much *better*, she thought admiringly. Years *younger*. The excavations revealed a firm jaw and a wide, full-lipped, sensual mouth in the context of which the tombstone teeth looked considerably less fearsome. Rather than a handsome face, Robbie's was a strong and a rather heroic one. The sort that remained set in the midst of the most violent hail or blizzard. The sort you could imagine rocks bouncing off.

Robbie clamped a hand to his naked chin and grinned sheepishly. "Yes. Thought it was getting a wee bit out of control. Any longer and I'd have needed a chainsaw to do it. Used up the village shop's entire stock of Gillettes as it was. No one's going to be able to shave their legs for a week until the new delivery comes over from Inverness. Sorry about that, Mrs. McLeod. Oh, have you met Mrs. McLeod, *Anna*…"

Hearing his low, warm voice pronounce her name was unexpectedly delicious. Suddenly aware she was gawping at Robbie like an idiot, Anna turned to shake hands. Mrs. McLeod was not the expected hair-tossing femme fatale, thrusting of breast, flashing of eye, and bent on removing local underwear for purposes entirely other than ironing, but a small, neatly-dressed woman, the only flashing thing about whom were small mauve-rimmed glasses. The only hint of Carmen about her was her hot-rollered, home-permed hair; to Anna's amazement, she looked well over sixty. Her prose, it would seem, was just as blue as her rinse. And, far from being an avid leg-shaver, her lower calves were covered with thick stockings.

In short, Mrs. McLeod looked as if she thought a leg wax was something one did to the nether regions of a dining table. She was also blushing violently.

"We're just going through Mrs. McLeod's new chapter," Robbie explained.

"So I heard. I thought it was wonderful," Anna said sincerely. "*Very* sexy."

Mrs. McLeod looked traumatised. Anna stared at her carefully. What on earth could this timid creature know about breasts bursting forth like dogs let out for a run and ejaculations like fire extinguishers? Certainly it made one keenly curious about *Mr.* McLeod.

"No, but I mean it," Anna assured her, as Mrs. McLeod shook her head. "You should be proud of it. I thought it was terribly good. And for what it's worth, I *adored* the bit about the fire hose." Anna had forgotten how one could discuss the most extraordinarily intimate things under the flag of literature. Her university days had included a number of racy tutorial sessions, including a particularly graphic one on the Metaphysical poets which had certainly put the semen in seminar. She would not have imagined that could be so spectacularly eclipsed by a discussion of firefighting equipment in a church hall on a Scottish island.

"Mrs. McLeod is very shy about her work," Robbie said, somewhat unnecessarily. "But she shows enormous promise."

Anna was touched and impressed by Robbie's determination to encourage what was possibly his only student. No wonder, with attendance like this, he had been so keen that she should come. But was that, it suddenly, miserably occurred to her, the *only* reason?

"As now, being three, we constitute a crowd," Robbie declared, gesturing Anna to one of the hard wooden chairs scattered around the bare and rather cheerless hall, "I'm going to give a reading from another work. I thought it would be valuable for Mrs. McLeod to hear how another author has handled sex."

Anna swallowed. Her lower bowels seemed to be in a constant state of excitement; either Nanny's champit tatties had had a deleterious effect or, suddenly, she fancied Robbie like mad.

She watched him as he rummaged in his battered leather briefcase and produced a bundle of paper, watched him clear his strong throat and run his deliciously clean-looking pink tongue over thick, dry lips before proceeding. She liked the way his mouth curled upwards when he spoke, as if he was constantly amused. Most of all, in profound contrast to Seb for example, she liked the way he didn't seem to take the whole subject of sex too seriously. The main amusement Seb seemed to have got out of it, Anna recalled, was laughing at *her*.

As Robbie began to read, Anna wrinkled her brow. The words sounded oddly familiar. As his voice rumbled, soft and low, never stumbling on or mispronouncing a single word, horror began to seep through her. *They were her words.* Robbie was reading *from her diary.* Uncertain what to do, blushing furiously, she gazed at the surface of the table at which she sat with Mrs. McLeod. *How the hell had he got hold of it? And did he know she had written it?*

She sat in stupefied silence and listened, unsure of what else to do. Unsure of what, exactly, the etiquette was when hearing ones most intimate and private thoughts read out in public. It was a miserable experience, not least because Robbie had picked a passage dating from a particularly unhappy period of her relationship with Seb, in which Anna had reflected on her own sexual inadequacy. She had, she remembered, originally written it in a self-deprecating way, trying it out as a possible passage for future use. Listening to it now she was struck only by the pain in the words, the sadness, and the sense of humiliation and betrayal beneath the thin surface of wry humour.

As a contrast to Mrs. McLeod's fire extinguisher, it could not have been more profound and, as she listened, Anna felt a black tide of remembered misery welling up inside. Seb had been *such* a brute;

listening to this rawly autobiographical account of their worst time together, Anna doubted whether her self-esteem would ever recover. No wonder, having gone through this, she had submitted meekly to Cassandra's excesses and leapt for Jamie as a drowning man might seize a lifebelt.

"*Brute*," gasped Mrs. McLeod, blowing her nose loudly as Robbie finished reading.

"That," he announced, "is the work of an extremely talented writer who understands completely that comedy and tragedy are often almost the same thing." Anna was amazed to see that Robbie's eyes, too, were shining slightly brighter than before.

"Who wrote it?" squeaked Mrs. McLeod timidly, dabbing at her eyes with an embroidered handkerchief.

There was a silence. Anna, puce with embarrassment, looked stonily downwards as Robbie darted a glance at her. Was he waiting for her to admit it? She hesitated.

Then came the interruption.

"I shay," demanded a loud, unsteady, shrilly patrician voice at the back of the hall, "ish thish Mishter Robbie MacAshkill's creative writing clash? I was told I'd find him here."

Robbie, his eyes fixed on whatever apparition had presented itself in the doorway, nodded in astonishment. Anna froze to the spot. *Those horribly familiar tones. It could not be. Surely.*

It was. "Eckshellent," pronounced Cassandra, eyes rolling, and swaying wildly as she advanced through the hall.

Anna leapt to her feet. The chair crashed to the floor behind her. "*Cassandra*. What on earth are you doing here?"

Cassandra clomped up, gyrated wildly to keep her balance, buckled suddenly on her leopardskin heels, and collapsed on the floor.

"I want to talk to someone about penishes."

Chapter Twenty-three

"FRIEND OF YOURS?"

As Cassandra lay crumpled and comatose at their feet, Robbie raised an ironic eyebrow at Anna.

"Not exactly. I was rather hoping I'd never see her again."

"Well, you probably won't from the look of her. I'd better call an ambulance."

"Och, there's no need to do that," piped up Mrs. McLeod. Anna and Robbie watched in astonishment as, with surprising strength, she dragged Cassandra's prone body across the dusty floorboards and deftly manipulated it into an upright position against one of the radiators. Propping the lolling head up straight, she began to slap Cassandra's cheeks. "Mr. McLeod comes home from the pub like this all the time."

Anna grinned to herself. This, at any rate, completely scuppered the theory that Mrs. McLeod's sexual fantasies were autobiographical. Or at least, that they were inspired by her husband.

Through gritted teeth, Anna offered to put Cassandra up at the castle. If nothing else, it would annoy Nanny. It was decided, however, that the rough roads up to Dampie might well finish Cassandra off altogether, and in the first instance she should go to Mrs. McLeod's cottage, conveniently just round the corner from the village hall. Once the long, slow process of moving Cassandra was completed, Robbie was dispatched to track down Zak. Cassandra, slipping in and out of lucidity thanks to Mrs. McLeod's face-slapping, had rather mysteriously revealed him to be in a Disco somewhere in the area.

"But there isn't a disco anywhere on the island," Robbie said, puzzled.

As they left Mrs. McLeod's cottage—a pin-neat, shining haven of order that could not have been less suggestive of her blatantly erotic prose style—Robbie brushed against Anna. She shuddered at the charge of desire that suddenly swept through her whilst trying to tell herself that the contact might have been accidental. The cottage was, after all, so tiny that only dwarf anorexics could have negotiated each other without colliding.

Listening to Mrs. McLeod sluicing down Cassandra in the bathroom, murmuring sympathetically as she did so, Anna tried to make sense of the afternoon's events. Neither Cassandra's sudden appearance, nor the means by which Robbie had got hold of her diary seemed to have any explanation whatsoever.

"I eventually tracked him down at the police station," Robbie reported, returning half an hour later dragging a thunderous-looking Zak who, once inside the cottage, immediately started to pick up and look at Mrs. McLeod's large, immaculately dusted collection of ornaments.

Anna tried, like a victim at a human rights trial, not to flinch at the sight of her former torturer. For Zak looked more evil than ever. His prep-school-perfect basin cut looked straggly and wild, its former white-blondness noticeably darker. It occurred to Anna to wonder whether Zak's platinum locks were in fact no more natural than his mother's; could Cassandra have really had her son's hair coloured to match her own? Could she really be so vain? Was the Pope Catholic?

"What was Zak doing?" she asked.

"Sitting in a cell. He'd tried to drive the car—called a Disco, by the way, so that explains that—but ended up smashing it into the postbox. Car's a write-off."

"The postbox? So at least he hadn't got very far then. The postbox next to the village hall, you mean?"

"No, the one on the other side of the island." Robbie passed a rueful palm through his hair. "The police were alerted after someone coming out of the pub saw a small boy driving a car at a speed in excess of one hundred miles per hour through the village. They would have got him sooner, only the person coming out of the pub was MacLoggie and, given his condition, his evidence was considered unsafe."

"I see."

"When they caught up with Zak, he was apparently sitting in the front seat listening to a woman talking dirty on a cassette recorder. Turned up full blast."

"Ugh." Anna tried not to remember the knicker-sniffing incident on her second day at Liv.

"How did you get him out of the police station?"

"They didn't seem too sad to see the back of him. They'll want a word with Cassandra when she comes round. Fortunately—for him at least—Zak's too young to have a criminal record."

"A record?" Zak's voice was scornful. "As if I'd want one anyway. No one has vinyl these days."

"Shut up," Robbie snapped at him. There was a smash as one of Mrs. McLeod's china shepherdesses collided with the tiles of the fireplace.

"*I* want to be a policeman," Zak announced defiantly, making no move to pick up the pieces. "*I* want to put people in prison."

Driving back to the castle in Robbie's rattling old Land Rover, Anna tried to stop her thighs shooting across the metal seat and cannoning into Robbie's every time they rounded a corner, which was often, sudden, and hair-raising. Either Robbie was a very bad driver, Anna thought, as her legs slammed into his rock-hard thighs, or…

"Hope Mrs. McLeod can cope with both Cassandra and Zak," she remarked, looking out of the Land Rover's broken window across the camouflage-coloured landscape. "But she did insist she'd have them until Cassandra gets…um…better."

"Mrs. M's a tough old bird," Robbie said. "We'll pick them both up tomorrow in any case. She probably wants them for material. Maybe her next chapter has a child in it."

"Talking of material"—Anna turned her head away to disguise the deepening vermilion of her face and unenthusiastically regarded the sodden, rendered walls of Dampie Castle as they jerked into view across the windscreen—"How *did* you get hold of my diary?"

"Oh, so you're admitting it was yours?" Robbie threw her an amused glance as the Land Rover plunged up the Dampie drive. "I wasn't sure if you wanted to. As it happens, I found it in the castle dustbin only this morning."

"*Dustbin?*" She remembered putting it there, of course, but what was *Robbie* doing rummaging in the castle refuse? Poetry paid badly, she was sure, but all the same…

"Yes. One of my jobs is to collect the local rubbish. You don't think I make a living being a poet, do you? Or through my creative writing classes, although I must admit that if I were a literary agent I'd probably be retiring on Mrs. McLeod."

"Are you *really* a poet?" Suddenly, the idea of a dustman who gave creative writing classes and was a poet into the bargain struck Anna as rather strange.

There was a silence. Robbie looked at her with a set face, then looked hastily back at the windscreen as the Land Rover lurched over another pothole. Then, to her relief, he laughed.

"No, of course I'm not a poet," he confessed easily. "As a matter of fact, I'm a novelist. Trying to be, at any rate. I'm writing a comic murder mystery set on a Scottish island."

"Oh." Was anything on Skul, Anna wondered, what it seemed?

"I'm here researching my characters, and being a poet was the only thing I could think of that wouldn't attract too much suspicion. Islands like this are packed with hawk-eyed old bards with beards. I managed the beard, as you saw, only I never felt it was quite me."

"It wasn't. It was a personality in its own right." Anna furrowed her brow. "But I don't understand why you felt you had to give creative writing classes."

"They were supposed to help convince people I was a poet. I never expected people to actually *come* to them. When, one night, the village hall door opened and Mrs. McLeod trotted in, I almost fell over with shock. When I heard what she'd brought with her, I almost died of it. Having said that, I think she'll have a great future as an erotic novelist once she's got a bit more, er, *front*." As his glance flickered, *possibly* involuntarily, towards her breasts, Anna's stomach lurched, in perfect synchrony with the Land Rover, in excitement.

There was a silence, punctuated only by the grinding of the Land Rover's engine.

"Yes. My character research has been rather more, er, *interesting* than I imagined." Their eyes met, briefly, before Robbie's swung suddenly back to the windscreen just in time to stop them smashing into a tree.

"Especially if you go through their rubbish," said Anna. "I suppose that was part of your research as well."

"Oh yes. There's a pivotal scene in my book where the maverick detective—"

"Unhappily divorced?"

"Yes, and with a drink problem of course."

"Of course. Smokes too much? Loves classical music?"

"Absolutely. Anyway, in this pivotal scene he's going through the dustbins in search of the murder weapon, so of course I had to know what the average islander puts out for the rubbish. You wouldn't believe some of the things I found."

"Like my diary."

"Yes. I hope you didn't mind me looking at it, but once I'd started reading it, I couldn't stop. It was so well written…"

Anna blushed again. It occurred to her that, although she knew next to nothing about Robbie, he was now familiar with her entire recent history. The humiliation of life with Seb, the near slavery of life with Cassandra, the boredom and disappointment of life with Jamie, he knew it all. Leaning very close to her, close enough for her to smell his aftershave and the faint mint of his breath, Robbie said softly, "You're not very lucky in love, are you?"

Anna shook her head. Until now, she thought, crossing her fingers behind her back. She was just closing her eyes and parting her lips when, with impeccable timing, Robbie's mobile rang. *Damn.*

After several minutes' terse conversation, Robbie snapped the mobile away. "That was Mrs. McLeod. She wants me to come and get Zak at once. Apparently he's sprayed the fire extinguisher all over her wooden floor. Mr. McLeod's just come in from the pub and gone flying."

Cassandra hadn't felt so dreadful in *years*. Someone, somewhere was plunging red-hot needles into her brain. When, oh when would she remember *cheap* alcohol disagreed with her? One never felt like *this* on Bombay Sapphire. Possibly because one could only afford *one* bottle of that at a time.

She narrowed her eyes as she took in her surroundings. Where the *hell* was she? Some poky, ghastly little bedroom, by the looks of it. Was it a nightmare? *Must* be. But only in the very *worst* of nightmares, thought Cassandra, cringing with disgust as her toenails scraped against the fabric, did people have *aquamarine nylon sheets* on their beds. *Or* wear baby pink bed jackets *with ribbons*, she thought, tearing frantically at her throat. Exhausted with the effort, she lay back and tried to make sense of the fuzzy images of herself rolling past the back of her eyes.

Dancing on the tables in some appalling pub—now *that* bit was obviously a nightmare. So difficult to work out what had really happened and what hadn't, but such, Cassandra thought, was the burden of the creative imagination. Some muscular man folding her tenderly into his arms—nothing remotely surprising about *that*. She could have sworn that somewhere along the line, that wretched ex-nanny of hers Anna, had been in the room as well—that *must* have been a nightmare too, even though she fully intended to drop in on her for at least a week's stay. A hideous thought suddenly struck Cassandra—perhaps this poky, chilly, ugly little room actually *was* in the castle. If so, she'd request a transfer to the master bedroom without delay.

What time was it? Cassandra raised herself on one elbow and peered at the bedside table, where she was gratified to see a number of her own paperbacks piled up. She was less delighted when her vision focused enough to reveal the plastic jackets and typewritten numbered labels of the public library—although this one said mobile library. Cassandra had not previously been aware one *could* borrow mobiles from a library. So that was what she'd been paying her bloody taxes for all these years. *Ridiculous.*

And what was *this*? Cassandra reached out and grabbed a handful of paper by the bed. Typewritten. Story by the looks of it. Someone had left it, perhaps by mistake. Anna, no doubt; she was so obsessed with writing she probably carried manuscripts round in her knickers. Well, Cassandra thought viciously, there'd certainly be plenty of room.

She may as well give it the once over; if nothing else it would send her back to sleep. Yawning, Cassandra pressed the papers close to her nose and began to read.

Five minutes later, she was sitting bolt upright, her hangover forgotten. This stuff was *sensational*. As she read on, Cassandra felt awe seeping slowly through her; either that, or she'd wet herself with excitement. She hated to admit it—in fact, she never had before—but there could be no doubt whatsoever that she was in the presence of a great writing talent. Someone who could knock herself, Jilly, Danielle, and even dear departed Dame Catherine into a cocked beach bag.

Damn. Damn. Damn. Cassandra rolled her bloodshot eyes hard at the ceiling. *What* an opportunity missed. How *could* she have been so *stupid*, so pig-headed as to have had the girl in the house with her and have *no idea* she was capable of this? When a soft Scottish voice suddenly enquired whether she was all right, Cassandra leapt a foot into the air and looked furiuosly at the small, timid-looking woman who had appeared at the foot of her bed. Doubtless one of the castle servants. "Do you always creep up on people when they're reading?" she snapped at Mrs. McLeod, looking in disgust at the rollers and tartan apron she was sporting. Really, Anna needed to take a firmer hand with the appearance of her domestic staff.

"I'm very sorry, Mrs. Knight. I didn't mean to wake ye up. But ye were so *quiet*…" Mrs. McLeod touched her rollers in panic. She'd just wanted to titivate her hair; one didn't, after all, get a great author staying every day of the week. Not that she had intended the great author to see her in her rollers; given Cassandra's condition when she and Anna had stuffed her between the sheets, Mrs. McLeod had not expected the great author to see anything for several days, in fact. "I just wanted to leave ye a couple of notes. Your son has been taken up to the castle and you're invited to stay there when you feel well enough to go. I'm very sorry to disturb ye…"

"Quite all right, quite all right," snapped Cassandra, relieved that this hideous little room wasn't the castle after all. The woman, however, was irritating—not only one of the servant classes, but a fan of hers as well. These grovelling old crones could be so *tiresome*. She knew the type—hideous old crumblies who crowded to her periodic bookshop appearances by the ambulance load and gathered dribbling and twitching round her table while she signed "To Edna" as quickly as she could before the reek of mothballs and Parma violets overwhelmed her. *Ghastly*.

Cassandra waved the paper in her hand impatiently. "Was quite enjoying this, actually. Rather well written. *Quite* impressed."

"Oh, Mrs. Knight, do you really mean it? I'm such an enormous fan of your work."

"Do I mean it?" Cassandra gazed dramatically up in the air. "Well, yes, actually, I do," she pronounced, patronisingly. "Must say, wish I'd known this was the sort of thing on offer. Could have written half of my books for me, ha ha." Anna bloody *could* have done too, with all the spare time she'd had on her hands, seethed Cassandra silently. Could have knocked off entire sagas between school runs. *Damn*. All that time she'd been suffering from writer's block herself and there'd been the literary equivalent of Dynarod just up on the next landing.

"Mrs. Knight…"

Really, the old girl was getting very excited. Gone quite red in the face.

"Yes, Anna certainly kept her light under a bushel." Really, it was *infuriating*. What a team they could have been. I, Cassandra thought wistfully, could have supplied the name and the reputation. All Anna would have had to do was bash out the books.

"Anna didna write it."

"Yes, well, I must say I found it hard to believe myself—plump, plain sort like that knowing about sex and all that. Still, the ugly ones are supposed to go like the clappers aren't they—so *grateful*. That's been my downfall really, being born beautiful means you don't *have* to try and so you don't tend to bother. Not that you'd know much about *that* of course, Mrs., er, um, but—"

"McLeod. *I* wrote it…"

"*As I was saying*, there are positions in here I wouldn't have dreamt possible—and the *language*. Very, very racy. If this doesn't get the gussets of Gloucestershire moistening, nothing will. And it's those gussets"—Cassandra raised herself on both elbows and looked aghast into Mrs. McLeod's blazing eyes—"that I need to reach. *What did you say?*"

"I wrote it."

"You wrote it? *You?*"

"Yes."

"*Fuck me.*" Cassandra fell back on her pillows, gasped, and stared at the ceiling. The answer to her prayers had just walked through the door in rollers and a tartan apron. "Mrs. McLeod, please sit down. Does the term *ghostwriting* mean anything to you?"

"Christ. *What* a day." At approximately the same time Mrs. McLeod drew a chair up to Cassandra's bedside, Anna pushed open the door of the castle dining room. "Oh, *Geri*. Wonderful. You're still here then. Thought you'd have given up on me and be halfway back to London by now." Was she imagining things, or did Jamie and Geri spring apart almost guiltily as she entered? Their heads seemed to have been practically *touching* as they pored over the maps spread across every possible surface of the room. Jamie seemed to be midway through a drain tutorial. But even *that* didn't explain, Anna thought, why they both looked so flushed.

"I'll get you some coffee," said Jamie, hastily beating a retreat.

Geri gave her an apologetic smile. "Sorry I was so vile to you this morning. I had the mother of all hangovers and I'm afraid you rather got it in the neck. Whatever I said, I didn't mean it. I take it all back."

"Oh, there's no need." Anna swallowed. "Quite useful, actually, some of it. What are you doing with all these maps?"

"Thought I'd try and give Jamie a hand. You know how I love to organise things."

"And *has* she *organised* things," Jamie exclaimed, returning with a coffee cup trembling violently in his hand, his wide-apart eyes shining. "She's been on the phone all morning ringing up rock stars to try and get them interested in coming to play up here. She talked to Robbie Williams for *ages*."

"Really? I didn't know you knew Robbie Williams." But much more amazing than that, Anna considered, was that Jamie knew who he was.

"Oh yes," said Geri casually. "He's one of Savannah and Siena's—"

"*Godfathers*," finished Anna. "Don't tell me."

"Yes, but he wasn't at the party because he was on tour. And sadly, he's on another one at the moment so won't be able to come and play Dampie for ages. But he's definitely interested."

"Meanwhile," Jamie was barely able to control his excitement, "we've had a breakthrough. Tell her, Geri."

"Oh yes, well, as Jamie said, I've been phoning round, and one of the people I called was Solstice. You remember—Jett St. Edmunds…"

Anna rolled her eyes. "Unfortunately I do, yes." Would the memory of him prancing around in a thong, she wondered, ever fade?

"Solstice are really huge now," Geri informed her, eyes wide with enthusiasm.

"They *are*?" Certain aspects, Anna thought, were pretty huge then.

"Yes. Amazing, I know, but they've become a massive ironic student hit."

Anna said nothing. A sense of impending doom seeped through her veins.

"They're really famous now," Geri pressed. "They've revived heavy metal single-handedly. They're on every chat show going. You can't open a paper without reading about them—and Champagne D'Vyne, of course."

"Champagne D'Vyne?" She'd been the blonde, tanned girl with the hot pink heels from the Tressell children's party, hadn't she?

"Jett St. Edmunds's new girlfriend. Dumped her last fiancé—one of the Manchester United squad she'd been engaged to for about forty-eight hours—to get in on the act with Jett. Self-publicist like her couldn't let an opportunity like *him* go to waste. He's massive, you know."

"So he used to keep telling me."

"Yes, well, it's great you know him, because he's coming to stay."

"*What?*"

Geri and Jamie nodded eagerly. "Most amazing coincidence," Jamie gabbled. "Geri called him on his mobile and it turned out that he's just come to the end of an extensive tour of British universities—"

"His Wold Tour, as he calls it," Geri interrupted. "It was a sell-out."

"And he's just, er, been playing at the, um, University of Achiltibuie, just over on the mainland. Better still," Jamie stuttered, "he's doing a live, um, album of all his concerts—"

"Which his record company want released as soon as possible." Geri regained the narrative while Jamie looked at her in open admiration. "But he now needs to shoot a cover and mix the tapes of all his live gigs. He's had a lot of trouble finding the right place to do it. So I told him all about the special acoustic effects of the dungeons here, and also that the castle not only looks stunning but also sits at the junction of every known ley line and is filled with cosmic forces."

"And is it?" Yet another fascinating fact about Dampie that's passed me by, thought Anna.

"May well be, for all I know," grinned Geri. "Anyway, Jett was thrilled and said he'd be right over with the boys."

"The boys?"

"The engineers," said Geri. "The rest of the band have gone back to London."

"But there's the girl," added Jamie.

"Oh yes, the girl." Geri smiled at him conspiratorially.

"*What* girl? *Not...?*"

"Champagne D'Vyne. Sure. They'll be here"—Geri looked at her watch—"within the hour."

"Perfect timing. Considering Jett St. Edmunds's soon-to-be-ex-wife is at this moment throwing up in a bathroom very close to us," Anna remarked grimly.

It was Geri's turn to look amazed. "Oh Christ, *yes*," she said, slapping her forehead loudly with the palm of her hand. "Meant to tell you. I met her on the sleeper. Completely went out of my head."

Anna looked at her searchingly. So *that* explained Cassandra's sudden advent. "Shame my address didn't then."

Geri had the grace to blush.

"Well, she'll be arriving here soon as well. We should," said Anna, "be in for an interesting evening."

Chapter Twenty-four

JETT ST. EDMUNDS WAS delighted. His two engineers, Bill "Newcastle" Brown and Tommy "Vindaloo" Jones, had finally finished setting up the mixing equipment in the dungeons and disappeared to the pub. At last, he was able to put his secret cover concept into action. Devising a way to get the rest of Solstice back to London so he could be photographed gloriously solo had used up practically every megabyte in his brain for the past few days.

Geri's sudden offer of a castle had seemed the answer to his prayers. Her assurance that Dampie was a fusion between Abbey Road Studios and Balmoral had failed rather spectacularly to deliver the former, but had not disappointed with the latter. The castle fitted the photographic bill—which Jett would do his best to get out of paying—superbly. Even as he lurched up the drive, Jett was planning how magnificent he would look against the battlements, aquiline profile silhouetted before a savagely beautiful sunset, hair lifted in the wind like storm-tossed waves, cloak thrashing as if possessed by the devil. Jett was very proud of his cloak, a sequinned, hooded affair in midnight blue bought in a rock auction in the belief that it had belonged to Steven Tyler; a belief Jett persisted in despite his subsequent discovery of the legend "Walberswick Amateur Dramatic Society" embroidered on the inside of the collar. He had not previously realised that Steven Tyler was a member.

All that remained to be sourced for the cover shoot were the pair of devil horns he intended to have protruding from his storm-tossed tresses. Plus, of course, some blood to drip from his hands and run in gory rivulets across his cheekbones. It had not been easy to brief the photographer on a dodgy mobile from the back of the tour bus, but he'd finally got the message, despite sounding doubtful about where to get the blood and the horns. Typical bloody photographers, thought Jett. Everything was too much goddamn trouble for them. Anyone with a camera thought they were goddamn Mario Testino these days.

He'd never been in favour of Seven des Roches, Solstice tour photographer and self-billed rock 'n' roll snapper extraordinaire; after all, what had been so wrong with Annie Leibovitz? But the record company's budget had ruled practically anything else out apart from an art student with an Instamatic. Which was more or less what Seven seemed to be. Still, Jett was confident of success. His visual concept was so strong it was practically foolproof. The whole idea of the title was rock and roll perfection; an idyllic fusion of the theatrical with the threatening, the light with the dark, the poetic with the diabolic; and the whole subtle, witty, and slightly mysterious. *Spawn of Satan*. It had a ring to it. Ten at least. He admired the array of gold skulls, snakes, and wolves' heads ranged along his fingers like knuckledusters; unable to pick just one for the shoot, he had worn the lot.

Call him a sentimental old fool, but something about the fistful of metalware reminded him of his wife. As he left the studio to make the rendezvous with the photographer, cloak swishing and swirling about him, Jett wondered how Cassandra was getting along. He hadn't heard from her for ages, not since the night Solstice had been playing the Enormodome in Portree and his mobile had gone off mid-set. Dragging it out of the bulge in his pants before a crowd of at least fifty had been bad enough; far worse had been Cassandra screaming at him about school fees and accusing him of being homeopathically disturbed. He had put the phone away conscious that he almost missed her.

"Mr. St. Edmunds? Over here." Having just managed to find his way out of that spooky goddamn castle and into the yard, Jett almost leapt out of his cloak at the unexpected voice. He whirled round to see Seven des Roches sticking his head out of what looked like an ancient, stone-built shed set slightly apart from the main castle building. Jett felt relieved; after three laps of the ground floor, including a terrifying encounter with a huge bruiser of a woman with a face like a road accident, even a seasoned performer like himself was beginning to feel a little self-conscious mincing round in a sequinned cloak.

Not least because it was so goddamn dark—he could barely see a thing through his sunglasses. As he approached the photographer, relief turned to surprise and then to terror. Seven's hands were dripping blood and there was a maniacal grin on his face.

"Gore galore," enthused Seven. "And guess what? I've found some horns as well."

Jett followed him into the building. The interior was gloomy, a sink at the murkiest end of it piled high with glistening organs. Some kind of big, hairy animal was hanging on the wall; beneath it, on the floor, was a bucket of what looked horribly like blood. Jett felt the gorge rise in his throat. "Fucking hell," he exploded. "What is this? Sweeney Todd's goddamn fucking sitting room?"

"It's a deer larder," said Seven, who had once had a girlfriend whose father owned a shooting estate. Although the relationship hadn't lasted more than a week, its enduring legacy was his name losing its T in a bid to sound more glamorous than the Steven he had been born, even if everyone assumed it was either a misspelling of Sven or he was a big Brad Pitt fan. His original surname, Stone, had gone through the same glitzification process with slightly more success.

"And look at this incredible stag." Seven directed Jett's gaze to the hairy animal on the wall. The vast, gutted deer carcass dangled rather abjectly against the roughly whitewashed stone. Jett stared with awe at the gaping cavern inside the massive beast.

"Horns on tap," grinned Seven. "We just pull them off and stick them on your head with a few strips of gaffer." Jett grimaced. The thought of pulling off the antlers made him retch. He could imagine the fur tearing, the sickening rip of muscle off bone. *Ugh.* "Or just hack the whole thing off," Seven continued cheerfully. "I've got a machete in my bag from when I was shooting the Nolan Sisters' comeback tour of Uganda."

"No fucking goddamn *way.*"

It took the photographer a further five tense minutes to hit on the inspired idea of Jett actually getting *inside* the deer carcass and standing facing front so its shoulders rested on his, its legs dangled down his back, and its head balanced atop his own, antlers soaring outwards. "Fantastic. Very His Satanic Majesty," Seven pronounced admiringly as Jett stood trying not to notice the still-wet insides of the animal and hoping it was water that was seeping into his clothes. At least the cloak was safe—Seven had thrown it over the back of the deer. "Looks awesome, I tell you. *Fantastic. Great.* Now just hang on while I pop on a bit of blood." Seven dipped a rag in the bucket and slapped it, dripping, across Jett's face.

"Hey, watch my goddamn sunglasses."

"*Fabulous.* You look *gorgeous.*" Seven prided himself on his professional patter. "Now we're almost ready to roll. Just come outside, that's right, take my hand and don't try looking from left to right—it'll all fall off. Thought we'd just shoot you with the castle in the background. *Awesome.*"

"Make sure you get my goddamn good side," Jett mumbled, feeling oddly helpless and vulnerable as he slowly emerged, clutching Seven, blinking, and covered in blood, into the daylight. He could only stare straight ahead. One unscheduled jerk of the head and the whole precariously balanced construction would collapse.

"Sure, sure." Seven rustled in the bag beside him, producing a plate and arranging something Jett could not quite see on it. "Now here. Just take these prawns. That's right."

"Prawns?" Jett was pleasantly surprised. "Great. Could do with a snack. Got any mayo?"

"Ha *ha*. Now *just* hold them in both hands and look satanic." He picked up his camera, thrust forward his hips, then swayed them from side to side in a grinding motion. "*Great*. Let's go. Wow. Fantastic. *Awesome*. Now we're really cooking with gas."

Jett stared at him from under the antlers and behind the ever-present sunglasses. "This is for the Polaroid, right? You're checking the position of the goddamn dripping dagger or whatever it is I'm really going to be holding."

"*Great*. You look *well* scary now." Although his pelvis was as eloquent as ever, Seven's face was now invisible behind his lens. "No, this is for the shoot."

"*Whoa*. Hold on just one *minute*." Jett tried to hold up a hand, but the deer carcass swaying on his shoulders prevented him. "Remind me again," he said in a dangerously level voice, "where the prawns come in?"

Seven lowered the lens. His hips stopped jerking. "You're joking, aren't you? They're the title, aren't they? *Prawn of Satan*."

Behind his mirror shades, Jett's eyes bulged with fury. "*Prawn of Satan?*" he gasped eventually. "*Prawn?*" he spluttered. "If anyone's a fucking goddamn prawn it's *you*. Of *course* it's not called fucking goddamn *Prawn* of fucking goddamn *Satan*." The deer carcass lurched and began to list dangerously to the left. Seven hastily put his camera down, rushed forward, and pushed it back on again.

"Well, it was very hard to hear what you were saying on the mobile," he said testily. "It sounded *exactly* like prawn to me. Thought you must be doing a tie-in with Iceland. You know, free kilo of crevettes with every CD. Lots of people do that sort of thing now, you know. Anyway, *anyway…*" he added hastily, catching Jett's murderous glare, "being a professional, I have a contingency plan. There is an alternative."

"So I should fucking goddamn *hope*," exploded Jett as Seven scuttled back inside the deer larder to emerge, a few seconds later, with a long, thin orange plastic device. A length of twine dangled out of the front of it. Jett glanced contemptuously in its direction before swivelling his incandescent, reflector-lensed glare back to the hapless photographer. "And what the goddamn fucking *fuck* is *this?*"

"A strimmer," said Seven.

"May I," asked Jett in even more dangerously level tones than before, "ask *why?*"

"Well," gibbered Seven, "I thought what you'd actually said might have been *Lawn of Satan.* As I believe I mentioned," he blathered helplessly on, "it wasn't easy to understand you on the mobile. I thought I could have you standing on some grass smeared in blood with your horns on, strimming with an evil expression…" His voice trailed away at the sight of Jett's face. Never had Seven seen an expression more evil. The trouble was, he knew if he snapped it, he'd never live to tell the tale. Let alone develop the film.

Jett's anger dropped several hundred degrees below freezing hatred. He took a few steps closer to Seven so the dead stag's nose pressed almost into the photographer's face. "*Lawn of Satan?*" he hissed. "*Lawn? Lawn?*" When did you last see someone looking like the goddamn Antichrist mowing their goddamn *lawn* for Chrissakes?"

"Well, take Haselmere any Sunday afternoon—"

"The name of the *alburm, you fucking moron,*" Jett cut in viciously, "is *Spawn of Satan. Spawn.* Not *lawn.* Not *prawn. Spawn.*" For a few seconds, Seven looked downcast. Then he brightened.

"There's a loch over there," he said eagerly. "We could borrow a jam jar from the kitchen and get some frogspawn. You could hold the jar up to the camera…" His voice trailed away again as he realised

Jett was no longer listening to him. His furious expression had been replaced by one of terror. Seven whipped round to see the largest, widest, biggest, ugliest, and angriest woman he had ever set eyes on stomping towards them from the direction of the kitchen. In her wake floated the vilest of cooking smells.

"And what exactly," boomed Nanny, striding up to Jett and prodding the carcass with a forefinger as thick as a tree branch, "do you think you are doing with tonight's dinner?"

Jett stormed back into his bedroom feeling rawer than a sushi makers' convention. The cover shoot degenerating into farce had been bad enough without that terrifying old bag bearing down on them into the bargain. Seven's offering her the prawns as a starter had only made things worse. Jett was not looking forward to the evening's planned big dinner party, despite being flattered that Geri and Jamie had decided to throw one in his honour.

The door, slamming shut behind him, echoed his feelings.

"Is that you, Wobblebottom? In here, darling." Jett's heart sank as he heard Champagne's voice issuing shrilly from the bathroom. In the three hours he had been absent, Champagne had managed to progress from the bed to the bath, a distance of a full ten feet. He stuck his head round the bathroom door to see her immersed in bubbles.

"Not *still* in the goddamn tub?"

Champagne pushed her hands into her hair and pouted at him. As her breasts travelled gloriously upwards at the movement of her arms, Jett was conscious of a tightening around his groin area hardly due to his skin-tight black jeans alone. Champagne's body was the most generously luscious he had ever seen, even if being first in line in the Looks queue meant she'd gone straight to the back of Brains. He'd heard that her beauty could drive men mad; but hadn't, until recently, appreciated in quite what way.

"Darling, I'm relaxing, yah?" Champagne beamed at him and raised a tanned, pink-toenailed foot from the foam. "Had an unbelievably exhausting afternoon. Waited *ages* for the maid to come and unpack my bag and in the end had to go down and drag someone up here to do it. Annie, I think she was called. Bloody useless, anyway. Hung my Gucci up all wrong."

Jett's heart sank. "That," he said evenly, "is the castle owner's fiancée. Your hostess."

"*Oh.* Well, I must say she was *very* unhelpful over doing my washing for me. Can you *believe* there's no laundry service here? She said she always washes her knickers in the *sink.*"

"Well, that won't be a problem for you. You don't wear knickers. Anyway, you better get ready," said Jett impatiently. "Dinner's in half an hour."

"Oh, *Wobblebottom.*" The special voice Champagne put on for wheedling purposes set Jett's teeth on edge even more than the maddening pet name. His bottom emphatically did *not* wobble. "You know I *never* eat in public," she purred. "Can't you get them to send me up a *tiny* vegetable consomme followed by a *minuscule* white truffle risotto and—oh, perhaps a *tiny* half-bottle of Krug as well? I *hate* to put anyone out, of *course…*"

For a moment, Jett flirted with the delicious idea of ordering room service from that terrifying bruiser of a cook. Better still, of getting Champagne to. "Well, come down for a drink at least. Be rude not to."

"Oh, if I *must.*" As Champagne rose, pouting, from the bath, water running down her breasts, hips, and pubic hair, Jett struggled to keep his erection under control. If Champagne saw it, all would be lost and he really wasn't in the mood. Her voracious sexual appetite could have left Casanova on his knees weeping and begging for mercy.

Galling though it was to admit it, Champagne was getting too much of a handful for him. His hands, at any rate, were getting too full of her rather too much; Jett wondered, quite literally, how much longer he was going to be able to keep it up. The years between his first flush of fame and recent revival had not seen an increase in stamina to match the decrease in hair. And besides, girls seemed to be getting more difficult to satisfy; Jett had no memories of seventies chicks being as goddamn demanding as their contemporary counterparts. Girls today seemed to expect more, and Jett had never met anyone who expected as goddamn much as Champagne.

In his defence, Jett knew his decline had been less spectacular than that of the rest of the band. Talk about the Mild Ones. By Solstice's former hell-raising standards, the pre-gig dressing-room conversations during the Wold Tour had been embarrassing. Less sex and drugs and rock 'n' roll than gardening, mortgages, and children. He was the only one even getting *divorced*, for Christ's goddamn sake…

Jett gazed out moodily into the impenetrable black beyond the windows. Say what you like about Cassandra—and he had, many times—at least she didn't want five orgasms a night. Didn't want any at all, in fact. Recalling the deep, deep, unmolested peace of the marital minimalist double bed, Jett sighed almost wistfully in the direction of the emerging stars.

"*Dah-dah*, yah?"

Jett was jerked out of his daydream to see Champagne standing in the bathroom doorway, arms raised in triumph and wearing a pair of snakeskin pants that must have been looser on the original snake.

Champagne wriggled her shoulders. "Like my bustier? Very rock chick, yah?" She tugged out a breast to expose the tip of a nipple and pouted at him again.

Jett stared at the complex structure of underwiring and cantilevering necessary to support and contain the flowing flesh of Champagne's cleavage. "Looks like something by Isambard Kingdom Brunel."

"Never heard of him, darling. This is Westwood."

Jett gritted his teeth. Champagne's obsession with fashion had been the one flashpoint of the Back From the Dead tour. Deriding their blow-dried, tight satin, and studded leather look, Champagne had attempted to shoehorn the whole of Solstice into Prada. The Mild Ones had finally seen red. As Champagne ordered him into a leather sarong, Nigel "Animal" Gurkin, drummer, father of five, resident of Tunbridge Wells, builder of dolls' houses out of matchsticks, and the Mildest One of all, had snapped. "We're a heavy metal band, you know," he had remonstrated, placing his glass of orange juice down on the table with slightly more emphasis than was strictly necessary.

If only we were, thought Jett longingly. For the money if nothing else. It was true that "Sex and Sexibility," the first single released from the *Ass Me Anything* album, had gone straight to number one on a riptide of ironic revivalism, but the unhappy consequences for him personally were the unwelcome attentions of that slumbering lion, the Inland Revenue. Then of course there was the yawning pit called the divorce courts down which he was pouring thousands despite a settlement seeming light years away. Talk about *nisi* goddamn work if you can get it, Jett thought sourly.

Last, but by no means least, was Champagne's conviction that, as a much-publicised, relaunched rock star in regular receipt of lavish amounts of publicity, Jett was rolling in money and it was her duty to get through as much of it as possible. His pleadings that a Solstice wold tour brought in significantly less than a Madonna-style world one completely failed to make an impact. Champagne had, Jett eventually realised, absolutely no idea of the multimillion-dollar difference between ironic and iconic.

At first he had thought she was joking when she'd asked him what she should wear to the Number Ten celebrity party this year. The thought of Champagne in Downing Street was an arresting one, especially after she had confided her belief that the Gulf War was caused by people queue-jumping at the Gulfstream factory. Even Cassandra had more of a grasp of foreign affairs than that, although she had once mortified him by insisting they stayed in the Hotel de Ville on a trip to Paris on the grounds that it was larger and more impressive than the Hôtel Crillon.

Jett sighed. He had passed from being an enthusiastic admirer of Champagne's frontage to looking forward to seeing the back of her. What had been initially good for his cred was proving disastrous for his bank balance. A Champagne lifestyle was not all it was cracked up to be. Yes, he was definitely missing Cassandra.

Zak stuck his fork in his glass and clanked it loudly backwards and forwards. Tendrils of venison stew sauce unravelled from the prongs and floated slowly in the water.

"Zak darling?" Cassandra smiled vaguely and beatifically at her son. "That's *such* a wonderful noise, but—"

"*Shut up*," snarled Jett as Zak, tiring of glass-banging, started instead to smash the silver cutlery hard against the polished surface of the table. In the shadows, Anna felt Nanny stiffen, yet Cassandra, most uncharacteristically, failed to fly like a wildcat to her son's defence. She seemed very calm. Probably still drunk, thought Anna. Yet, for someone recovering from an industrial-strength hangover, Cassandra seemed in an unusually good mood. Even more amazingly, a whispered conversation with Robbie had revealed that it was something to do with Mrs. McLeod.

Anna shot an amused glance across the table to Robbie, intercepting an amused one from Geri to Jamie. Those two, thought Anna with a twist of the lips. Obvious enough what was happening *there*. They'd bonded over the tearooms and toilets—talk about lav at first sight. Just as well she wasn't the jealous type. Besides, discussing books with Robbie made such a welcome change from Jamie banging on about drains.

Robbie looked so handsome in his dinner jacket, the miraculously white and crisp collar of his shirt—could she detect the skilled hand of Mrs. McLeod here?—contrasting with the high, outdoor colour of his rugged, sensual face. Looking at his eyes, shining large, amused, and amber in the candlelight, Anna felt for the first time in her life that here was a man she could trust. Except for keeping the dreaded beard at bay—his five o'clock shadow was now edging rather more towards midnight.

"Darling, what are you doing *now*?" Cassandra's urgent whisper suddenly cut across her thoughts.

"Willy tricks." Zak, smirking ostentatiously, was busy pressing down hard on his leeks with a fork so the white centre shot out at a distinctly penile angle.

"Behave your goddamn self," snapped Jett, raising an eyebrow and grinning apologetically to Cassandra.

To Anna's amazement, Cassandra not only grinned back but, in addition, shot Jett a coy look from under her eyelashes. In Jett's mirrored lenses, the candlelight glowed softly in reply. What *was* going on there? The expected hysterical scenes following Jett and Cassandra's discovery of each other in the castle had not taken place. And that was *before* Champagne D'Vyne had appeared.

Champagne had arrived at the dining table forty-five minutes late. "Sorry, yah?" she trilled, tossing her long blonde hair back over her shoulders. "Had to write my column, yah?" She rolled her brilliant green eyes theatrically. "Deadlines are *such* a bore."

"You're telling me," muttered Jett. Champagne's weekly newspaper column, in which she chronicled her dizzyingly glamorous social life and in which Jett had recently made his debut portrayed as the author's adoring lapdog, had done his street cred almost as much damage as Champagne herself had done his bank balance.

The rest of the company exchanged looks. Along with everyone else in the Sunday newspaper-reading universe, all those present, apart, perhaps, from Jamie, were aware that Champagne did not write the society column that appeared weekly under her name. It was well known that the only person for whom Champagne's deadlines were a bore was the unfortunate hack on the paper whose job it was to extract the column from her.

Having arrived for dinner fashionably late, Champagne soon found herself in the considerably less chic situation of facing Jett's ex-wife across the table. "Is this some kind of *joke*?" she had, after a freezing silence, demanded of the hapless Jamie who was doing the introductions. Stamping her metal heel so hard it drew sparks from the flagstones, Champagne treated the assembly to a display of explosions worthy of the millennium celebrations and a stream of eye-watering expletives that would have left a battleship crew gasping but left Zak in raptures.

By way of a finale, Champagne stormed off as best she could given that at Dampie storming off anywhere involved waiting in the hall for the one local taxi for up to three hours. And there was another curious thing, thought Anna. Jett had seemed almost relieved to see the back of her, even if the two engineers he had brought with him had looked rather regretful. In the end, it had been they who took Champagne off in their gaffer's van, thus freeing up three portions in total of Nanny's venison stew to be divided among those left behind. This had not been a blessing. The rule that each mouthful must be chewed thirty-two times could have been invented for Nanny's cuisine. Then doubled.

"I can't eat any more of this crap." Zak suddenly spat out a mouthful of venison casserole on to the table. Jett immediately cuffed him across the basin cut.

"Gosh, the wind's getting up, isn't it?" Geri said loudly and distractingly, as Nanny smashed plates together on the pretext of collecting them. Outside, the gale was slapping itself against the windows almost as hard as Jett had just smacked his son. And, no doubt, almost as hard as Nanny would like to smack Geri.

"Nanny'll soon fix that," said Jamie, grabbing the chance to make amends with both hands. "She's amazing. Full of ancient lore. Whenever there's a storm, it always calms down after Nanny goes to the shore and throws a pudding into the sea."

"*Pardon?*" Cassandra, evidently glad of the excuse, put her fork down in surprise. Anna blinked. Even *she* had never heard this one.

"Ancient tradition," Jamie added. "Feeding the waves, she calls it."

"Eat *up*," Jett ordered Zak, who immediately stuck his tongue out even further.

"Tummyache," he muttered.

"Oh, Nanny's got a cure for that as well," Jamie burst in eagerly. "She'll have you hanging upside down like a shot."

"*What?*" Cassandra and Jett peered into the shadows where Nanny lurked with awe and interest, as if observing a strange and wonderful beast.

"That's her cure for stomachache," Jamie gabbled, thrilled that Nanny was receiving the respect she deserved from some quarters at least. "Hanging people upside down by the heels."

"Really?" Cassandra looked impressed. A speculative light shone from Jett's eye. There was an astonished silence, in which it was hard not to notice that Zak was the stillest and quietest of all.

Chapter Twenty-five

"WILL YOU…?" JAMIE LOOKED apologetically at Anna. The question, raised after dinner in the sitting room while Geri had gone down to the kitchen to, in her words, "put a bomb under Nanny with the coffee," was not entirely unanticipated.

Anna had been expecting it for days, ever since she had caught Jamie kissing Geri in the ruins of the wine store. After which Geri had studiously avoided her—that had been Anna's interpretation, at least, of the fact Geri had suddenly been rushing back and forth to London on "urgent business."

"Would you mind very much giving me back the, um…"

"Ring? Not at all." Anna delved frantically in her pocket to produce the small box. It was, more than anything, a relief to hand it over. Apart from all its other unfortunate associations, the responsibility of carrying it around all the time had been onerous but she had not wanted to risk leaving anything but the box in her room. She passed the ring to Jamie not entirely convinced it would reach its next rightful recipient. The wine store roof, after all, had yet to be replaced.

"You don't mind?"

"Of course not. You'll be much better off with Geri." The odd thing was, Anna believed it. Even before the wine store incident, she had caught a number of looks passing between Jamie and Geri that were of a far more incendiary nature than anything she personally remembered. Perhaps it was because they were such opposites—fiery, capable, earthy Geri, highbred, dreamy, and romantic Jamie. Although the dreamy bit might be in for a shock; Geri, Anna knew, would not stand for any shirking in bed. Jamie would be expected to stand and deliver.

"Thanks." Jamie swiftly pocketed the ring. "I'm glad you think so. She *is* wonderful, isn't she? So capable and full of energy."

Anna nodded, looked around the room, and reflected that it was just as well. Her gaze fixed on the telltale black sweep of fungal damp on the wall behind the sofa.

Its disintegration was a grim reminder that at Dampie decay was not a slow, gentle, faintly melancholy process, but a vital, thrusting affair. Less a case, Anna thought, squinting at the fat black beads against the whiteness, of watching paint dry than watching it warp, bubble up, split, and eventually slide defeated off the damp walls. She shuddered. Call her spineless, but all her previous sense of abject failure had disappeared, to be replaced by the profound relief of knowing she was not spending the rest of her life in this place.

"I hope you'll be very happy," she told Jamie.

"I'm sure we will," Jamie assured her, his gaze following hers to the wall. "Geri's fantastic at DIY, you know. I've never seen anyone handle a grout gun like her." His eyes shone with mixed adoration and admiration. "And she loves the traditions—all the history…"

"Yes," said Anna. "And that's all great. But you know you've got to sort out one thing. Once and for all. Otherwise it will never work."

Jamie swallowed and dropped his gaze. "I'm going for sex counselling, if that's what you mean…"

"Good," said Anna. "But I didn't mean that, actually." As Jamie looked at the floor, Anna pressed on, suddenly feeling this was the best and ultimate service she could do her friend. After all, Geri had, in a roundabout sort of way, rescued her from an untenable situation and provided an extremely neat, if unorthodox, solution. She wanted, Anna decided, to give Geri the best wedding present possible, one that owed nothing to Jerry's Home Store and decoupage waste paper bins.

"I mean Nanny," she said.

"What will you do now?"

Anna, face buried in the thick, salty matt of Robbie's chest hair, heard his question reverberate powerfully through his rib cage. She raised herself slowly until she was sitting up on top of him, pushing aside her tousled hair so she could see his eyes. He looked serious.

"I don't know," she replied truthfully. In view of where careful plotting had got her before, she had decided not to have a plan for her future. "I'm taking things as they come," she smiled at him. Inside her, Robbie's just-spent penis stirred enquiringly. She'd already had three orgasms, each one longer than the last. And miraculously, so far, no sign of a UTI.

Although it applied to every other encounter she had had, Johnny Rotten's famous pronouncement that sex was "two minutes of squelching" was a glorious misrepresentation of Robbie. Unlike all who had come and gone before him, Robbie did not thrust immediately into her, dragging a host of delicate, dry, and protesting internal organs with him.

Robbie's—surprisingly expert—method was to slowly raise her to a pitch of wet and gasping expectation, guiding her with flickering tongue and precise, circling, lust-slicked finger through hoops of quivering delight to the brink of back-arching ecstasy. Only then were her vaginal muscles allowed to clamp the great rod of his penis. Only then, as she swayed poised on the cliff of juddering delight, did Robbie finally fire into her and combine with her yelps of pleasured pain his groans of discreetly profound ecstasy.

But his greatest skill of all was that he managed to do it all without making her feel for one second self-conscious. Merely conscious of the fact that he found every inch of her, every ridge of cellulite, every careless bruise, every soft white swell of excess flesh, every split nail quite literally delicious. He had an earthiness about him, an unbounded, unabashed joy in the carnal. Oh, the blessed, sweet relief of being in the hands of someone *normal*. A pleb, rather than a Seb.

"Will you come and live with me?" he suddenly asked her, clamping both strong, warm hands around her waist. Anna luxuriated both in the question and the feeling of strength and security. It was tempting. And she knew there was only one answer. No.

"I'd love to. I really would," she mumbled. "But I just couldn't stay here, I'm afraid." Before coming to Dampie, Anna had never really considered herself a city girl. Now, however, even the thought of the Circle Line with signal failure filled her with eye-misting nostalgia.

Robbie pushed both hands through his thick hair. At the sight of the abundant bush in his armpits, Anna felt the familiar, dizzying plunge in her pelvis. *Oh God.* Was she making the right decision?

"Of course we wouldn't stay here," Robbie muttered, sitting up and sucking at her nipples. "We'll go back to London and write."

"But where will we live? I haven't got a flat. Or any money."

"Don't worry about that. I have. Rather nice one in Belgravia." Beneath her, he was grinding gently up and down. Anna gasped as the red waves began to rise in her once again.

"*Belgravia?*" she murmured into his salt-tang hair as he pulled her head down to kiss her. She winced as the Brillo Pad brush of his bristle scraped hot and rasping against her cheek.

"Family flat. But only I ever use it."

Anna spat out Robbie's tongue and looked at him in dismay. This had a horribly familiar ring to it. She shot a suspicious look at his naked little finger. At least *that* didn't.

"Family flat? So your father is…?"

"An earl." Robbie looked at her shamefacedly. "I'm awfully sorry. I didn't want to tell you. I gathered from your diary that you weren't too keen on the aristocracy."

"So you are?" Anna gazed at him stonily.

"The Honorable Robbie Persimmon-MacAskill. But don't hold it against me. I'm all right really, I promise you."

Anna looked searchingly at him. Then she grinned as she felt his penis, formerly growing limp with despair, begin to swell within her once more. "Talk about an ingrowing heir," she whispered.

"So will you move in with me?" Robbie gazed anxiously at her.

Anna's breasts bounced wildly as her shoulders shook with laughter. It was *too* ridiculous. The penniless poet had turned out to be yet another scion of the privileged classes. "I guess I'm Hon for it," she spluttered, grinding herself down on him once more. "Get to it, big boy," she shouted joyfully. "*I want you to come inside me like a fire extinguisher.*"

"Will you come back to me?"

Jett saw the windscreen plunging towards him as Cassandra, shocked at the question, jerked her foot suddenly down on the accelerator. The car plunged forward almost into the back of a swaying beige Volvo with a sticker in the back window proclaiming "It's Hard to Sit Down When You've Been to Harrow." Cassandra stared at it and said nothing. For possibly the first time in her life, she seemed to be choosing her words carefully.

"I've missed you," Jett persisted. It was true. Without Cassandra exploding every five minutes, his life had seemed flat and without drama. He had not realised until now what his marriage had meant to him, how addicted he had become to their screaming rows and steaming exchanges of vicious insults. How addicted to the wonders of W8 as well, as many weeks of crummy tour hotels, student digs, and B&Bs had helped remind him. The horrors of a bed and breakfast in Peterborough run by a couple called Ken and Flora and called Kenora still had him waking sweating in the night.

Nylon sheets. As slippery and electric as an eel. Jett had not realised until skidding up and down that Peterborough single bed, how large lying down each night in Provençal lavender-scented sheets of Irish linen had previously loomed in his life. And who was to say, if they persisted in going through with this stupid and expensive divorce, that both he and Cassandra wouldn't be condemned to nylon sheets forever. Catching their toenails for the rest of their lives, sliding around on seas of tequila sunrise orange, aquamarine, and bright purple. Breathing their last on sheets alive with static.

"We suit each other, you and I," he added persuasively. Funny how a master lyricist like himself, from whom choice phrases usually flowed like the cleansing swirl down a lavatory, found it so hard to express himself in real-life situations. Cassandra was the same— celebrated author and yet unable to utter a word about what was really important. Mind you, Jett thought, nothing new there.

"Come on, Sandra," he urged. "You know I've got a bit more dough now after the tour. And there have been a million orders for *Spawn of Satan* already and it's only been goddamn released today. I can keep you in the manner to which you used to be accustomed."

"Actually," Cassandra said regally, drawing herself up at the wheel, "now I've hammered out the deal with Mrs. McLeod, I'll be quite nicely off myself, thank you. We've got the summer paperback market stitched up well into the millennium." She beamed through the windscreen. Getting Mrs. McLeod to write her books had been an infinitely more satisfactory arrangement than bothering to do it herself. Far better to become a brand and just slap her name on whatever McLeod produced. Her writer's block may have lifted slightly, but not enough, she knew, to power her through another six-hundred-page Torremolinos beach special, and certainly not at the speed McLeod could write. The old bag could leave a jet ski lagging behind. How *clever* she had been to find her. How *inspired* of her to turn up at that ridiculous, rustic creative writing class. Suddenly, Cassandra's satisfied smirk twisted into an unbecoming scowl. "Though if anyone's been stitched up it's *me*," she added bitterly. "That *bastard* Robbie MacAskill got McLeod a shit hot agent and she's getting a straight fifty percent cut. Bloody cheek. After all, it's *my* name the books go out under. *My* reputation at stake."

"Well, she *is* doing all the work, isn't she?" Whoa, Jett warned himself, seeing Cassandra's furious face. You're almost there. Don't fuck it up now. "But yes, I quite see your point," he added hurriedly. "Your reputation, absolutely."

Cassandra's stony profile softened, although how seemed a miracle, given the amount of plastic surgery it had undergone.

"Come on, Sandra," Jett wheedled. "You know you've got a soft spot for me."

"I've certainly got a spot for you," said Cassandra levelly. "And don't call me Sandra. You know I hate it." Her lips tightened. Cassandra loathed being reminded of her real name.

"Aw, baby. You know you're the only one for me." Jett's voice began to take on a desperate tone as the outer darkness of rootless drifting and grubby groupies beckoned. As the image of Champagne D'Vyne raised itself terrifyingly before him, he cringed inwardly. The day she had walked out of his life had been better than jamming with Hendrix. Not that he *had* jammed with Hendrix. But he had once judged an organic lemon curd competition with Paul McCartney.

"But what about Zak?" demanded Cassandra suddenly. "You were so horrible to the poor darling before."

Behind them, Zak was too busy carving up the cream leather of the hired Rover's back seat to listen. He sat back to admire his handiwork. "SHAMPAIN." *What* a woman. He almost regretted now finding her phone number and writing it in every service station telephone box they stopped at with the words "FOR FREE SEX FONE" scrawled above it. He sniffed loudly. That funny white powder he had found on the top of the loo in Champagne's bathroom after she had gone had really made his nose run.

"Listen to him," Cassandra declared dramatically. "He's *terrified*. And there's the problem of his school as well. We can't live in London—no one will, um, rise to the challenge of him. Every London prep school I tried"—Cassandra's voice rose—"said there was a basic problem with home discipline and they couldn't help until that had been rectified."

"Which means a good nanny," said Jett.

"Exactly." Cassandra pressed her foot down in helpless fury. The back of the Volvo loomed large again. Even if she took Jett back and—miracle of miracles—they managed to find a good nanny, the old problems were bound to start again. She sighed. It was a vicious circle. Good day school meant good nanny which meant Jett trying to jump on them which meant goodbye nanny which would now mean goodbye school as well. Talk about a Catch-22.

What she wanted was someone who could control Zak to the standards of the strictest schools whilst being completely without charm for Jett. What we need, she thought, is a battleaxe. A nanny of the old school. Of the old *everything*. Damn. She could have *sworn* she'd met one of those lately…

What we need, thought Jett, is someone who will be as firm as a goddamn Gucci heel with that brat. Someone who will put the fear of God into him and give the goddamn little sod the hard time he deserves. Christ, but his memory was bad. He was *sure* he had seen the fear of God in Zak's eyes recently, but goddamn it if he could remember where. He had a vague memory of someone very big and frightening looming out of the shadows...

"Do you think," Cassandra said suddenly to Jett, "that we could somehow persuade—"

"That old nanny of Jamie Angus's?" finished Jett. They looked at each other in wild—and in Cassandra's case reflected—surmise.

In the back, Zak, who had suddenly tuned into the conversation, yelped in terror.

"Don't worry, darling," Cassandra beamed, turning round. "Everything's going to be all right."

Beautiful People

"Give my love to the Queen," Dad shouted from the other side of the train window, his voice faint through the thick glass.

"I will!" Emma laughed, not caring if the other people in the train car stared. Let them stare.

As the train pulled out of Leeds and her parents' faces, half proud, half anxious, slid past, a mighty wave of excitement passed through her. She was going to London. To seek her fortune, like Dick Whittington in the books at the nursery she worked at. Or had worked at.

She fought through the jumble of people and luggage at the end of the carriage. "Is anyone sitting here?" she asked a grey-haired, grey-suited, grey-skinned man, whose pink newspaper was not only the one colourful thing about him but who also occupied an entire four-seater table area. If he'd paid for all four seats so he could spread out his *Financial Times* to the max, then fine, Emma thought. But she doubted this. He didn't look the extravagant sort.

"No," the grey man admitted. From behind his glinting glasses, he scanned Emma as she edged into the seat, feeling, despite herself, rather self-conscious. Of course, she didn't care a button what a stuffy, miserable, old wrinkly like that thought about her looks, but even so, it would be wonderful to have the kind of whippet-skinny figure that allowed one to slide swiftly into confined areas. But her build required a little more room.

Of course, she wasn't fat; far from it, but she wasn't thin either. She defied anyone not to be plump when they lived with her parents however. Mum put out two different types of potato every Sunday teatime—roast and mash—and there was always pudding and custard to follow. And Emma had never known the biscuit tin to be empty, even in the most difficult times, and there'd been a few of those. In fact, the leanest times were when the biscuit tin tended to be at its fullest.

But physical appearances didn't matter so much anyway, Emma reminded herself—not in the business she was in. It was how good you were at your job—and she was very good at hers. Too good in fact now, with all the extra qualifications she'd spent the last two years getting at night school. Especially as Wee Cuties, the nursery in Heckmondwike that employed her, was uninterested in keeping up with the latest educational theories. It was time to move on. And, without mortgage, without fiancé, there would never be a better time to do it.

Should she stay, she would probably remain at Wee Cuties for the rest of her life, as most of her colleagues seemed to be planning to—the ones, that was, who were not planning to defect to the soon-to-be-completed supermarket, which was rumoured to be offering better wages and longer holidays. And while Emma sought both, she sought also excitement, challenge, and possibility, none of which were normally associated with supermarkets.

And so it was, when first her eye had fallen on the ad in the Yorkshire Post, that a thrill of recognition had gone through Emma. The ad leapt out at her immediately. "Nanny Sought. Smart Area of London. Well-behaved Children. Excellent Pay and Holidays." With shaking hands, she copied down the details—Dad hated his paper being vandalised.

The train was hot. So that it would not crease, Emma removed the pretty fawn jacket with its nipped-in waist bought, along with the skirt, especially from Whistles for the interview. In the shop, the pale brown had perfectly complemented the chestnut shoulder-length hair that was, Emma felt, her best feature, with its flash of red threads in the sunshine. She crossed her feet in their smart, low-heeled brown pumps at the ankles and tapped her fingers on the new matching handbag. Perhaps she looked too smart, but better to be too smart than too scruffy. After all, Mrs. Vanessa Bradstock, the mother who would be interviewing her, had sounded very grand on the phone.

Stepping out of her carriage in St. Pancras International, Emma's gaze swung automatically upwards to the great glass arc of roof flung above the station, through which poured sunlight from an optimistically blue sky.

London was as fast moving and purposeful as a colony of ants. To the right and the left of her, people swarmed off the train, darting towards the shining chrome barriers in a jostling, heaving mass, weighed down with rucksacks and briefcases.

All the rush and running made her feel she should run herself, and Emma found her pace quickening past the glossy shops in the terminal; no scruffy cafés these, but smart bookshops, glamorous French patisseries with aluminium chairs outside, and fashionable florists whose chic bouquets arranged tastefully round the door bore price tags that made Emma gasp. She lingered in front of the great glass window of Hamley's toy store, her eyes running greedily over the big, shiny, colourful, wonderful things on the other side of it. The idea of bringing a small present for her future charges—if the interview with Vanessa Bradstock went well—came to her. Emma ventured inside, amid the lights and pounding music, and quickly picked a little stuffed pink cat for the girl—girls always liked cats—and a small rubber train for the boy. She had yet to meet a boy who didn't like trains.

❖ ❖ ❖

Emma looked just right, Vanessa thought gleefully as she opened the front door. Fat, in other words. Size twelve at least, to her own carefully preserved ten. Fourteen even, at a pinch, and there was certainly more than an inch to pinch there. Oh yes. Emma was certainly not the long drink of water Jacintha, the last nanny, had been.

One should always employ fat girls. They were so grateful and had absolutely no self-confidence. This girl, with her brown hair—not a highlight to be seen—and almost makeupless face had low self-esteem written all over her.

"You're late," Vanessa said challengingly. Best make it clear from the start who was in charge.

"I'm sorry," Emma said immediately, even though she did not consider the fault to be hers entirely. It would have helped a great deal in finding the house—one of a row of red brick Victorian terraces with pointed roofs and small front gardens—if she had known it was in Peckham and not posh Camberwell, as for some reason had been put on the letter.

"My last nanny's father was a peer of the realm," Vanessa loftily informed Emma. "She was excellent. So if you get this job, you'll have some very big shoes to fill." She glanced at Emma's shoes and twitched her lips disapprovingly. They looked plain and brown and possibly from Office Shoes.

Emma's reaction was not what Vanessa had expected. Instead of looking cowed and terrified, as had been the intention, this girl from the north turned her brown and direct gaze on Vanessa and asked her, in a quiet yet steady voice, why Jacintha had left, exactly.

Vanessa, while unpleasantly startled, nonetheless realised she had to give an answer. The windmills of her mind whirred in panic as she searched for one. That The Honourable Jacintha had left to go and work for the family of a famous writer had been a bitter blow. A more famous writer, Vanessa corrected herself; she herself had a newspaper column and was extremely well-known. In media circles. Her lack of influence in more general circles had been unpleasantly illustrated by Jacintha's resignation.

"The Honourable Jacintha had been with us for some time," Vanessa hedged. "It was time to move on."

"How long?" Emma asked steadily.

Vanessa pretended to think hard, as if the answer—six weeks—had somehow been lost in the midst of much more pressing concerns. "Three months," she asserted, with an imperious toss of her head that warned Emma that she proceeded any further down this track at her peril.

Emma added the toss to her store of impressions about Vanessa. Her main impression was that she was rather cross and unhappy looking. But why was a mystery. Her house was big and roomy, if not particularly tidy. She clearly had money. She was also very attractive, slim in a close-fitting white T-shirt and long purple denim skirt, her pink-sequined flip-flops revealing tanned feet with red-painted nails. Her shining blonde hair was brightly streaked, but so finely it looked natural, and much chopped about in that artful way that only real good hairdressers could pull off. She had big blue eyes, which were pretty, if bulgy. And good skin, even though her face was rather red. So what did she have to look grumpy about?

Perhaps Vanessa was unhappily married. Perhaps with an overbearing alpha-male husband. Yes, that could be it.

"Sit down," Vanessa said, sitting on the edge of the battered mock-Georgian sofa.

It seemed to Emma that—beyond the obvious about driving licence (yes) and criminal record (no)—Vanessa was soon struggling for questions to ask her. She subtly took over herself, conducting her own interrogation of her employer to be. Vanessa seemed to know little about her children. She had no idea what Hero and Cosmo, as the children were apparently called, liked to eat, what books they liked to read, what games they liked to play, or whether they had special words or names for favourite people or things.

The husband Vanessa may or may not have been unhappily married to worked, it emerged, for the Foreign Office and had been sent to Equatorial Guinea, wherever that was. He would be back in several weeks. "So you see, I really need someone urgently. Now," Vanessa emphasised, skewering Emma with those bulging blue eyes.

But it did not seem to Emma that this urgent need was reflected in the salary offered, which was low. On the plus side, she would be living in, and while she had not been expecting luxury, the fact that the tall house seemed to get colder the further up you got was discouraging. Even more so was the tiny bedroom at the top she was shown into, with the peeling wallpaper, collapsing curtain rail and light fitting that appeared to be masking-taped to the wall and ceiling respectively. Next door was the children's bedroom and, next door to that, the playroom. The "nursery suite" was how Vanessa referred to the whole.

Emma went back downstairs with Vanessa, full of uncertainty. Should she not get out now? Go home? She could always write off for other jobs, after all.

"You can start immediately," Vanessa offered. Or, possibly, instructed.

"But I haven't seen the children," Emma pointed out quickly. If they were awful too, that would decide it.

"Hero! Cosmo!" bawled Vanessa.

The children appeared at the door. Hero, the solid little three-year-old, had a solemn little face and hair so flaxen, so impossibly white, that it seemed lit from within, a silver flame. Cosmo, at four, had eyes that were deep, sunken, and anxious, and his hair was a caramel pageboy, striped with lighter gold. They regarded Emma suspiciously, but that, she felt, was understandable enough, especially if five nannies had come and gone in the last twelve months.

"Ask me if I'm a passenger train or a freight train," Cosmo demanded suddenly in a low, growling voice.

Emma thought of the toy train in her handbag. She had been right, after all. Was there any little boy who didn't like locomotives?

Vanessa rolled her eyes. "God. He's absolutely bloody obsessed with trains. Just shut up, will you, Cosmo? You've driven all the nannies mad with this. Another reason why they've all left," she groaned at Emma.

But Cosmo, ignoring his mother, was looking at Emma expectantly, his blue eyes round through his blond fringe. She sensed it was some sort of test. She smiled, stooping down to his level, and felt the difficulty of doing so in wobbly high heels and trousers that bit at the waist and round the thighs. She looked into his uncertain little face. "Are you a passenger train or a freight train?" she asked, obediently.

Cosmo shuffled his little feet on the carpet. His fingers were joined together and pointing forward, and both arms were revolving by his sides, imitating the moving parts of a locomotive.

"I'm a passenger train," he told her now, his four-year-old face entirely serious.

"Can I get on you?" Emma asked.

"No," said Cosmo, causing Emma's heart to sink rather. Her initiative had been rejected. "You can't get on me," Cosmo added, earnestly, "because I'm a special train. But you can look at me. Woo woo!" And with that, the little boy steamed out of the sitting room.

"See what I mean?" steamed Vanessa. "He wants to be an engine driver. I ask you, is that what I'll be paying millions in school fees for?"

Emma looked at Hero.

"And Hero's obsessed with cats," Vanessa added, as if this too was a crime.

Emma hardly heard. She was looking into Hero's blue eyes, in which she had spotted an unmistakeable, hungry look that was nothing to do with food but everything to do with the need for affection and attention. It twisted her heart.

"I'll take the job," she said, reaching for her handbag. "And, actually, I've got a couple of presents for them."

Farm Fatale

BANG ON 8 A.M., the car alarm that had been shrieking all night finally stopped. After a two-second pause, the road drills began. Rosie could hold back no longer.

"Mark? You know we've been talking about moving to the countryside…"

"*You've* been talking about it, you mean," corrected Mark, hunched over his bowl of Cheerios and flicking rapidly through the newspapers. "I don't believe it." He groaned.

"I know." Rosie pressed her hands to her ears. "They only dug up that patch a week ago. Something to do with cable TV.

"Not that," said Mark, his spoon dripping milk as he shook it at the center spread of a tabloid. "This. The *Mail*'s got Matt Locke. We've been trying to get him for ages."

"Who's Matt Locke?"

Mark looked at her, exasperated. "Honestly, you're like that judge who asked, 'Who is Gazza?' Don't you ever *read* the papers?"

"You know I don't. Apart from the horoscopes." No doubt, Rosie thought, she was missing something, but she failed to share the awe with which Mark regarded newspapers in general and his job on one in particular. After all, it wasn't as if he was setting the national agenda, exposing Nazis, or bringing corrupt politicians to book. As far as Rosie could make out, Mark's job as assistant editor on a Sunday lifestyle section mostly involved rewriting other people's articles—"tickling up" as he called it—and attempting to persuade celebrities to give interviews about everything from their cystitis (for "Disease of the Week") to the contents of their refrigerator (for the "Chillin'" slot).

"Matt Locke, m'lud," Mark explained with elaborate patience, "is an extremely successful singer. The chisel-cheeked champion of howling rock 'n' roll angst, he burst on the scene two years ago with the number one platinum album *Posh Totty*, an epoch-making elegy to soaring strings, gutsy guitar, melancholy blues, and a touch of country and western, following it up with the even more successful *What Did Your Last One Die Of?* Then, at the height of his fame, he crashed and burned amid claims that the stress was too much."

"Oh," said Rosie, peering at the newspaper photograph of a girlish-looking youth with elaborately tousled hair and huge lips. He did not look particularly stressed. Actually, he looked half asleep.

She winced as the road drills outside changed to an even more brain-penetrating key. "Darling, you know you said you'd think about it. The countryside, I mean."

"Recycled interviews, of course," Mark muttered, pressing his nose almost against the newspaper. "Nothing that's not been printed before. Apart from these aerial pictures of Matt in his garden, although they're so blurry it's probably one of the gnomes."

"Two-thirds of people living in cities want to live in the country," Rosie persevered, hoping she'd remembered the figures properly. "Thousands are migrating every month."

"So if we stay in London," Mark said flippantly, "everyone else will eventually leave, house prices will go down, and we'll end up with a mansion on Regent's Park Road."

"Oh, *Mark*."

"Look," Mark said, putting the newspaper down at last. "I know I said last night that I'd think about it, but it was the wine speaking. I don't want to leave London. I'm a townie born and bred. Crowds and noise are my lifeblood; filth is my friend. I can't breathe anything but carbon monoxide. A landscape of brutalist shopping precincts, down-at-the-heel Tube stations, and municipal concrete bunkers is the only sort of scenery I have time for. Besides," he added, stretching with satisfaction, "I'm going to be promoted. At long last, the paper's going to give me a column of my own."

"It *is*? But you never mentioned that last night."

"Well, it's not quite sorted out yet."

"So it's still 'Driving Miss Daisy' for the moment?"

The main column in Mark's section, "Driving Miss Daisy," recorded the adventures of Househusband, a stay-at-home father who looked after his infant daughter, Daisy, while his wife, a successful futures trader, went to work. Desperate for a column of his own, Mark despised the weekly chore of extracting the material out of Househusband and writing up the results himself. The fact that Househusband was incapable of stringing a sentence together, much less coming up with ideas, was, as Mark often savagely pointed out, not unconnected to the fact that he was the brother-in-law of the paper's editor.

Mark's brows drew together crossly. "For the moment, yes. But they've obviously given me that to train me for better things." He raked a hand through his rumpled golden hair. "Rosie, I can't leave. I'm on the brink of a promising career."

"Look," she said persuasively. "Why don't you ask the paper for a writing contract? Or go freelance, if they won't do it. You'd enjoy it much more. We could live anywhere we liked then. You can't really want to stay here." The hand she waved at their rented flat's dust-bloomed windows jerked involuntarily as a backfiring car joined the shrilling symphony of drills. "Imagine. Clean air. Cottages with roses round the door. Sun-dappled country lanes, empty of traffic."

Mark merely shrugged at this. Her dreams, Rosie realized miserably, were not his. In which case she'd target his nightmares, namely the dentist and going bald. "Water that doesn't cause tartar buildup behind your teeth. Rain that's clean and doesn't poison your hair follicles." As he still looked unimpressed, she added desperately, "Struggling into the office on the crappy, broken-down old Tube with your face pushed into someone's bottom. Or armpit."

"You don't have to struggle on the Tube anyway," Mark cut in self-righteously. "You're a freelance illustrator. You can lie around all day if you want."

Rosie rolled her eyes but refrained from pointing out that the endless illustrations for the food and horoscope pages of various glossy magazines in which she seemed to have become a specialist left little time for bon-bons on the couch. The fact that paintings of scallops and Scorpio were relatively poorly paid was, Rosie thought, another argument in favor of the move. Her fees would go further in the country.

"But what about everything we'd leave behind?" demanded Mark. "Restaurants, the theater, the cinema, and all that."

"But you decided a while ago we couldn't afford to eat out anymore," Rosie said gently. "We never go to the cinema and I can't remember the last time I saw the inside of a theater." In fact, she added silently, the most cultural thing we've probably done all year was eat Marks & Spencer's ravioli in front of *The Charlie Rose Show*. "We don't really make use of London these days," she pressed. "If you went freelance, we could live anywhere in the country. So why not live somewhere that's nice?"

Mark's handsome face was preoccupied. He was, Rosie knew, searching for the defining argument against, the ultimate no.

"But I'm on the fast track. The managing editor told me the other day that anything could happen. Which can only mean one thing. They're seriously thinking about giving me my own column."

"But wasn't he just saying anything could happen now that everyone's combining jobs because of the cutbacks? I mean, now the fashion editor's the foreign editor, too, so he's got a point."

"As I believe I mentioned," Mark said defensively, "the only reason Tallulah covered the military coup in Zwanwe was because she was doing a bikini shoot in the disputed border area at the time. Getting her to do a few interviews while she was there was only sensible."

"Even if her scathing criticism of the local warlords' dress sense wasn't," muttered Rosie, suddenly tired of arguing. "Darling, listen to me," she pleaded. "Moving out's not a mad idea. A recent survey said seventy-one percent of all people thought the countryside was more peaceful than the town. Fifty-four percent like the feeling of space and, um, fifty percent like the trees and forests." She was gabbling now, she knew.

"Fascinating," said Mark. Rosie looked at him sharply. Was he being sarcastic? The smooth dips and planes of his face, however, expressed only thoughtfulness.

Rosie waited, stiff with hope, watching Mark anxiously. Odd how, straight from bed, clad only in crumpled boxer shorts and an ancient T-shirt, he still managed to look devastating. She drew her toweling robe around herself, conscious of gray calves so long unshaved they probably needed a combine harvester by now. "So what do you think?" she ventured.

"I think," Mark said, slinging the spoon back into the pool of milk in his bowl, "that I might suggest it to the editor as a features idea."

Rosie ground her teeth and decided to drop the subject of the countryside. For now.

About the Author

WENDY HOLDEN WAS A journalist for the *Sunday Times*, *Tatler*, and the *Mail on Sunday* before becoming a full-time author. She has now published nine novels, all top-ten bestsellers in the UK, and she is married with two young children. Her novels include *Beautiful People*, *Farm Fatale*, *Simply Divine*, *Gossip Hound*, *The Wives of Bath*, *The School for Husbands*, *Azur Like It*, and *Filthy Rich*.

Krestine Havemann

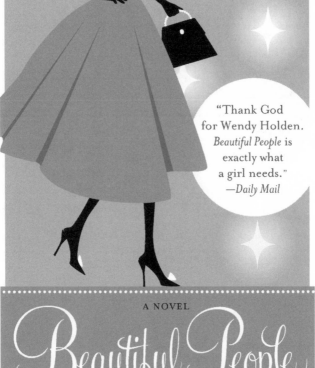

"Thank God
for Wendy Holden.
Beautiful People is
exactly what
a girl needs."
—*Daily Mail*

A NOVEL

Beautiful People

wendy holden

INTERNATIONAL BESTSELLING AUTHOR

Beautiful People
WENDY HOLDEN

A witty, utterly addictive novel from bestselling author Wendy Holden, *Beautiful People* is a tale wicked in its observations yet buoyant at its heart: an irresistible confection you'll want to devour immediately.

Darcy—a struggling English rose actress
when The Call comes from L.A. An Oscar-tastic director. A movie to make her famous. The hunkiest costar in Hollywood. So why doesn't she want to go?

Belle—a size-zero film star
but she's in big, fat trouble. Hotter than the earth's core a year ago, she's now Tinseltown toast after her last film bombed. Can she get back to the big time?

Emma—a down-to-earth, down-on-her-luck nanny
trying to weather London's cutthroat childcare scene and celebrity mom whirlwinds. What will it take for her to get back in control of her own life?

Jet to London, Hollywood, and Italy; toss in a passionate star chef, a kindhearted paparazzo, and a reluctant male supermodel; and find Wendy Holden at her best—a smash international hit.

Praise for *Beautiful People*

"Holden's satirical humor and adept writing shine through. Glitzy fun with appeal for readers of Emma McLaughlin, Plum Sykes, or Lauren Weisberger."
—Library Journal

"Holden's novel is the literary equivalent of a big-budget romantic comedy with an all-star Hollywood cast in which everyone's stories overlap. And it is equally as carefree and enjoyable. With clever dialogue and a great spectrum of personalities, Holden's big book of celebrity obsession and the price of beauty is fast-paced, realistic, and hugely entertaining."

—Booklist

978-1-4022-3715-7 • $14.99 U.S.

A
Comedy of
Country Manors

Farm Fatale

wendy holden

INTERNATIONAL BESTSELLING AUTHOR

Farm Fatale
WENDY HOLDEN

A witty, beloved novel of heart and heartland, *Farm Fatale* skewers the culture clash of city vs. country in the snappy, observant style that made Wendy Holden famous.

Cash-strapped Rosie and her boyfriend Mark are city folk longing for a country cottage. Rampantly nouveaux riches Samantha and Guy are also searching for rustic bliss—in the biggest mansion money can buy. The village of Eight Mile Bottom seems quiet enough, despite a nosy postman, a reclusive rock star, a glamorous Bond Girl, and a ghost with a knife in its back. But there are unexpected thrills in the hills, and Rosie is rapidly discovering that country life isn't so simple after all. Or is it?

Praise for *Farm Fatale*

"Wendy Holden writes with delicious verve and energy."
—Mail on Sunday

"Clever, naughty."
—Sunday Times

"This lighthearted romp, surprisingly unpredictable, smart, and fun, is refreshing fare readers can turn to."
—Publishers Weekly

"A light, sexy, and entertaining novel…will please fans of contemporary and comic romances."
—Bookreporter.com

"Every character here is deliciously ridiculous, and every rustic detail a grand satirical opportunity."
—Baltimore Sun

"Wickedly funny."
—Kirkus

978-1-4022-3716-4 • $14.99 U.S.